Also by Christopher Dickey

With the Contras: A Reporter in the Wilds of Nicaragua
Expats: Travels in Arabia, from Tripoli to Teheran

INNOCENT BLOOD

A NOVEL BY

CHRISTOPHER DICKEY

SIMON & SCHUSTER

SIMON & SCHUSTER
Rockefeller Center
1230 Avenue of the Americas
New York, NY 10020

SIMON & SCHUSTER and colophon are
registered trademarks of Simon & Schuster Inc.
Designed by Edith Fowler
Manufactured in the United States of America

10 9 8 7 6 5 4 3 2 1

Library of Congress Cataloging-in-Publication Data
Dickey, Christopher.
   Innocent blood : a novel / by Christopher Dickey.
      p.   cm.
   I. Title.
PS3554.I318I56   1997
813'.54—dc21   97-6778
                                                   CIP

ISBN 0-684-84200-9

Citations from the Qur'an are adapted from
the translations of A. Yusif Ali and
Marmaduke Pickthall.

For James
father and son

Are the people of the townships then secure from the coming of Our wrath upon them as a night-raid while they sleep? Or are the people of the townships then secure from the coming of Our wrath upon them in the day-time while they play? Are they then secure from Allah's plan?

—THE HOLY QUR'AN,
  Surah 7:97–99

*C-130 rolling down the strip,
Airborne daddy gonna take a little trip,
Mission unspoken, destination unknown,
Don't even know if we're ever coming home.*

—RUNNING CADENCE FOR
  U.S. ARMY AIRBORNE RANGERS

I

The Cherisher

Thou canst not make those
To hear who are
Buried in graves.

—*THE HOLY QUR'AN,*
Surah 35:22

I I come from Westfield, Kansas, down near the Oklahoma border. Flat lands. Pickup truck lands. American heart lands. A long way from anywhere else in the world that you could think of, even farther from any place you could feel for. Which always struck me as strange, because we were all from somewhere else. The Parcells down the road were just as Irish as they were American, even though their folks had probably been in the country for two hundred years, rednecks the whole time. My first girl was Mary Hagopian, and when we were thirteen and out in the bed of her father's truck and talking and talking, and making out a little bit, she told me her family was Armenian. Who were Armenians? Or the Swedes and Danes, like old man Syerson, who owned all the Hardees in three counties, and who I worked for, for a while. Or the Browns and the Jacksons and all the other Anglo-Saxon-nothing names, made up or borrowed, that belonged to the blacks in Westfield before some of them started calling themselves Muhammad or Abdullah.

My name is Kurtovic. Nobody thought about it. My father originally came from what we used to call Yugoslavia to Westfield on a teaching contract—teaching high school French—which was one of four languages he picked up in the years right after World War II. My father had fled Communism and won asylum in America. I was never really sure just how, or who he'd worked for in the late 1940s. You didn't talk about history much in Westfield, and the

13

mechanics of immigration are not so important in America, once you're here.

By the time I was born my father was the basketball coach for the Westfield High School Vikings, a job he kept until he died of a stroke at the age of sixty-four. The seizure hit him in the family room one night after the rest of us had gone to bed. I woke up and heard the crackling of static on the television. My bedroom was just off to one side and I'd grown used to falling asleep with the sound of the late-night news, then Johnny Carson, droning beyond my door. But it wasn't like him to leave it on. I found him with the blood from his nose already congealed along the side of his face and his eyes like glass in the silver light of that dead screen. I was fourteen. He had been, more or less, an old man when I was born. I was the third of his children, by far the youngest, and the only son.

My mother stayed mainly in the house when I was growing up. She was, when I was little, a beautiful woman. Blond and blue-eyed with fresh skin that almost glowed. Her charms, I realize now, were much appreciated around town. But she spoke with a slight accent. There wasn't really much to it, and you could never have guessed for sure where she was from. But people in Westfield always knew she wasn't from around there. Blood doesn't matter, I guess, but accents do. She'd go into a drive-in sometimes, and the guys would say they couldn't understand enough to take her order. After my father died she got a job at the Wal-Mart, and by the time I was sixteen she was remarried to Calvin Goodsell, the manager of the hardware department, which at that time included sports equipment and guns and ammo as well as drills and saws and miter boxes.

I felt sorry for my mother. Goodsell was an asshole and he didn't make her very happy. But, then, she was not a happy person to begin with. Even when she was married to my father they would fight and she would seek refuge in our old station wagon. She would storm out of the house and just drive away. And drive and drive. Alone, I thought. She would be screaming, hysterical, and my father would not even raise his voice. "Now, darling," he would say, "you don't mean that." And she'd just get more furious, and then she'd leave. And I would be terrified that she would not come back.

When I was very little it was an unfocused fear. But by the time I was ten or eleven I knew enough to mull on it and make it worse. She would be driving to Arkansas City, I thought, to get liquor. Because our county was a dry county. No booze at all. And when she would come home, she'd smell of it. My father would sit quietly—it is the quiet that I most remember about him—and wait for her to get back. Sometimes the fight would begin again. But more often he would stay in his chair and watch her pass to the bedroom and watch her close the door.

By the time my mother married Goodsell she had begun to get very fat, and, with the excuse that she was not drinking, she discovered Valium, then Percodans. And of course eventually she was doing all of them in greater or lesser amounts.

She would never have Calvin over to the house when he was dating her. They would always go out to dinner—and sometimes to the Ramada, I think it was. So he never saw the way the dishes piled up, and the scum, and then the mold that you had to scrape off the plates if you wanted to eat off of them. Eventually she started buying paper plates and, still, no one did the dishes. I ate at work, mainly, and at school.

My sisters could have helped, but they were out of the house and married by the time my father died. And they just didn't. Joan moved away to St. Louis where she worked for a while in real estate and married a guy named Carlo Piscatori and started putting on airs and having kids. And she never did want to know much about me or the rest of us after that. I think she called Mom once a month or so. The conversations were brief and after a while didn't even end with "I love you."

Selma and her husband lived in Westfield, but Selma's life was so shitty that she didn't have much time for me or the house or anything else. When I was little, she'd been the one who took care of me most of the time. She was the one who listened for me in the night when I cried. Then Selma got married and her husband, Dave, made sure she paid attention to him, and only him. Seeing her meant seeing him. So she wasn't far away at all, but instead of seeing her I just missed her. Dave was an ex-Marine who worked as a state trooper. A rough son of a bitch who thought being a rough son of a bitch was enough to get ahead as long as you were in uniform. But it wasn't and he lost his job as a trooper. And when he came home, usually around dawn, from his job as a Wackenhut guard, he made Selma pay. Not long before I left Westfield I got into a fight with Dave. But it wasn't so much to protect Selma, I realize now—I think I even realized it at the time—as it was to get something back from Westfield. Sometimes it's only violence that can get something back for you.

In the seventeen and a half years I spent growing up in Kansas, I don't think anyone who knew us knew that my father's family was Muslim.

My mother was Catholic. My father had paid her way to the United States from Zagreb in 1954, the year before Selma was born. I always thought he married her for that skin of hers, and that beautiful hair. But the details, I just don't know. There's so much you don't learn as a child in America. So much that doesn't make sense. Of course I knew where Yugoslavia was on the map. My mother showed me Zagreb. She was proud, or maybe smug is a better word, that it was on the globe that she bought me one Christmas. My father's hometown, a place called Drvar, was not. "Really even this is not his village," she said. "His people were from Ljeska Župica. Can you even say that word, my love?"

I tried but could not. "Never mind," she said. "And thank God you do not need to."

Our house was empty of mementos. Certainly there was nothing there you might have identified with Islam. But there was almost nothing you could have identified with Yugoslavia.

When I was about eight and very bored one afternoon and alone as usual after school I climbed on a chair and pulled down the steps from the trapdoor in the attic and spent a couple of hours rooting around up there—not looking for history, really, but for something, anything, that would satisfy my aimless curiosity. As I think on it, the attic was remarkably neat. Probably Mom couldn't be bothered to put things up there. That was my father's job, and he did impose some order. I found a box with a few old toys. I remember I found a kind of toy pinball machine and got excited, but the batteries had corroded inside and it wasn't any good anymore. There were other boxes full of dusty old books with gray covers: *Foreign Policy Journal.* There were trunks, old trunks, the big green kinds with shiny studs on them and latches you had to shut with a padlock. But there were no stickers on them from faraway places. There wasn't very much in that attic in Kansas to satisfy even the curiosity of an eight-year-old, except for a pair of large engravings. One showed a quaint old town with a bridge across a gorge. The glass was shattered in the frame as if it was hit with a fist, and instead of being repaired it had just been put up there in the attic. I couldn't remember seeing it before, and I couldn't read what it said at the bottom of the print. Much later I realized it must have been the bridge at Mostar. A tourist attraction of sorts. It was still there the first time I visited the city. But now, of course, it's gone. The other engraving was of a cave. Deep and dark. It frightened me so much that I dreamed about it. And once I woke up screaming. But I was so ashamed that I couldn't tell my mother why I was crying when she came to my bedroom. I couldn't tell her I had slipped up to the attic. I didn't dare. So the secret of the cave stayed with me, scaring me for months. And I'm not sure it had left me completely even when I joined the service.

Maybe if Dave had not been a Marine, I would have joined the Marines myself. When you're seventeen that line about "a few good men" sounds very important. It has the steel edge of certainty about it at just that moment when you aren't sure what the hell you want to be. And I was not at all sure, just then, who I was. But if Dave had been one of the few, I figured they could count me out.

Originally I thought about flying. Who doesn't when he's a kid? I thought Navy-Pilot-Right-Stuff and breaking all the barriers. Or Air Force, which was a little closer to home. Sometimes on the road to Wichita you'd see fighters roaring out of McConnell and feel your blood rise with the thunder of the engines. The whole time I was growing up, for as long as I could remember looking up at the sky and the clouds, I saw vapor trails. They were part of my dreams. But I knew enough, even when I was seventeen, to know that most of the men like me who went into the Air Force wound up as techies on the ground. I didn't want to join the military to do lube jobs on landing gears. I wanted to know about combat. I wanted to know how I'd do with that kind of test.

In the end I joined the United States Army. There was a recruiting office set up in a booth at Town East Square in Wichita, and I hadn't planned to sign up that weekend— Easter weekend, 1985—but there it was and I did it.

It's amazing how little they want to know about who you are or where you came from when you fill out those forms. They worry about your age. Have you crossed the line of legal consent before you sign up to kill and be killed? Do you have the right number for your deductions and your taxes? Communicable diseases are a significant concern. They wanted to know was I homosexual.

But they don't really care much, anyway not at first, where you're from, what your true faith is, who your family are. You give an address like every other address in America. Just a street and a number, a town and a state and a code. It's for the mail, that's all. Your address isn't you. They ask your race. Caucasian, that strange way of saying white. Or black. Or Hispanic, as if that were a race, or Oriental or American Indian or Polynesian. Half the list is about the spectrum of skin tones, and within that half, given that the Army is full of soldiers from places like Puerto Rico and Samoa and from the reservations—the not-quite Americans of the not-quite-united states—there are some nods to ethnic background. But Caucasian? That's white and that's all they've got to know. And then when they've asked that question about race they let it go, as if they didn't care and couldn't see, even though they don't see much else. They're blinded by white.

They don't really ask your religion. ("Optional," it says on some forms.) Decisions aren't supposed to be made on the basis of race or creed. Sure, you're always writing this stuff down, filling out papers for their statistics. But then your race and creed and ethnic origin—so much of what makes you "you" in other countries—is reduced to the safety of numbers in democratic America.

Dave and Selma lived in a semi-detached house in a little development not far from the Wal-Mart. They were that next step up from mobile homes, these "villas," but they didn't feel a lot more permanent. They were just so many walls that white trash blew up against.

And there was Dave standing in the door.

"What you want, Hunk?"

When I was seventeen, eighteen years old I couldn't get

over the idea that I was too skinny for six feet three. I wanted to feel lean and taut, but I was awkward and brittle. Which probably was one reason I wanted to go into the service. But, yeah, everybody called me "Hunk." Some asshole was looking over my shoulder when I signed up for gym one day and saw me fill in my mother's maiden name: Unkovic. So I became Hunk. I didn't say anything about it. But when people used that name I shrank a little, and hated them a little for making that happen. And Dave, I hated him anyway.

"Selma here?"

"She's restin', Hunk."

"Un-hunh. Well. I got something I want to talk to her about. She's not asleep is she?"

"Don't know. Don't think so."

And don't give a shit, I thought.

We just stood there looking at each other, like there wasn't anything else to say. The front door opened right into the living room and I was watching for Selma to hear us and come out from the bedroom, but she didn't. Moths were swarming around the bulb over the door and around our faces. Finally one hit Dave in his half-open mouth and he spit and brushed it away. "Hunk, you come back tomorrow."

"It's no big deal, Dave. But I'm leaving tomorrow and I just wanted to talk to Selma about, you know, mail and stuff."

"What time you leaving in the morning?"

"Real early. Before sunup."

"Guess you'll have to call her."

"No, man. I want to see her."

"Don't think so," he said, drawing himself up in the doorway, trying to bulk up and intimidate me like I was some traffic violator or small-time criminal perpetrator. "Now you just run along."

There's something in the glands of men like Dave that just picks fights. They're like roosters in barnyards, but most of the time they've got no hens and poor Selma, God love her, she paid for whatever Dave was missing. I don't think he even got much release out of beating her. It was just something he did, like jerking off. He knew I knew that Selma was hurting. She'd have a black eye; maybe a loose tooth. But he was going to face me down. And we stood there for a minute again, in silence, the bugs flying around our faces. And he was thinking we'd go through the whole predictable ritual of confrontation, the shoving and name-calling and the first hits, and then he'd come in on me fast and beat the living hell out of me. He was getting primed.

I knew Dave. I knew this house and I knew, asshole that he was, he kept his Wackenhut club next to the door. He'd shown it to me a couple of times. It was a full yard of hardened rubber with a flexible steel core and little ball bearings at the ends, a billy club gone high-tech and lethal. At least that is what you were supposed to think. Dave used to like to pick it up to make a point. Used to like to hold it in his hand and feel its weight. Used to play with it some-times when he was sitting there in the living room talking on the phone.

"Well, let me come in for a second," I said and started to shoulder past him. He pushed me against the doorjamb. I put my hand behind me to get steady and just looked at him. I don't know why I was so calm, but I was almost limp against the doorway with his hand on my chest and his face in mine and the stink of stale beer and sticky saliva in my nose and—and I felt the end of the club in my hand.

Part of me had thought this through. Part of me had thought about Dave, and that stick. Maybe it was a dream. Maybe, having lived through this before in the quiet of my sleep, it was easier to handle now. But in that minute I broke all the patterns I'd learned. And didn't shout or shove or call names. I just set out to take Dave apart as quickly and effectively as I could.

I pushed off from him, into the house, and stepped back, just to get a little room for maneuver. Didn't threaten. Didn't gesture. Didn't scream. I just started swinging that damn club, and hard, damn hard. The first blow glanced off his forearm with a crack. He grabbed his wrist and that exposed his head just long enough for me to catch him with the backswing on the side of the skull behind the ear. That loosened his joints a little. Once. Twice. Again. And he wasn't defending himself much anymore. He went down. I wanted the face. I wanted the teeth. But he was starting to curl up like a fetus as I kept swinging. Nine, ten, eleven. It was strange. I think I was actually counting out loud. I don't know why. I don't know what number I was looking for. Then just for a second the son of a bitch caught the end of the club. He wrenched, twisted, and pushed and knocked me off balance. I fell back over the little coffee table, but held on. Dave was dazed and he couldn't quite get up and grip the end of the stick at the same time, and anyway it was slick with his blood and snot by then. I twisted it once more and got clean away. And I just kept beating him, wanting to be sure he wasn't going to get up for a while. You don't let someone like Dave get up.

Selma grabbed me from behind. She sank her fingernails into my cheeks near the eyeballs and I had to drop the club for a second to get her hands off my face and throw her back across the room. She stumbled and lost her balance, knocking over a trophy on a chest of drawers. Then she picked it up, the first weapon that came to hand. But I had the club again, and she shrank back.

Maybe we talked. Maybe we said something to each other. But I don't think so. The only sounds that come back to me are the animal sound of my lungs and heart and the Velcro rasp of my tongue inside my dried-up mouth.

"You okay?" was all I remember saying. And all I remember from her was the fear and—yeah—the fascination in her eyes, like she hadn't ever seen me before.

When I reported for duty in Wichita the next day, the scratches from Selma's nails still made jagged stripes across my face, like tribal scars.

II   I did basic training at Fort Benning, in Columbus, Georgia. I heard from my mother a couple of weeks after I started that Dave had recovered, but slowly. He hadn't pressed any kind of charges against me. That wouldn't be his style. And, still, Selma stayed with him. Otherwise, not much word from Westfield, and not much time to think about it, really. I was settling into the new universe of the Army. My home became the barracks, my town the fort. And it was a nice town. It had class, I thought. The senior officers lived in big white houses on tree-lined streets that looked out on the golf course. (There are thirty-six holes at Benning.) The lawns were tidy and large. Sure, you knew this was an Army installation: in the middle of the main post the three jump towers were two hundred feet high, painted red and white, looking like stickmen from space. There were sheds filled with rows and rows of swing-landing trainers for paratroopers, soldiers twirling from them like chickens on conveyor belts. There were tanks and Hum-Vs and mortars in their own special parking lots, and warehouses so tightly guarded and rigged up with electronic surveillance that they set off your fuzz-buster whenever you drove by. No question, this was Army. But in every corner of the base, the buildings were as orderly as the Main Street America you see in old movies. There were even white clapboard churches with little steeples.

My mother actually wrote to me a couple of times, but

23

I couldn't quite write back. And then she stopped and I didn't really care too much. Just about all that was left of my family was trouble, and I had another world to live in, now, and other concerns.

Ranger school was the first real test I faced in the Army, and I knew it would be. Even when you're in basic you're getting psyched for Ranger, if that's the way you plan to go, and you could see it coming at you across the calendar like your personal doomsday. You convinced yourself no amount of PT was enough, you had to do more pushups, run longer distances, break your body down so it could come back strong at just that right moment when you'd need it—but you knew those moments were going to stretch into days, and weeks, and there was no way you were going to hold up. No way.

Even south Georgia was cool before dawn. The streetlights of Fort Benning glowed sulfur yellow along the roads, but on the path I took there were none. I was running by feel, navigating by shadows, letting my mind drop into that hole where the sound of your shoes hitting the ground goes, that hollow sound that sucks you in with it. I liked to be at that place where the sweat begins to pour off you and you think "Sweat," and if you slow for a second at that hour it starts to cool and you think "Cold," and if you keep going you think "Quit. The Pain." But, hey, you do keep going. And all you hear is the rhythm of your feet. I've talked to some people who say that while they're running they think. I guess I did, too. But I never remembered what it was that I'd thought. It was like sleep. Whatever it was that went through my mind only came back in pieces. No, I ran to keep from thinking. And I ran a lot in those days to become a Ranger.

The shower was the reward.

"I am fucking wiped out," Clifton shouted over the

water. "Wiped fucking out." He'd been running, too. And we were going to be running some more. This was a pre-run run, for those of us with Ranger in our gut.

Water. Love the feel of the water on my face. Love to breathe it.

"You don't know what tired is," I said.

"We gonna be drones," said Clifton. "Fucking drones."

"If we're lucky." The water drummed against my eyelids.

"RE-COG-NIZING!" I shouted.

"Recognizing-that-I-volunteered-as-a-Ranger-fully-knowing-the-hazards-of-my-chosen-profession-I-will-always-endeavor-to-uphold-the-prestige-honor-and-high"—Clifton had been shouting in one long breath but now he stumbled for a second—" 'esprit-de-corps'-of-the-Rangers." Clifton took a quick breath and shouted back at me. "ACKNOWLEDGING!"

"Acknowledging the fact that a Ranger is a more elite soldier who arrives at the cutting edge of battle by land, sea, or air, I accept the fact that as a Ranger my country expects me to move further, faster and fight harder than any other soldier.—NEVER!"

"Never-shall-I-fail-my-comrades . . ." he went on.

"GALLANTLY," I answered, reciting lines about respecting superior officers and keeping neat. Then I called out "ENERGETICALLY!"

And now we were in chorus:

"Energetically will I meet the enemies of my country. I shall defeat them on the field of battle for I am better trained, and will fight with all my might. Surrender is not a Ranger word. I will never leave a fallen comrade to fall into the hands of the enemy and under no circumstances will I ever embarrass my country.—READILY!

"Readily will I display the intestinal fortitude required to fight on to the Ranger objective and complete the mission, though I be the lone survivor.

"RANGERS LEAD THE WAY!"

It was easy enough to memorize the creed. The first letters of each paragraph spelled R-A-N-G-E-R. Sometimes I faltered around the housekeeping details, the neatness of dress, the care of equipment. Of course the lines that you actually learned first were "Surrender is not a Ranger word," and "Though I be the lone survivor."

The Appalachian forests where we did our mountain training were dark and open. The huge trees cast such black shade that only a few things could grow down below—ferns, hopeless little saplings, poison oak, and huge thickets of mountain laurel, the trunks twisted and hard, the leaves shining like polished leather. Every afternoon, almost so you could set your watch by it, the rains came.

When you're humping on the twelfth mile of mountain trail, straight up half the time, straight down the other half, the rains make your life miserable. You start to lose your footing at every step, and you cling to roots, to branches, to anything you can grab ahold of to help you move. Then, when you don't want them to, they grab you. "Wait-a-minute vines," we called them. After a couple of days all of us were hurting bad, banged up from slides on narrow trails.

We stopped to regroup in a shallow depression among some laurel. Sunset was about an hour away, but here the twilight was deep already. The downpour seemed to increase right as we stopped, the rain falling in sheets that made it hard to see more than a few feet in any direction. It was dripping off the bills of our caps and the hoods of our ponchos like a liquid veil. But you didn't want to stay still too long because the damp and the chill started to catch up with you.

"Infantry sunshine," said Clifton.

"Yeah," said Hernandez. "That tells you somethin' about the infantry." He was trying to whisper, but the rattle of the rain on the leaves was so heavy that the words came out in a hoarse shout.

I didn't say anything for a minute. I was afraid if I started talking I'd lose my focus, give in to the cold and the ache and let myself slide.

"We're close," said Jackson. "Real close."

"Yeah, you got it," said Hernandez, hunkering down under his poncho. "But close to what?"

"Unless we fucked up, Alpha is defending a position on this hill. Should be this slope."

"You think we got the right mountain?"

Nobody said anything. I was wondering if the rain could get any heavier. If it did, I figured we'd be swimming instead of walking. "Hey, I don't know," said Jackson, "but look, if we've plotted this right—" He started to reach for the map, but there was no point. Might as well throw it in a lake and try to read it underwater. "That path we came off should take a bend to the left in a couple hundred yards and work its way along a rock face. Alpha's supposed to be in a kind of a cut just above it. Right?" said Jackson. A couple of us nodded. "But they—this rain. They must be in the middle of a waterfall right now."

We all thought about this for a second. Nobody wanted to give Jackson right. But he could be right about this.

"Where do they move?" I said.

"Damned if I know. I don't think they know."

"They come back around the cliff," said Hernandez.

"Jesus, think what the footing's like."

"Let's go for them," said Jackson. "In this rain, in this dark, if we're guessing right we can catch them crawling."

"They're gonna be looking for us," said Clifton.

"Yeah, but if we move in this rain they're not gonna see us," said Jackson. "Their thermal sights, their NVDs, they're all gonna be fucked."

"That's why we love the rain, right?" said Hernandez, pulling on his collar with both hands as if that could stop the steady flow of water now running in rivers against his skin.

"Fucking love it," I said.

I was convinced Jackson was an asshole. In fact I knew he was, and part of me wanted to see him prove it to everyone—including himself—with this stupid deployment in a downpour. He was too deep into the game. This stuff wasn't in the mission profile. But we all moved out. We spread out on each side of the trail and in seconds we started to lose each other. Clifton became a blurred outline to my right. Jackson disappeared altogether to my left. We moved slowly, so slowly that it was hard to judge the distance we traveled. We were trying to stay parallel to the trail, but we only had a notion of where the trail was from the map burned into our minds and, sometimes, a break in the intensity of the rain. It seemed to have a rhythm to it, like the sky was heaving, throwing water at us, then holding back a little, then throwing some more. The leaves under our feet were slick, floating on mud, and the moment you put your weight wrong you slipped. As we got nearer the cliff trail the angle of the slope increased and it wasn't just Alpha that was crawling. If Alpha was there at all.

A chill was working its way into my shoulders and the back of my neck, crawling down my spine, creeping under my ribs like a sickness. The tops of my legs ached. My right ankle, which I'd sprained any number of times as a kid, and which never was strong, had begun to throb and cramp. But I kept moving. "Focus," I kept telling myself, repeating the word into my teeth, feeling the muscles of my face harden with it. "Focus." An enormous, rotting tree blocked my way. Down to the right, the trail would let me get around it somehow. But our orders were to stay off that path. I looked down there to see who else was moving, but with the light gone and the rain still coming, I couldn't make Clifton out. Couldn't see anyone. Jackson was gone, too. I listened. Nothing but rain and leaves. I felt my way along the moss-covered bark. The wood was so full of rot it crumbled in my hand like wet paper. I figured it must be about seven feet high, and I didn't have any idea how far it might go in either direction. I inched along the side of the tree until I felt the stub of a broken limb that seemed strong enough to step on. But even with that leg up, I couldn't get any purchase on the wet moss and the wood. I pulled my combat knife and used it like a pick, stabbing my way along the green slimy surface of the tree.

And then, in a second, the rain stopped. I was grunting and hammering the blade into the rotting wood, and the forest fell silent. I froze and listened. There were scattered drops of water falling from the leaves. Nothing else that I could hear. And then I could see, coming at me, another curtain of water. If God had had a garden hose he couldn't have made a cleaner line of water clattering down through the leaves. It was an onslaught, a stampede of rain. And I was over the tree and sliding down the other side, working my way through the light brush again toward the objective.

My head was pulled back so fast and so hard there was no time for thought and the blunt edge of the knife half-strangled me as I went down.

"You're dead" was all that the breath in my ear said. Real quiet. No anger. Just a little adrenaline behind it. And dead right. I sat down where I was. The soldier from Alpha disappeared into the dark and rain before I could make out much more about him than that he'd left his kit somewhere. He was in his green T-shirt and his camouflage pants. He was black. He was moving fast.

"Now you men may think this is show-and-tell, but you better take a look at what I'm showing you if you want to live to tell about it."

Everybody tried to be serious, but there was something about the sergeant with the little bottles that made you want to laugh—at the same time your flesh was starting to crawl. He was standing on the tailgate of a transport truck and we were standing in the high grass, getting ready to start the phase of the program in north Florida swamps, and he was giving us his little talk on snakes, scorpions, and spiders.

"You men—any women here?—no—you men are going to be walking into the poison capital of America this morning. Things that crawl, things that fly, things that swim, things that rub against you while you're marching and creep in with you when you're sleeping. Here at Eglin we've got them all."

He told us about cottonmouths and copperheads, timber rattlers, some of them as big around as your arm, and coral snakes, those quiet, colorful little serpents. "If you are bitten you probably are not going to feel much. It's going to get a little numb around the bite. Then the poison goes to work on your nervous system. Maybe your skin gets real sensitive, maybe light starts to hurt you, your heart starts beating so fast you don't know what's happening, you go blind, you shit in your pants. We can't tell you exactly what is going to happen to you, but if you don't guess right about what bit you, and fast, then you are in trouble."

"Excuse me, sir."

"Yes, sir."

"What's the procedure if we're in trouble?"

"Medevac. We'll get to that."

I could hear Clifton talking under his breath and I nudged him. "But will Medevac get to me?" he whispered.

The sergeant didn't have as much to say about scorpions. Maybe he thought their looks made the point. It was a relief to hear that we probably wouldn't die from a scorpion sting. It was pretty obvious that the sergeant was bored by scorpions.

If you listen to enough of these talks, you realize that there are some medics who are just repeating what they're told to repeat, and some who are really into it, and the ones who are really, really into it have their favorites. This sergeant, you could tell, liked spiders. He held up a tarantula that looked big enough to eat a sparrow. "You wake up one morning with this crawling across your face and—nothing. This is not Hollywood. Pick it up and put it in your pocket if you want. Impress your friends. I'm not saying it won't bite you. But your tarantula is not going to take a big piece out of your day.

"This, on the other hand"—he held up a bottle with something inside that looked like a big black grape with legs —"is a problem. This is a black widow. Take a close look. There's nothing on eight legs that looks like this, and, as I say, it bites you, you got a problem."

I'd never seen anything quite like it, that's for sure, and I was fascinated. You hear about black widows from the time you're a little boy. Kids spook each other with stories about how horrible they are. And there's no mistaking them. They look like finely engineered bits of evil, black as space, with that red hourglass on their bellies. Why so damn black? Why the red? Why an hourglass? They're not natural. They don't blend with anything. They're just there, evil and alien and waiting to kill you.

"Two tiny red dots may appear where it bites, but you might or might not feel it. Then the swelling begins after a few minutes. Cramps. Pain that makes you scream. Your muscles go stiff. Sometimes you get an erection—yeah, but it doesn't go away. Your penis swells and you can't urinate. You get chills, you get rashes, and your muscles tie up in knots, and, if you're lucky, you get to somewhere where there's antiserum. You do not have any in your kits. And if you are not lucky—well, the best way to deal with this situation is to stay alert in the first place."

"You," said a whisper just behind me and talking to me. "You are one of my dead men."

I turned enough to see a black soldier, but there wasn't much I could tell about him. He was almost as tall as I was, but his frame was heavier. I expected him to smile, but he wasn't giving anything away. "By that big tree day before yesterday," he said.

"Alpha."

"You got it."

"Brown recluse," said the sergeant, holding up a bottle with a little shriveled spider in it that looked a lot like something you'd find in the dust that settles in the corner of a tool shed. "We have more problems with these than any other spider at Eglin," he said. "If it bites you, probably it won't kill you, not directly, but you might wish that it had. The area around the bite goes pale and you feel a stinging sensation, or a burn. Then the hemorrhages start into the skin around the bite, the flesh starts to decay, and infections can start very easily. There may also be internal bleeding, convulsions, cardiovascular collapse. Death.

"So—your tarantula, which looks big and hairy and dangerous, is not. Your black widow is dangerous as hell, but you know it when you see it. The brown recluse, which will be hiding in the kinds of dry places you're going to want to sleep and to rest, is the most dangerous of all, in my humble judgment, because it is the one you forget about. Any questions?"

I had a question for the soldier behind me, but when I turned around he'd gone. I wasn't going to look for him. But I could feel a good hate for him coming on, and the idea that he wanted that didn't make it any better.

We saw plenty of snakes in the swamps at Eglin Air Force Base, especially cottonmouths. We would spend five, six, sometimes almost eight hours paddling through the cypress stumps, then wading over and around them, and on top of them. They stabbed you and tripped you and snagged you. And more than once, a cottonmouth came gliding toward us across the black surface of the water, then made its way right through the momentarily frozen collection of humans. Soon we quit caring.

That first night we tried to be sure there were no scorpions in our boots, no brown recluses lurking in the site we chose to sleep in. But who could tell? None of us was bitten by anything but mosquitoes and chiggers. By the second night we were so beat it didn't seem to matter.

Eglin, on the edge of Florida's armpit, bracketed between towns called Niceville and Valparaiso and Bagdad, is a special, humid little corner of hell. You spend sixteen days there rotting on the move. When you first get into the Zodiacs you think you're going to keep your feet up and fairly dry. But you cramp in the same position after a while. The rubber on your ass, the mosquitoes and gnats in your face, the sweat oozing from every place in your body and turning to lines of cheese in your groin, all that breaks down your good intentions pretty fast and you let your feet drag in the cool when you get a chance. Then they turn white and wrinkle. The calluses you've built up in basic and with all the running and marching and the action in the mountains, they all peel away.

Your brain starts to unravel a little, too. One afternoon on a small rise in the middle of the swamp I saw a cluster of flowers. Not just ordinary swamp flowers, but a selection of daisies like something from a florist shop. And I thought, Isn't that pretty? and Isn't that weird, here? and then, It's not here. I just looked at it, and looked at it. Still there. But I didn't want to reach out and touch it because I knew it wasn't.

"You lose something?" Hernandez asked when he saw me move my hand through the air where the flowers were not.

On the morning of about the twelfth day it turned strangely, suddenly cool at night and we all slept with a chill on us, then woke up early. Clifton sat up, rubbed his eyes. I shined my flashlight low in his direction and it caught what looked like a wrinkle on the earth behind him. "Freeze," I whispered hard. He did. "Stand up and—and don't look back until you've taken a couple steps forward." A copperhead had slithered in under him while he slept, for the warmth, but he'd been so completely out of it that he hadn't moved the whole time. I was frightened for him and my pulse was racing. When I saw that he actually saw the snake I was relieved, too.

"There is something they're not telling us about this place," said Hernandez after the first night marching in the desert at Dugway Proving Ground in Utah.

"What they are telling us is bad enough," I said. "My feet are like hamburger. I'm so tired I'm seeing things. My stomach's got a knot in it, and I don't know if I'm coming down with the flu, or just beat to hell, or one of these goddamn chemical agents is doing something to me. How are you feeling?"

"Same as you—that's what I mean. I think there's something leaking, you know? I think they didn't clean it all up. But, like, I can't use the antidote because I don't know and the antidote fucks you up."

"I was kidding. The detector says there's nothing."

"Yeah. But maybe they fixed it."

"Aw, shit, man. Leave that alone."

"And what about biological agents? What about those? Anthrax? Q-fever? Shit."

"Shut up."

"Suppose there are some of those little anthrax spores around? Just leftovers? All you got to do is breathe one in. Bingo. One hundred percent dead."

"Shut the fuck up. We are here and we are not going to get out of here, and it ain't going to make things better if we make ourselves crazy." We didn't talk after that. Maybe we were afraid to.

It was the middle of summer but we were in the high desert, six thousand feet up, where the air is crisp and light shines through it with an edge. All night long the black of the sky had been perforated by the stars as brilliantly as the dome of a planetarium, but now that I could lie back and look at them for a second, some were already disappearing behind the first light of dawn. Soon there would be only the planets and the sliver of the moon, and then the sun. But I couldn't sleep, and as much as I tried to concentrate on the stars my mind wouldn't let go of the random facts we'd been taught about chemical warfare since the first days of basic.

Night is the best time for chemicals, I thought. A calm, cool night, a light breeze. Perfect for killing. Sun causes most of the chemical agents to break down. Sunlight alone can reduce by sixty percent the area covered effectively by nerve gases. A high wind can carry lethal doses of some nerve gas for a hundred miles, but it's unpredictable. It can dilute the gases, too. You pop the top on a night like this, though, and—what kind of gas would it be? What did they try out here at Dugway back in the 1960s? What didn't they try? They only taught us about the obvious stuff. Your mustard and your blister gas, a big favorite of the Russians that left you writhing in pain and your skin peeling off your body like a slug covered in salt. These were called "harassing agents." They weren't necessarily going to kill you, but they took you out of action fast. The first thing they destroyed was your eyes.

Then there were the ones that were meant to be lethal: choking gas like phosgene, the big killer in World War I, which shut down your lungs; and blood gas, usually based on cyanide, which threw you into convulsions before you suffocated and died.

And night was the best time for them all.

I never could identify the planets, except to know they weren't stars. Venus. Mars. Love and war. Silver blue and red, they said, but I wondered if I was just imagining the colors.

Some of the nerve gases had exotic names, almost mystical-sounding, like Tabun and Soman. Others were cold and technological, like car models, CMPF and VR-55 and VX. They were very sophisticated and the formulas could be adjusted so that the lethal effects lingered effectively for twenty minutes in some cases, up to two thousand seven hundred hours in others. In a war the nerve gases probably were not going to be used on the front lines, because they were too dangerous for your own men. They were designed mainly to go at the rear guard, the airfields, and, while nobody said it straight out, the civilian population. They were the most terrible of the chemical weapons because you didn't have to breathe them to die. You just had to touch them, and you didn't know when you had. You couldn't see them, or smell them. You could only feel what they did to you. People would drop quickly, like victims of a plague in the Bible, and they might never know what hit them.

Back in the heyday of Dugway our American scientists would have shot these agents in rockets and artillery shells, sprayed them like insecticide from crop dusters, drenched this wasteland of sand and mesquite, Gila monsters and sidewinders with the most evil compounds they could devise, sure that the Russians had developed something even worse. They experimented a lot with delayed delivery systems, devices like mines left to go off when the enemy had overrun your position. If any of those were forgotten or misplaced they could still—

But this was not what I wanted to think about. "REC-OGNIZING that I volunteered . . . ," I started repeating to myself, but repetition didn't work. My mind kept veering back to the gases. Now, I thought, they sent Rangers here to train, with our feet raw and rotted and bleeding from the swamps, with our systems overloaded with fatigue, and marching hour after hour in MOPP-4—full chemical, biological, and nuclear warfare gear—the rubberized suits with the activated charcoal lining and the drawstrings and Velcro and the hood and the gas mask, of course, and the straw to drink your water from a sealed bottle like a huge fly sucking from a flower. And then sometime we'd cross the very same ground MOPP-0, more or less normal combat gear, the suits and masks stowed and no protections at all but the little antidote kits we were told not to use until convulsions started. Were they just training us, or testing us? Or testing the equipment and testing the effects, years later, of the chemicals? Who the hell knew? But—every one of us felt something was wrong. But—even if nothing was wrong, we were told, we would think so. A big part of chemical and biological warfare was the way the stuff worked on your mind when you started to think about it.

Time to take a shit, I thought, and moved as quietly as I could over a low rise near the camp and dug a little trench with my knife. As I squatted and looked around I saw another soldier at the limit of my vision in the rose-gray twilight. He was black and I couldn't begin to make out his features, but if he saw me at all he took no notice. At first I thought he was there for the same reason I was, but then I saw he was pulling off his boots. I finished my business and watched. He was taking a kind of bath with water from his canteen, rinsing his hands, splashing his face, rubbing behind his ears, over his head, even washing his feet. The idea of the chemicals must really have gotten to him, I thought. He's trying to wash them off. Now he was standing with his hands resting on his chest and his head bent down a little bit, like a vertical corpse. This wasn't decontamination. I couldn't figure out what he was doing. I stayed there in the shadows, watching. He was facing the stain of light just starting to spread across the eastern horizon. And he dropped to his knees and put his head to the ground.

Damn, I thought. I'll be damned. I wanted to laugh, but I didn't. I moved closer. The morning was as still as pond water and I had to take care. Even the sound of my pants legs rubbing together could have been heard. As it was the sand slipping beneath my boots filled my ears with its noise. About thirty yards away I could start to make out the soldier's features. It was him. Alpha. His eyes were closed and as he kneeled his head touched a stone on the ground. He was muttering to himself with his ass in the air. It would have been so easy to put my knife to his throat the way he had put his to mine. But I left it in the sheath. Weird and funny as the spectacle seemed that first time that I saw it in person, I recognized it from travel movies on late-night TV and old cartoons on Saturday mornings as the ritual of prayer. This wouldn't be the moment for revenge, I thought.

He stood again, unmoving, then shook his head slightly as if waking from a deep sleep. He didn't look in my direction, but I heard his voice.

"You know how I got you in Georgia?" he said.

"The noise," I said. "Climbing over the tree."

"No, soldier. The smell," he said, turning to look at me, his eyes white and clear in the dawn light, and angry for reasons I could not penetrate. "The white devil stinks," he said.

He walked away and I let him go. I was tired, too tired to move, too surprised to think of anything to say. He disappeared over a small dune. I had been crouching and as I stood up I realized I'd grabbed a handful of sand. My knuckles were white around it. Funny how fear and anger can leave your brain calm while your body ties in knots. I stared at my clenched fist. I loosened my grip. The rough grains slipped through the creases of my hand like time.

III   I led an oddly peaceful life at Hunter Field near Savannah, Georgia, improving my leadership, survival, and killing skills and falling in love and thinking about raising a family. The Army gave my life an order it hadn't had, if not quite the order I'd expected.

In my first year, in fact it was at Eglin in the swamp one night, an idea came to me that helped me to endure. I kept focusing on it for the rest of the time I was there, and then at Dugway, too, and eventually it took shape in my mind as something that was mysterious but gave me power: there is strength in submission. I thought in those days that the notion was original, a kind of pact I made with myself. It wasn't like me. My way had been to never give in, ever. But I focused on this notion and built on it and repeated it to myself like I was going to work myself into a trance with it, convincing myself that you could give in and be strong at the same time. And in the most basic sense it worked. I stayed on duty, stayed on track. I guess I just knew that if I talked and acted in the Army the way I had done all my life in Westfield, always ready to fire back at any insult, real or imagined, always letting people know what I thought of them, well, I wasn't going to make it in the Army. And I did want to make it. I really did. Especially as a Ranger.

I wanted to erase my past and make of myself something completely new. I wanted independence from everything I'd known, from my mother and sisters, from the memory of my father, from the boredom of the malls and the backyards. But I didn't have a clear idea, really, what that new me would be like. A Ranger. Yeah. Maybe an officer someday. But I couldn't quite picture that life. I defined myself entirely by what I was not. So I learned in those days to give in and to let the world I'd entered make of me what it would. I learned not only to take orders, but to absorb them, endure them, digest them, internalize them, even, in a weird way, to enjoy them. Eventually I was fascinated by the discipline itself.

There was a part of me, I believed, that could become a machine.

But by the end of three years, when I was based at Hunter and a fairly skilled survivor and quite able to kill on full automatic, I'd started to lighten up.

Partly, it's a fact, you have to have a sense of humor to do demolition work, and by then that was my particular specialty: knowing how to blow up the enemy, and keep him from doing the same to me. The basic techniques are no-brainers, like most of what you do in the Army. Setting up a Claymore mine by the side of a trail, for instance, is at most a problem of style. Any fool can read the directions, figure the pattern of the blast, and set the detonator to fire. The most basic tripwire uses a clothespin and a plastic spoon. Nothing exotic about it. But the trick is in the precise positioning, and in the camouflage. You want to be able to deceive and eliminate someone who knows every bit as much as you. In the killing game you have to imagine constantly that your enemy is smarter, more creative, and more committed than you are. If you believe that, then there is always the incentive to think. There is always the little adrenaline rush of fear. And you live longer. Get it wrong just once and, as one of my instructors used to say, there's nothing left of you but pink smoke. You can be deadly serious about this stuff. But if you are, you'll likely be dead sooner rather than later. You have to stay loose. Alert but loose. And to do that, sometimes you have to laugh.

The other reason I lightened up was Josie.

The base itself was a decent enough place to live, and the South, with its slow ways, was generally pretty kind to me. Even now, when I see Spanish moss and live oaks, palmettos and sawgrass, I get this weird rush that's partly the security of familiarity, partly the thrill of battle. We spent a lot of time crawling in that gray sand and red clay, hiding among those leaves and burying ourselves in the pinestraw, hardening our bodies, working on our timing, refining our discipline, simulating death. And then we'd play—at the beach, in boats, and, for a while in my case, at the service clubs. But after I met Josie other women and other worlds seemed a little bit beside the point.

I first saw her, as it happened, in a filling station. I had an old Nova I picked up at Benning for eight hundred dollars. One stifling Sunday in June it just barely limped into the Fina station outside Hunter's Montgomery Gate, then died on me. There was nobody around. Even the car wash was shut. I tried to make a few adjustments myself, but the engine still sputtered and coughed, strangled and croaked, and I was stupid with the heat and couldn't begin to figure out what to do. I could feel the sun burning through the shirt on my back. Sweat was running into the corners of my eyes and as I was wiping it off, smearing grease across the bridge of my nose and feeling just about as grungy as I could get, I looked up and saw her smiling, sipping a Pepsi. She was leaning on the fender of her old Triumph convertible in front of Road Savannah Import Auto Repair, a little junkyard of rusting Alfas and MGs that looked like it was closed, too.

"Need some help?" she called out.

I looked out at her again. I still wasn't sure she was

talking to me. I could feel the blood rushing to my face and I fooled around under the hood. I was clueless before she arrived and now I was completely distracted. She walked over and stood behind me, still sipping the Pepsi. I felt, well, kind of trapped.

"Looks like nothing's open around here," she said. "Should have known on a Sunday, but sometimes Jim Bob works odd hours. Sure you don't want some help?"

I figured it was time to cut my losses. "I'm not much of a mechanic," I said. "Got any ideas?"

"Mmmmmm," she said and reached over to the distributor cap and twisted it a little bit. "Try it now."

With that a process of trial and error began that lasted the better part of an hour. Josie, I'm sure, realized at the time what it was all about: a kind of greasy courtship ritual staged to the sound of a revving V6 and the smell of unleaded octane. But obvious as it was, the fact of what was going on is only clear to me now, much later. Obvious as it was.

Her hands were what fascinated me first. I liked the kindness of her face and the warmth of her brown eyes. Through her cutoff jeans I could see she had beautiful tight hips and her breasts moved easily under her shirt, but I was trying not to look at all that too much. She had thick golden brown hair. Later, I would love the dense feel of her hair in my fingers and the smell of it next to my face as she slept. But that first day, that first hour it was her hands—those long, delicate fingers—that impressed me. In the gunky, steamy little hell of my Chevrolet engine they seemed angelic.

"Look, I have to buy you dinner after all this help," I told her.

"That's okay," she said. "I've got a date."

"Then let me buy you a drink or an ice cream or something right now, maybe the Crispy Chick is open."

"Maybe I'll have a sweet tea," she said. "But not at the Crispy Chick."

"Anywhere."

She smiled at me and said nothing. And then her face got very serious and she looked into my eyes, and still she didn't say anything.

"I don't really know this town too well," I said. "How about if I follow you?"

We drove out of Savannah.

I'd thought we were going around the corner. But when we turned from DeRenne onto Abercorn she shot off down the road like she was making an escape, and I followed as well as I could in the Nova, the old crate rattling and squeaking and complaining. I was wondering why I hadn't just left it behind at the filling station and gotten in the car with her, or asked her to get in with me. I guess because she didn't offer or ask.

We were headed south, out of town, and every time I guessed where she might stop we just kept on going, past the medical offices, the pawn shops, and the malls. The Taco Bell and Godfather's Pizza and The Kettle were all passed by. Was she taking me home? Now there was an exciting thought. When we came up on the English Oaks Garden Apartments I imagined, maybe because she was driving an English car, that she might turn in. But no. And not at the Timberland Apartments or the Spanish Villa Apartments either. When we stopped at lights she just smiled, then took off too fast for me to ask a question. She just kept driving on toward I-95, then even past that. We were fifteen miles from Hunter and I was wondering if she'd decided to lose me, but I couldn't catch up with her. Not in that Nova. She made a quick, hard turn off the highway onto a back road and headed east through pine woods and low marshes where the pavement seemed to rise out of the land like a spine. I just settled in behind the wheel, and followed.

If we'd been driving straight off the edge of the earth I'd have followed that Triumph. The wind whipped Josie's hair into knots and curls, and every so often she'd take both her hands off the wheel and run them through the tangle to try to tame it. The late afternoon sun was giving everything a warm glow, and the sight of her face in that kindly light when she looked back over her shoulder at me was as exciting and as strange, it seemed at that moment, as anything I had ever seen.

She stopped at last at a bait and tackle shop by a little pond on a dirt road in a place I did not know.

There was a long wooden dock out on the pond where you could fish for bass if you wanted to, and it was open on a Sunday afternoon in case there were those who did. Inside they sold fiberglass rods and spinning reels, and also bamboo poles with bobbers, and Buck knives and landing nets and Slim Jims and Vienna sausages and pickled eggs and Yoo-Hoo chocolate sodas and, if you had the need for them, six-packs of beer and shotgun shells. And in an old Frigidaire in a corner behind the counter they had big plastic jars full of tea.

It was real sweet, with just the right edge of lemon. When I think about it I can still taste it.

There was a thin summer haze above the lake. The twilight was blue and gray, but where the water rippled with a rising fish or a beetle skimming across the surface it shimmered with the last pink light of the sun.

"This is a fine place," I said.

"You approve?"

"Ah? Approve?" I lay back on the dock and stared up at the early stars and breathed in the summer air. "I love this place."

"I'm glad."

What did we talk about? The weather, a little. So hot but now so nice. Her car and mine, but cars didn't seem so interesting anymore.

"I am—you're going to think this is weird, probably."

"Mmmmm" was all she said.

"I just have this rush of happiness right now like I can't

tell you. I don't know any other way to say it. I'm happy I'm here in this place. Happy I'm drinking this tea. Happy I've met you and happy I'm with you. And that's the truth. And I don't know the first thing about you except that you know something about cars, and you know this place, and you're beautiful and—I'm just really happy to be here— with you. Right now—and I know all this is just incredibly uncool—but right now I wouldn't want to be anywhere else in the world with anyone else in the world."

It was all true, but I couldn't believe I was feeling it or saying it. Sometimes the right words never come to you. And sometimes the right words come out all wrong. But somewhere in what I said I guess there was something that was right enough. Josie leaned over and kissed me and then sat back, and I felt like we were much younger than we were, like we were little kids on a pretend date. And I liked the feeling.

"Are you from Savannah?"

"Hinesville," she said. "I think the boys at Fort Stewart call it Hooterville." I blushed. "Daddy says we've been in these parts since Oglethorpe, in Hinesville and Savannah and the Sea Islands. Not that it counts for much when you go to buy groceries. And you?"

"Kansas," I said. "Near the Oklahoma border."

"How do you like the Army?"

"It's a place to be, I guess. Did you grow up here? Go to school here?"

She'd gone away to school, she said: to Atlanta, first, and then to college outside of Washington, D.C., for a couple of years. Now she was back for the summer, she said, or maybe for longer. "I'm thinking of working with my father. Daddy's got a pulp business. And Mount Vernon College doesn't teach you much about the pulp business."

"But don't you want to get away from here?"

"From here?" she said, sipping her tea. "I've been away. I couldn't wait to get back."

"Your friends, I guess, and—"

"And the place itself. A lot of Savannah is a pit. That's a fact. But this land around here, just this little pond and places like it, I love them. They're home to me. Don't you feel that way about your home?"

"Not so much. I guess the Army's my home."

"Well, it must be hard."

"Sometimes. Hey. Listen, I—I hope I didn't sound too crazy a couple of minutes ago."

"No. No. You were sweet. I didn't know anybody on the base could be that sweet. But you must, well, it must be very lonely. Why are you smiling?"

"I'm thinking, Not now. Do you have to go on that date?"

"Mmmmmm."

"Can we do something later this week?"

"We'll see." She was taking the last sip of her tea. Then she stood up. "Got to go right now, though."

"Well, would it sound too dumb if I asked you, you know, what this afternoon was about?"

"I liked your engine. Daddy has a V6 like that in one of the old crates on the farm. We used to play around with it when it broke down. It's the only engine I know besides the Triumph. So maybe I was showing off a little bit. And, then, I liked you. I don't know anybody from the bases. We don't have much to do with the military in Daddy's business and mostly we just stay away from them. But you seemed so, you know, so easy. Relaxed."

"I blow things up all week long. I've got to relax sometime."

"Sounds interesting," she said, standing next to the door of her car. I wanted to devour her, to tear off her clothes and mine and make love with her there on the hood of the car, or the vinyl seats or the grass or the gravel. I wouldn't have felt or seen a thing but our bodies. But she kept me a little distant. Controlled. And all we did was to kiss, slowly, very slowly, so I could feel all the texture of her lips, so soft, with mine, and breathe a little bit of her breath, and touch the back of her neck, then the smooth curve at the base of her skull with my fingers through that thick hair and pull her body next to mine and feel just the light touch of her breasts against my chest. I was about to go crazy.

"Got to go," she said, putting the tips of those long fingers up against my lips.

"Oh, God."

"I'll be at the office tomorrow. Call me. Rankin Pulp Mills. Ask for Tyler Rankin's office."

The drive back to Hunter Field was long. She drove fast and knew the roads. I didn't. Then she turned north and I turned south. She waved casually, then took hold of the wheel with both hands and was gone. By the time I got back to the city limits I was very, very lonely. And even I realized I was in love.

I sat in the car in the dark in the parking lot. "Time to get a life," I said out loud to no one in particular.

I don't know if I ever understood Josie, although I tried very hard to. We fought so much. We were so frustrated. The things that interested her, apart from me, were not things I'd ever thought about. The questions she asked were ones I did not want to answer. The time and attention and the caring that she demanded were more than I ever thought that I could give. But I did try.

"Tell me about your grandparents," she said one October afternoon as we were sitting on the wide wooden porch of her father's house. She had her own place, at the other end of the property, a very simple house that must have belonged to a sharecropper once but had been made, by her mother, comfortably genteel. Just two rooms and a sandy yard shaded by a pair of live oaks. But we'd had Sunday dinner in the big house and we were still sort of lazily recovering. Her father and her uncle had driven off to look at some other piece of land he was thinking about buying. Her mother and aunt were upstairs. I could hear their voices through the bedroom screens, but couldn't make out what they were saying, and didn't try. Babies must hear voices like that in the womb, the background noise of security and home.

"Not much to tell, as far as I know. Mr. and Mrs. Kurtovic, Mr. and Mrs. Unkovic. I've never met any of them. Never even gotten a birthday card."

"That's sad."

"Not if you don't think about it. So let's not."

"Wouldn't you like to meet them?"

"What would we talk about? How would we talk at all? Do you think they speak English?"

"There must be somebody."

"Please don't push this."

"It's not like you've got anything to hide."

"No, it's not. But it's not like there's a lot to show either."

"Are you going to take me to Kansas to meet your mother?"

"Someday."

"Maybe after Christmas?"

"Maybe. Or maybe never."

"Kurt."

"What?"

"Kurt, you need your mother. You need your family."

"Look at those foals running up and down in the paddock."

"Kurt."

"Please."

"Kurt. Do you want to have children? Do you want to have grandchildren?"

I sat back in that big cane chair and, feeling the pressure behind my eyes of unexpected and unwanted tears, turned my head away.

"Talk to me, Kurt."

But I couldn't. For a minute all I could do was shake my head. And then I had to speak very slowly, and to think more than I wanted to about what I was saying. "You know I love you."

"Yes," she said evenly.

"Could you say that you love me?"

"I do love you."

"Why?"

"That's silly."

"No, it's not. At least not for me. Because—I do know why I love you. There are so many reasons, but I know all of them. And I don't know why you love me."

"But—"

"Let me finish. Please . . . please let me." I was thinking I was about to make a terrible mistake. Some bit of emotional survival instinct was telling me very urgently to shut up. But I couldn't.

"I have loved you," I said, "since the first day I saw you last summer when I didn't know anything about you—and everything I have learned about you since then has made me love you more. And not just you. But everything that is around you and part of you. Your parents. Your home. Your uncle and cousins and your friend Ginny who came down to visit last week. You have a whole life and I'm just part of it, but that's fine. That's better than fine, to be part of your life. And when I sit here on the porch like this and listen to your family and look out on your land and think about you being here next to me, I feel like I belong here. But how can I? I don't come from here, and there's a whole other life on the other side of that fence at Hunter Field. I go back there and it's like there's a switch that goes off and Corporal Kurtovic takes over. And I get through each day and do my job well, and then as soon as I can I come to you. But Josie, that is all, absolutely all, I can handle. Two lives, you see? One in the Army that's an obligation. And one that is you. Please don't ask me to deal with any more."

"I don't understand," she said.

The stillness of the afternoon closed in around me.

"I don't understand," she said again. "I'm not asking you to choose me or the Army or this life or that life. If you feel you've got to make a choice, it's not because of anything I've done."

"Honey?" It was her mother's voice from upstairs. "Could you come up here?" I wondered if she'd been listening. I wondered if she was giving me my break. Anyway, I took it. I shouted that I was going to take a little walk, trying to control my voice, but I'm sure it sounded strange.

If I'd had a gun I would have squeezed off the whole magazine. If I'd been on the base I would have blown something up. Behind the wheel of a car I would have driven like a madman. Which is probably why the survivor in me kept me out of the Nova just then. I was looking for violence. But, finally, the only thing that came to hand was a twisted branch of oak lying on the ground. When I picked it up to bash it against the trunk of the tree it was so rotten that it fell apart in mid-swing.

"Better stick to grenades or whatever you use," Josie said, a little out of breath after running to catch up with me. She put her arms around me, pinning my hands to my sides. "We're going up to the Rileys' in Savannah. Come on with us."

"I don't think so."

"Then be in my house when I get back."

"What time?"

"It'll be late."

"Maybe I better not. I've got to be up early tomorrow."

"You do what you think you have to," she said.

I thought that I would not be there. I went through all the motions of staying away. I went back to the fort, drank a beer, turned on the television and drank another beer, and one more. And the flag and anthem came on and I was still awake in the darkened room, with the only light coming from the screen. And a chill went through me.

As quickly as I could, I turned on first one lamp, then the other, and I dressed again and went out and began to drive.

I'd worked so hard, so damn hard, to win Josie. And now I was throwing it all away and I could feel despair and anger building in me enough to make me blind. For five months, now, I'd forgotten just about everything else in my life. I went through the routine at the fort with no heart and little interest. Every morning was an exercise of will. And now this. I wasn't sure I could stand to see her this night.

Before, when we had known each other for about six weeks, there had been a kind of strange incident. My unit went off for training with the Bundeswehr in Germany, doing low-altitude, low-opening drops, which were danger-ous as hell, and training and drinking and bonding with these guys who had hundred-word English vocabularies while we had zero words of German. It was the kind of thing we always did. You make a lot of buddies around the world as a Ranger. Friends are harder to come by. And when I got back to Hunter Field I was more excited than I could remem-ber being in a real long time because I'd see Josie. But when I called her at the office, her dad said she was out. And when I called her at home I only got the machine. So I waited a day. It was all I could do. And made all those calls again. And then in the evening I'd gone out to her house, parked my car down the road, and walked in along the little path that ran by the creek near her backyard, and just opened the door and went in. She almost never locked the place.

And when she got home I was sitting in the dark and could see her in the doorway. And him, too. I looked at him quickly and her carefully as they said good night. He was about my size, but soft. Easy to take. There was a little of the same feeling you get in a defensive ambush. You don't want to fire and give yourself away. But you're ready, and you see them and they don't see you. Control. Control. Control, I told myself. Just sit. Wait. Listen. Watch. Control yourself and you control the situation.

She shook his hand. Damned if she didn't. Then kissed his cheek. "You be careful driving home," she told him. And turned around and closed the door and turned on the light and saw me and flattened against the wall.

"You scared the shit out of me," she said.

"I'm sorry," I said, and wanted to say, "Who the fuck is he?" but for once had better sense, at least at that moment. "Are you glad to see me?"

"Not right here right now. No."

"Well, I've got to tell you, I'm very damn glad to see you and I'm sorry as hell that I surprised you. But I just had to." And once again, by luck or instinct I guess, I said the right thing, because first she said I should leave, and then she asked me if I wanted some coffee before I went, and I didn't go out the door until dawn.

Now I was on the same path again, walking along the side of the creek in the moonlight, but things were different. I loved her now too much and if there was another man there—

Darkness is a terrible time. Even if you know how to use it and move in it, when darkness surrounds you so do the ghosts of all your fears. I don't care who you are, or how you bluff yourself or others, the ghosts are there. And now as I saw the house in sight and her car not there, I felt a rush of fear and anger, all of it a little clouded by the scene in the afternoon and the beer and the memory of that time before. And I knew if that man was in the door with her, or any man, there wasn't going to be enough control this time. I wasn't courting her anymore. This was not an open game. I had given myself over to loving her and in that there would be no compromise.

The front door was locked and I jerked the handle so

hard I might have broken it, but it wouldn't give. The back door had a chain across it, but swung open enough for me to break it with the side of my hand. The wood was soft and the screws gave way with only a little noise. There was no sound in the house.

Before I went into the bedroom I listened. There was enough light from the moon sitting low on the horizon to see every wrinkle on the unmade bed. But it was empty. I went out to the main room and sat in the big chair and waited.

The sound of her tires on gravel woke me up. The glow of the headlights swept across the ceiling and went out. I could hear her fumbling with something under the windowsill. She was looking for the key, I thought. Yes. I heard it turn in the door.

"Kurt?" she said. "Kurt." There were no lights on, but she walked over to me with that confidence she always had: in her place, among her people. It was even her moonlight. "Kurt," she said, kissing me, "I'm home. Are you?"

IV "Is this the residence of Kurt Kurtovic? If it is, this is his sister, Selma. Could he please give me a call? Soon?" I heard the answering machine as I walked in the door.

Selma never called to say hello. She never called at all. But there was so much potential for bad news with my relatives that I couldn't bring myself to pick up the phone. It was late November and the heat was on too high. The house felt airless. I was tired and spent. Josie was coming over from the mill. We were going to go to a movie. That was as much energy as I was willing to muster. The phone clicked off.

For a few seconds I thought about some of the terrible things that could have happened. Visions of disaster sprang up randomly, like silhouettes on a rifle range. Maybe Selma had killed Dave at last, or he'd put her in the hospital. But no, even then she wouldn't call me. And there were also, as I thought about it, less dramatic possibilities. Maybe she had some excuse for not coming to the wedding. That would be a relief.

But the wedding was still months away. The Rankins were planning every last detail for their only daughter. And Selma would wait until the last minute to not show up. Without even thinking, she'd make her absence an embarrassment. No, that wasn't it. But it would be something like that. Something simple. Something stupid.

The disaster could wait, whatever it was. I erased the message.

The delicious shock of cold beer in my throat settled me. It was the moment every day when I turned from a Ranger back into a human being. I sloughed off my uniform, carried the can of beer with me into the shower, and closed out my mind with the pleasure of being clean. It wasn't exactly like the ritual of Superman stepping in and out of a phone booth, but it would do. In a couple of minutes the transition was complete. The part of me that knew all about killing was safely stowed out of sight. The regular guy engaged to a beautiful woman emerged. And the kid from Westfield was somewhere else completely, all but forgotten.

"Sugar, you ready?" Josie shouted through the screen door as she let herself in. "It's a long movie and I don't want to be late, you know?"

We went to see *The Abyss*, a picture that tried to span alien worlds from the bottom of the sea to the farthest reaches of space, complete with elastic-looking extraterrestrials, as if you could find something out there, or down there, that would explain all the fear and uncertainty you feel about—anything here on earth. "Close Encounters of the Wet Kind," said Josie as we brushed the popcorn crumbs off our laps and worked our way out of the theater with the rest of the crowd. Then we were in the hot night air of the parking lot and I was fishing through the pocket of my jeans for the keys and she said, "Would you have died for me?"

She didn't ask questions like that very often, and when she did they made me angry. Very angry. "Sure, darling. No question," I said. I could feel the blood rushing to my face. In the movie, Mary Elizabeth Mastrantonio died for Ed Harris so they could get out of a trapped submarine. Then he beat on her chest, plugged her in, and she came back to life. A good scene, I guess. Josie had cried a little. Maybe I did, too. But dying was serious business for me, not teenage small talk. Dying was what I was supposed to be ready to do for my country and my buddies and because I was a Ranger all the way. But it wasn't a subject I wanted to dwell on. And there was that call from Selma. *The Abyss* had helped me put it out of my mind, but this kind of talk was bringing it all back.

"He didn't die for her," I said, opening the door of the Nova.

"But he was ready to."

"She died for him. And *he* brought her back."

We drove in silence for a long time.

"Why are you so angry?" she said.

"Let's just say I've got a lot on my mind—and one thing I don't want to have on it is you dying."

"Well, let's just say what it is that you've got on your mind, Kurt. How about that?" She leaned over and kissed me on the cheek, then slid her body next to mine, but her touch made me cringe a little. She backed away again. We drove along for a few minutes in silence.

"There's some kind of trouble back home."

"Home in Kansas?"

"Selma called and left a message but didn't say what it was about."

"Maybe it's nothing."

"Maybe."

Josie moved over next to me again and ran the back of her fingers gently along the side of my face. "Whatever it is, Sugar, we'll take care of it." She kissed the tips of her fingers and put them against my lips.

The red light on the answering machine was flashing like crazy when we got back. There had been a lot of calls:

The first was a hang-up.

So was the second. Then Selma. "Kurt? Kurt? You there? . . ." *Click.*

Another hang-up.

"Sergeant Kurtovic, this is Dr. Carlson at the Westfield Medical Center. Could you please call me this evening or at the office tomorrow? We need to talk about your mother. My office number is—" I stopped the message, found a pencil, wrote down the pertinent information. I was very methodical. Josie watched.

"You want a beer?" she said.

"Later." I listened to the purring tone of the phone ringing at the doctor's house. His voice was thick when he said hello.

"Dr. Carlson?"

"Yes."

"This is Kurt Kurtovic returning your call."

"Yes," he said. "Yes, yes," he repeated, pulling the words into focus. "I suppose your sister has given you an idea of your mother's condition, but I thought you might want to go over it a little more to see whether you want to try to come back to Westfield for—for a few days."

"I haven't talked to my sister," I said.

"I see. But you are aware of your mother's condition."

"Negative."

"You don't know."

"I don't know, doctor, but I would appreciate it if you could please tell me what is going on. Is my mother sick?"

"Yes. She is doing a little better today, but she—"

"What's wrong with her?"

"—but, as I was saying, she has a serious condition."

"What does that mean? Is it her heart? Her brain? Is it some kind of cancer?"

"No, no, it's not cancer. It's related to her liver," said the doctor. "But—"

"So it's the drinking."

"Probably. But the critical symptoms are in her esophagus. There is a swelling of the veins inside the esophagus, like varicose veins if you know what those are."

"That doesn't sound so serious."

"These veins are very fragile. Last night there was an incident and your mother was hospitalized. She's still in intensive care."

"Incident?"

"A hemorrhage."

"From her esophagus? From her throat?"

"That's right. She lost a substantial amount of blood but we were able to stop the bleeding."

"And she's okay now? Or what? Is she critical? I mean, how is she feeling?"

"She's off the critical list, Mr. Kurtovic. But there are some important decisions to be made and I thought you should be informed."

"Where's her husband?"

"Calvin is taking it all pretty badly. He was with her when she started bleeding. He brought her to the hospital. I've given him a sedative."

"If she's getting better, I don't see what I can do by coming back."

"We're not sure how much better she's going to get," said the doctor. "There may have to be an operation. But with her weight problem she's not a very good candidate."

"Candidate?"

"For surgery."

"Doctor, you're not giving me a very clear picture here. Do you need my approval for an operation for some reason? I don't see why."

"No. But it may be advisable for you to be here."

"Let's try to be very clear here, doctor. Do you think my mother is going to die? Is that what you are telling me?"

"I can't say that and won't say that. But that's not the most important reason for you to come back. She wants to see you. Improving her frame of mind might improve her chances of recovery."

I thought for a minute about whether I would be able to get emergency leave, and decided I could. "Tell her I'll be back as soon as I can get there."

Josie was sitting in the shadows in the corner of the living room listening. "Assholes," I said as I hung up. "Doctors are assholes. He tells me that Mama is getting better, then he tells me I'd better get back to Kansas as soon as possible." I opened the door of the refrigerator and stood in the cool that poured out. Josie stood behind me in the pale light and I tried to explain what was wrong with my mother, but I didn't have much of an idea. The conversations left me with images of blood pouring out of my mother's throat, but that was all I really understood.

The intensive care unit had six people in it that morning. I'd gone first thing and I'd gone alone and, not asking any questions, I went from cubicle to cubicle looking at each of the patients. Tangles of tubes led into them and out of them, dripping liquids and spewing oxygen and sucking urine. Machines beeped with the regularity of heartbeats. Here was a man with a horribly inflated belly; there was a shriveled woman, her mouth opening and closing silently like a fish gasping. Another individual with bandages across its face might have been a female, might have been a male: the body was slight beneath the sheets and the face beneath the gauze was flat. A woman in her seventies lay with a kind of noseclip feeding her oxygen, but she moaned with every breath. A little boy looked like he was sleeping peacefully, except that there were wires around him everywhere and a man who sat beside his bed was crying softly. I did not find my mother.

"Can I help you?" said the duty nurse.

"I was looking for my mother—Mrs. Kurtovic."

The nurse looked at her clipboard, flipped a page up, then back down, as if to show she was doing her job. "We don't have a Kurtovic here," she said.

Calvin screwed up, I thought. Typical. He tells me she's in intensive care and she's not. But I was relieved. "I guess she's been moved."

The nurse flipped through the clipboard again, then went over to her counter and looked through some index cards. "I don't believe . . . ," she said, letting the thought trail off as she read names. "I don't believe that we have had a Kurtovic in here."

"Goodsell. I'm sorry. Probably the name was Goodsell. God. I don't know what I was thinking. Can you tell me where she's been moved?"

The nurse looked at me for a minute, directly into my eyes. "Goodsell," she said without expression. She glanced down at the clipboard again but didn't appear to read it. "Number four," she said.

"Where's that?"

She pointed to one of the cubicles I'd just passed, where the old woman had been moaning, half conscious, her eyes closed, with the oxygen tube up her nose.

I stood beside the bed trying to discover—in that yellow and gray hair slick from repeated sick sweats, in those features that seemed to have fallen off the bones beneath, in that voice moaning low in a singsong of pain, in some piece or part of the woman before me—my mother. But it took a long time for the features to assemble into someone I recognized. A long, terrible time.

I touched her hand and she opened her eyes. They were so blue, still, so much hers, but so tired and so frightened. She started to speak but her throat was dry and the words came out hard. "Baby, you came. You didn't—" She tried to clear her throat but it was obvious that it hurt her. "Not supposed to talk."

"I'm sorry you're sick, Mama, but I'm glad I'm home. Don't worry about talking now. Just wait and rest and get better and then, you know, I was thinking you could come down and visit in Savannah for a while."

"So proud," she said. I leaned toward her face, trying to be careful not to brush against any of the tubes leading into her, and kissed her forehead. "Shhhhh," I said. But suddenly her eyes filled with anxiety again. "Under bed," she said. "Look under bed."

There was an old shoebox, the top loosely closed over it.

"Father's—your father's papers," she said.

I held the box uneasily in my hands, not sure what to do with it.

"Open," she said. "Look." A few papers. "Look close."

The first papers were covered with elaborate engravings of the American eagle. I'd never seen anything quite like them.

"Savings bonds," said my mother. "When you were born."

There was a small, battered book with a soft black leather binding, like a psalmbook, but drawn on its cover was an odd design in gold that I couldn't understand. I flipped through the pages, filled with meaningless writing, some of it underlined. "Koran," said my mother, but I didn't look up. Searching for some word or phrase in a language I could read, all I could find were, on the last page, a few equations scribbled in pencil in my father's writing. Beneath the book there were other papers, too: discharge papers from the U.S. Army, with a picture affixed of a young man in uniform I could only barely recognize. A chill went through me. My father never said anything about being in the Army.

"Hello, Kurt." Selma's voice. I turned.

Dave was standing behind her, his face still showing marks from that night in '85, the broken nose never quite fixed. I looked him in the eyes. He looked back, then away, then back again.

"Oh, Mama, how are you today?" said Selma, rushing up to the side of the bed. My mother smiled and tried to lift her hand to take Selma's. For a second all I could focus on was the blue of needle bruises beneath her skin, and the rust-colored stains of disinfectant.

"Hello, Dave," I said.

"Glad you could make it," he said. "Kurt."

V

Something like hell was taking shape somewhere above us. The Specter gunship had opened up before it was supposed to. Its twin cannons, the Bofors guns, and the 105mm howitzer were all rocking and rolling. "American Express" Jenkins called the Specter because, yeah, Rangers "never left home without it." But it was just about to kill us now. You could feel the floor shake and the air ripple with the explosions. You could hear the columns of the subterranean parking lot groaning and smell the cement dust, bitter with lime, that fell in flurries from the ceiling, clinging to your tongue as you waited, breathless but silent, to make the next move. There was no light, not even enough for the night goggles. Our new NVDs had their own infrared source. They were supposed to acquire man-size targets at fifty meters. But all I was picking up were silhouettes of my own men, and only when they crossed the goggles' field of vision, a forty-degree tunnel of green shadows. We were moving ahead on four senses across an architect's drawing we had in our minds. Above us the thunder was growing.

One shaft of light, then another, exploded across our eyes. Flashlights. But they weren't looking for us. They were just trying to find their own way in the dark, and as they scrambled into a Jeep Cherokee they still didn't see us. There were four in all, all wearing the khaki uniforms of the Panamanian Defense Forces and carrying M-16s. Three were pretty big men, and one of those was pretty fat, too. But the fourth was slight and wiry except for a little potbelly: the profile we were looking for. I swung my face and goggles toward the captain. His hand was in the air, fist clenched. We were frozen, watching his arm and fingers as he signed like a deaf-mute, but in our own language, with its own meanings. Jenkins, working the line near the left wall, would take the big man opening the driver's door. The captain would get the one headed for the death seat. The fat man was mine.

The thudding of the combat above us drowned the muffled reports of our rifles and the screams of the targets. I remember a flicker of terrible fascination as I watched a burst of three rounds, then three rounds again, tear into the body of the fat man, knocking him around like an inflatable doll springing leaks. One caught his femoral artery close to the groin, and in the green light of the goggles the black stain spread across him like he'd pissed in his pants.

I was closest to the car. The little man was already inside. He'd dropped his rifle somewhere, but he was reaching for his pistol, it looked like a 9mm, trying to wrench it out of a stiff leather holster. Before he could see me I was sitting next to him and the muzzle of the AR was up against the base of his skull, just behind his right ear. "*No te muevas!*" I shouted, my mouth almost touching his head.

"NVDs!" I heard the captain yell, and I pulled the lenses away from my eyes. A Maglite focused in on the prisoner's features. They were dirty from the dust falling around us, but they were clear. Too clear. We were looking for a subject with skin as rough as a pineapple. "Negative," said the captain. I put my hand over the subject's face, feeling it. The subject tried to bolt, grabbing for the door. Then there was a little bullet hole in the Cherokee's Plexiglas window with a few bits of bone and brain spread around it.

No time to fuck around. The NVDs went back on and we plunged again into our tunnel of shadows, heading for a steel-framed door at the end of the parking lot. Most of it was made of bulletproof glass as thick as a phone book. A couple of ribbon charges took care of it. But three feet away was a second door, just as thick. It was a lockout chamber, like the double doors of a bank. Whatever element of surprise we had, we'd lost it now, and I was on point alone. The space was so small there was no room for anyone else with me, and no way they could cover me. I had nothing in my hands but the explosive charge, like a sheet of dough, and the detonator.

I love C4. It's so clean, so predictable. Water doesn't affect it, or sweat either, for that matter. And when it blows, there aren't many fumes the way there are with commercial dynamite or TNT. But even so I was holding my breath in this closet that was filled now with shards of glass as thick as gravel. I focused as much as I could through the NVDs. The door began to tremble and clatter against my hands. What looked like crystal spider webs appeared magically in the glass in front of my face. Someone was shooting. A pistol. The bullets weren't making it through.

I stepped back around the corner and triggered the charge. The second door blew and the team poured fire into the room. But when we entered there was no one there.

"*Shiiit,*" I heard myself whispering. "Shit. Shit. Shit." But nobody else heard and if they were saying something, I couldn't hear them. The building was starting to shake like an earthquake, but all the force was coming from above.

We'd entered what looked like the waiting room in a dentist's office, with a coffee table and a little sofa now splintered and perforated. A lot of pictures had fallen off the wall and onto the floor, but a few still hung on unsteadily. They looked like the oil paintings in Wal-Mart. They were all of children, some boys, some girls, but all of them with big, tear-filled eyes.

To the right, across the room, was another reinforced door, this one solid, with no glass. A display case had fallen near the door, spilling its contents onto the shag carpet. It must have been a collection of some sort, because there were toy toads all over the place, all shapes and sizes, their evil little faces peering out of the pile like gremlins. I pulled the case out of the way and blew the door. Jenkins took point, then ducked. A pistol flew by his head. He ducked again. He stood up a little straighter and motioned me in with his head. There was a woman up against the wall, her hands flat against it as she looked into the darkness with no idea what was coming after her. She was the only person in the room. *"No dispare!"* she was screaming. *"No dispare!* No shoot!" Her face twisted by fear, creased by glowing shadows in the green light, she looked like a Halloween witch. I thought for a second she was wearing a helmet, then realized she had a scarf on over curlers.

Jenkins grabbed her and spun her up against the wall. She couldn't see what had taken hold of her. She screamed. She tried to kick out. But he just went about his work, strapping her wrists together with plastic cuffs. *"El jefe!"* Jenkins was shouting. *"Dónde está el jefe?"*

Her boss was gone, she screamed. She didn't know where he was. *"En Colón. Ya no está. No se! No se!"*

"Vámonos ya!" the captain shouted. "Now. C'mon! Now!"

The percussion of high explosive on the floors above sounded like it was right on target. Too bad for us. Bits of ceiling were dropping all over the place. Jenkins steered the woman in the dark, pushing her ahead. At his signal, I dropped back and set up a Claymore with a fixed trigger wire. If anybody tried to get in or out that way the whole room full of big-eyed children would be a kill zone.

On the last turn of the ramp before the exit from the parking lot, the captain stopped us and we flattened against the wall. Starbursts of light started erupting in the shadows. Men were coming down into the dark, trying to find their way with cigarette lighters. A couple of them were shirtless. Others were wearing only their underwear. We followed them with our rifle barrels but let them pass as they headed deeper into the building. We inched upward toward the light from the outside. Even at the other end of the lot it flooded our vision. We stowed the NVDs. We loaded fresh clips.

I could see the woman in curlers screaming, but there was no sound now but battle. Three cars were burning at the entrance, and in what little space was clear we could see the Panamanians had set up a machine gun. But there was no one operating it. A lone man, just a kid, was sitting in the protection of the wall near the exit with his knees pulled up and his arms wrapped around them. His head was down, then up, then down again. He was trying to decide what to do. We were still down the ramp in the dark. He couldn't see us yet. But he would if we moved any farther. He could count his life in seconds now, I thought. Then we stopped.

The captain was on the radio. With a gesture of his head, he ordered Jenkins to keep a closer watch on the woman. She had stopped screaming or struggling. She looked like she was going into shock. She twisted her head toward her back, trying to draw attention to her hands. They'd begun to swell. Jenkins unsheathed his knife and she froze. But all he did was cut the plastic cuffs. Then he pulled her arms around in front of her, one at a time, watching her closely, and put new cuffs on her. I saw him looking at her fingers. He laughed and gestured for me to look. Her nails were polished, but not just painted. There were designs in red. Spider webs.

Behind us and below us was a fierce explosion. The Claymore.

The captain signaled the squad to hold position. We were going to wait. I didn't like it. You start to shake when you wait. But there was nothing else to do.

From where we were the only view out of the parking lot was that fraction of sky at the entrance, and that was glowing orange. Spotlights swept through the smoke from above. The barrage from the gunships overhead and the tanks that had rolled out of the Canal Zone now became more sporadic. You could make out small-arms fire and sometimes hear it answered by the blast from an Abrams tank.

There wasn't much to do but try to stay alert. I watched the kid near the garage entrance. He's going to live, I thought. All he's got to do now is surrender. Then, a strange thing, he started slapping himself on the face. The fucker's got no idea, I thought. No idea. Then suddenly he stood up.

Wait, I thought. Wait. Just wait a little longer and you'll make it. But I guess he'd spent all that time getting psyched. He didn't wait. He crawled over and lay down behind the machine gun and before he could pull the trigger I sent three rounds through him lengthwise from behind. The woman in the curlers had had her eyes closed, but now she opened them to see this boy curling and crumpled like a worm on a hook, gasping and puking, and she started to scream again and this time we could hear her. But when Jenkins pointed his finger like a pistol at her face she shut up.

A couple of hours after dawn, the main force of U.S. troops entered the Comandancia and found us waiting there for them.

The phone was ringing at Josie's house, but nobody was answering. I called her parents. But their line was busy.

There were other soldiers waiting for the phone. So I took a shower and went for some breakfast.

It was a strange war, this Operation Just Cause. Except for the kills, it was a little like training. We performed our mission in the foreign country in the early morning, then went back over the line into the Zone, and there it was still America. The lawns were trimmed just so. The houses had barbecues out back. You could buy pink lemonade in the PX. Only the plants were different, really: bigger, broader-leaved, darker green. And there were the vultures that circled overhead all the time. I'd never seen anything quite like them. I thought they were seagulls at first, but too big, too black. They soared in great swirling formations above Ancon Hill. The first day it passed through my mind that they might have come for the war, which continued just across the street into the afternoon.

The coffee didn't calm me down. I tried Josie again. And

her parents again. No answer either place. I wanted to tell her that I was okay. I knew she'd be worried, and I wanted to make her feel better. There'd been a fuckup at Rio Hato and 850 Rangers had jumped into the middle of a shooting gallery. As I heard the story later a couple of the new super-secret Stealth fighters that were supposed to clear the way dropped bombs on open fields instead of the two main barracks. By the time the Rangers were over the jump sight there was so much lead in the air one of them got a bullet through his head while he was still in the door of the C-130. The commander ordered a low-altitude drop—so low the chutes barely opened before the Rangers hit the ground. They were busted up all over the place. Four got killed. I didn't know what they were hearing about all that in Hinesville, but I wanted to be sure Josie knew I wasn't one of the ones who was hurt.

Finally her mother answered the phone.

"Mrs. Rankin?"

"Kurt? How you doing, Sugar? It looks like hell down there. But they just keep running the same tapes over and over again on the television."

"I'm okay. I'm okay. It was a little hairy this morning, but, okay, I'm all right. I just didn't want you all to worry. Especially Josie. Is she okay?"

"She's fine, Kurt. But she's not here. She's been out all morning. Where can she call you when she gets back?"

"I have to call her. Look, when you see her could you please, please ask her to be at her house at five this afternoon? I'll call her there, then, for sure."

"I'll tell her, Kurt. We've all been so worried. Now you stay safe."

"Don't worry about me. I'm through for the day," I said. But I was wrong.

The hunt for Panamanian dictator Manuel Noriega was not going well. We'd missed him in the PDF headquarters.

Probably he wasn't anywhere near there. And by the afternoon suspicions were growing he might have gotten away. Maybe to Cuba. I guess some of our commanders started to take this personally.

The captain kicked the foot of my bunk. It was just before three in the afternoon and I'd had maybe two hours of sleep. I was drenched with sweat and my eyes felt like they were full of sand. "We got another mission," said the captain.

Our particular unit was supposed to be used to back up other special operations units—sometimes SF, sometimes Delta. We were tasked in ways most Rangers weren't, and we figured we were ready for anything just about anytime. We were supposed to be good at improvising, which meant sometimes we got called in to do something when somebody couldn't make up his mind just what thing he wanted to do. That was the truth in this case. Someone up high had realized that if they kept knocking down buildings with main battle tanks every time a sniper from the Dignity Brigades let off a couple of rounds, there wasn't going to be much of Panama to save. Around the PDF HQ the Chorillo neighborhood's clapboard houses and shops had burned like kindling. (I don't think anyone ever did know how many people died there. But a good guess was a hell of a lot.) Now they were worried about a district called Cholula where there were some big apartment blocks with a lot of guns in them. One of these was holding out like the Alamo. They wanted Rangers to take it and, if Noriega was inside, to get him alive.

"I joined the Rangers," said Jenkins. "Not a fucking SWAT team. I ain't trained to arrest nobody and read him his rights."

"Listen," said the captain. "I'll tell you what our mission is here. It's to get into that building, have a looksee, disarm or neutralize whoever we have to, and get out alive. But the last point first: get out alive."

The building was twelve stories, a block of public housing with some windows boarded up and others draped with laundry that blew in the wind. The paint was coming off the side of the building in peeling sheets. The concrete underneath was rotten from one-hundred-percent humidity. And on top of that, fifty-caliber rounds had knocked a lot loose. Most of the action looked like it was near the roof.

The plan was simple. We were going in with the better part of a company. First we'd secure the main stairwell, cover the corridors, and try to take care of the gunmen on the top. Then we'd start a more thorough search.

God, what a shithole that place was. I was positioned on the fourth floor, looking down a long hall without a single lightbulb working and a shattered window at the end. A couple of the doors were broken down. You couldn't say when. The walls were covered with graffiti and on one was the red, white, and blue flag of Panama. A corner was loose and the whole thing was rippling and flapping in the breeze from the window. Other doors were made of iron bars. The place looked like a prison, but the bars were to keep people out, not in. Standing at the entrance to the stairwell I couldn't see into any of the apartments and couldn't be sure what would come out. But I could smell plenty: shit and the sea, piss and cornmeal cooking, all at the same time. Yeah, people were cooking. They've got to eat, I thought. Wouldn't mind eating something myself.

One of the barred doors on the left of the corridor swung open about ten yards from me, and before I could think about it a little boy with a tamale clenched in both hands, a filthy striped shirt, and no pants at all was standing with the red dot of my laser sight on his forehead. He stared at me, not sure, I think, what he was seeing. Then he started to cry. It's weird how that sound of a child crying cuts through other noise. Even with the shooting outside and up on the roof, his wails filled the hall and filled my head.

"Shut up, kid!" I shouted. "Shut up!" The laser dot danced around on his face. Still he kept crying.

An adult stepped into the hall from the right, then dove back when I shot a burst into the ceiling.

Now the kid was really screaming, but he wouldn't move.

"Somebody get this kid!" I shouted at the top of my lungs, wishing I knew the phrase in Spanish.

Nothing happened. I gestured with my hand, then with my rifle. The laser was a red stripe flashing across his body, but still the boy wouldn't move.

Then from the same door on the right, I saw two hands appear, low, at the level of the little boy, reaching for him. They were a woman's hands, and they were empty. That was all I could be sure of. And whoever they belonged to, the little boy knew her. He ran into them and they pulled him out of my sight. I heard the baby whimper a couple of times, then be quiet. Only then did I realize the shooting outside had stopped.

Any change in the objective situation makes you nervous. The silence made me nervous. And then the alarm on my digital watch started beeping. Four-fifty P.M. Josie was waiting for my call, and I wasn't going to make it.

"So, how are you?"

"Your folks told you I was okay, didn't they?"

"Yes. But they told me you were going to call at five, too."

"Darling, come on. I mean, I don't want to make a big deal out of it, but there's a war going on down here."

"I see that on TV. Looks like it's about over."

"Well, it's been pretty intense today. For me anyway."

In the silence between us I could hear the voices of another couple on another line, but too faintly to tell what they were saying.

Josie spoke first. "Don't you want to know how my day has been?"

"Yeah, sure."

"I drove into Savannah in the morning to buy Christmas decorations at the Altar Guild shop. I was going to do a big number in my house. But then I decided not to buy anything."

I could hear the other people's voices on the line again. Finally I said, "I thought you wanted us to have our own tree. I was thinking about you decorating it. It made me feel good."

"I was thinking about me decorating it alone. It didn't make me feel good."

"Is that what's wrong?"

"My fiancé is in the middle of a war zone. I could be a widow before I'm a bride, and he wants to tell me how exciting it is. And it's Christmas. He's not here. Okay. But he can't keep the simplest promise: a phone call."

"I said I was sorry about that."

"But I haven't finished telling you about my day."

"What now?"

"Selma called."

"What's the matter? Mama's still getting better, isn't she?"

"Nothing serious. I guess. She's not back in intensive care or anything, but Selma says your mother was wondering if you were going to call her. Did you try?"

"I wasn't sure—you know, with the hospital switchboard. Sometimes it's hard to get through, even in the States, and from here, and I thought maybe she was even going to be out by now . . ."

"Well, she'd like to hear from you."

"But I was calling you."

"Maybe you'd better call her."

It was easy to get through to Kansas, in fact, and I thanked God that Kansas couldn't call me. Since my mother's sickness the family had been closing in on me. Selma had taken to calling Josie at all hours to share her many problems with her new "sister"-to-be. I'd even heard from Joan, my oldest sister in Missouri, before I left the States. She talked about her husband's money. I was polite, but that was enough.

"Mrs. Goodsell, please. Room B-302."

There was no answer and the switchboard picked up again.

"What name was that?" said the operator.

"Goodsell," I said. "Or maybe Kurtovic."

"Goodsell. Yes. She's been moved. I'll connect you."

Electronic chimes played "Home on the Range" while I was on hold.

"Hello?" The voice was thick and weak.

"Mama? Mama, it's Kurt."

"Oh, my, Kurt. I—I've been thinking about—I—I— There's a nurse. Can she? Can call back?"

"Mama, what's the matter?"

There was noise in the room at the other end of the line. The receiver banged. And then I heard what I thought was my mother's voice, but half screaming, half choking.

"Who is this?" asked a new voice, the nurse's voice, on the phone.

"This is her son, Kurt. What's happening? Is she okay?"

"She's just having a little setback. We—we really need to attend to this. Can you call back later?"

"Yes, yes. When?"

"Later," she said and hung up.

Routine saves your life when you can't think at all, and sometimes it saves your sanity when you think too much. Tired as I was I cleaned my rifle, and repacked the basic contents of my rucksack. I didn't have a lot of personal stuff except for the Koran, and I wasn't really even sure why I had that. I couldn't read it. I'd started squirreling little things away in it: Little notes to myself. A birthday card from Josie's mom and dad. A couple of ticket stubs. And my father's alien registration card from the 1950s, which had on it the same picture as his Army ID. I hated the fact that my mother's sickness and my sisters' lives were invading my life. I had thought I'd gotten away from all that with the Army, with Josie. And I wanted to get back to getting away as soon as Mama was a little better. But this mystery about my father did interest me. I was waiting for my mother to really get better so we could talk about all that. Whatever it meant.

I tried to study the numbers my father had written in the Koran to see, once again, if I could make anything out of them: 114, then $29 = 3\,(1) + 10\,(2) + 13\,(3) + 2\,(4) + 2\,(5)$ $\{42 = 2$ or $5\}$. I thought they must stand for something pretty simple, but damned if I could figure out what. Sometimes I could fall asleep trying to sort them out. I would have liked to sleep. But this night I couldn't. And I couldn't find the energy to get up, either. I was, despite myself, worried about my mother and I was furious with Josie for being angry with me.

"I'm sorry, baby. I know it's late but I couldn't get a line out."

"Kurt. Listen—"

"No, you listen. I'm just calling to say I can't stand it when we fight. It makes me crazy."

"Kurt, honey, listen to me. You haven't called Kansas tonight."

"No."

"Oh, Kurt, I'm sorry. So sorry. They called here, Kurt. I don't know how to say this but to say it—"

"She's dead."

"She's dead, Kurt."

VI The cold light of the winter sun was shining bright and clear and I could follow the shadow of the airplane over the contours of the land. There was a white sheet of snow on the gentle hills of eastern Kansas, but you could still make out the patterns of the fields below where the earth was ploughed and rough and waiting for spring, or where winter wheat had sent its first green shoots up in time to brave the ice. In some places the earth had warmed enough to burn brown ragged holes in the white. The bare branches of the trees were so sharply visible in that crisp air that even at ten thousand feet, starting our descent toward Wichita, I thought I could focus on their frost-covered twigs, their last dangling leaves. Somewhere deep in my head I could remember the fresh cold clean air of Christmases, of vacations, that I'd forgotten. I reached for Josie's hand and held on to it, but I couldn't take my eyes away from the window.

"... Advent calendars," she was saying, and when I didn't say anything she repeated herself. "When you were a little boy did you have Advent calendars?"

"I don't know."

"You know. Like a big card full of windows and you open one every day and see a shepherd, or a Wise Man?"

"We did," I said. "Yeah."

"Remember the suspense?"

"Suspense? I guess."

75

"Who else would the last one be on Jesus' birthday but Baby Jesus? But you open up a little paper window each day and there's some new face to see."

"Yeah, I remember."

"Kids love opening those windows. Didn't you?" Josie was nervous, I suppose. She was talking on and on like she did not normally do. "Even when you've done it for years it's something to look forward to. You know?" she said. "Counting down to—Christmas morning."

"We didn't have them every year. Sometimes, I don't know, we'd forget. But, yeah, I liked them. A lot, I guess."

Josie's hand, that beautiful hand, felt strange to me. There was contact, but no current.

I didn't want to have to talk. I wanted to watch the land and feel the sensation, part sadness and part excitement, that was building up inside of me. It was the feeling of home. Here in the plane, looking out the window, it could still be an idea, memories, dreams untouched by the people, living or dead, that I really didn't want to have to see or deal with. Here at ten thousand feet, as I saw those empty fields below me, the feeling of home was pure.

"Can you see Westfield?" Josie asked. But I just shook my head, and she was quiet for a little while, until we were almost touching down at the Wichita airport. "Is someone meeting us?"

"I hope not."

There was no one at the airport. And when we found the cemetery outside of Westfield there was no one from my family there, either. The funeral had been held ten days before. My sister Joan wanted it done right away, she said, "so I can spend at least part of my holidays with my kids." And so it was. That I couldn't get away from my unit was "really such a shame," she said. "I'm so sorry, Kurt. But everybody else is here already," she said. "We'll all be thinking of you." I told her I would be thinking of all of them, and I would come back as soon as I could, and I let it go.

When I told Josie over the phone from Panama what was happening with the funeral in Kansas, she was furious for me. "They've got to wait," she said. "Or at least they've got to have a service when you come." But they didn't wait for the burial or the service. It was all wrapped up two days after Christmas in a corner of Highland Cemetery. Joan managed to get a Catholic priest to come over from Ark City. I hadn't ever heard his name before. It was all over before I could even get out of Panama, and the truth is I would have been relieved if I could have left it like that. But, again, Josie wouldn't let it lie. She wanted to come with me, to be with me, she said.

"So here we are," I said, getting out of the little car I'd rented and looking around for someone to tell me where I could find the grave. There was a man working on the engine of a backhoe. When he looked up I recognized him as someone who'd been in high school with me, but not in my class. His skin was flushed and red, his features were sharp, and his eyes were milky blue. The face came back to me from the hallways of Westfield, from the bleachers at Vikings games. But I couldn't remember the name.

"Hunk!" he said. "How you doin', boy? I hardly knew you."

"Hey," I said. "You working out here?"

"These last six months. I tell you, it ain't easy when the ground's froze. Plays hell with the backhoe."

"Looks like it's warming up."

"Hope so." He finished wiping grease off his hand and shook mine. "Sorry to hear about your mama."

"Thanks. Yeah. You know where the grave is?"

As we walked toward the southeast corner of the cemetery I saw that Josie was standing beside the car. She was waiting for me to call her, or to make some sign. But I wanted to find the grave, and see it, and be alone for a minute, and not to talk about it. More than anything, I wanted not to talk about it.

"Guess you couldn't make it back for the funeral 'cause of Panama," said my gravedigger friend.

"Yeah."

"You sure kicked some butt down there, I'll tell you."

"Yeah, I guess."

"Let's see now. It should be right over . . ." He bent down and brushed some snow off a little metal plaque with a number on it. "Nope," he said.

"My father's grave is over there," I said, pointing to the far side of the cemetery.

"Yeah. Un-hunh. But your mama's here someplace," he said.

I guessed that was Goodsell's idea, to keep them apart.

We walked to another low mound, where some wilted daisies were anchored against the prairie winds with a rock. A vase of plastic roses had tipped over. He brushed off the plaque. "This is it," he said. "We're waiting for the stone. Not sure what's happening with that. Takes a while sometimes."

"Thanks a lot."

"Must be pretty hot down in Panama, hunh, Hunk?"

"Yeah. Thanks."

"How 'bout I buy you a beer when you're finished up here?"

"Got to go see my family. But thanks."

"I had a cousin was down there a few years back. He said it was Sin City. I hear there was massage parlors open right through the war. That right?"

"I didn't see that part of it. But, you know, I'd kind of like to be alone right now. Thanks."

"Sure. Maybe we'll catch up with you later."

"Maybe."

"How long you going to be around?"

"Not sure. Okay?"

"Hey, yeah. Okay." He went away.

There it is, I thought, looking at the dirt and snow and dead flowers and the plaque with a number but no name. "There it is," I said to the wind. "There it is." I took a deep breath of air that was turning bitter cold as night came on.

The door of my car slammed and the noise was like a trigger.

I turned and sprinted, scrambling, attacking as I headed for the little Chevrolet and Josie. "What the fuck is the matter?" I shouted. She was standing with her back up against the car. I was right in her face. "I want to be alone for five minutes at my mother's fucking grave and you have to fucking slam doors and throw a fit."

"Calm down," said Josie. "Calm down!"

"You fucking calm down! Shit!"

"It's cold. You took the keys to the car with you. I just wanted to turn on the heat."

"Take the fucking keys. Take the fucking car."

"Kurt. Come on."

I threw the keys at her. "You're not helping. Not at all. You wanted to come here, you wanted to do this. Why? I don't need this. Not at all." I slapped the roof of the car and darts of pain shot through the cold muscles and bones.

"You fucker," she said, getting in the car, slamming the door and knocking down the locks. She shoved the key into the ignition and cranked it up, threw it in gear, and spun gravel off the back tires that hit me like spent shrapnel. She tore out of the cemetery drive and drove to the top of the hill on the main road half a mile away. Then she pulled over onto the shoulder. She was still in sight.

I started after her, wanting to finish this fight somehow, wanting her to see that I was right. Then I stopped; then I began to run. Easily. Deliberately. Disciplined. By the time I reached the car I had chilled out. But Josie was there crying, her head on the steering wheel. I tapped on the window. She shook her head. I tapped again and waited for her to look up and told her silently through the glass, "I'm sorry." She looked at me with those honey-colored eyes and they were full of tears and desperation like I had never seen in her. "Please," I said.

She rolled down the window and kissed me. I felt her tears against my face, lines of cold running down the smooth warm skin of her cheeks. Leaning in through the window, the car door was still between us, but I kissed the tears away as best I could; kissed her lips, and her closed eyes. "I'm sorry," I said. "I'm sorry."

"Come on, baby. Get in," she said. "I'm sorry, too. I know it's hard." She started the engine again.

"Head on back toward I-35," I said, and we drove down to the Comfort Inn, at exit 222, just across the line in Blackwell, Oklahoma. I don't remember that we said anything to each other on that drive.

"Hell of a homecoming," I said as I looked around the room that could have been in any motel in America.

"We shouldn't have come," said Josie. "I was wrong."

"No. No. You—I mean, I told you that this isn't really where I belong. I thought—you know I thought for a minute when we were flying in that maybe it was. But it's not. Look at this. We're not even in Kansas. Joan's gone again. And Selma? And Dave? We going to go pay our respects to Calvin Goodsell? I mean, wow. What a family."

"I thought you said you'd patched things up when you were out here before."

"Yeah, well, yeah. I guess. But all I want to do now is get out of here."

"Okay."

She surprised me.

"Okay," she said again. "I can't fight it anymore, Kurt. I just can't. And I'm not going to fight with you. This was all a big mistake. If you don't want to see Selma, I can understand. I'll meet her, or whoever else, some other time. Or never. Let's just go, now."

"Right," I said, feeling as if I'd been rescued from a nightmare, and feeling, too, like I might have been saved from myself. But when we checked with the airlines, there were no flights out of Wichita to Atlanta until the one we were on the next afternoon, and we were both too exhausted to drive to Tulsa or even to Oklahoma City.

Defeated by logistics, I gave Selma a call. Having gone through the motions this far, I figured I might as well follow through. It was fate. We agreed we'd meet at the Peking Palace in Arkansas City. It was neutral ground, and you could get a beer.

"U.S. BEGINS TROOP PULLOUT IN PANAMA," said one of the headlines on the *Wichita Eagle*'s front page. "ARMY SEES INVASION A BUDGET-WAR BOOST," said another. Noriega was still hiding out in the Vatican embassy, where he'd gone a couple of days after we missed him. The fighting was now completely over. The streets of Panama City were a chaos of looting and vigilantes. But to read the paper you'd have thought this one man was just the last detail that needed mopping up. "They'll get him out sooner or later," I said out loud. "And it says here the brass are happy." Josie looked up from the crumpled second section of the *Eagle* they'd found for us behind the bar at the Peking.

Selma and Dave were late. They'd probably been fighting. I didn't want to think about it. So Josie and I read the paper, eating Chinese munchies, talking little and about things that didn't count. "They're pleased because this operation was a complete success. They think that means they'll get more money out of Congress. But, damn, can you imagine if it wasn't a success? We started out with twelve thousand men in the middle of the country—two-thirds of the people we used in the whole operation. And of course they're not talking here about how many Panamanians got killed. Hey, who the hell knows?"

"Think Noriega is going to—"

"Here's Selma," I said.

She looked okay, which was a relief. Dave was breathing whiskey.

"You must be Josie," said Selma. "You are just about the prettiest thing I ever did see. Don't you think so, Dave?"

"Kurt is a lucky man, I'll say that," he answered. They'd been rehearsing the lines in the car, I figured. We arranged ourselves in the booth and ordered beers all around. We talked about the bowl games the day before. I'd missed them, so Dave could fill me in. The gridiron was safe for us. The Huskers were wiped out by Florida. That was the big news. And basketball was just getting started up. Kansas looked to be in the top five again. And the high school scene was getting hot.

"So how's it look for the Vikings this year?" I said.

"Shit. They look like shit, except for this Chuck Bolide. This kid can do twenty-five, thirty points a game. He's going places. But he can't do it by himself. He's Duke Bolide's kid brother. You know, Duke who played for your dad?"

I didn't really, but said I did. "Whatever happened to him?"

"He's working up at Highland Cemetery. You might've seen him if you went up there today."

"Oh, yeah?" I said, remembering that milky-blue stare.

"Duke's a friend, you know," said Dave. "A good man."

"Ain't Mama's grave in a pretty place?" said Selma.

"Real pretty."

"If you could help us out a bit, Kurt, I know just the stone for it. It's pink granite with a little kind of medallion of the Virgin in one corner. I know that would have meant so much to her."

"Yeah, that sounds nice. How much do you need?"

"About five hundred dollars."

Dave broke the silence, tapping his finger hard on the newspaper lying on the table.

"Look at this. 'Kwanza.' Did you read about this stuff?"

"No."

"It's black pride shit. It's like we've got Christmas, Jews have Hanukkah, and they've got to have this Kwanza stuff. Can you believe it? Some kind of Black Muslim shit."

"Never heard of it."

"You better think about it. Because soon, you'll be celebrating it. Don't want to offend our Afro-American brothers, do we?"

"I thought religion was going out of religious holidays," said Josie, who should have known better, from what I told her, than to give Dave an opening.

"No, ma'am. What's going out of the holy days is Christianity. That's what's disappearing. Our traditions, our values. Hell, you come from Georgia, don't you? You know what's happened down there. There's parts of the state as black as Africa. Juju and voodoo and I don't know what else. Am I right?"

Probably Josie recognized her mistake. Anyway she said nothing. Selma looked at Dave's broad, rough face with an expression as blank as a sheet of paper.

"You sure this Kwanza thing is Muslim?" I asked, finishing off my beer and looking for a waitress to bring me another one fast.

"Or voodoo. What's the difference? Mumbo jumbo. You're too young, I guess, to remember Cassius Clay. Hell, I'm too young. And Lew Alcindor? Now we got Muhammad Ali and Kareem Abdul-Jabbar." He leaned across the table and put his face close to mine. "Abdoooool. Can you believe that shit? Is that just about the most niggery thing you ever heard? And it's everywhere. Everywhere!"

Was he testing me? I didn't think so. I didn't think he'd make that mistake, even as drunk as he was. He was trying to relate to me the best way he knew how, in a bar, talking sports and niggers, one white man to another.

"Shit," he said again, sure he was convincing me. "But

at least—at least—and I'll give them this—at least they are trying to preserve their racial purity. I don't think they've got shit to be proud of. But at least they're thinking about pride, in their background, their ancestors. But not your whites. No, sir. Your whites are just giving up. We're paying the bills for other people's purity, so welfare mothers can keep dropping their litters, and pushing drugs, and ripping off the society the white man built. You know?"

"Amen," said Selma.

Josie's face had a look of strained formality, like a student in a manners class.

As for me, I wrapped myself in self-control like it was a poncho and I was waiting for this drizzle to pass so I could move on.

"Whites are scared for the most part. I tell you the truth, I think there's more nonwhites I respect than there is whites. The black man and the Jew, working together, have made the white man ashamed of himself and opened the way to the mongolization of the race."

"The what?"

"Like a mongol dog, all mixed up like Heinz 57, and you don't know where the hell it comes from. 'Cause no pride. That's the problem. No pride. The whole damn Western civilization. From flush toilets to 747s, and no pride in it. And do you know why?"

"I swear," I said, "you sound like a preacher sometimes."

"I have done a sermon or two," said Dave.

"Christ the Redeemer Church up on Route 77," said Selma.

"I'll be damned," I said.

"Me, too," said Josie.

"But do you know *why*?" Dave thundered, not wanting to be drawn away from his point. "Because the Jewish-controlled media have made us ashamed of our uniqueness as a people. First their aim is to destroy our identity—like our Christian identity—and then it is to destroy and enslave us. And—you mark my words, brother—they have almost succeeded."

"And what if your mother was Catholic, say, and your father was a Muslim?"

"That's what I'm talking about. Just exactly," said Dave. "You see niggers with white women on the streets today and you're not even supposed to look twice. The Jews say that's supposed to be natural. But you won't see no Jews marrying outside their own kind. And no Muslims neither. But to mongolize the white race—oh, yeah. That's just fine."

"Suppose I told you Selma's father—my father—was a Muslim?"

"What the hell are you talking about?" said Selma. "You don't think it's hard enough being a Catholic here in Kansas?"

Josie laughed. And Dave had finished his sermon. At least out loud. But you could see his mind was still revving like an out-of-tune engine on a hot day, banging and knocking even when the ignition was turned off.

"Have they still got that chicken-and-peanuts?" I said.

"Moo shu pork!" said Josie. "I love those little pancakes."

I rejoined my unit on January 8, 1990, a day after it got back to Savannah. Josie went back to work at the mill. And we did our best to pick up life where it was before Panama; before Westfield. We made plans for the wedding. But Josie no longer insisted on inviting people from my family, and when her mother raised the subject, Josie just said she didn't think it was really necessary: both my parents were dead. She didn't use the word "orphan," but whenever I heard these conversations or heard of them, that's what I thought. And as for Selma and Dave, after Westfield I don't think Josie much cared if she saw them again or not. Better not, in fact.

We talked a lot about our future—about my future—

that spring of 1990. The world was changing too fast for the Army to track, much less a single soldier. The years ahead looked like times of peace and cutbacks. For forty-five years we'd lived and breathed the Soviet Threat. Now—it was gone. Some of our commanders told us the changes in Moscow were just a trick to catch us off guard. But I'd been in the Army long enough by then to know budget bullshit when I heard it. You could look at the map. Suddenly all those places we used to call "strategic"—weren't.

"So what's the point?" Josie would ask.

"A paycheck," I'd say.

"You know where you can get a better one," she'd say, meaning her father's mill.

And sometimes we'd fight, and sometimes not. We knew the script really well after a while; it was just a question how we played it one day or the other.

"You're too old to be doing what you're doing," she'd say.

"But it's what I know how to do. It's what I love to do," I'd say. "It's what I am."

And so the conversation always went, and wasn't resolved.

And she, who always knew so much about me so long before I did, knew it was over. In March, while I was away in the California desert on an exercise, she sent me a letter telling me she thought it was better if we put the date for the wedding back from June to September. And I realize now that those first weeks of summer in 1990 she must have been looking for a way to tell me there wasn't going to be a wedding. And everybody must have known but me. I'd go to the Rankin house like I'd done, now, for more than a year, but feel like a stranger. Tyler would be busy in his study. Mrs. Rankin—Myrtice—would bring me lemonade or a beer, whatever was my pleasure, but wouldn't sit down with me to talk. Too busy in the kitchen. And Josie would come back from work and I'd ask her what was wrong, and she'd say nothing.

On July Fourth weekend the Rankins had a big Sunday dinner, with long tables set up on the lawn between the house and the pond and a buffet of Waldorf salad and ribs and fried chicken, stewed stringed beans and fried grits, watermelon, devil's food cake and angel food cake and strawberry shortcake, and lots of ice cream, and pitchers, of course, of good sweet tea. A lot of the people from the mill were invited. So was I.

"Watermelon. Oh, my, it's so good when it's cold like this," said Myrtice. "When I was a little girl, my mama wouldn't let us even think about eating watermelon until after Fourth of July. 'Not ready yet,' she'd say. 'Not just yet.' And, naturally, we couldn't think of anything else. So when July Fourth came and we tasted that first bite of watermelon, Lord, it was better than Christmas."

"I love it, too," I said. "Josie, aren't you going to have some? I think I'm going to have another slice."

"Let's go for a walk," said Josie, putting her arm through mine.

We had crossed the paddock and were on a trail through the stand of pines when she said, "Kurt, you know what I'm going to say." And I said I did. But still, I said, she ought to say what she felt. And in the most reasonable voice you can imagine she said, "I'm not going to marry you, Kurt."

"Can I ask why?"

"Oh, you could tell me. I could tell you. We could fight. Again. But Kurt, I still care for you and I don't want—"

"Maybe just a little explanation? Just a few words to keep in mind? Is it my job? My—I don't know. My family? I guess it's not my mouthwash, is it?"

"Very funny."

"But if you still care for me—"

"Marriage is about the future, Kurt. And you don't see that. You see us together now. But you don't see us together ten years from now. You don't see kids. You don't see—the future."

"I guess I have enough trouble in the present."

"In the past, Kurt. Your trouble's in the past. But you don't see that either. You don't even want to begin to look at that." She started to cry, but wouldn't let me hold her. Then she dried her eyes and we walked in silence.

I didn't fight. We followed a path that took us by the field where the cars were parked. "I don't think I can really go back to the party," I said, stopping in front of my old Nova. "Give me a kiss," I said. "And don't drink all the sweet tea."

As I drove away I felt a sad sense of relief, and the barest suggestion of fear.

If your job is killing it's hard to throw yourself into your work unless there's a war. In August 1990 Saddam Hussein gave us one. It took a while for anyone to figure out just what our role would be, but as we readied ourselves in Georgia the commanders I trusted never seemed to doubt that a fight was coming. We put aside the skills of the jungle and picked up what we needed for the desert. Our uniforms changed color, from shadows of forest to shadows of sand and rock. Worries about rust and corrosion gave way to worries about dust. And more than ever the night became our day. We were trained and honed and ready to kill. Once we moved out it would be easy enough to quit thinking. There was the smell of sand and oil and the sour tang of iron to keep me company.

II

A Taste of Death

Only he who is saved
Far from the Fire
And admitted to the Garden
Will have attained
The object.

—THE HOLY QUR'AN,
  Surah 3:185

VII
One by one I unfolded the two blades and the four screwdrivers and opened the jaws of the pliers, then folded them back into place so that all were neatly contained in a little rectangular block of hinged steel. Then I started the process all over again. The business end of the pliers folded out first. Out of the handles flipped the smooth blade and the serrated blade, which was dangerously sharp, the flathead screwdrivers, the Phillips screwdriver, the can opener, the awl. The little multipurpose SOG Paratool was a new one and all the hinges were stiff. Opening it up, then folding it back into itself, again and again, loosened them. And it gave me something to do as I listened to the rain on the roof of the tent.

Your fingers bring comfort in moments of high-stress boredom. A cigarette; a rabbit's foot or rosary or just a bunch of keys: things held in the hand. They have functions, and maybe they're symbols, but that can't explain entirely the satisfaction they give. Even the feel of a sharp blade catching lightly in the whorls of your fingerprint as you run your thumb across it is kind of satisfying. To make things move repetitively, mechanically, half-thinkingly with your fingers is really very reassuring. And if you do demolition work, I believe, you feel that sensation even more. You are aware of your hands in ways that other people probably are not.

When you're working with C4, for instance, it feels just

like the modeling clay you used to play with in school. You squeeze it and mold it and work it in your fingers to warm it up, then you shape it as you have to: just basic forms, mainly cones and slabs, but still your fingers are making something. Working with the fine wires of another man's bomb, untangling the purpose of each strand, is as delicate as a surgeon's work. But doctors only risk their patients. We risk ourselves, so when our hands are steady, no hands are steadier.

They're also terribly exposed. When you're first training and you put on a bomb disposal suit you realize you've got fire-resistant fabric and sixteen plies of bullet-proof Kevlar wrapped around your body, a chestplate made of fiberglass and foam, an extra cover for your helmet, an acrylic mask for your face, guards for your shins, and a flap with extra layers of Kevlar to cover your balls in case the thing blows. But your hands are out there on their own, naked.

I unfolded the pliers again, opened the jaws, closed them. Perfect for cutting most wires, and good backup for crimping blasting caps; an all-around useful tool for field-expedient situations, when you have to cobble together defensive devices or shaped charges.

Now all we had to do was get in the field.

Our units should have been some of the first to land in this sandpile, but as it turned out they were among the last. The generals at CENTCOM had taken one look at all that flat land around Kuwait and figured it was textbook-made for heavy metal. They'd use tanks and Bradley fighting vehicles, artillery, and airplanes—especially airplanes. You could run in the desert, they figured, but you couldn't hide. And they could go to work with all their most expensive toys, proving how well each and every one of them functioned, or not. It wasn't a war for a few men carrying rifles and knives, C4 and pliers.

Rangers are basically low-tech types. Sure, we've got the laser sights and computerized navigating systems and night-vision goggles, but while most of the rest of the Army is fascinated with gadgets, we're moving in the other direction. We like things simple, physical, understandable. The first page of *The Ranger Handbook* carries standing orders that date back more than two hundred years to Rogers' Rangers in the French and Indian War. They're folksy as hell, like something you'd find hanging on the wall at a Cracker Barrel country store along the interstate, but they still make the point. "Don't forget nothing," the list begins, and it's true, you're always checking and double checking. "When you're on the march, act the way you would if you was sneaking up on a deer. See the enemy first," it continues. "Tell the truth about what you see and what you do. There is an Army depending on us for correct information. You can lie all you please when you tell other folks about the Rangers, but don't never lie to a Ranger or officer." The list concludes: "Let the enemy come till he's almost close enough to touch. Then let him have it and jump out and finish him up with your hatchet." We'd progressed from muskets and hatchets. But not by much. At least not in spirit. Moving quietly, gathering intelligence, killing at close quarters, these were supposed to be our things. But now that we were here it was clear this was a big, noisy, eyes-in-the-sky war. A standoff war. If, in fact, there was going to be any war at all.

I unfolded the long blade on the tool, the one with a serrated edge like a bread knife. It was good for cutting rope and webbing, but unless you locked it in place by refolding the tool shut, with just the blade exposed, it could flip back down on your fingers and give you a nasty slice, which it almost did.

"Shit," I said, breaking the silence in the tent.

Jenkins took this as an invitation. "Listen to this," he said, reading from a little pamphlet we got on "Customs and Courtesies" in the Middle East. " 'It is "natural" for an Arab to speak with double meanings—and the American who fails to watch for these can make foolish mistakes. If something is threatening to an Arab or puts him down, he will simply reinterpret the "facts" to suit himself—which is perfectly correct by his code.' They sound shiftless as hell to me. Guess that's why they call 'em sand niggers," said Jenkins, tossing the pamphlet onto the floor and lying back on his cot. "You read this thing?"

"A couple of times."

He raised an eyebrow. His face was so red from the sun that little white lines showed on his forehead. His brows were so bleached they looked like a couple of woolly caterpillars. "You got anything else to read?"

All I had, in fact, was my father's Koran, and an English translation I'd picked up from a black Muslim of some sort selling books and perfumes on a street corner in Savannah. I hardly ever looked at these books myself, and sure didn't drag them out in public. Most of the time they just anchored my kit bag, squirreled away like porn in the bottom of a bedroom drawer. "No, nothing," I said.

"Can you believe it's fucking pouring rain in the middle of the fucking desert? We come out here to kill and all we do is rot. You got any letters I can read?"

"You think I'm going to show you my letters?"

"Not the ones you write. Do you write any? I just saw you open a couple that had stuff from the newspapers in them."

"It's stuff my sister sends me from Kansas." I pulled a pile of envelopes out of my kit bag and tossed them to him. Selma had never written me a letter in my life before we shipped out for Saudi Arabia. But with all the talk about war, and the TV filled with scenes of troops in the field, knowing somebody in the middle of this big event was, for Selma, like knowing somebody in the audience for "Oprah." You could almost touch the celebrity. So Selma told people she had to do her bit for her baby brother. But she still couldn't bring herself to scratch out more than a couple of sentences. She just started ripping articles out of the local paper and sending them to me with "Thought you'd be interested" written at the top, or "How about this?," or no explanation at all: Westfield High sports scores, articles about local Kansas boys and girls serving with the forces in Desert Shield—but not about me—and every so often an article about homemade letter bombs. I guessed she figured I'd have a professional interest.

A lot of times they were just one or two paragraphs long, and didn't really tell you much. Sometimes I'd heard about the incidents, sometimes not. Sometimes there wasn't even a date on the articles, and I wasn't sure where Selma had found them. But the general impression was that the U.S. mail was about as dangerous as Saddam's Scud missiles. There were a lot of misfires, sure: Someone sent a bomb to Bob Dole, the senator from Kansas, but it never went off. "I guess that's one thing about slow mail," said Dole. "The battery died." But just before the Panama action, a federal judge in Alabama opened a shoebox wrapped in twine and a pipe bomb blew him halfway across the room, fatally filling his guts with sixteen finishing nails. Other bombs were defused at the District Court in Atlanta, and at offices of the National Association for the Advancement of Colored People in Jacksonville. And in Savannah—it had been really big news just as I was about to ship out for Panama—a black lawyer was killed by yet another bomb. It looked like somebody was trying to start a race war. Dave, always on the lookout for a possibility like that, brought up the bombings at the dinner in Ark City. What did I think about it, he wanted to know: "I mean, as an expert and all that." I told him letter bombs weren't my thing. Still, those were the cases that Selma followed most closely with her scissors.

"You ever think twice about opening these up?" Jenkins asked, holding one of Selma's envelopes to the light.

"I got a weird family, I guess," I said.

"You and everybody else. I ever tell you about my uncle Jack the pig fucker?"

"The one with the prize sow?"

"The very same."

"The one who truly was happy as a pig in shit?"

We both laughed. I looked at the nylon ceiling. "But that was a joke, right?"

"I'll tell you my aunt Gladys wished it was."

I always figured Jenkins made up that stuff. But it wasn't until a long time afterward that I thought about why. He was one of those soldiers who have a great ability to keep the people around them cool. He might not work at it, or even think about it, but the skill came naturally to him. If there was tension in the air, like there so often is, he'd make a joke or tell a story that would take the edge off before things got dangerous. Partly he was just having fun. But I think, now, there was more to it than that.

Jenkins came from a place called Social Circle, Georgia, which I also thought was a joke the first time he told me. But it was a real-enough town. You drove right by on the interstate between Atlanta and Augusta. I never went there with him because he never wanted to. He said his only real regret in the Army was that he was stationed so close to home. If you even mentioned dropping in on his family, he'd look at you kind of slyly and say, "Yep, I hear Uncle Jack's prize sow has got a fine new litter." And that would be the end of that.

We spent a lot of time together, me and Jenkins. And if I had come a little closer to actually marrying Josie than I did, I might have asked Jenkins to be my best man. I'm pretty sure of that. When the thing with Josie ended, he made it easier for me to lighten up. I guess I took all that for granted. I didn't wonder until later if maybe he spent so much time with me because he really was worried about me.

The rain was splashing in the sand outside the tent flap. A soldier carrying his kit was walking through the downpour, coming in our direction. He was tall and taut. And black. And I recognized him, as much as anything, by the way he moved. He stopped for a minute in front of our tent and looked down the row like he was searching for an address. He looked straight at me with that hard angry face I'd been seeing in my nightmares since Ranger school. Then he smiled. "We're in God's country here," he said. And that was all, and he went on.

This had been a shit assignment. Schwarzkopf didn't want us. Our commanders weren't sure how to use us. The longer we were held in reserve, the more tightly wound we got. It was like seminal backup. We were all on the verge of fights all the time. And now this. I slogged over to the headquarters compound to be briefed on a new make-work assignment. As I went I suppressed the urge to look over my shoulder. I didn't like the sensation. I'd have to come to terms with Alpha one way or another.

Even if it means doing nothing, the Army finds something for you to do, and Jenkins and I and a couple of others were detached to teach Saudi junior officers the basics of special operations. I hadn't exactly volunteered, but I was happy to go. Teaching gave me the chance to blow things up for an audience.

Any demolition man gets a rush when he sets off good charges, well constructed and laid, with good target analysis and the minimum amount of explosive: just enough to get the exact job done. For a demo man, accomplishment and annihilation come in the same package. But we're not the only ones who get the thrill. Any man has an urge to build and an urge to destroy. You can see it from the time little boys make towers out of blocks just so they can knock them down. Demo men act out that scene on a big, grown-up scale, and get paid for it. The destructive power of modern explosives—and their precision—are awesome. You set off some C4 fireworks and the spectators are as much fun to watch as the blast. Besides, after six weeks in the desert I hadn't seen anything but canvas, steel, and sand. Any glimpse of anything resembling civilization would be welcome, even if it was just the outskirts of Riyadh.

The course started every morning at eight, and a lot of the Saudi officers came late. Motivation was not their strong point. Neither was their attention span. It was like they could never get enough sleep. And my biggest worry all through the course was that they'd slip into dreamland and blow themselves or someone else to smithereens. But a few were squared away, and some were better than that. One of my best students was a lieutenant named Khalid al-Turki. He'd been to school in Texas. "I just love America," Khalid liked to say, whether you asked him or not. He also loved country music. Garth Brooks. Alabama. Reba McEntyre, even some old Willie Nelson, as I discovered when I heard him humming "Mamas, Don't Let Your Babies Grow Up to Be Cowboys" one morning as he practiced crimping blasting caps onto time fuses. You'd have thought he was shelling peas.

"It's good to stay cool. But not too cool," I told him, taking the fuse and crimping the cap onto it with my folding tool. "This is one of the most basic operations in demolition. If you pay attention you'll never have a problem. But if you get sloppy—I know some guys walking around with hands that look like this." I held down three of my fingers so only my pinky and my thumb were sticking out.

"Go Longhorns!" said Khalid.

After a couple of days and a few sweaty scenes on the firing range, we were getting pretty familiar.

"Listen, Sergeant Kurtovic—is 'Kurt' okay? Kurt, you've got to see a little more of my country."

"Maybe someday."

"No, c'mon. I know they're trying to keep you low-profile. Kind of hard to do when there's 500,000 of you floating around, you know? But hospitality is important here. Let me invite you to my house. All of you in the course. We'll have a little party."

I couldn't really imagine what a Saudi party would be like. Tea and goat? But I told him we'd try to fix things on our end if he fixed things on his. "Let me make *all* the arrangements," he said.

It was late at night and Alpha didn't expect to see me standing in the door of his tent. He looked me straight in the eyes, but I had the odd feeling he was focusing on something else.

"You're with the 163rd," I said.

No reply. Like mine, this wasn't a unit you talked about.

"It's been a long time since north Georgia."

"A long time. What do you want?"

"My name's Kurtovic."

"Griffin," he said, but made no effort to get up and shake hands.

"I see. When I saw you the other day in the rain I thought, well, you might be able to help me with something."

"Really? I'd be surprised."

"All right, look, I'll just tell you what I thought. First, if you were still that wild man from Ranger school, you wouldn't be in the 163rd. I figure you've given up that white devil shit or you wouldn't have a prayer of security clearance. But, second, I figure you know something about the Koran." He really did look puzzled. "And I'd like to know more about it."

"What's your interest? You Jewish?"

"Hey, you said it: We're in God's country. We've got Mecca right around the corner. And, no, I was raised a Catholic, sort of."

He squinted a little.

"I just want to know more. We're going to fight a war for these people, I'd like to know what they believe in. A friend gave me a copy of the Koran and a translation before we shipped out, but I can't make anything out of it."

"What makes you think I know anything about this?"

"I've seen you pray. And when I had your knife on my throat I heard you preach."

"I don't know what you think you're doing, sergeant. But you're walking close to the edge of real trouble here."

"I'm not fucking with you."

"I can't help you."

"Okay. Okay. But—maybe you could tell me one thing. I swear, it's stupid, but it's driving me crazy."

"Yeah."

"Alef. Lim. Mam."

There was a long silence. "Alif. Lam. Mim," he corrected.

"Whatever. You know what I'm talking about. A lot of the chapters start with words like that and, as far as I can tell, they don't mean anything at all."

"Code," he said.

"It is?"

"Those are Arabic letters."

"What's the key?"

"Who knows?" said Griffin. "The NSA's never cracked it." He smiled. "It's God's code," he said.

It was the password into a long night, anyway. Griffin said he'd always been puzzled by these words, too, and once he'd opened up even that far, he wanted to talk. I didn't give as much about myself. He said he'd come to the conclusion at about the end of his first year in the Army, not long after Ranger school, that he was going to have to make a choice, and he chose his career. Islam had helped him, he said, but his ideas about it evolved. "It gives a man pride. It gives you a place in the universe." And the way he understood it then it gave him the drive he needed, the hate he needed, to push himself that first year. Now, maybe he still believed, but he didn't need the old hate. He wished he could find a way, being here, to make a trip to Mecca. But he didn't need to advertise his beliefs. He'd come back another time. "For now, anybody asks, I tell them I believe in God Almighty, but don't have much time for churches."

"Good line," I said.

"It's true enough," he said. "I've got the polygraphs to prove it."

Khalid was wearing his uniform when he picked up Jenkins and me for the party. But he was driving his personal car. I didn't know there was such a thing as a Mercedes 1000 SEL, but in Saudi Arabia you see quite a few. Instead of silver chrome, they're trimmed in gold. Inside, the seats are so soft they cuddle with you, and the stereo penetrates to the bone. Khalid had k.d. lang on full blast. If the men on the street hadn't been wearing white sheets and the women weren't covered in black, you'd have thought we were back in the Midwest. We passed Safeways and KFCs, Dunkin Donuts and Cadillac dealers. "Trail of Broken Hearts" played on.

"Got a surprise for you," said Khalid as an electronic gate opened and we drove up to a huge house with pink marble columns. The floors inside were glistening stone, covered with Oriental rugs so soft and fine you wanted to take off your shoes to walk on the silk. Every room had crystal chandeliers, and straight through at the back was a swimming pool under tinted glass like a greenhouse—but not to keep it warm, to keep it air-conditioned. A barbecue grill was flaming in a corner. "I thought we'd have a cookout," said Khalid. "Or, rather, a cook-in. We've got steaks, spuds, brews, the works." Some of Khalid's fellow officers were there already.

And there were girls. They arrived in stretch Mercedes limousines driven by Pakistani chauffeurs. They were clustered in the back like crows in a cage, their bodies and faces covered completely in black. But as they walked into the house they shed the layers like butterflies coming out of cocoons, and by the time they reached the pool, they were dressed for Malibu.

"Is this the Playboy Channel?" said Jenkins. But as we stood there I got the feeling we were the ones on display.

Most of the women were older than us. Some must have been in their early forties. Some were dark-haired, some blond. One with greenish-brown eyes and long red hair was wearing a lime-green bikini that almost glowed under her thin silk robe. Heavy gold sparkled around her wrists, and at her throat was a tight golden necklace with an emerald. Her skin was so white and smooth that you could almost see through it to the fine blue veins beneath. Maybe she was thirty-five years old, but she must have taken a bath in milk every day of her life. She was the first to talk to us, and as she spoke she rested her hand lightly on her chest, showing off long red nails and a huge emerald ring.

"Thank you for coming to protect," she said in awkward English with a French accent.

"You're welcome, ma'am," said Jenkins. "Our pleasure."

"Our pleasure," I repeated.

"It is nice here, no? It is not what you expected, maybe."

"Not really, no, ma'am," said Jenkins.

Another woman came to listen to the conversation. She was taller, darker, slimmer, but with big breasts. Her eyes, outlined in black so they looked even darker than they were, followed our eyes to her chest, and she smiled. "Saudi Arabia is more fun than you think," she said.

"Yes, ma'am," said Jenkins.

"Enjoying yourselves?" said Khalid, coming up behind the women. He'd changed into Bermuda shorts and a Long-horns T-shirt, with a baseball cap backwards on his head.

"I think they are a little surprised," said the woman with the dark eyes.

"Well, boys, we'll just keep this as our little secret," he said. "Wouldn't want the *mutawa'in* to give us any shit. Pardon my French."

"The religious police," added the woman with the dark eyes.

"They are beasts. But they will do nothing to you, that is for sure," the redhead said to Khalid. "And even if you were not you," she said, "they will do nothing now."

"Why's that?" I asked.

"I have some connections," said Khalid.

"No one has better," said the blonde, sociably taking his arm.

"Want another beer?" said Khalid.

Jenkins and I both drank too much too quickly that night. The smell and touch of women, even when we were just standing around, really disturbed me after so many weeks in the desert. And after Josie. I'd only been with one other woman after we broke up, and her only one time. Now surrounded by women in this weird closed society, looking at almost every inch of their skin in this place where they were normally covered head to foot, drinking beer in a country where liquor was banned, having married women come on to me in a place where you could get executed for adultery, talking American, eating Kansas beef, no less, and getting drunker by the minute, I felt like a spectator, sometimes like a performer, but never completely part of the show.

All I really wanted to do, and all I might have managed, was to talk. But none of the women wanted to talk about anything that meant anything. It seemed natural to me, for instance, to ask what would happen to Saddam.

"Oh, ever since you said you would protect us we are not worried," said the blonde, and there wasn't a lot to say about the subject after that.

"What are these religious police?" I asked her.

"They are very boring," she said. "Shall we find some place to sit down?"

I knew she wanted sex. I thought I should, too. But I didn't. At least not with her, not in this place. Nothing felt right to me. I drank more. All I wanted was for the party to end, to go back to the base, to get some sleep.

Khalid brought me another beer. "What do you think is going to happen to Saddam?" I asked him.

"Gotta kill the mother," he said. "If you don't he's going to take revenge. Simple as that." He took a swig of beer. "We Arabs are famous for that, you know. Ten years. Twenty years. Two generations. However long it takes. We don't forget. We take revenge."

"Sounds like the Mafia."

"Does it? I always thought it was more like a Western. You got a showdown, you shoot to kill. One man walks away. Call it fate, call it justice. Anyway it's simple and it's final. If not, things can get, you know, complicated." He toasted me with his beer can and moved on.

I noticed for the first time that there were couples, now, in the pool. Others were wandering back into the house.

"Come," said the blonde, taking my hand.

"Listen," I said. "It's not you. But I just don't feel like doing anything." Her face changed quickly. It was like watching a mask drop. She turned my hand over in hers and looked at the palm like she was going to read it, then pushed her nails into it like a cat sharpening its claws, and turned and walked away.

I went off in search of a bathroom. The house was like a hotel and as I looked through it I heard Jenkins's voice coming from one of the rooms. It was obvious he was getting more out of the party than I did.

"Raunchy," he said next morning. "Truly raunchy. But I tell you, I Am In Love. Did you know Muslim men can have four wives? I think I've found myself a home."

"Could be dangerous."

"No shit. You could be fucked to death."

"I think just about all those women were married already."

"Yeah?"

"What's her name?"

"We didn't get that far," he said.

VIII

The air was thick with grease and gritty with soot and the rain was black as it fell. Even with the low thrum of the silenced engines in our ears, you could hear the water scouring the sides of the helicopter like sandpaper. During the day visibility was less than a hundred yards. Now, at night, no stars showed, no moon penetrated the clouds. But there was still just enough ambient light for the pilots' night-vision equipment. The Al Burgan and Umm Gudayr oil fields were burning bright, like geysers straight out of hell. Ahead of us, to the right, lights from Kuwait City showed dirty yellow near the coast.

I could barely make out the shadows of the pilots in the cabin. Their faces never bent toward the instrument panel. Their concentration was total. The closer we got to our insertion point the closer we came to power lines that marched across the desert three by three suspending dozens of high-tension wires that would smash the choppers and fry us inside if we hit them.

When our mission came, we only had thirty-six hours to plan every detail. Flight paths, insertion points, attack plans, possibilities for exfiltration: there was, at almost every turn, a good chance to die. But without this mission, we would have had no part at all in the biggest war since Vietnam. And there are some fates that your career commanders consider worse than death. We'd only come as far as we had in Saudi with the pretense of performing search-and-rescue work if the war dragged on, and it was only just before it started that they found an assignment more suited to our skills. This mission was to search, for sure, but also to kill and capture.

The map of Kuwait looks like the profile of a hawk facing to the east. Virtually all of it is flat desert. Topographical colors distinguish between regular sand and wet sand, sea-level terrain and slightly-higher-than-sea-level terrain. The highest point in the country is only 235 meters. The border with Iraq runs all along the top of the hawk's head and down the back of its neck. At the hawk's shoulder, following a line that seems to trace the top of his wing, is the border with Saudi Arabia. And just beneath the beak, at the throat, there is a bay. Kuwait City is at the southeast corner of the bay, where the top of the hawk's puffed-up chest would be. Most of the rest of the country's people live along settlements dribbling down the coast on the main road leading south to the Saudi border at Khafji. But another road does run to the west, skirting the bay until it reaches the town of Jahra, right at the throat of the hawk, then turning north through the lowest point in a little rise called the Mutlaa Ridge, and driving straight on to the Iraqi frontier, forty-eight miles away. Our insertion point was in this area near Jahra, at the throat.

The road between Kuwait City and Jahra goes through about six miles of open terrain, but there is a turnoff to the right that leads to a spit of land jutting into the bay at a place called Doha. Near its tip was a military base, Doha Camp. Along the upper shore were beach bungalows near a little port for wood-hulled sailboats, and the power station. Members of the Kuwaiti opposition pinpointed this area as the fallback command center of Saddam's top officials in Kuwait City. Drones had taken pictures showing a steady flow of soldiers in and out of the bungalow the Kuwaitis wanted us to target. And we knew the whole area was heavily protected. A SEAL team had tried to infiltrate near the site the week before to get firsthand intelligence, but got stuck in the sludge-filled tidal pools and was nearly shot to bits by the batteries on shore. A chopper managed to extract them, but it got shot up, too, and it crashed as it returned to base. Two men died in the incident, officially ascribed to bad weather.

You'd have thought that mess would have compromised our mission, and if there was a command center it would have been moved. But Kuwaiti opposition sources insisted activities around Doha continued normally after that.

I didn't feel good about the intel on this mission. Not good at all. But intel was not my business, so I didn't say anything. That the Iraqis were sloppy made me feel a little better. Like the lights on in Kuwait City. Why wasn't everything blacked out? But when the enemy is sloppy, he's also unpredictable.

Everyone knew the ground war was beginning. We'd been bombing the hell out of Baghdad itself for more than a month. B-52s dropped so many tons on Iraqi lines northeast of Kuwait the whole area must have looked like a waffle. Now President Bush had issued an ultimatum and a deadline, it had passed—and that was the last we heard before we went in. But there wasn't any doubt in any of our minds that, whatever Saddam did now, the allies were going to roll. From our base in Saudi we'd watched and listened to huge squadrons of allied planes flying overhead.

The Longest Day must have been like that in Normandy, you thought, and it was a show to stir the blood of anyone who'd been made the way that we were made. Rangers remember D-Day. They take a lot of lessons from it: the way C Company of 2nd Battalion climbed the cliff at Pointe-du-Hoc to take out the gun emplacements raining fire on Omaha Beach. Rangers remember that in the trenches around the fortified house, two of their number were killed, and sixty-nine Germans died. And they also remember something about the Navy and the Air Force. The big guns and the bombers laid ten kilotons of high explosives down on Pointe-du-Hoc in the weeks before D-Day.

As much as landed on Hiroshima. But the fortifications were still in place at Pointe-du-Hoc, and so were the Germans. It was the Rangers' rifles that took out the Germans, and their thermite grenades that took out the big guns.

In my first couple of years in the Army I used to visit the museum at Fort Benning as often as I could. I wanted to know everything about those traditions that were becoming my traditions. You could say I was obsessed, reading all the time, every history of Ranger actions and engagements and special forces operations, from Rogers's outfit around Lake Ticonderoga to Merrill's Marauders in Burma. Anything I could get my hands on. But it was D-Day that got to me. I even used to dream about it—an image that came to me from just a few sentences in one account, about a Ranger sergeant in one of the landing craft that was hit before it made it to the beach. One shell blew away the front of the craft, killing a lot of soldiers and drenching the rest in gore. Another hit the side. The sergeant was trying to pick up a 60mm mortar to carry with him when there was yet another hit and he went over the edge, into the water of the Channel. Weighted down by his radio, his grenades, his gun, and his mortar, he sank into the sea. And he never did remember how he got to the beach after that. But in my dream, I knew.

He walked. Like slow-motion in a movie, like a man in space, like the aquanauts in *The Abyss*, he walked, not breathing but not thinking about breathing, just burning adrenaline and fear and hate and glory, safe beneath the surface, he walked toward shore and screams and explosions. In my dream I could hear the water giving way to air around my head and shoulders, and the silence giving way to thunder. And then I would wake.

The chopper bucked into the air, then plunged back down again like a roller coaster. We'd dodged the power lines. We were seconds away from insertion. I peeled the Velcro cover back from my watch face. It was 2:08 A.M. Kuwait time, February 26, 1991. We were out, on the ground, and taking up defensive positions. No contact with the enemy. The second Blackhawk came in. The second squad poured out and deployed. Now we had a full contingent of security teams, the assault team and the "support" team that I was on. The choppers disappeared into the wet smoke like they'd never been there at all. We were twenty-four men alone now in the middle of enemy territory. We waited, watching. The captain scanned the immediate area with a night-vision device. Then he put it away. We were all letting our eyes adjust to the dark. For a march like this, we needed to use our natural senses.

We were south of the Jahra road in a low depression, well covered by the night and the smoke and the rain that wouldn't let up. But we couldn't stay there. Our plan was to move north until we picked up a dirt track that led to the Jahra road, cross it, and continue on for about another two miles across country. There we would link up with Kuwaiti Resistance and head northeast toward our primary objective, the bungalows, and close in on the temporary command center of the Iraqi governor. We were betting on confusion. Theirs, we hoped, not ours.

I was cold and wet and wanted to move, but as I lay there letting my eyes bring into focus whatever they could my nerves settled, my pulse slowed. I could feel control working itself through me from the back of my neck, through my shoulders and into my guts and thighs. It was good to rest for a minute. We didn't have to cover much distance, but each of us was carrying close to one hundred and fifty pounds on his body. Most of the weight was in bullets and water, but each man adapted his equipment to his needs and his mission. I went light on bullets, heavy on Claymores, and C4 was stuffed into every corner of my pack, shoulder straps, and belt.

The curse of adapting your own kit is that you're the only one who can be sure you're not missing something. I'd checked, rechecked, and checked again, maybe half a dozen times in the last three hours before we boarded the choppers. The night before, lists of what I needed came into my head when I was on the verge of sleep. I'd wake up and write down whatever it was that occurred to me, then doze off again. I had to have everything on me. Everything on me had to work. And I was even willing to bear the weight of a little backup. I carried the standard crimper and demo knife, and I carried the little folding tool, too.

There were some pieces of equipment that no one bothered with. None of us brought much MOPP gear. If Saddam hit us with nukes or biological weapons or whatever, well, we were fucked. The most we carried was the mask. It was bulky, but the air was so poisonous already from the burning oilfields that I was glad I had it and I thought I might use it.

Nobody took sidearms. No sense weighing yourself down with 9mm Berettas that need their own ammo and, compared to the rest of the infantry's arsenal, rank as peashooters. But I went lighter than most on conventional firepower. Other members of the squad were lugging SAWs, the little machine guns you can carry like a rifle, or M-16s with M203 grenade launchers under the barrels, and what looked like golf bags full of AT4 disposable rocket launchers. My only conventional weapon was one of the little M231s the Bradley crews use to hose whatever crosses in front of their firing ports. It's just a little bigger than an automatic pistol, and it's not worth much at a distance. The magazine empties forty rounds in less than three seconds. You've got it on safety or it's on full auto. That's it. But the 231 uses the same rounds as the SAW and the M-16. And if you take out two of the three buffer springs, it reduces the rate of fire. Great in close combat. And I wanted something I could hook and unhook from my LBE quickly when I was setting up charges in the field. This was a compromise. I'd been experimenting with it in training at Hafr el-Batin. I thought it would work. Anyway, it was too late to change now.

We moved out.

Jenkins and three other men took deliberate strides toward the higher ground. And froze. You could see by the way they waited that something wasn't right. Then they motioned us up to move on up and past them. In the shadows and rain I saw the something that they had seen. Bats, I thought. Or birds. Or—what? Huge and wounded and flying crazy, now close to the ground, now high up in the air, as if they'd lost control. Victims of the wind. There must have been a dozen of them, two dozen, maybe more. You couldn't tell. They moved in a flock, or in a swarm. I didn't like these flying shadows. I couldn't place them. I was spooked. But we kept moving steadily across their path. There was no way to avoid them.

Like a thing you can't see in the ocean that curls around you in the sandy water, one hit me on the neck and the side of the face. I grabbed it and held it, gritty and wet in my hand. I felt it. Rubbed it. Crumpled it and tossed it behind me. A plastic bag. Polyethylene throwaway bags are littered everywhere in the desert. They blow for hundreds of miles across the bare sand until they find a twig or wire or fence to cling to. The wind that night collected them from all over Kuwait and funneled them toward us.

After about two miles on a heading due north we reached the abandoned site of a highway under construction and came to a track angling to the east. We were on course. There was no sign of soldiers, no movement. But there was what looked like a Bedouin tent. Next to it in a crude pen you could just see the outlines of camels. There must have been several people inside. There was a good chance there were dogs, too. But the rain and the wind helped us here, pounding on the heavy wool walls of the tent, humming through the ropes, the oil smoke deadening scent and covering motion. No dog barked.

The horizon to the north and west started to glow in bursts, like brief dawns, beautiful and dangerous. The light silhouetted the contours of the land and anyone moving across it. A few seconds later the wind brought us the rolling thunder of the bombs. We slowed down. Our eyes had to readjust.

We were getting near the main road. We knew that

where the track ran into it there was a checkpoint. The officers with the thermal imagers could see an Iraqi APC and two Range Rovers with what looked like several men around them. But it was really impossible to judge. The terrain was giving us no cover to move closer, and the weather hid the Iraqis as much as us.

We deployed slowly to the south and east for several hundred yards to skirt the checkpoint, keeping the Iraqis between us and the distant flash of the bombs. We were looking for ditches or, better yet, culverts to take us under the highway. But there were none in sight and as we got closer to the road, we saw something else. Posted like markers every hundred meters were Iraqi soldiers. Vehicles moved along the highway, sometimes from the west, sometimes the east, usually with their parking lights on. We watched, looking for a pattern, but the traffic intervals were fatally random. Crossing the road would be like spinning the cylinder of a .38 and pulling the trigger. You know there's only one bullet in six chambers. But if you lose, you're lost.

I saw Jenkins moving low and fast toward the soldier nearest us. The Iraqi was wearing a poncho that flapped in the wind, and a helmet pulled down low. He was leaning against an oil drum. Not real alert. If you were watching at the right second you saw his head whiplash back and a hand pass under his chin in a quick, hard move, sawing just a little to cut through the gristle. Jenkins hugged the body to him from behind, holding the corpse so it wouldn't flop. Then he let it drop to the sand, and put the poncho and the helmet over the barrel. Good idea, I thought. In the dark, the other sentries wouldn't see a gap in their line. Then Jenkins fell back to the cover of a low dune. A car was coming, driving with parking lights. It passed the dead sentry. Didn't seem to notice a thing.

There was more good news. A concrete barrier about a yard high ran right down the median strip. That would give us some cover. There was no sign of sentries on the other side. We waited for pauses in the traffic and crossed as we could in twos and threes, plunging over the barrier, then running low and hidden from view to the far side of the road. Most of us got across okay. But in the murky night it was hard to calculate the speed of oncoming cars, or how much their lights might pick up our movement. Just after I landed on the far side of the barrier, a big four-wheel drive bore down on me, coming twice as fast as I'd thought, and about to catch me like a deer in its headlights. I sprinted bent over, with my knees near my face, balancing my pack, sprawling into the sand. The car passed.

As we moved on away from the road we were getting closer to the water. The sand was sloppier, and in patches there were thin stands of seagrass to trip through. We'd gone about another mile before we could start to make out the shape of another Bedouin tent. A storm lantern, like something from an old coal mine, was hung from one of the posts. A small flock of goats was bedded down on the edge of the light. What was happening inside was impossible for me to see. Somewhere out of sight I knew the platoon security teams were deploying, ready to fight and fall back if this wasn't the contact we were looking for.

The assault team squad leader took off his helmet and advanced slowly toward the tent opening. When he was sure he was in view, but still about fifty yards out, he shone a flashlight into his helmet so no glare was cast beyond its rim but anybody looking from inside the tent could see it clearly. Two long flashes, one short. A long pause. Two long flashes, one short.

A round bearded man wearing Bedouin robes came out. He took the lamp off one post and moved it to the next. Yes! I thought. The linkup was made.

Now the fat man was talking to the captain. Another character came out of the tent. He was clean-shaven, wearing a windbreaker, and moving like a soldier, taut and aware.

He shut down the lamp. Again, we waited a few seconds for our eyes to adjust, and now we were moving again with these two as guides.

They were taking us to the bungalows up the coast from Doha camp. One of those was supposed to be the Iraqi governor's fallback command post, a secret hideout where he could direct a rear-guard action, or make his escape if Kuwait finally got too hot for him. He was supposed to be personally close—a cousin or something—to Saddam himself. If we couldn't get the Butcher of Baghdad, this man was supposed to be the next best thing.

The objective was set back from the water about a hundred meters, on a low rise. Small dunes and depressions gave good cover for a man on his belly, and the seagrass offered still more concealment. The rain and cold and our night assault suits cut down on the chances of observation by infrared and thermal imagers. But you couldn't eliminate the risk that someone would see you. Not altogether.

Our recon so far showed a surprisingly small—very small—number of soldiers near the target house. They weren't posted as sentries, they didn't surround it in any way—at least not that we could see. They were just sort of milling around. Several were smoking cigarettes. Some were sitting with their backs to the wall of the house, hunkered down, like they had no direction or orders. It didn't look like any command post I'd ever seen, even if it was disguised. But that wasn't my call.

The randomness of their movement made it easy to kill some of the soldiers, but hard to take them all out quickly and quietly. Jenkins and the rest of the assault team went to work with knives and silenced weapons. We were wearing headsets. They could talk to each other if they had to, but they didn't. I set up a thin perimeter of Claymores. I waited for my signal, and I watched the others in action. The light from bombs going off across the bay showed on the team like a strobe in a disco. Their dance was careful, silent, bloody, weirdly beautiful.

The captain called me in to blow two entrances to the house, one through the door, and one, with a five-second delay, through the wall on one side. There wasn't much to the door, in fact. We could have kicked it in. But that would be like saying, "Hi, I'm here. Kill me." I set off the first charge and the silent phase of the operation ended. One member of the team with a SAW hosed down anything that might be moving in a line with the blasted front door. The second charge blew. The main assault plunged into the house through the hole in the wall.

Then the firing stopped. I was covering on the outside, but I could hear the men talking on the headsets as they worked their way through the three rooms. There was no one there. And nothing. No furniture, no radio equipment, just garbage and, in one room, stinking little piles all over the place. The house was stripped. The soldiers in the area were using it as a latrine.

"I guess we're in the shit now," said Jenkins.

"Get those Kuwaitis in here quick," said the captain. When they arrived, he clicked off his set but I could make out some shouting from inside the house.

The captain came back on. "Demo," he said, and I went inside.

The fat bearded Kuwaiti was doing all the talking. The captain was pointing a flashlight down at the floor. The other one, the wiry one with the good moves, was hanging back, interpreting when he had to, with his Kalashnikov at the ready. Jenkins was positioned in a corner of the room, ready to cover the captain, keeping an eye on the thin man.

"I bromise you," said the Kuwaiti with his thick accent. "Fi haga. Fi haga zein."

"He says there's something important in there," the thin man translated. There was a strange tone in his voice, like his teeth were clenched.

The fat Kuwaiti was on the floor, pulling up a piece of plywood with his fingers. I levered one side up with my knife. Beneath was a slab of metal with two dials on it. I thought for a second it might be a radio, since that's what I expected. But it looked more like a refrigerator, the kind you used to see in country stores with popsicles inside, but with a combination lock. A safe of some sort. I could make out the word "Revco" near the top dial. The Kuwaiti looked up over his shoulder and smiled, like we were all supposed to be happy now. He tried to twist the dials, but they would barely turn. This close to the salt water and sand, they'd corroded and frozen.

"What is that supposed to be?" said the captain.

"*Ibn sharmuta,*" growled the thin man. "*Ibn sharmuta!*" He booted the fat Kuwaiti in the side, practically rolling him over, and shoved the muzzle of his Kalashnikov into his gut, right at the solar plexus. The sound of the detonations was muffled by the fat man's flesh as the thin one squeezed off a three-round burst that tore up through his lungs and heart, exploding out through his shoulders and neck.

Jenkins moved. The muzzle of his rifle was square against the back of the thin man's head, just above the collar. For a couple of seconds the only sound was the rain and wind and the faraway thud of bombs. Then the Kalashnikov clattered onto the floor.

The captain grabbed the thin man, threw him against the wall, and got right in his face. Jenkins repositioned the muzzle of his rifle under the man's left ear. "What the fuck? Explain this!" shouted the captain, ready to finish with him. But the thin man was cool now. Very cool.

"This was Jaber's house," he said. "That is how he knew who was here. But he was lying. You see this? He has money here. All this work, all this risk? He put all of us in great danger. And why? So he can get his gold. He could not wait to get his gold."

"You knew this?" said the captain.

"No. I saw the safe there and I knew. No question. I did what had to be done to a traitor. It was clear. He was under my command. I did not want to waste time, and we do not have time to waste now."

The captain looked at the bloody mess on the floor that used to be named Jaber. He looked at the safe and turned to me. "Blow it," he said.

It took a couple of minutes to shape the C4. The problem isn't to blast the door off a safe, it's to preserve whatever is inside. The charge has to cut, and very precisely. As I worked I heard the captain ordering Jenkins to keep the thin man covered. I was finishing the second charge. Then we heard the Claymores going off on our perimeter. The security teams posted outside opened fire.

The captain listened for a few seconds to reports over his headset. The security team on our eastern flank was taking fire from what looked like an Iraqi platoon and reinforcements were coming up. The captain ordered a withdrawal to our first rally point.

"The safe?" I asked.

"Leave it," he said. "And bring this man with us. But without his weapon."

We reached our first rally point under fire and there was no way to hold it. The Iraqis were bringing up tanks. Somebody fired an AT4 and its 84mm rocket hit one of the tank's treads. It stopped. But the turret still turned. It started pouring machine-gun fire in the direction of the security team, then cut loose with its big gun. A second AT4 missed, and now the second tank opened fire. The thin man and I were hunkered down in a shallow dip with a couple of inches of water in it, and I was starting to shiver. So was he.

"I am Rashid," he shouted above the noise.

"Kurtovic."

"What?"

"Kurtovic."

"What do we do now?"

It was a good question. The choppers were supposed to come for us at 04:52. No question of that now. We'd have to find a safer rally point, hole up, and make a new action plan. But we wouldn't get that far unless we got enough close air support to cover our retreat—and soon—before light.

"Wait," I said, and pointed to the sky.

The A-10s came in low and fast and blasting away, their rapid-fire cannons stitching everything in their path—men, tanks, sand—with massively heavy rounds of depleted uranium. We started to fall back. The moves were classic: cover, retreat, cover. It was a disciplined scramble into the desert, south toward the tent where we'd met up with Rashid and the man he killed. He guessed where we were going.

"This won't work," he said. "The tent's out in the open. We'll be trapped inside. We should bear east." I took him to the captain, who listened, considered, then called for the sat com. It was dead. One of the two we had had gone out just after we landed. But this one had been performing okay. The operator checked it again. It had taken a spent round.

"Better it than you," said the captain.

"I'm not so sure," said the operator.

The captain nodded for a couple of seconds, thinking. He looked at this guy Rashid. "Tell me about this place," he said.

"We've used it before in the resistance," said Rashid. "But not so much that they know about it. It's not far from Doha camp, but it's not a place they think to look, especially now, especially for American soldiers. And there's enough cover for us to deploy and take care of ourselves."

The captain nodded. "Let's go."

We made it across the Doha road just as the first hint of dawn was coming and, still headed east, we could see what looked like towers and metal structures. Shit, I thought, a refinery. The last place I wanted to be in the middle of a shooting war. But no, as we got closer I could see the outline of a rocket ship. Not a missile. A rocket ship. And across a huge parking lot the domes and towers of castles. A sign was now visible, barely, in the black dawn. "Entertainment City," it said.

IX   The rides were gone. The dodgem cars had been carted away to Baghdad, just like every Chevrolet and Mercedes in Kuwait. If there was a merry-go-round or a roller coaster, it had been dismantled and shipped north long ago. But the fantasy fronts of the rides and restaurants were still there—the Space Needle, the American Railroad, the ticket stands. It was Kuwait's little answer to Disneyland and it was more than empty, this place: a fairground where the fair had moved on, or been blown away. A fiberglass clown had been shot up and beheaded. Donald Duck had a bullet between his eyes.

In the background, all around us, the sounds of artillery, of bombs, of airplanes; the roar of the burning wells. But at least there were no Iraqis here. At least not yet. The drizzle went on and on. The sun did not rise, but the sky grew lighter until we reached the dirty twilight that served as day. The night had beat us down, but we set up a perimeter as best we could. I wondered if we could claim the first liberated territory in Kuwait. A Luna Park.

There was nothing to do during the day but try to sleep in shifts in the shelter of a place called Sinbad's Cave. Our communications weren't completely shut down. We had several short-range emergency radios, PRCs. They were designed to signal, then guide in rescue choppers. But they only worked for voice or code transmissions in short bursts when planes were directly overhead, and it took hours to coordinate a new plan. We were too close to the middle of the action to be extracted, day or night. The allied forces were moving up fast, now, from all directions, encircling and closing in on the defenses of Kuwait City like a hand squeezing an egg, and with just about as little resistance.

To me it would have made sense to stay where we were. But in the early afternoon the order came through for us to make our way—they didn't tell us how—to an extraction point north of Jahra, at 04:00 hours. They couldn't do anything before that because there was too much rock and roll going on all over the theater now. They needed until then for deconfliction, they said, so our own planes wouldn't shoot down our own choppers. There was nothing to do but wait until night, and try to rest. And in those long uneasy hours, in that place filled with the spirits of children who fled and laughter that died, I thought a lot about my father, and about all the things I never knew about him.

He must have been lonely those first years in America, cut off from his home and his people, before he sent for my mother like a mail-order bride. Or was he excited by this new world of his? If he missed his people, why didn't we ever hear about them? Grandfather Ali, Grandmother Zein. Their names were about all I knew about them. Did my father have an accent when he arrived? He never did when I knew him. Had he gone looking for other Muslims in America, from Yugoslavia or anywhere else? I doubted it. I guessed he stopped thinking about religion the day he put the Koran in the safe deposit box. He had spent—I had to think for a minute because I'd never actually done the calculation before—seven years in the United States, in Kansas, before my mother arrived. He'd come in the summer of 1947, started teaching in the fall. I remembered when I was nine they gave a dinner for him for his thirty years at the school. Thirty years. What could Westfield have been like in those days before interstates and airports, air-conditioning and shopping malls? A main street in the middle of America, nothing more or less. And nothing like the places he'd come from.

"How well do you know your father?" I asked Jenkins, who was lying beside me in the shelter of Sinbad's looted cave.

"Let me sleep, man. Let's save the energy for tonight."

"You okay?" As I looked at him more closely I saw that the dark, wet fabric of his uniform was covered with blood. "Are you okay?"

"Grazed on my left shoulder, that's all," he said, shivering. "Gives me a little twinge when I raise my rifle, but no problem really." He looked down at himself. "Oh, you mean this? The sentry last night. A real gusher." Jenkins moved closer to me for the warmth, but half turned his back.

I'd wanted to ask him how much he knew about his father's life before he was born. Maybe anybody's father is a mystery that can't be solved. There is a life there, a world of romances and fears, of wants and needs—a whole person —who is your father before his children were born. And you've got no idea about him, really. And even in the time that you do know him, what do you know? He's loving you or scolding you, ignoring you or paying attention to you. Those are the main things you feel from him. But they don't have much at all to do with the way he seems to anyone else. Maybe if you both live a long time you can get to know each other as adults, and that's different. But I couldn't tell you. The man I knew as a child was a man no one else had known, and the man known to everyone else was a stranger to me, even in Westfield. And before Kansas, no one that I knew could tell me what he was like. I tried to imagine my dad as a young man, but I just couldn't. I couldn't at all. Even the image of his face as an old man, the only way I'd ever known him, was clouded in my memory. The image I carried of my father was of his size. I'm as tall, now, as he was. I was just about to catch up with him when he died. But all I can ever remember was looking up at him.

My father was a quiet man whose passions mainly showed—only showed—in his work with the Vikings. Around the house his silences were what disturbed me most, and I can't think of a time when he raised his voice, or his hand either. But on the court, at his job, he changed. To see him at the games fascinated me and, yes, frightened me a little bit. There was a kind of intensity and almost a desperation that I never saw in him anywhere else. When a game was close he would clench his teeth and shout at the same time, the veins standing out along his temples and a little ridge of foam along his lips, like something terrible inside him was trying to get out. But most people just thought he cared too much about basketball, and there was no way to care too much about basketball in Westfield.

He was a man who was always trying to improve the way people did what they did, but except for the kind of thing he was taught in clinics and workshops, there wasn't much science in his coaching. He would just get inspirations for improving the way the boys on his team ran, or conditioned themselves, or passed the ball, or did layups. It all made for a pretty strange style of play, but if one or two members of his team were talented enough, they could get away with it, maybe even do better with it, and he would figure he was doing the right thing. When I was young, he tried out a lot of his ideas on me in the backyard: these inspirations that were supposed to turn my clumsy ten-year-old scrambling into all the right moves. But with me they never really worked. And he would try to hide his disappointment. He was always quiet with me. But each of his disappointments killed me a little.

I moved still closer to Jenkins and tried to run through a mental checklist of my gear. Again. And once more. Hoping not just to reassure myself, but in the process to sleep. It didn't work. At least not at first. I wound up watching Rashid moving around the camp, checking the perimeter, talking to the captain. He was far too busy for a guide and translator from the Kuwaiti Resistance. But by instinct I trusted him. He was the first Arab I met who seemed really professional, really competent and confident; much more than most of the Saudis we'd worked with, including Khalid. Rashid didn't seem to need sleep. Carefully, methodically, he checked on each of us, watching in every direction for some sign in the distance. His intensity was cool, and his control was something else. Even the shouting before he killed Jaber, as I thought about it, seemed tightly controlled. And then the way he'd snapped back into complete calm when the last of the three rounds drilled up through Jaber's gut. He was like a controlled explosion. The kind that gets the job done.

I closed my eyes and smelled the air. It was still fouled with oil smoke, but there were moments when some of it seemed to have been washed clean. A cool curtain of oxygen would pass over my face like a current of springwater in a muddy lake, chill and clear, that seems to come from nowhere.

When you're lying up the mind wanders for hours in that narrow space between sleep and waking. Through half-opened eyes I watched Rashid run half-crouching from one position to another and wondered where he might have trained in special operations. Then, in the next second, I was thinking about Griffin, about north Georgia and Utah and the tent in Hafr el-Batin—and the Koran—and about Christmas. I hadn't seen Griffin since Christmas.

God, what a miserable time that had been. For weeks before Christmas came, I would wake up every morning with sadness in my veins like a drug. I couldn't focus; could barely do what I had to do. Khalid got in touch with me a couple of times, but I blew him off. Selma actually wrote me a real letter, but it was about her own depression as the anniversary of my mother's death approached, and I didn't read past the first paragraph. I gave up reading almost entirely and tried, in every spare minute, to sleep. The Koran and the translation stayed at the bottom of my pack. To read them in public, by then, would have been to ask for a fight. And I was too depressed even for that.

There was a lot of anger among us in the camps. "The Saudis stole Christmas like the Grinch," Jenkins kept saying. We were not supposed to decorate, or pray, or sing. And the men started to hate everything about the Saudis. Everything. Including and especially the Saudi religion that the Americans were supposed to worry so much about offending, because this was Muslim holy land, and we were supposed to be defending these Muslims and their God— and their oil—and forget about America's own God, and even about Jesus Christ. . . . No, it wouldn't have made much sense to try to read the Koran in front of the other soldiers in those days before Christmas.

Listening to all that anger, I might have shared it. But I didn't. I began to feel like it was aimed at me. It was a strange thing, but every joke, every insult, every remark about Muslims and ragheads and camel fuckers stung me like ice on an exposed nerve. I was blond, blue-eyed, all-American. Nobody figured they were talking about me. And I got an idea how a Jew feels when someone who doesn't know talks to him about kikes. Or a closet homosexual when his boss talks about cocksuckers. But I was even more vulnerable than that, because I wasn't sure what my secret really was.

I thought Griffin might be able to help, and I wanted to talk to him some more. But in those last few days before Christmas I couldn't find him. And even if I'd been stupid enough to ask where he'd gone, I wouldn't be finding out. Not where his unit was concerned.

Christmas morning brought CARE packages to a lot of soldiers. The Army had saved them so there would at least be that much to raise spirits. But for those of us who got no packages, the holiday was that much worse. And then came dinner. Turkey and cranberry sauce, but served cold. Every bite of it fed the anger of soldiers who were missing Christmas, missing home, more than they could say.

The singing began at the other end of the chow line. It was one voice at first, low and mournful. It was gospel music. I'd never heard it quite like that before, and didn't know the song. But other soldiers, black soldiers, did. A lot of them did. "I said I wasn't gonna tell nobody—but I—couldn't help myself." And they began to join in, until, soon, all the soldiers who knew the song—all of them black soldiers—were singing.

The rest of us were excited. Sure. Any music would have been good. But then you wanted to sing along and—it wasn't yours. You didn't know the words. Maybe some of the white soldiers knew "We Three Kings of Orient Are" or "Silent Night," but not enough to compete, and those carols were as flat as a kazoo up against that gospel excitement. The white soldiers began to wander away. And the officers, you could see in their eyes, figured they had a problem on their hands. One by one, with nudges and pats on the back they encouraged the spur-of-the-moment Desert Shield Christmas Gospel Choir to break up, and finally it did. But one of the last to stop singing, and he didn't do it until he'd finished the song, was Griffin.

He was part of something, I thought to myself as I shivered a little, still wet and waiting under the fiberglass mouth of the cave for the order to move out. What was I part of? A creed I couldn't understand? Or the Rangers? "Blood, guts, sex and danger, ain't no stranger to an airborne ranger." I repeated the running cadences over and over to myself, wishing I really was running. And then I fell into a full sleep.

X   Like stray dogs making their way out of a forest, the Iraqi deserters wandered toward us from the city they'd pillaged for six months, and now were abandoning. A few buildings were burning in the low skyline on the other side of the bay, but the air, dense with drizzle and smoke, blotted out most of the scene. The men we saw were just the spill-over, the stragglers at the far edges of the exodus that was now under way. But there were enough of them coming to make our position impossible to sustain. We couldn't kill them all. We couldn't take them prisoner.

Rashid was talking to the captain. They were arguing, negotiating, planning. It was hard to say just what they were doing. Then he made his way toward me and asked if he could borrow my little M231 "for half an hour." He needed a pistol, or the next best thing. I looked over at the captain. He nodded. I didn't like parting with my weapon. But this was a situation, hiding here in the shadows of the Sinbad cave watching deserters slipping through the edges of the park like phantoms, that could not last.

Rashid slipped the 231 inside his windbreaker. Thirty minutes later, he was back, carrying four Iraqi uniforms. He gave three to us, and put one on himself. He asked for another 231 magazine, then went back out again. A few minutes later he was back with more uniforms and two Kalashnikovs.

The captain had been on the PRCs, but one after another he'd used up their batteries, and the last one was about to fade. He studied the terrain with his binoculars. Rashid borrowed rounds from another soldier—he guessed he was wearing out his welcome with me—and went out again. The captain outlined the plan, which I think most of us had guessed the gist of anyway. The only way to make it to the extraction northwest of Jahra was to cross the road, and that was now jammed with cars, trucks, tanks, and soldiers headed north. No question of American troops slipping across, and not much sense in fighting through. But there was enough confusion for a few more Iraqi soldiers here or there to blend in, especially after dark. Rashid would do whatever talking was required. When we made it to the extraction point, we'd use the last PRC to bring in the choppers and explain the change of clothes.

An hour before dark, we had enough uniforms and as many AKs as we were going to get. Some of the other men were able to put the baggy Iraqi fatigues over their own. The one I got was too small to do that. It was as wet as my own, and the soldier it belonged to had worn it for months, then died all over it. I put it on anyway. It was that or stay in Entertainment City. No choice there. But the stench of the dead man stuck in my nose and the slimy memories of him inside the fabric crawled across my skin.

"Make sure the AKs are operational," the captain ordered. All of us were trained to strip them blindfolded, and most of us had broken them down already. The weapons were more dangerous to the man firing than the man being shot at. "Only carry what you can put in your pockets," said the captain. "Take water. But no LBEs, no packs." So no Claymores. No C4. The only ammunition we had for the AKs was already in their magazines.

This was all wrong, I thought. We weren't trained for this. We were exposing ourselves to enemy fire and to our own. On the faces of the other soldiers I could read the same worries. But I put my folding SOG tool in my pocket and the basic demolition kit, the crimper and the nonsparking demo knife, in my belt at my back, ready to go. In the last shadows before dark we spread out as far as we dared without losing each other, and slipped out of the park.

Our march was much slower now than when we came in. We were moving with the same pace as the defeated. In every direction you could see Iraqi soldiers wandering across the sand, shuffling north through the twilight in shock. The Doha road was crossed with no problem. There were a few trucks moving on it, but they paid no attention to us, and that gave us confidence about what was to come. Skirting the edge of the bay we trudged through low grass and thorn bushes with plastic bags fluttering from their branches. Ahead of us we could see the glow of bombs and artillery. Above us was the constant roar of low-flying aircraft. We wanted to hit the road north of Jahra at the Mutlaa Ridge. The highway narrowed there from four lanes to two. There was bound to be a lot of confusion, and if we could approach the road at a right angle we could minimize the time spent crossing it. But as we moved up the gently sloping side of the ridge we started hitting the strands of barbed wire that marked off minefields. By the time we were halfway up we'd been funneled into the dense stream of men and trucks creeping through the pass.

The A-10 is a noisy plane, made to create havoc on the ground. It's officially called a Thunderbolt, and if you see it in action you know why. As we got to the highest point on the highway, we heard one come in right over us, following the contour of the road, headed north. Then another. Another. Another. Their bombs flashed like sheet lightning on the desert ahead of us. Waiting for their thunder, I counted the distance. They were less than five miles away. More jets came in low and fast. They were crossing and crisscrossing over our heads. More bombs hit. The traffic, which was barely moving before, now stopped completely.

Iraqis were leaning out of their vehicles trying to see

what was going on. A man hanging from the side of a truck suddenly dropped to the road in front of me. His face was inches from mine and he looked straight into my blue eyes. He didn't say a thing. He just dove under the truck.

The sky was vibrating with the sound of jets, the ground erupting with bombs. And the targets they were hitting got closer by the second. Several blasts surprised us from behind, just north of Jahra where the highway narrowed. The planes were cutting off any retreat. Now the whole line of traffic was under the gun. Headlights were swinging wildly in every direction, ordnance flashed, phosphorus burned white, trucks glowed red with flame. Some drivers tried to wheel their vehicles around, swerving through the desert—and into the mines. Men were running away from their trucks, but in one second the concussion of the bombs would shatter their insides, in another second incendiaries swept around them in waves of flame. Clouds of fire mushroomed from the line of traffic in front of us. And behind us. And there were screams. There were so many screams. Thousands of screams. All lost like whispers in the exploding air.

The only way off the road that would take us in the direction of the extraction point was through a minefield. The captain signaled to me. One truck had made it about thirty yards out before a tire exploded. The driver ran a little farther, then tripped a mine himself and died. For us that corpse was a beginning. We could follow the tire tracks and the footprints, but when those ran out I had the point.

On my belly I wormed through the sand, feeling for mines with my fingers, hoping I could remember enough about the Russian-made Iraqi devices to defuse them in the dark. Each of my hands walked over the sand, each of the fingers sensing the way forward, looking for the touch of metal or wire prongs. An inch at a time. Then I used the blade of my knife in the same space, probing beneath the surface. The rest of the squad followed my trail. We were deafened by the exploding highway. We had no shelter from the raining debris. We struggled against the need to rise, to run, to flee as fast as humanly possible. We just kept creeping out of the inferno the only way we could, one inch at a time.

I touched metal. I felt over the top of it lightly like I was reading Braille. It was still warm, a piece of scrap that had fallen back from the explosions on the road. We edged farther along. Where were the mines? Where were the fucking mines? They were there, somewhere, but thinly scattered, and the failure to find them was shaking me. When minutes passed and there was nothing, instead of thinking we might be in the clear I had to be afraid there was something I'd missed. Fantasies would flash through my brain that, behind me, the squad was gone; blown away by my mistakes; their destruction unheard in the deafening explosions. I twisted to look back over my shoulder. The first eyes to catch mine were Jenkins's. He looked right at me and managed a smile. And in that second, I'll tell you, I loved him for it.

The blade of the demo knife hit something, but with all the noise I couldn't hear the metallic click I'd normally expect. I concentrated with everything in me, nudging the wet sand away, and felt the rough texture of a rock. And we moved on.

A scream was close behind me. A terrible scream, in a voice I knew. "Medic! Ah, fuck. Water!" It was Jenkins. A glob of white phosphorus thrown up by the explosions on the road had fallen on his back. It seared through his shirt and skin and started burning into him. He was close enough for me to smell the flesh, but I couldn't turn around full circle on ground I hadn't covered. Over my shoulder I saw the medic, scrambling over the bodies of the men in front of him to get to Jenkins. They were handing the medic their canteens. He had one in each hand and was dragging two more—dragging them outside the cleared line we'd made. My muscles clenched waiting for a canteen to hit a prong, trip a wire, but there was nothing. And now the medic was lying on top of Jenkins, trying to steady him as he poured water on the phosphorus. But Jenkins, even Jenkins, couldn't hold still with that kind of pain, and a lot of water was spilling uselessly to the sides of the hole the phosphorus made as it bored into his back. He was coughing, choking, and his body started to buck violently. The phosphorus must have hit his lung. Then he was still.

My hands were not. A chill was running down my arms from the base of my skull, every nerve was tingling and my hands were shaking. "Ah, God," I said. "Ah, God," I prayed. My hands started to steady. Enough anyway. Enough to keep working.

I could hear shouts behind me. It looked like one of the soldiers was trying to get up, trying to make a run for it, and two others were dragging him back down.

Metal. Cold and flat and circular. I cleared the sand. I felt over the top of the thing, felt—the detonator, right where I thought it should be. The concentration it took spared me, a little, the horror raining down around us. There was nothing in my mind, then, but the messages my fingers brought me, and that unvoiced, half-finished prayer. I unscrewed the detonator and threw it away. The mine was safe. We moved on.

We were inching forward and downward. I felt the hard surface of a track, a path, a road. A dirt road, graded and leading northwest from Jahra. Ah, God. Ah, God! I felt over it faster and faster. It was well-traveled enough, recently enough, to suggest safety.

Now we moved fast, running double-time to the extraction point, moving like Rangers again. It was almost 04:00. We were going home.

Tracer rounds cut across the track in front of us. Another burst. We hit the ground.

I was near the captain and he had his thermal imager out. At almost precisely the extraction point there was a company of Iraqi troops. From the discipline showed by their deployment, they must have been an elite unit. And from the way they'd fired in our direction, they must have had night vision or thermal imaging equipment. The minute we went down, they stopped shooting. They thought we were Iraqis, too. They didn't want to kill us. But they were pulling out. And they weren't taking stragglers.

Our problem was: they weren't pulling out fast enough.

Our captain was on the PRC trying to communicate, but the choppers weren't in range yet. They had to be almost directly overhead for it to work, and if they came too close, they'd wind up with enemy contact they didn't expect. It was 03:57. The captain started repeating a warning signal over the radio. Again and again. Now we saw more tracers. But these were firing into the air. There was a long pause. I can't tell you if it was seconds or minutes. Then the rockets from the choppers started to come in one after another. Four in all. The captain had his ear glued to the PRC. He shouted for us to fall back—and fast.

After a couple of minutes' running we heard a jet pass overhead. A mushroom cloud went up where the Iraqi company was. A fuel-air bomb. The force of the blast blew us back, sucking up gales of wind and dust.

We waited. There was nothing else to do. No one else was coming for us. Not this night. The window was closed.

We settled in, shivering now, just waiting for dawn and new orders. The thunder died slowly, like a storm that passes out to sea. And at sunrise the air was still.

The bits of paper that descended from the clouds fell as gently as a light spring snow in Kansas. Rashid picked one up and translated it. The war was over.

It was just as well. No orders had come, and none were going to. The battery in the PRC was dead.

We decided to head back toward Kuwait City. Since we were wearing Iraqi uniforms, we'd have to figure a way to surrender to our own troops. We followed back along the dirt road and turned with it toward the killing fields of the night before. The rain had washed away our tracks, and with them the path we'd followed out of the minefield. Jenkins was out there somewhere among low mounds of sand, but we couldn't see him.

In the gray, grim dawn the road through the Mutlaa Ridge was a gridlocked slaughterhouse that stretched as far to the north as we could see. The sound of the bombs had stopped. The artillery was still. No A-10s hosed down the terrain with their rapid-fire cannons. No screams floated on the air. But as we trudged closer to the scene there were other sounds. Far in the background were the roaring oil wells sending tornadoes of flame and smoke into the sky. And closer at hand—here—and here—and there in the distance—and almost anywhere you turned, there was music. All at the same time you heard marches, military and triumphant; and the mournful wail of Arabic love songs; and the sound of rock and roll. You could hear the excited voices of news announcers. All over this scene of hell, the radios in cars had been left on.

The engines—many of the engines—were still running. A truck on its side spun a wheel like a dying turtle trying to right itself. A tank idled on the slope of a dune like it was still waiting to charge, but no one was alive inside to give the order. Instead of ammunition it was loaded down with blankets, bedspreads, silks, and calicos looted from Kuwait. The cloth spilled onto the drab sand of the desert like silent explosions of color in the morning light.

As the Iraqis fled they'd grabbed everything and anything they could: clothes and washing machines, stereos and beds, food and toys. Barbie dolls and Ninja Turtles, stuffed animals and radio-controlled cars, all scattered, melted, distorted by the heat and flame. It was looting, pure and simple. But it was looting for homes, I thought. These were things for the wives and the kids of soldiers who'd been stuck in this desert shithole for months, and probably never wanted to be there to begin with, and this was going to give them something, at least, to show for all they went through. You couldn't justify what they did. But you could understand it. Or, at least, I could.

We moved slowly through the wreckage, careful to avoid the little bomblets scattered everywhere. That fatal traffic jam, up close, was like a funhouse fantasy of corpses petrified by fire, too horrible not to look at, creatures molded out of charred, crisp, stinking stuff in positions of escape, or fear, or, in a few cases, caught completely unaware. We could have been any of them. In the back of one truck, soldiers still sat awkwardly on benches. Some faced straight ahead, their scorched skin without eyes or lips. Two of the dead men were embracing each other in fear, like children in the dark. In another truck, burned hands still gripped a steering wheel, bonded to the plastic by the heat. But there was no body attached to the hands, and no sign of what might have happened to it.

I heard the flutter of the Blackhawks before I saw them. They were coming in low and fast over the highway. One banked hard for a looksee, and we looked right back at it, straight up the barrel of the door gun. "Americans!" we shouted. "Rangers! Hoo-ah!" I stripped off the top of my Iraqi uniform. So did the others, shedding the shirts like a discarded skin to reveal us there in our whiteness and blackness and God-bless-America non–Arab-ness. The chopper circled again.

I was exhausted, fighting to keep my eyes from rolling up into my head. And I saw that one of us, I'm not even sure which one of us, was standing there among the carcasses of machines and men with his arms stretched out parallel to the ground, like a man on a cross, with his rifle in his right hand. And for a second I wasn't sure what the hell was going on. And then the part of my brain that still functioned kicked in and I remembered our recognition signal for link-ups when other communications failed. Now I held out my arms. Others held out theirs. And there on that highway of death we stood like crucifixes with AK-47s, and waited for the choppers to get the picture. And waited.

"They're gonna fuckin' kill us right here," someone said. The Blackhawks circled. Hovered. We were frozen in their shadows. Then the door gunner waved, said something to his pilot, and the helicopters made one more broad sweep, then settled into a clear space about two hundred yards away. They kept their engines running and their wheels inches off the ground as the men inside poured out.

Their captain looked over the scene and started radioing orders, keeping our captain standing beside him in silence and, I thought, anger, but wasting no time. Only when he'd finished were all the introductions made. They were a Special Forces unit attached to Psychological Operations. The Cleaning Crew.

This was a high-profile site, right on the main road north of Kuwait City, and reporters and cameras were going to be here soon, one way or another, so they wanted to sanitize as much as they could before that happened. Leave the machines in place. Just tidy up the rest of the mess. The human mess. They needed extra help and there was no one around alive just then but us. They handed out the gloves and what looked like Hefty bags.

"How about some water," I said. An ordinary request, but I heard the anger in my own voice.

"Who's he?" the Cleaning Crew captain demanded, pointing at Rashid. "Prisoner?"

"Kuwaiti Resistance," said our captain.

"Don't fuckin' worry about him," I said. "There's a dead American out there somewhere." I pointed toward the minefield, and started to walk toward it.

"Halt," said one of their sergeants.

"Fuck you," I said.

"Halt. Right there." It was my captain. "We'll send a team for Jenkins. Don't worry. But nobody's going to try to get to that place the way we got there last night."

A sergeant on the crew started tossing bottles of water

to us. "Let's get a move on," he said, looking around and identifying the first areas to be policed. He spotted the truck with the charred soldiers inside. "There," he said. "Captain? We're going to need a lot more body bags, more crew, and the dozers."

"Already on the way," said their captain.

The sergeant stepped up into the bed of the truck and started shoving bodies off benches onto the sand. He didn't have much trouble. They were dry and light. They came off in pieces.

There were a lot of papers littered in the wreckage. Big wooden crates with rope handles had been blown out of one truck, and the Iraqis' records of the occupation were scattering in the wind. A couple of the Cleaning Crew set about gathering them again for intelligence purposes. Beside a gutted torso I saw what looked like a personal diary and picked it up. I held it out in the direction of a soldier gathering papers. He shook his head. No point, he said.

"I'll take it," said Rashid. He leafed through it.

"What's it say?"

"That he was married last October and only got to spend one week with his wife." He flipped a few more pages. "That he was lonely . . . and scared."

"Yeah. Ain't we all."

"But that he trusts in God."

He put the diary under his arm and looked at the torso near our feet, then at the Cleaning Crew going about its business. "Fucking shit," he said, pinching the bridge of his nose like he was trying to stop the pain in his head. "I am really tired," he said. "And you know what? I'm gone."

He started walking, alone, down the road toward Kuwait City. Another sergeant from the Cleaning Crew stopped him, but Rashid looked over at our captain and our captain cleared him to leave. As he walked, Rashid shed what was left of his borrowed Iraqi uniform. He stepped out of the battered boots. He stripped off the pants. For a few seconds, still walking, Rashid had on nothing but his BVDs. Then he grabbed some white cloth from a roll of it on the back of a tank, wrapping it around his waist and throwing it over his shoulder like a toga; walking upright, proud; walking away from us and all that we had done.

A pair of heavy-lift choppers were following the road, coming up from the south with small bulldozers suspended under their bellies. More choppers arrived with men to reinforce the Cleaning Crew. Our captain had another discussion with their captain. And it was on those helicopters that we were taken out at last.

As we wheeled up toward the smoke I looked for Jenkins's body, west of the road in the sand. I thought I saw it, but I couldn't be sure.

"Captain!"

I didn't know if he knew who I was anymore. Or who he was.

"Captain, don't let them bury Jenkins out there!" I shouted. "He's got an Iraqi uniform. They're going to bury him with *them*."

"It's okay, it's okay," said the captain, shaking his head to bring it in focus. "I told them."

" 'I will never leave a fallen comrade to fall into the hands of the enemy.' " I shouted the line from the Ranger Creed.

"There's no enemy down there," said the captain. "War's over, remember? No enemy left."

I looked out the door of the chopper. Rashid was walking somewhere below us on the road. But there were small groups of people emerging now from the buildings in Jahra, from the desert tents, from the sand itself, walking along the highway to Kuwait City, wearing their pure-white robes, waving flags, celebrating the victory, looking at the aftermath. From the air, as we flew away, Rashid looked like any or all of them.

XI   I needed peace. Like a withered vine needs water, I needed something that would lift me up and bring me life. And give me peace. The old discipline and control, the training and beliefs, they weren't working for me anymore. I wasn't connected to anything. And not to anyone. My mind turned in circles around thoughts that came at random, scattered points of anguish and fear that had no ties between them except more anguish and fear: the silver light of the television playing across the face of my father; worries about bills in Savannah and Selma in Kansas; a backhoe on frozen ground; bulldozers in the desert; a dragonfly floating across the surface of a Georgia pond like a Blackhawk over the sand. Everything came together, but nothing could be resolved. And I felt like my soul was dying inside me.

The sight of Jenkins's cot without him in it was the last image burned into my eyes before I fell asleep, and the first thing I saw when I woke up. We'd worked and trained together. We partied together. Twice we'd been in combat together. We were buddies. Part of a team. "He knew the risks" is what we always said when one of us died. And that's what I told myself. But knowing the risk of being killed seemed different, now, than the risk of being dead.

Without moving, I focused on his bed. When I fell asleep, there was a pile of stuff on top of the cot, and beside it a neatly closed box. When I woke up the box was gone. Someone must have come and taken it away. Before you go out on a mission you divide up your personal effects. The stuff you want shipped home for your family to see goes in the box. And Jenkins's box already was on its way. The rest, you figure it's up for grabs if anybody wants it. I could see a couple of *Penthouses* and some bits and pieces of gear.

Under my cot where I'd shoved them I could feel my own small pile of belongings, my own half-empty box of personal effects. Selma's letters were inside the box, in case she wanted them back. And my father's Koran, and the translation. I opened the box, flipped through the envelopes, but couldn't bring myself to read the letters and clippings. I picked up the Koran and studied it like it was an object: a puzzle. There had been times when I tried to match the passages underlined by my father with the English translation. It wasn't an impossible job. The translation had a column of Arabic, and right beside it the column of English. But matching the characters of an alphabet I didn't know or begin to understand could take me hours, and when the match was made the translated passages didn't seem to have any deep meaning. Sometimes they didn't have much meaning at all.

I let the translation fall open on my chest wherever it would. And it was a single phrase in the third surah that caught my eye. "Every soul shall have a taste of death," it said.

I must have read those eight words before. At one time or another I'd gone through about half the book. But they hadn't meant anything to me the other times. And now they touched me. In ways the words alone couldn't explain, the phrase moved me. It was a physical sensation. " 'Every soul shall have a taste of death,' " I read out loud.

"A taste of death." In my gut I felt the meaning that I needed. This soul—this Muslim soul—experienced things. The immortal soul I'd heard about from my mother's priest and preachers on TV seemed to me as hard to grasp as the smoke that floats up from a candle when the flame is blown out. The soul they talked about in church—my soul, they said—didn't seem to have much to do with me. It was as distant and mysterious as God himself. They weren't talking about the spirit that was hurting inside me now. But in this phrase in this book I found a soul that lived. It tasted life. And if it tasted death, too, that was just one important experience in the long life of that soul. Of my soul.

You'll say I was exhausted, seeing a bunch of flowers in the swamp where there were none to see; finding an answer to prayers I couldn't even finish. But I'll tell you revelation is different than that. It touches you in every nerve. It pumps through your veins. It brings you life and it takes away the fear of death. And it gives you peace. My eyes began to cry. I let them. There was no one to see. And inside myself I was as happy as I could remember being for a very long time. I closed the book and folded my hands over it on my chest. I'd keep that one phrase to remember. I could keep myself going with that, I thought.

But I did not announce my new understanding to the world. It was still so special, and so fragile inside me, that I didn't want to risk discussing it with anyone. And, anyway, who could I trust? Were there Saudis who could show me the way? I didn't think so. They were so corrupted, so hypocritical. "They have made their oath a screen for their misdeeds," I read and understood. Did the Nation of Islam hold the key? Not for a white boy. And even Griffin, when he told me about his revelation, was not able to touch me with it. Could scholars give me more of what I discovered for myself? No. They could interpret words, but they couldn't reveal the spirit. It was up to me, myself, to find the meaning.

And so, without explanation to anyone, but without embarrassment, I began to read more seriously than I had ever done before. Some of the passages made very little sense to me. But others were electrifying. This book was not like a collection of Bible stories you could follow easily.

There were mysteries here, like the code at the beginning of so many chapters, that I guessed I would never solve. And maybe that was the point. But there was also a lot that was perfectly clear: rules laid down for men and women to follow. Rules from God, but rules for humans. Rules for people who felt real love and anger, lust and hunger, happiness and fear. Rules for souls that lived.

In the couple of days spent waiting for transport back to Georgia, every minute I could spare was spent with the Book. This faith and revelation, now that I began to understand it, was all so different from what I'd thought before, or what we'd been made to think. Where were the veils? I couldn't find them. Where was it forbidden to drink? What was advised against was drunkenness, but wine was something you found in heaven itself. This Allah was not some foreign God, but the same one Moses worshiped, the same one who created in Mary the miracle of the Virgin Birth. Just like you can feel the rocks and olive trees in Israel's soil when you read the Old Testament, in this Koran you could smell the desert, and you could live, in a word or moment, among the tribes being civilized by His revelation. Rough as it was, I could understand His justice, and see where it could apply today.

Still, I didn't pray. I was working, I was traveling. These were my excuses. But there was another thing, too. I wanted to understand completely, in my own mind, what it meant to pray.

In the plane from Riyadh to Hunter, I sat in the back row beneath a cone of light while everyone else was asleep, looking at the passages that puzzled me or moved me or helped me to define the new world I thought I would make for myself. Only now and again did I look at the footnotes in the book, and then just to learn who was who, not to take the translator's word for what it all meant. There were references to the closest followers of Muhammad: Abu Bakr, Ali, Othman. And to his wives.

My eyes blurred on the page beneath the reading light and one of the holy names came back to me as part of a memory I wanted to be rid of; something from a few weeks after Josie and I broke up. It was when Jenkins—ah, Jenkins —and I had gone to the Canton Inn. It was just outside Savannah, just a place to get drunk and maybe get laid by some Korean or Philippine bargirls, and just sort of generally forget about things. Jenkins thought it would be good for me.

One of the women in the bar was called Girlie, she said, and she laughed. I laughed, too. I didn't believe her. But she put her hand down to her throat and held up a little gold necklace that spelled out, yes indeed, G-i-r-l-i-e in flowing script. I took another long pull on my beer and smiled.

"You want to dance?" she said.

I didn't.

"C'mon, soldier," she said. "You made to dance. Look at those legs." She ran her hand up the inside of my thigh. She turned her head and winked at another one of the girls.

"No, no," I laughed. "No!," and grabbed her hand.

She was just a little taller than the other girls, and she seemed prettier. "You so biiig," she said.

"I bet you say that a lot."

Jenkins spit some beer out, some of it through his nose. "Ooooh," he said, wiping the back of his hand across his face. "Be nice, Kurt."

"Come on, Kurt," she said, picking up my name. "You dance with me." She took me by the hand and onto the floor and by now I'd given up. And I enjoyed. But I couldn't shake the idea I was in a movie. The cheap strobe on the dance floor flickered through heavy smoke. The whole scene looked like a Chuck Norris version of Vietnam before the action starts. Girlie had been with a couple of friends, Filipinas like her. One was sitting by the bar alone twirling her leather cigarette pack on its corner. The other's face was pocked, you could see that even in the low light, and her sleepy eyes and narrow lips and dished-in profile gave her a weird lizardy look, but she was moving in on Jenkins, hot and heavy, slithering over him on the barstool, and he was giving as good as he got.

"You like the Doors?" I shouted at Girlie.

"Sure, sure," she said. "Jim Morrison."

"I was thinking of *Apocalypse Now*," I said.

"What?" she said.

But the Doors weren't on tonight. The next song that came across the speakers was something country by Garth Brooks. I raised my hands in surrender. "Girlie, I really can't. Let's sit down someplace like—outside."

"No can do," she said. "Buy me a drink."

"One drink."

"Champagne."

"I choose."

"Champagne," she said.

The people out on the floor were lining up. Some of the Filipina girls were in jeans and boots and knew all the steps already, holding hands crossed with their partners, sashaying like dancers on the Nashville Network. The girls who didn't have men were dancing with each other, just to be on the floor.

Girlie was wearing a cowboy-style shirt with the tail tied in a knot above her bellybutton and cutoffs sheared and raveled in an even line with her crotch. "Where'd you get those legs?"

"What?" she said, and put her mouth to my ear. "What?" she said, and ran her tongue along the ear's inside ridge so the hair on the back of my neck stood up and I wanted to scream. "Champagne or zombie punch," she said. Ginger ale or Hi-C. Ten dollars a glass. But what the hell. I didn't like all these preliminaries, all this hanging around. But I never was one of those soldiers who can say, flat out, "Let's fuck." I had another beer, and watched some trouble brewing at the other end of the bar.

If you wait long enough and drink long enough in a dump like the Canton Inn, you can depend on a fight. And sure enough one came. And it got bloody faster than I expected. A redheaded boy got a broken bottle in the face. I remember watching with a little rush of horror as the son of a bitch who was after him, a short dark man with a death's-head tattoo on his right arm, twisted the jagged circle of glass across the kid's nose and just under his eyes. Lucky he wasn't blinded. A friend of the redheaded kid caught the tattooed man across the back with a Spyderco blade and opened him up like a filleted fish.

I didn't have anything to do with this fight. Not directly. And didn't want to. But the blood and fear always leaves you a little excited.

"C'mon, Girlie. Let's get the hell out of here."

She didn't say anything but let me pull her along the edge of the room to the door, moving as close to the wall and as far from the fight as we could, watching the action flickering beneath the strobe. She stopped and tried to pull away from me when we got clear of the building and into the carpark, but without any energy. She was gulping air and I thought for a second she was going to be sick but she leaned against the side of my car and closed her eyes and let her breathing even out. "Is terrible," she said. "Why they do that?"

"Come on."

"Where we go?"

"I don't know. McDonald's. Bojangles. My place, your place. Let's just get out of here before the police come or—"

Right then the tattooed man spilled out the door and wheeled around to face whatever was coming after him. In the yellow sulfur light his shirt and the skin under it and all down the back of his pants were black with his blood.

We burned rubber out of the lot. Adrenaline and desire were pumping so hard in my system I gripped the wheel tight for a few minutes just to steady myself. "You mind if

I just drive for a while?" I said when I'd already been driving for a while. Girlie moved her body next to mine like a cat looking for warmth.

"You're from the Philippines?"

"Mmmm," she said.

"Where?"

"You know Philippines?"

"Manila. Subic Bay."

"Mindanao?"

"Heard of it, I think."

"Why you ask?"

"You know, just want to talk a little, I guess." I could feel myself getting hard just from the feel of her leaning against me.

"I got idea," she said, pulling my zipper down slowly. I tried to watch the road as I got the sensation of metal separating over the head and the shaft of my dick and the elastic of my underwear as she pushed it down off the flesh and started to kiss and suck just under the head.

"You like?"

"Yes I like. But I can't do this and drive." I had my fingers in her hair and pulled her up and held her next to me. We were about a dozen miles out of Abercorn now, passing the lots full of RVs and the last of the car dealerships. It was late. Everything was closed, and the summer night was blowing through the windows warm as bathwater. I turned hard into the drive of a used-car lot, running up over the curb to get around the chain across the entrance, and pulled in back of the offices, where the only light was from the moon. The second I stopped and turned off the engine she was back down on me, taking it as deep into her mouth and throat as she could.

I pulled her head up again and kissed her. She was small enough for me to pick her up, almost to cradle her. She struggled for a second, trying to turn and go down on me again, but I didn't need that. I kissed her face and neck and she settled into the bend of my left arm. She plunged her tongue into my mouth but I pulled back slowly from it, keeping my own tongue on the tip of hers until we were barely touching. She giggled. I laughed. She smelled like sweat and Ivory soap and something else, like jasmine maybe. I started pulling at the pearlized snaps on her shirt with my teeth, untying the knot with my right hand, feeling just the tip of her nipples with my tongue, with a finger— now unbuttoning her cutoffs and pushing them down. She pulled her legs free from them and spread her legs wide like she was going to welcome the world. I ran my hand behind her knee and felt the contour of her ass, then drew my fingers up through the hot wet space between her legs. There was no hair on her anywhere. None at all to cover the wet, slick smoothness of her cunt. "Get on me," I said. "Get on!"

"You got protection?"

"Get on!"

"I got," she said, fumbling with her right hand for her bag on the floor of the Nova. Her left arm was caught under mine but she didn't bother pulling herself free. She tore the edge of the foil with her teeth and rolled the sheath down over me, then swung her leg on top and started to guide me in. My hands were around each of her arms. I stopped her.

"Just the tip," I said, and held her above me, feeling her muscles tense around me, looking at her body glistening now with sweat, her small hard nipples black against the moonlit silver of her breasts, her stomach muscles clenching as she gripped me inside her. "You come," she said. "You come!"

"No," I said. "Not yet."

She leaned forward and put her arms around my neck, shrugging off my hands and settling down onto me now, moving gently in a circle, stirring. I reached under her with both hands, gently spreading and massaging her from behind.

"Girlie?" I said, looking at the gold chain around her throat. "Is your name Girlie?"

"Lots of pilipina girls name Girlie."

"And you?"

"Maybe not."

I pushed into her a little more deeply. She put her forehead down on my shoulder and concentrated, making me feel every inch inside her.

"Maybe not? Then who?"

"You know name of Aisha?"

"Eye-shah?"

She didn't say anything for a second, concentrating, then drawing out her words slowly, two or three at a time, making the phrases fit into her slow, controlled rhythm. "You ever hear of Muhammad?"

I couldn't believe this. I pushed back from her and looked her in the face. Her eyes were closed. I couldn't read her. "Yes," I said.

"Yes?"

"Hey, maybe I'm a Muslim."

"You full of shit," she said, playing at biting my ear; closing down hard on me inside her.

"Have it your way."

"Muhammad an old man . . . many wives," she said. "He like fucking . . . all the time. . . . And youngest of all . . . Aisha . . . he love her sooo much."

My groin was drenched and I was throbbing but I was holding back. I wasn't going to come yet. Not yet.

"And you know . . . how young Aisha?" Rising slowly, putting her hands on mine and spreading herself wider with them. Now settling. Rising. "You know? . . . She ten year old. . . . Little Aisha. . . . Soooo good girl . . . so little girl."

She started to shake. Sobbing. And still crying when it was over.

In the dull light before sunrise I woke to the sticky feel of the vinyl seat and the smell of sex and the steam of the summer in the South.

"You okay?" I said.

"Yeah. Fine."

"So tell me again about the Prophet."

"I make it all up, Jack."

"Kurt."

"Soldier. I make it all up."

She opened the door and stood outside, putting on her shirt and cutoffs, twisting the side mirror to see her face, running her fingers through her hair and shaking it out.

"You take me home," she said, talking through the hairpins in her mouth.

"Aisha?"

"My name Girlie," she said. "You pay cash or Visa?"

Now half asleep in the passenger compartment of the C-5A that was like a little movie theater with no screen, the scene moved through my mind in fragments. I thought it was just a fuck at the time. But ever since, and especially now, remembering it left me feeling deeply, desperately unclean.

XII

"Kurt? Come on in. How you doin'?"

"Fine, thanks, Tyler."

"You've caught me all alone here, I'm afraid. The ladies are out."

"On a Sunday afternoon?"

"Can I offer you something?"

We walked together into that big kitchen where I'd spent so much time when I was courting Josie. The place still had a familiar—a family—feel to me, even if the courting seemed so long past that I couldn't remember what it was like.

"What can I do for you, Kurt?" said Josie's father, pouring me a glass of cold sweet tea.

"I hope I'm not interrupting something."

"Just going over some papers."

"Well, I wanted to talk to you, Tyler. I'll get right down to it. I'm getting out of the Army." I took a long drink. "I see you're surprised."

"I'm sure it's the right decision."

"I think so."

"And there's something I can do for you?"

"Not really. Not right now, anyway. I'm planning to travel for the next year or so."

"Whereabouts?"

"Europe. You know my folks were from Yugoslavia. I thought I'd go check it out."

"Sounds like it's pretty dangerous over there."

"Yeah, well. Probably not where I'm going. I've had my fill of wars."

"I guess. Josie told me she heard you were in the Gulf."

"Yeah."

"But, Kurt, you'll excuse me. I don't see what this has to do with me."

"Well, I'm trying to plan for the future a little," I said. "I'll be leaving the service in September. I saved all through the time I was in the Gulf. I mean, what would I spend money on? Right? And my mother made me a beneficiary on her life insurance, and there were my father's savings bonds: $24,200 worth, as it turned out. All in all, I figure I can scrape together about $72,000."

"That's a decent amount for a man your age."

"It's not nothing, I guess. It's enough to buy a few nice things, which doesn't interest me, or to take a couple of years off, which does. It's enough to get me to my father's village."

"And when you leave there, where do you think you'll go?"

"I can't know that, really. But—and this is why I stopped by this afternoon—I was thinking I might come back to Savannah. It feels as much like home as any place I know."

"I see."

"And I was wondering, when I do, if you might help me look for a job."

"Or give you a job."

"Well, yeah, if I'm good enough for it. It's not like I haven't worked before."

"No. It's not like that. But right now, I just can't say. A lot can change in a couple of years."

"I'm counting on it. But—"

"But, I don't think so, Kurt."

"What do you mean?"

"What I said."

"You used to talk to me all the time about what I could do at the mill. Maybe security. Maybe management."

" 'Used to' was more than a year ago, Kurt. And you're talking about one or two years from now. Things change. So does the business. We're laying people off, not signing them on."

"Is that the real reason?"

Tyler knew what I was asking. "It is" was all he said.

I looked around at the kitchen in silence. The tidy cabinets painted white and light blue, the soapstone counters, with a bowl of fruit always off to one corner. A farm kitchen. A rich man's farm kitchen. The stove looked big enough to roast a steer. Beside it was a butcher block so old, so used, so often sanded down that it dipped in the middle. On its side was a rack of half a dozen cleavers and knives.

I was still in control. I got up and took a deep breath. "But that's right now," I said. "The layoffs are right now. Maybe in two years we can see how things are going."

"Why, sure. Sure, Kurt. Send me a letter before you head back this way. I'll give you an answer straightaway."

"That'd be fine," I said. "That's all I'm looking for, really."

"Can I get you anything else? I've got to get back to my papers, I'm afraid."

"Well, you know, what I'd really like is one of these peaches," I said, picking one out of the bowl and pulling a knife out of the rack. "Is that okay?"

"That's what they're there for," he said, shifting his weight from one foot to the other as he leaned against the counter.

I started to cut into the skin, but the knife didn't have much of an edge. Like I used to do when I was in the kitchen all the time, I pulled out the sharpener and honed the blade. "Remember when this was my job at Thanksgiving?" I said.

"Yeah," he said, as flat as that.

"Mrs. Rankin used to say nobody could put an edge on them like I could." I looked up at Tyler as I finished peeling the peach over the sink, trying not to make too much of a mess. "I'll tell you," I said, "there's no peaches in the world like these." I rinsed off my hands and the blade, wiped it with a paper towel, and put it back. Tyler was watching me very closely.

Sometimes, you know, you live up to the fears other people have about you. But I couldn't figure out what was bothering Tyler. Not really. I pulled the knife back out of the rack and made like I was wiping the blade again, just to see how he'd react. I didn't like the look on his face.

"Sorry if I was imposing," I said.

He should have said, "Come back anytime." But "That's okay" was all he did say.

"Anyway, thanks again." And I was out of there.

Rolling down the driveway I felt like there was something wrong with me, even though I knew there wasn't. "Planning for the future," I told Tyler. "Planning for the future," I said out loud to nobody in the car. "Fuck the future!" I shouted, just to hear the sound of my voice again. Then I pushed down the accelerator and tried to let the car take over my thoughts. I was going to leave Savannah behind. Fuck it. I was going to leave America behind. I was tired of looking for myself in the Army, at the Rankins'— in other people's homes.

The idea that I belonged somewhere else had been growing in me for a long time. "You belong in the Rangers," I used to hear people say. But all they meant was that the man fit the job. Americans don't know about belonging, I thought, and now that I'd begun to find my faith, I wanted to find my history, too; to find just that place where I belonged in every sense—belonging to the land, to the people, part of their blood, their past, their future.

By the summer of 1991 I had been in the United States Army for six long years, seen action in two wars, Panama and the Gulf, and learned enough to know that blood, guts, sex, and danger were short-term highs: addictions, in fact, for a lot of people. And not just the soldiers. No, sir. We were the players. But the whole American people was addicted to our show.

America's wars, when I was in them, were waged like football games. We were all supposed to file into the stadium and play, then win and walk out. They were made for TV. Whatever the conflict was it shouldn't go on too long. People get bored and restless. So don't get in unless you know how to get out. And the violence should be visible without being too disgusting, too real. So when I watched the videos of my last American war, I saw a lot of Nintendo-style pictures of smart bombs finding hard targets. There were dramatic scenes of poor Iraqi fuckers surrendering to us in wholesale lots. But that highway through the Mutlaa Ridge, we didn't see much of that. No bodiless hands gripped the steering wheels. No Ranger lay screaming in the sand while white phosphorus burned through his back and lungs. No. The Cleaning Crew had done its job. Ours was a sanitized win. Just one hundred and forty-six of us dead and some fairly vague and undeterminable statistic of them. Then on to the next war.

There'd be someplace in the world nobody ever heard of, and Washington would declare it of vital strategic importance. Then you needed a bad guy. In the old days it might have been a whole country full of people, like the Japs. But the USG couldn't get away with that pure public racism anymore. Not quite. So the bad guy had to be one individual bad guy, and when he was identified, he suddenly became the single most dangerous man in the world. Kaddafi or Noriega, Khomeini or Saddam. Washington would make him a dark star: the Threat, the Monster, the new Hitler. And we'd push him and prod him and fuck with him, whoever he was, like an animal in a cage until he swung a claw out from between the bars. Then we'd go and fight our war and get out. We'd declare victory whether there'd been one or not. And people would believe it, at least for a while.

When I drove out to Tyler's place, I'd half thought we could talk about all of this. We had some good talks in the old days and I thought that, whatever happened with Josie, he and I would still be able to communicate. But he'd had his papers to attend to. And maybe I was wrong about him. Maybe, before, he wasn't listening either. Beyond being polite maybe he just couldn't be bothered. He was so American that way. Just couldn't be bothered.

I thought about what was happening in the land of my dead parents. Even the little news we got said there was something evil there. But who could be bothered about it? None of the great nations that got together for the war in Kuwait could agree on a goddamn thing when it came to my parents' people. Not for the Croats. Not for the Bosnians. We never heard the word "strategic." No threat to America was found. The buildup for intervention never began.

Tyler hadn't had the time to hear any of this. And whatever happened, I wasn't going to bother him again.

When Josie called, I'd already made that decision.

"You listen to me," she said with that voice that steamed like dry ice when she got angry. "You stay away from my family."

"I just wanted to talk to Tyler about—"

"With a knife?"

"Josie? Hey, Josie. Reality check. Who's getting paranoid out there, you or your father?"

"I'm not going to engage you on this. I'm just going to tell you, very simply, leave us alone."

"Sure," I said and hung up. She didn't call back. Neither did I.

■

There were a lot of days in the long months from the fall of '91 to the spring of '92 when I felt like I was moving in slow motion. Everything in my life was changing. I was leaving the Army, heading to a part of the world I'd never been to, looking for part of my past I'd never experienced. But every single day had its own routine, too, and they all blended together. I'd started running again, and running hard, in the early mornings. But I also started reading. For hours I'd work through passages of the Koran, trying to discover their meaning to me. "Every soul shall have a taste of death." But I also read the Bible, because I realized there were so many parts of it that I only half remembered if, in fact, I ever knew them at all. And they were part of the meaning of the Koran. Moses, Jesus, other prophets. They're all there, but in a kind of shorthand. "We believe in the Lord of the Worlds. The Lord of Moses and Aaron." I read history. I'd start with the military campaigns, then work backward to find out how the war started, then further back to previous wars, and the personalities of the men involved, and their biographies. It was like my soul had just waked up and was dying to know what the world was about. And when I could find books about the Balkans, I read them. But there weren't many. Not in 1991.

As I could, while I was doing my discharge paperwork and selling what I could of my possessions and making my plans, I tried to follow the Balkan troubles from Savannah. But Georgia was not much interested in the drama of Yugoslavia. From the little news items you saw in the papers or on television it seemed like one day they were all celebrating democracy and freedom, and the next day they were all at war. This made no sense to me, but there was no one in Savannah who knew enough to tell me what was happening. Do you remember that summer in the Balkans? Probably not. It sounded so confusing. But it was not really mysterious. Every horrible event was predicted. You could see each atrocity coming like a telegraphed punch. But nobody wanted to believe it.

Yugoslavia was coming apart. The Roman Catholic Croats and Slovenes identified with the West and wanted nothing to do with the Eastern Orthodox Serbs. The country tore right down the center. And the Muslims of Bosnia and Herzegovina were caught right in the middle.

By the time I sold the Nova and my stereo and gave away the few other things I owned, the war was on. Slovenia and Croatia seceded. Real fighting began in Croatia. And this was all-out war. A city no one in the United States had ever heard of, a place called Vukovar, suddenly started making headlines as a city that was under attack—that was in ruins—that was erased.

"Sounds like it's pretty dangerous over there," Tyler said. Yeah. But Bosnia and Herzegovina were still riding it out. Still at peace. Still, in fact, unheard of by just about anyone reading the papers in America.

"Kurt, is that you?" It was early evening and the yellow light shining over the door made Selma look old. Not just tired, but old. It was the first time I saw that.

"Come on inside. It's freezing. You going to be staying for Christmas?"

"I don't think so." I took a deep breath, trying to loosen up and shake out some of the memories held in this airless house near the Wal-Mart. It had changed some. There were little figurines on the mantel above the fake fireplace: a man with a white wig playing a lute to a woman with a fantastic piled-up hairdo; a rabbit with one ear drooping, painted in a kind of red-and-white checkerboard pattern.

"That's nice," I said. "You've put out a lot of Mama's things."

"You're not mad, are you?"

"No, no, Selma. It's nice to see them."

On a shelf in a corner there were three little china boxes. Two of them were pink. I picked up the blue one and shook it. There was a lonely rattle inside. "I can't believe it. Where did you find these?"

"Mama had them put away in the attic, all wrapped in a box."

Inside was a little white tooth, almost like a kernel of baby corn. The edge was a faded brown. "Was this really mine? What else did you find?"

"I got new frames for those two engravings by the door."

There was the ancient bridge across the narrow gorge, as foreign and exciting as a fairy tale. And framed beside it the mouth of a cave.

"Oh, wow. I was just thinking about these pictures, wondering what happened to them. I'm going to go find those places."

"Why don't you stay for Christmas?"

"No. I don't think so."

Dave's steel-spined club no longer leaned against the side of the door. It was nowhere in sight, and neither was he.

"So how's your life, Selma?"

"Quiet. Yeah, you could say that. Real quiet."

"With Dave?"

"He's busy. Got all kinds of projects these days. No time for me." She shook a True Blue out of a pack on the coffee table. There was a lighter in the shape of a hand grenade, but all it did was spark. "You know, if we're going to have this thing here, you'd think he could put some fluid in it." She found a match in her purse. "No time for nothing, that's Dave these days."

"Second job?"

"Ha! I wish. What Dave's got is 'projects.' Him and that Duke Bolide and I don't know who else."

"Duke who?"

"Used to work up at Highland Cemetery."

"Oh, yeah. What kind of projects?"

"You don't want to know. They think they're going to save the country."

"In Kansas? How's that?"

"You think they tell me? And, believe me, I don't ask. I just know it gets Dave out of the house, and that's fine with me."

"Me, too." I looked at the engravings again. "Selma, did you find anything more that was put away about the family? Maybe letters with addresses on them? Something like that."

"Oh, Kurt, I'm so sorry. I wish I'd known you was interested. Mama had a whole bag full of letters from back home. But I couldn't read any of them, so I just kind of threw them out."

"I see."

Selma noticed how long the ash was getting on her cigarette and cupped her hand under it. "Can I get you something to drink? A beer maybe?"

"Just something nonalcoholic. Water's fine, if that's all you got."

"How about some coffee?"

"Fine."

She got up off the sofa, still cradling her hand under the ashes, and disappeared into the kitchen. She banged around for a few minutes, knocking an ashtray against the side of the can as she dumped out the butts. Probably she spent all day sitting in that kitchen watching the soaps on that little black-and-white TV they had in there, drinking coffee, smoking cigarettes, talking to people on the phone. It was easy enough to imagine what her life was like now. It was just about like it always was, only maybe now with Dave gone so much she didn't get beaten so often.

"You know," she shouted from the kitchen, "I think I might have saved a couple of things." She put a mug of coffee down in front of me. "You want to come upstairs and see?"

There were two bedrooms at the top of the narrow stairs. One was used for storage, except for a little corner where Selma had her sewing machine. The other was where she and Dave slept. It was a real small, real cramped place. The king-sized bed took up most of the floor. The only window gave out onto the back, looking at the windows of another row of semi-detached houses. There was a mirror on the ceiling, which I didn't want to think about. And there were mirrors on the sliding doors to the closet, which Selma rolled back to show me a little built-in chest of drawers. She took something out of the top one. "Hold out your arms," she said, like she was going to wind yarn around them. She laid a neatly folded silk nightgown across them. Then she piled on a couple of lace teddies, some frilly underwear.

"This is quite a collection," I said.

"Victoria's Secret."

"Dave must like it."

Selma sort of snorted. "Oh, hell. You think I'd put this on for him? No way. This stuff is for me." She smiled and shook her head. "Victoria's Secret is my secret," she said. "And it hides some of my other secrets. Here." She pulled a big white, almost square envelope out of the bottom of the drawer and looked at the front. The address was to our old house on Sherwood Lane. The stamps had been torn away, probably by my mother to give to somebody else's kid. Selma turned over the envelope. There was a return address on the back flap.

"Who's it from?"

"From Mama's cousin, Anna something-or-other." She looked at the envelope. "Anna—and I can't pronounce the rest." Anna Koromitza, Kaptol 31, it read. Zagreb, Yugo-slavia.

"What's inside the envelope?"

"Oh, maybe you remember it. Mama used to put it up

every Christmas on the table by the entrance when we lived on Sherwood. I was just thinking about it this morning." She pulled it out of the envelope gently, as if that would keep it from shedding the dust of glitter glued on too many Christmases ago to remember. "I think it's about the prettiest Advent calendar I ever did see," she said.

I don't know if my hand really did tremble, but looking back it seems to me that it did as I opened up those little paper windows. Every one of them held the memory of a six-year-old, a seven-year-old, an eight-year-old. I wasn't sure they were memories I wanted to touch.

"Mama and Daddy used to have a fight every year about this thing," said Selma, tearing off the address on the back, then slipping the envelope into the bottom of the drawer, daintily packing away Victoria's secrets on top of it. "I don't know why, really. I mean"—and her voice sounded almost like a child's—"isn't Christmas supposed to be a happy time?" She pressed the piece of paper into my hand and put her head on my shoulder. She started to cry. "I miss Mama so much," she said.

III

A Portion of Wrath

It was We who
Created man, and We know
What dark suggestions his soul
Makes to him: for We
Are nearer to him
Than his jugular vein.

—*THE HOLY QUR'AN,*
  Surah 50:16

Lay not upon us innocent blood:
for thou, O Lord, has done as it
pleased thee.

—*JONAH* 1:14

XIII

The statues in the park were strangers. They were of men whose names were not names I'd ever heard of, written about in stone in words I couldn't read. It was three in the afternoon and I was the only person there. The light was fading already. The rain was falling in heavy drops through the bare branches. I tried to picture it in the summer when the light lasted and the sky cleared. There was an old pavilion in the middle of the park. Did bands play there? They must. I wanted to try to see the place, to smell it, feel it, to *be* in it like my mother must have been when she was young. But the only pictures that came to mind were like something from those postcard-colored movies they made in the 1950s, scenes of women with parasols listening to men with epaulets playing tubas. I knew the vision was wrong, but it was the only vision I had. And in the grayness of the winter afternoon, even that faded. The unfamiliar heroes looked back at me with hollowed-out eyes full of unexplained rage. A chill of cold water ran down my spine. I sucked the air and rain through my teeth and moved on up the hill toward the cathedral.

If I could get through this first day, I thought, I wouldn't be so lonely here. "It's going good," I said to no one. "It's going good."

I had landed at the airport in the late morning with no visa and no idea where I would stay, and been prepared for almost anything but the ordinariness of what I found when

163

I walked into the terminal. There were some sandbags and armored personnel carriers outside. You could tell there was a threat of war. But there wasn't the feel of one. Inside the airport, the staff were mostly in the tourist mode they must have used for all those people who visited Croatia's islands before the fighting. The posters for the beaches were still on the wall. The people in uniform were courteous. They smiled. They told me I could get my visa at the booth over to the right.

"Kurtovic? You are from where?" said a young woman behind the counter. I waited a second for her to look up at me. "Born in Kansas, in the United States," I said. "But my family is from here."

"So, why you are here? To visit family?"

"Yes."

"You have been before?" she said, making notes in a ledger book. I said that I had not. "Where you stay?"

"With my family."

"Address?"

"Thirty-one Kaptol." She looked up at me for a minute. She studied my name and her handwriting in the ledger.

"But, to tell you the truth, they're not expecting me."

"Ah," she said, as if that confirmed something she'd already thought. "Maybe you need hotel. Good one for you is Astoria. Anyway, I write it down." Then she pasted the visa in my passport: a piece of paper with a red-and-white checkerboard on a shield, the Croatian coat of arms.

The first part of the Yugoslav war was starting to end by the time I arrived in my mother's city in February 1992. Zagreb was picking itself up, getting organized again in the lull after the fighting. But nobody believed the war was over. And of course it was not.

On the way into town from the airport the city seemed more modern, and more cold, than I expected. Farmland gave way quickly to rows of three-story houses with red tile roofs, then high-rise concrete apartment blocks. The backwardness I thought I'd find wasn't there. But neither was the magic.

The Astoria was a little hotel on a street of gray buildings and half-empty shop windows not far from the center of town. There was one room left, they said at the desk. Most of the floors were filled with refugees. The room was small and dark and everything inside it was brown to hide the dirt, or because of the dirt. There were cigarette burns on the spread and on the floor and even on the toilet seat in the bathroom. As soon as I'd dropped my bag I was out of there. No sense getting depressed for nothing, I thought. And I was hungry. But the man behind the front desk, formally dressed in uncleaned clothes, his collar covered with flakes of dandruff, told me the restaurant had stopped serving lunch. I walked back and checked. It was a Chinese restaurant, it turned out. And yes, it was closed.

"Maybe," said the man, "you can find something in Gornji Grad. The old city near the cathedral."

"Okay, but can you tell me where this address is?" He glanced at the piece of paper but didn't seem to focus on it. He thought for a minute, like an actor on a stage, very serious. "Is near cathedral," he said, "in Gornji Grad."

When I was out on the street walking through the early dusk and rain, I wasn't hungry anymore. The atmosphere started to sink in on me. In the windows of the shops there wasn't much to see, just patches and pins for sale with the red-and-white checkerboard of Croatia on them, and empty shoulder holsters, and hunting knives, and camouflage pants and camouflage caps and camouflage uniforms for children. Even for little children. Sometimes the windows displayed dishwashing soap or a bottle of whiskey alongside the homemade uniforms and the holsters. They weren't so much shops as garage sales. But the city, in its heart, was so old that it surrounded me with its dignity. I came here to be— here, I told myself, to share in that dignity, that history. And then there was the park, so orderly and Old Worldly. And so lonely. And all those white stone faces reminding me of the things I didn't, and couldn't, know.

Still, I was here. The city was giving me something. Maybe not the details of history. But the feel of it. "It's going good. Yeah!" I smacked my fist into the palm of my hand and picked up my pace, feeling the skin tingle a little with the cold. The street opened out into a big cobblestone square busy with trolleys. Above them stood a huge statue of a soldier on a horse who pointed his sword above the crowd. Bronze braid was spread across his chest. A bronze feather stood out from his hat. And behind him I saw the steeples of the cathedral.

I walked fast up the hill. A smell of coffee slipped through the wet air for just a second. There were little cafés along the street. It wasn't even four o'clock yet, but the lights inside were on already. People were pressed around the bar. Many of the men were in uniform.

The nearer I got to the steeples, the faster I walked. The lower mists of the clouds were drifting over and around them and the light was almost gone. In the middle of the square a gold Virgin stood on a pedestal in the middle of a fountain, but I hardly noticed. A car skidded to a stop just behind me. I waved an apology and backed up against the Virgin's fountain and kept looking up. Sharp-winged birds flew out of the mist and into hidden nests high in the steeples. And there was something else up there, like rough claws against the clouds. Twigs? There were plants growing out of cracked stone. The rain and moss and bird shit of centuries were caught up there in those towers, and a lot of it probably older than America itself. It seemed the most incredible thing. And on each side of each of the steeples there were clock faces, dark red and dripping with rust. They were too ancient to work and I wondered when and how, exactly, they had stopped. There must be a legend attached to their frozen hands: some earthquake, some war, some mutiny or revolution or execution I'd never known about.

Anybody in the café across the street could explain it, I was sure.

The hunger was coming back. I glanced at my digital watch: 4:18. I looked back up at the steeples. They read 4:20. They were working. They were right. Even with their creaking gears and their rusting faces, the eight clocks of the cathedral steeples kept the time. They hadn't stopped at all. But I had seen what I expected to see, and been wrong, and that bothered and embarrassed and, yeah, scared me a little bit. I didn't really have the feel of this place at all.

The drizzle and the fog clung in the creases around my eyes and the stubble of beard that I hadn't bothered to shave away for—I wasn't sure how long. For a couple of days now, anyway. The stone cold of the street was starting to work its way through the soles of my shoes into my bones. I was so tired. I should get inside. But the café didn't look welcoming any longer. I didn't feel confident enough, just then, to talk to strangers. And what language would we speak? I didn't want to stand at the bar in silence. I looked for a street number. Time to search for Cousin Anna. Maybe at least I could get that done. And right there, right in front of me, just to the right of the cathedral on the gates that led back to the buildings behind it I saw the address: 31 Kaptol. This was the place! I was right where I wanted to be and hadn't known that, either.

A nun carrying a plastic bag full of groceries was just going through the gates, walking down the long row of arches. I caught up with her as she was unlocking a door to go inside. "Excuse me." She looked at me like I was a little boy who had wandered into her classroom by mistake. Whatever it was she said, I didn't understand a word of it. "Anna Koromitza?" I said.

"Anna?"

I nodded. She spoke. I shrugged helplessly. She spoke again and put up a hand to show me I should stay where I was, then she went inside and closed the door behind her.

Maybe ten minutes passed, or maybe less. Long enough for me to get impatient and wander out to look at the steeples again, and wait, and wait some more and lose whatever adrenaline had woken me up again when the nun had recognized Anna's name. If she had.

"You asked for Anna Koromitza," said a man's voice. I hadn't heard him open the door. He was short and gray and a little heavy. His hair was mussed and his rough wool sweater didn't fit him quite right, like he'd pulled it on in a hurry in the morning, then never bothered to straighten it out.

"She's my cousin," I said.

"You are?"

"Kurtovic," I said, reaching out to shake his hand. "My mother was Mary Unkovic. She is Anna Koromitza's cousin."

He didn't bother with his own name. "Unkovic?"

"Yes."

He fit my mother's name into some particular place in his mind. You could see it register. "Come in," he said, and I thought I was getting someplace. But once I'd stepped into the bare front hall, he stopped me again and left me standing as he went up the stairway and disappeared.

At least it was a little warmer here. There was a faint smell of cabbage cooking. A couple more nuns came in. They looked at me standing in the entrance hall like I was a delivery boy waiting for a package. Then they went upstairs. I wondered if one of them might be Anna. I tried to brace myself for the idea of meeting a relative in a black habit with her head covered in white. Finally the man came back to the top of the stairs and motioned me to come up.

I followed him down a long corridor with what looked like small offices and classrooms on each side, then down another set of stairs. The cabbage smell got stronger. And when we stopped we were in a kitchen. A thin, hard-looking woman sat at a wooden table peeling potatoes. Her hair was covered by a plain gray scarf. I couldn't tell if she was just a cook or a nun in work clothes.

"Anna Koromitza," said the rumpled old man.

She wiped her fingers on a rag. Her flesh was cool and lifeless as we shook hands. She didn't get up from her chair, and as I began to talk, she went back to peeling the potatoes.

"I'm really happy I found you," I said. She nodded as the old man translated. "My mother always wanted me to visit Zagreb. She told me so much about this place. It really is beautiful." Again she nodded and listened, and peeled potatoes, and then spoke to the translator.

"She asks if your mother is well," he said.

It took me a few seconds to say anything. "My mother died," I said. "It's been almost two years. I thought Selma or Joan wrote to you."

Anna Koromitza slowly dug the eye out of a potato, then looked up, talking to the old man.

"She says she is sad about this news, and she wants to know if your mother died in the Church."

This woman was just a cousin, but so many times, I remember, my mother had talked about her when we got those cards at Christmas. What exactly my mother said, I couldn't tell you. I never paid that much attention. But the idea was that this Cousin Anna was real family. And real religious.

"It was God's will," I said, hoping to God that we'd find some other thing to talk about. Cousin Anna nodded and spoke in short sentences. The old man translated in simple language. But I don't think there was any emotion lost in the process. No, I said, I did not have a wife and I did not have children.

"Why is that?" she wanted to know.

"I haven't found the right person," I said. And even though I thought clearly to myself that she was not much interested, I tried to explain a little more. "I would have liked to," I said. "But my job, my life, made it—"

Anna started talking to the old man, then got up and carried her potatoes over to the stove and dumped them in a pot of boiling water. She walked back and stood by the table. It was my cue to leave. "Keep translating," I told the old man. "Tell her that I would have liked to build my own family, but that I was in the army, and it's hard for a soldier like I was. But that I've come back here to try to find the family that is left to me. Anyway, to—"

The old man stopped me and started to translate. And Anna Koromitza repeated one word in Croatian.

"You are a soldier?" the old man asked me.

"I was."

"And you have come here to fight the Chetniks?" Anna's eyes, and the old man's, too, had suddenly taken on some life and interest.

"No. No, that isn't why I came. I wanted to meet Anna and whoever she could introduce me to, and stay here for a few weeks maybe, and then go to my father's village near Drvar. I really don't know anything about his family. I was hoping you could help. Do you think he's got any relatives here in Zagreb?"

Anna said something to the old man, which he didn't translate right away. She checked on her potatoes, adjusted the heat, walked out of the room, and closed the door.

"Wait a minute," I called after her. "Is that all?" I opened the door, but didn't see her in the corridor.

"I think it is time for you to leave," said the old man.

"What?"

"She said that if you wanted to ask questions about Muslims, maybe you should go to the mosque."

I went back to the hotel. I tried to sleep. I thought about eating, but did not. I couldn't bring myself to leave that narrow brown room at the Astoria. And every single thing I thought about doing to take myself out of myself, like running or walking, like just moving for God's sake, was blocked in my head before I could start it. "Not now," I told myself. "Not now. If ever." I was frozen with frustration and fatigue. No one at the mosque was going to know anything about my father. The mosque. What the hell was I thinking? What did I know about mosques and Islam and calls to prayer? Just about as much or as little as I knew about Holy Communions and Holy Ghosts and Sacred Hearts. Which wasn't much. "Did your mother die in the Church?" Hell, yes. In her heart. While she was puking blood, while the blue unoxygenated life of her was pumping out of her mouth, she was trying to talk, calling to God and trying to call for a priest. Oh, yes, she was. And who came? Nobody. Just nurses. Because old Father Milligan had some engagement that night and couldn't quite be found in time. Did she die in the Church? Where she died was in the hospital vomiting blood.

And I had been so far away.

The Zagreb night was long and the blanket was thin. I wanted some weight on me, but couldn't find the energy to get up and get my parka. And when I finally fell asleep it was only to wake up again at two, and at three, as if some clock in my brain was warning me not to slip too deeply into unconsciousness. It was like I was trying to fight off hypothermia, but the cold was inside me. And after I woke at four, the feeling of desperation left me almost breathless, like my heart and lungs were shutting down and only my brain was working, and it was working overtime.

The door rattled on its hinges. A man's voice was shouting outside, angry, wrenching the handle, beating a fist against the door, slapping the wall beside it, growling and moaning in words that I'm not sure anyone could have understood. When he threw his weight against the door the first time, cracks of light showed around the sides. That gave me a second to move. The next time he threw his weight against it, the door gave. He staggered into the room, shouting and looking around, and didn't know I was there until I stepped from the bathroom behind him, rushed him, and pinned him doubled over against the chest of drawers. The corner of it caught him right in the solar plexus and winded him bad. His gut was heaving and I had his face flat against the glass on top of the chest. Two, three times I smashed his face down until the glass cracked into shards. I leaned down over him, breathing hard myself, listening. I couldn't understand what he was talking about, but I could sure smell the alcohol on his breath. His face and eyes were full of blood, his nose was broken and bleeding. I glanced out the open door and saw women in old bathrobes and men in their underwear coming downstairs and gathering in the hall. The man I had ahold of started trying to shake himself back into some kind of consciousness. I smashed his face again, then brought him up off the chest of drawers and wheeled him around to face the spectators, holding one of his arms locked behind him, clutching his hair and pulling his head back with my other hand. I wanted to show them real clear the ugly mess I'd made of him. And they did see it. And they froze like stone.

"Anybody speak English?" I shouted. They looked at each other. "Anybody want to tell me what the fuck this is all about?"

One of the men, a big man, looked like he half wanted to fight, half wanted to talk. Finally he spoke. "Is wrong room," he said.

"You're damn right it's the wrong room. I'm trying to get a little sleep and this guy breaks in like Godzilla."

"He think his wife here," said the bystander.

"His wife not here," I said.

"Is wrong room."

"Yeah, yeah." The groggy husband I was holding up started to stir and struggle again. The bystander stepped forward. "You take him," I said. "He's all yours." And the big bystander half picked up his friend, half dragged him, toward the stairwell. I closed my eyes for a second and tried to lower my pulse rate, then turned around to go back into the room, but it was a disaster now. The door was smashed, and there were long splinters of broken glass and stains of blood all over the floor. And anyway, I wasn't going to sleep now.

Zagreb's streets were empty and freezing and badly lit in the last hours before daylight crept into them. It didn't take me long to cool out as I worked my way through the lonely shadows from one side of the city to the other. At least the sky had cleared. And there were times when I looked up and saw bright stars. I traced my way along the street map, navigating by luck and guesswork. Sometimes I passed little groups of drunken soldiers, but nobody bothered me. Then as I got closer to the mosque, the neighborhood where I was walking didn't seem like it could be the right one. It was so tidy and so middle class, and so ordinary. What did I expect? I wasn't sure. But I kept thinking I was lost. Then the street I was on ended at a parking lot and a few hundred yards beyond that there was a big, odd, modern building set on a rise in an open field. A few lights were on inside, but only the bare outlines of the building were visible in the dark. A tower—a minaret. And a dome that looked like it was split in half. I couldn't believe this was the place. But there didn't seem to be any other possibility. The only other buildings were a church in the distance, with a cross clearly visible on its top, and a little farther on a power plant, its huge tower steaming into the icy sky.

One car, then another, and then a small bus drove into the parking lot, and the men inside made their way up the path and the stairs to the building. I watched from the shadows, then followed behind. The door was open. I walked in. And no one took much notice.

The lobby was like a community center; cleanly decorated in plastic and bright colors. The ragged-looking men gathered there were having cups of coffee. There were twenty or so, some of them wandering into other rooms, some just sitting on the white molded chairs smoking cigarettes and waiting for the sleep to clear from their heads. They looked like farmers, for the most part, with rough red hands and red faces. Not so different—not really different at all—from most of the men I'd seen in Zagreb. Against the black night outside, I could see all of us reflected in the plate-glass window, transparent as ghosts. And for a second, searching among those faces, I couldn't find my own.

I took a cup of coffee and asked if anyone spoke English. The young man everybody turned to was a little taller than the rest.

"Salaam aleikum," I said as I shook his hand.

"Aleikum salaam," he said. "What can I do for you?" No accent at all that I could make out.

"Are you American?" I asked.

"Went to college in Syracuse for a couple of years."

"And played ball."

"You got it."

"Well, I can tell you, I am truly happy to meet you." Here, at last, was somebody I could talk to. "Kurt Kurtovic," I said.

"Aliya," he said. "People called me Al. You just arrived?"

"Just yesterday. Between jet lag and one thing and another, I couldn't sleep."

"And what brings you to the mosque?"

"I'm—I came for prayers."

My voice surprised me. This was not the moment I meant to choose for the first time in public, among other worshipers. I'd wanted to wait until I got to Ljeska Župica. It must have been one of the last places where my father prayed before he left his homeland, before he gave up praying for good. It seemed like I'd be bringing things full circle. But now, at this moment this night, the wait seemed sort of pointless.

I'd been thinking all through my walk across town:

why was I being so shy? For months I prayed in private, in my room. But either I believed, or I did not. And if I did, there was nothing to be embarrassed about. This waiting to pray in public in my father's village, like some kind of coming out, did not seem right. My prayers, after all, were supposed to be to God, not to my father.

"You are welcome," said the kid from Syracuse.

"Allahu akbar," came the deep voice, singing low over the public address system. *"Allahu akbar,"* the recording went on. I didn't know the Arabic, really, but I knew the gist of it. "God is great," the call to prayer began, summoning the faithful to wake up before dawn, telling them prayer is better than sleep.

Together we washed our faces, then our arms and hands, first the right, then the left, from fingertips to elbow. The ritual was deliberate, and functional and spiritual all at the same time. For me, who learned it as an adult, maybe it meant more. You cleaned your thoughts at the same time you cleaned your body. The link was conscious and clear. And at the end of it, shoeless, with even your feet cleansed, you presented yourself to God.

Beneath the high, sterile ceiling of the mosque surrounded by its bare, modern walls, we stood and spoke the praises of God and of his Prophet, peace be upon him. We knelt, we touched our heads to the ground. We stood. We finished our prayers. And it was only then, looking up, that I saw a couple of men who were different from the rest—from the rest of us, I was thinking. They were Arab. And one of them, behind his beard, looked familiar. He was thin and his body was tight and he moved like a fighter. His dark eyes, intelligent and aggressive, had known me before, too. I could see that. We had known each other—on those long days and nights, on that long bloody highway, in Kuwait. There were tears in his eyes that I would never have expected to see there. He took my head in his hands and kissed me first on one cheek, then the other.

"Rashid," I said. "Well, I'll be damned."

XIV

Highway signs are mysterious and disturbing things after a civil war. Place names carry new and tragic memories, but the signs don't change right away to tell you that this city or that is not part of the same country anymore, or that checkpoints and lines of artillery and mines have to be crossed to get there, or that thousands of people died in that place. They don't tell you that the place itself might not exist anymore.

If I had come to Yugoslavia a year before, it would have been simple to drive south and east through Bihac to Drvar, and from there to Ljeska Župica. There were still signs pointing the way. But the war had cut the roads. Drvar was on the other side of the Serb-held territory of Krajina, and the only way I could think to get there was to head southwest toward the coast, then work my way up through Bosnia and Herzegovina.

Rashid went with me. In fact, from that first morning when we drank the last of the mosque's coffee, he barely left my side.

"Important things are happening here," he said, swirling the coffee around in its plastic cup.

"More important than Kuwait?" A vision skirted through the back of my head of Rashid walking away from us on the highway of death. I started to say something, but he cut me off.

"More important. For any Muslim, much more important. And now you are here. And Muslim. It's incredible. You are so American."

"My father was Muslim from Bosnia. He came to the States in the forties."

"He is alive?"

"No. He died a long time ago. I want to see his village."

"I am sorry to hear this about your father. But—you are not here for the war?"

"That's not why I came."

"You are a good soldier. A fighter. This is strange for you, to be a tourist," he said.

"Really? You think so?" I remembered the crawl through the minefield. And the night and the phosphorus and Jenkins. "Aren't you sick of wars? It's time to move on, man."

"We're not making these fights," Rashid said, waiting for me to look up from my cup of coffee, then searching my eyes. "We're not the ones making these wars," he said again.

" 'We' who? Listen, Rashid, buddy, this isn't even my fight, and my folks came from here. I don't see how this is your fight at all."

"Do you believe in justice?"

"Justice? Un-hunh." I was tired of all this talk. "You know, I'm really glad to see you. I can't tell you how glad. I'm not sure why you're here, but I'm glad you are. But it's been a real long couple of days, and all my plans are changing already." I could hear my voice starting to ramble. "There's a lot—a whole lot—I'd like to talk to you about. But I've got to regroup right now. I've got to go back to my hotel. There's a mess waiting for me there you won't believe. And I want to head out for my father's village sooner rather than later."

"How are you getting there?"

"Renting a car."

He smiled. "It's going to take you three days at least," he said. "And I think you will never get there." He explained about Serb-held Krajina and about the roads. "Do you speak any Croatian?" he asked.

"No. Do you?"

"Some."

I was impressed. "Maybe I can hire someone to translate." I was thinking maybe someone like Al, and looked to see if he was still around. But he wasn't.

"To drive to Drvar? How much money are you going to pay them? And nobody here is going to go with you. The war in Bosnia is going to begin in a few weeks, maybe a few days—"

"You know that?"

"Everybody knows that."

I shook my head. So much frustration. So little sleep.

"How long did you want to stay in Drvar? One day? Two days?"

"I guess. I don't know. I really do not know."

"I have to go to Bosnia this week," said Rashid. "Today." I was staring at him. "Drvar is not close to where I'm going, but it is not so far. If you want, I'll go with you there, and then we will see what happens." He read my face for reaction, and I tried to read his. "Maybe you can come with me where I'm going. Anyway we can take the car I have. What you rent here will not get you to there."

He wanted me as a fighter, I thought. I don't want to fight, I thought. But all I said was, "That's an offer that's hard to refuse."

My rucksack was in the hotel lobby, with some of my loose clothes stuffed in a plastic bag and my toothbrush lying on top of it. A pimple-faced teenager sat near it on a brown sofa, and when he saw me looking at it, he sprinted up the stairs.

"One-twenty-one," I said to the man behind the desk, whose clothes and dandruff were the same as the day before. "Finished cleaning the room?"

Instead of the key, he handed me a bill calculated in local currency and totaling 643 U.S. dollars.

"You're kidding."

"It is the door, and the chest. And we have to replace rug and even sheets on bed. These are imported things. Very expensive."

"You're kidding," I said again, stuffing the plastic bag and toothbrush into the rucksack and swinging it onto my shoulder. I was angry, but I'd half expected this. I put a hundred-dollar bill on the counter.

"What is this?" he said.

"All that I'm going to pay."

He shook his head and pushed the money back at me. I didn't pick it up. "Let me talk to the manager," I said.

The seedy little man picked up the telephone and plugged a wire into the switchboard, then started shaking his head even before it had a chance to ring on the other end. "He is not in," he said, and pushed the house phone toward me across the counter so I could hear for myself. It was one of those heavy old black phones, and all I heard was a crackling busy signal.

Rashid was behind me. He put his hand on my shoulder and looked down at the bill. He made a low whistling sound and wandered over to the opposite corner of the lobby again, near the entrance. "Try the manager again," I said through clenched teeth.

There was a sound of footsteps coming fast down the stairs. It was the heavyset bystander from the night before. And the pimply kid. And the drunken husband himself. His nose was taped and the rest of his face, held together with sutures and Band-Aids, was different shades of purple and brown. They were all in a mood to settle scores, I figured. Even the kid looked, now, like he was ready for a fight. I still had my rucksack on my shoulder, my hand on the phone.

Rashid shouted something as he put his hand behind him inside his parka, reaching for whatever he kept in his belt at the middle of his back.

I thought he was bluffing. Apparently, so did Scarface, who headed for me like a linebacker. He was still crazy, still stupid, still stinking of alcohol. I hadn't moved, and didn't until he was a couple of feet from me. Then I swung the old phone with a solid backhand that caught him across what was left of the bridge of his nose. He half screamed, half roared and grabbed his face. The phone clattered and spun across the floor. The man behind the desk was shouting. Rashid was shouting. But the boy and the bystander weren't moving. Rashid had not been bluffing. His Heckler & Koch 9mm was extended at arm's length.

The brawling husband was crawling, shaking his head, all but blind from the pain. The little gray man behind the counter was flushed red, more from fear than anger I'd say. And Rashid just stood there as cool as a cop on a firing range.

"Put the phone on that, too," I said, patting the hundred dollar bill on the counter. "And keep the change."

Rashid's Land Cruiser was just outside. On its side was an insignia with an open book and Arabic writing. I threw my rucksack in the back, then took his pistol and covered the door of the hotel as he jumped in the driver's seat and we took off.

"Shit, Rashid. What is it exactly you told me you're doing here?"

"Refugee work," he said.

By the time I woke up, we were getting off the main highway at Karlovac.

"There's food in the back," he said. Pizza, in fact, and some cola.

"All the comforts of home," I said. The pizza was cold, but I was starving. The cola was cold enough, and the fizz in my throat woke me up. "Thanks for back at the hotel," I said. Rashid was watching the road. A mix of snow and rain was falling, but he was driving fast. He paid close attention to what he was doing. "And for Kuwait," I said. "That's twice you've helped me out."

"We are friends," he said.

The closer we got to the sea, the higher and rougher the mountains became, the more twisted the road, and the crazier the traffic. Rashid drove with all the concentration of a kid in a video arcade.

"Are we in a hurry?" I said.

"Maybe," he said. "We go fast when we can."

The windshield wipers were working full time, but the sun, low on the horizon near the sea, broke out enough to send shadows through the car and across our faces. There was always a reserve of tension in Rashid's features. I remember thinking about it for the first time that afternoon. You couldn't call the look fear. But you got the feeling, when there was nothing much going on, that there was something there inside him that was not quite right, like a man who's been told he's going to die but can't yet feel the pain.

"So, tell me about Kuwait," I said.

"It is a long story."

"It's a long ride."

"Correct." He took a breath. "I was born in Kuwait. I grew up in Kuwait."

"Yeah."

"But I am not Kuwaiti." He said this with a sort of grim smile. "I am Palestinian. From Jaffa," said Rashid. "My mother was only three when she left."

"Are your parents still living?"

"Yes, thanks to God."

"I read that the Palestinians supported Saddam."

"A lot did not. We fought against him. You remember?"

"I do."

Rashid concentrated on his driving for a minute. He was trying to get by a large truck on a tight curve. A little Fiat-type car came around the bend and we squeezed three lanes out of two.

"There were more of us fighting Saddam than there

were Kuwaitis. Do you remember Jaber? The son of a whore who almost got us killed? The one with the safe?"

"I remember." Especially I remembered him dying with Rashid's gun shoved in his gut.

"He was Kuwaiti. He wanted everyone to fight for him. But all *he* wanted was to get to his money."

The drift of the conversation was reminding me how little I knew about the Middle East, and about Rashid. "I don't really know anything about Palestine," I said.

Rashid looked at me. He was surprised, I think. Then something in front of the car caught his eye. "Checkpoint," he said as we slowed to a stop in a long line of traffic.

A tall man in camouflage fatigues wandered down the road looking at the drivers and passengers and the interiors of the cars. His AK was slung across his back and he didn't look too steady on his feet. "Slivovica," said Rashid as he watched him. "These people are always drunk."

Rashid got out of the car and took the soldier aside, talking to him behind the truck in front of us, out of sight of most of the other cars. At one point Rashid reached behind his back for something and I thought, Oh, shit, but all he pulled out was his wallet. He showed the soldier an ID. The soldier looked at it closely, like a gorilla checking out a banana. Then they both looked at me sitting in the Land Cruiser. The soldier seemed satisfied. He came over, leaned across the driver's seat, and exhaled plum brandy. "American." Yes. "Good," he said, pointing his thumb in the air, then wandering down past other cars.

"They like Americans?"

"Today, yes. Tomorrow, who can say? But he liked the money I gave him." The line of traffic began to move again.

"Palestine," I said. "Can you go back there?"

He looked at me again with a mix of surprise and disappointment. "Our family was driven out of Palestine in 1948," he said. "Now Israelis live where my mother was born, Israelis have my grandfather's shop. They claim it all belongs to them. All that they stole. You know, my mother still has a key to our house in Jaffa? She still has the deed. My grandfather took it with him. He thought he would be going back. The Arabs were going to get it all back for us." A line of muscle hardened in Rashid's jaw. "But he died in Kuwait and he never went back. So we lived with the black-eyed Arabs of the desert. Others from Palestine lived with the Egyptian boot on the back of their necks. We lived— wherever we could live—and we waited. But all the Arabs did was lose more, even Jerusalem, until Al-Aqsa was in the hands of the Jews. And we lived with those shit Kuwaitis, and we built their country, and they lost even that—and then they blamed us. They are pigs, these people."

"I mean, I don't know anything about it. I guess that's obvious. But there was that big peace thing last year."

"Arab politicians selling out—again," said Rashid. "This is not peace. This is surrender."

"It's complicated," I said.

"That's American bullshit," he said. "There is justice. There is injustice. It is simple."

"Well, it's not my fight."

"It is the fight of every Muslim."

It was dark now, and I was watching, half-hypnotized, the headlights weaving across the roadside, the oncoming cars, the rock faces to one side and the open sky above the sea on the other, as we worked our way along the coast. "Then why are you here?" I asked, finally. "Why aren't you fighting in Palestine?"

"This is also the fight of every Muslim. It is a question of justice. And someday," he said, "someday there will be justice."

"So, let me get this straight. You want to fight for Palestine, but right now you are going to Bosnia."

He let himself smile. "And lucky for you," he said.

■

We missed our prayers. The demands of travel made it impossible to stop. But in Split we spent the night in a little house full of other men. There was a small crowd still awake smoking in the kitchen. Some were Arabs. One was black. That surprised me. But there was a mist of sleep lingering between my eyes like fog in a valley and I could barely say hello. When we found a bed, I was out. But before dawn, we made fajr, the first prayer, once again. And as much of a struggle as it was to rise, to wash, to clear my head, I could feel myself falling into that routine, that rhythm, that had begun to comfort me so much.

After prayers, Rashid handed me some papers in a half-crumpled envelope. Permissions. I couldn't read anything on them except my name, but they looked official. "How'd you manage these?" I said. "We have some good people," he said, "and we have good money."

Once we were back on the road the papers, along with Rashid's other persuasive techniques, worked just fine. By noon we were in Livno. The map said it was in Bosnia, but Croatian flags were flying everywhere. We took time for prayers in a deserted mosque. After that, I drove. And the roads got worse. And lonelier. At one point we stopped and Rashid peeled the Arabic signs off the doors, and splashed mud on them to erase the clean squares they'd left behind. "We can't be sure who we'll meet up here," he said. But for hours we met no one at all.

The road, rutted and potholed, and covered with snow, twisted high along the sides of mountains, sometimes along stony cliffs, other times through dense forests as dark and sinister as those in fairy tales. We were constantly in four-wheel drive, but even so there were times when no wheel got any purchase on the road and we would slip toward the brink.

"Do you want me to drive?" said Rashid.

"Not unless you want to."

"You are a good driver," he said.

We were talking less and less. The only sounds inside the car were the groan of the suspension, the growl of the engine, the loud whirring of the heater fan. We were enclosed, protected, but it was easy, too easy, to imagine tumbling over the rocks, cracking open the car, and us inside it.

I have never liked heights. I've jumped out of more airplanes, and walked over more rope bridges, and rappelled down more cliff faces and from more helicopters than I could count. But never once without fighting a fear that was just about to freeze me. When I was younger, the first few times in a jump tower, my legs locked up on me and it was all I could do to move. Later, I learned to eliminate the fear by concentrating on the routine procedures, or on other concerns, like who might be shooting at me as I came down. But now, driving along these twisted roads, there were times when I was looking out into the abyss, and the old fright was creeping back into my muscles, tying me up. The edge was so close. The car could surprise me, the machine could betray me. Too close. I was struggling to keep it on the road, and to keep myself loose.

Once, after we passed Glamoč, I thought we'd have to give up. The road went through a small valley, then climbed back along the face of the mountain and got narrower and narrower, with only dirt and a little gravel under the snow, and then it was just one lane. And then not even that. Part of the surface had actually dropped away and a huge crack in the road had been filled with logs—not spanned by them, just filled with them, lying sideways in the hole, some of them projecting out over the drop—and they looked very damned unsteady. We both got out to examine them. This cobbled-together road was not quite as wide as the Land Cruiser.

"We can do this," said Rashid, stepping gently across the logs to the other side. He almost slipped on their icy surfaces.

I wasn't convinced. But the road behind us was already

too narrow to turn around. We'd have to back up a long way, and that could be almost as treacherous. It was beginning to snow again. In fact, we didn't have a lot of good choices. If we didn't make it across the logs, I'd probably never get to Drvar. And we might get stuck on this mountainside for the night. Maybe longer. But if we tried to get across the logs and sideslipped too far, the car would go over the cliff. Whoever was inside driving would die.

"I hope you're right," I said.

"I'll drive, you guide," said Rashid.

"No, buddy. It's my trip."

He looked at me for a few long, slow breaths. "And God's will."

"Yes, and God's will."

"Fold back the mirror on the right side, and don't worry about the paint," he said.

"Yeah. I'll try not to."

I inched the car forward in its lowest gear, and tried to concentrate on Rashid in front of me, or even on the rock wall to the right, but it was impossible not to look down to the left. All I could see beneath me was air. If I opened the door and stepped out, I'd be in free fall. The valley floor was maybe a thousand feet away, and mostly lost in the swirl of snowflakes and the blank gray currents of the clouds around us. The nerves in the back of my neck were tingling, and every muscle in me was drawing tight. I could feel the tires moving over every pebble, every grain of ice and snow that squeaked and crunched beneath them as I approached the logs. The tires touched them and rolled up on them and over, slowly, one, two, slowly, a few more, the logs started to shift, and the left front tire, closest to the edge, started to slip, and the whole front end of the car was losing its grip.

"Keep coming," said Rashid. "Keep coming!" he shouted, as he climbed onto the front bumper. With his weight there, the tires gripped. The logs balanced. We kept inching forward. He was out there now on the front of the car, outlined against the sky and the space beneath it. He never took his eyes off me. "Keep coming," he said. And then he was just mouthing the words. "Slow. Come on." The metal on the right side of the car was grinding, grating, screaming against the rock face. The front tires slipped over the last log and crunched into the snow. But the rear tires were starting to slip on the ice the front ones had made. "Don't stop!" Rashid shouted, and started scrambling onto the hood of the Land Cruiser. He lunged for the luggage rack and I could hear him clambering over the roof to the back of it, putting more weight on the rear tires. They slipped. They sideslipped and, in bursts, they spun on the ice. But they held just enough, just long enough for the front ones to really take hold on solid ground, and start to pull. The car bumped and jolted the last couple of feet, and finally left the logs behind.

Rashid's face appeared upside down in front of me, peering from the roof. He smiled and whistled that low whistle of his, but I couldn't hear him through the glass. He motioned me to drive forward a little farther, so he'd have room to stand, and he slid down off the roof on the far side of the car. He looked at the door and shook his head. "You open it," he said. "No handle left." He swung himself into the passenger seat.

"I can't believe we made it."

"Thanks to God," said Rashid.

"Yeah, with a little help from his friends," I said, but Rashid didn't say anything. I pulled forward another few yards to a point in the road that was still wider, set the parking brake, and got out. My legs could barely hold me. I had to lean against the side of the car as I pissed. After that, Rashid drove. And he got us to Drvar a couple of hours after dark.

XV I had seen the cave. In the attic, in that old framed print when I was a little boy, I had seen it and studied it and even dreamed about it, I think, but never known exactly what it was. And then, there it was, on the far side of the river in Drvar, halfway up a cliff face, with all kinds of signs that pointed to it from the town. "Titova pecina." It was Tito's cave, Rashid said. It was a tourist attraction. Or at least it had been before the memory of Tito, like the state of Yugoslavia he held together, fell apart and faded away. There was even a big motel in Drvar, built for schoolkids and sightseers before the troubles.

Now we were the only strangers in town and it was easy to get the idea that nobody wanted us here. When we signed into the motel after that long day driving across the mountains, two men with guns who'd been waiting near its door stood looking at our registration forms while we filled them out. They looked closely at my name.

"What is your business here?" one wanted to know.

"We're here to see the cave," Rashid told them. He introduced us as graduate students working on a project about World War II. I was American. He was British, he said, even producing, to my amazement, a UK passport. The men didn't interfere with us, but they watched us.

"What happened to refugee work?" I asked Rashid when we were in our room.

"You have questions to ask," he said, "and you need a reason to ask them."

188

"How about, 'My father came from near here, and I'd like to know more about my family'?"

"And if your father is a Muslim, and the man you are asking is Serb? No. Kurt, my friend, as far as these people are concerned, we're not even in Bosnia-Herzegovina. For them this is part of Krajina. They've been building up their forces here since last summer. Believe me, you do not want to be someone they don't want you to be."

Early the next morning we walked to the cave. There was no way I could not go. The armed men were still there near the motel entrance, sitting in their car. They watched us leave, then followed from a distance.

It was an ugly little city with a big paper factory. There was a stink of pulp in the air that reminded me of the worst of Rankin Mills. The streets didn't show much life. But you couldn't say they were peaceful. They'd emptied out the way streets do when people are scared to walk in them. No one strolled. No one chatted. The clumps of men in front of a few shuttered shops had guns on their shoulders, and when they talked, they looked around to see who was coming, who was near. The whole place felt uncertain and evil. When we got to the little museum at the foot of the cliff where the cave was, and went to the ticket booth, the two men following us seemed to lose interest. But they wouldn't need to look far if they wanted to find us. The whole town was watching us.

Inside the booth, a fat, middle-aged woman in what looked like it used to be a uniform was making tea over a little burner. When she slid back the glass you could smell stale sweat inside. "Ask her if she has any brochures in English," I said to Rashid.

"I speak English," she said to me. They didn't have any information left in any language, she said. Rashid suggested maybe she could tell us something about the place herself. Bored, she looked at the teapot about to boil. Rashid allowed as how we could pay her a little something extra. She turned off the burner.

"Is cave of Marshal Tito," she said. We waited for more. "In 1944, this Partisan headquarters. On day of 25 May 1944, Nazis make big offensive. Airplanes. Bombs. Many, many German soldiers. Almost catch Marshal Tito. But he escape." She stepped out of the ticket booth and pointed to the top of the cave. "Up rope. There." Then she stepped back into the booth. The show was over. Rashid gave her a Deutschmark.

We climbed to the mouth of the cave. Snow had melted and dripped and frozen again on the steps. It looked like we were the first visitors for a long time, and neglect had made it a stupid, dangerous climb. Once we got inside, there was litter on the floor and around the small waterfall at the back. It had been almost fifty years since the Communist leader of the Partisans hid in this place, and for most of that time it was a kind of shrine. And for some of that time it was, in a strange way, part of my childhood. Now I was standing in it, and it was full of trash.

"Let's get out of here," I said.

I took one last look around. "What do you think happened when Tito got away, and the Nazis took this town?" I asked Rashid. But he was already headed back down the steps. I hadn't really expected an answer. I hadn't really needed one.

Ljeska Župica, the birthplace of my father, was not so much a village as a hamlet, a collection of houses scattered around a mountainside. There was no main square. There was no main street with shops on it. There was no mosque.

Rashid pulled to a stop at the bottom of a narrow lane that led to one of the few houses with smoke coming out of its chimney. "What now?" he said.

I got out of the car feeling a rush of energy. "Look around, I guess." The scene was beautiful. Heavy, fast-moving clouds were rolling in front of the sun, and the view was spectacular. Free-form light and shadows swept across the land. Everything was covered with snow and even barbed-wire fences were glistening with a layer of ice. On the hill above us were thick stands of pine, their branches drooping under the snow like they'd been flocked for Christmas. And below us in the valley a small lake turned slate gray one second, under the clouds, then sparkled a brilliant blue the next, under the sun. "Is it beautiful enough for you, Rashid?"

"Where are the people?" was all he said, his voice low. "Where are the animals?"

We walked up the lane and found the door half open. Rashid called out something in Croatian, but there was no answer. We knocked. Still no answer. The shutters were all closed. The only light was behind us. As we entered we moved apart and stepped clear of the door until our eyes could adjust, moving slowly, getting a sense of the place. Even without a gun in my hand, the moves were instinctive. And moving like this I missed the gun. I saw Rashid shake out his right hand to loosen it up, and unzip his parka for quick access to the middle of his back.

It wasn't much of a house. Basically just two rooms downstairs and a kitchen. A small home for people with a simple life. But whatever they'd had was gone now. Cupboards were open, and what hadn't been taken away was broken. The walls were bare, and a couple of framed photographs were smashed on the floor, old pictures of old men rigid with dignity. Bits of torn paper fluttered across the room like leaves as the wind blew in behind us. In a corner were a couple of slivovica bottles. There was no other sign of life or, for that matter, of death. The fire in the heating stove was almost out. Rashid poked through some half-burned papers. "Legal papers," he said. "Deeds, I think."

"What the fuck is going on here?"

It was a relief to step into the light again. But the beauty of the landscape didn't excite me so much now.

"Where are the animals?" Rashid had asked. And now I wondered, too.

Several hundred yards away, we could see smoke coming from another chimney, high up near the forest, and it was while we were walking toward it, crunching through ice-covered snow up to our knees, that Rashid saw the cows. There were three of them dead and bloated in the field. They'd been shot with automatic weapons, then left to rot.

Someone was inside the second house. The door was locked and bolted. I knocked. Rashid shouted through the door and at the windows. No response. I slammed my hand against the door, then against the shutters. "Come on!" I shouted. "Come on! All we want to do is talk." But no one answered. They were not going to talk to us.

"I can't fucking believe this, Rashid. How far have I come to get to this place?"

He was walking away again, even higher up the hillside, toward the edge of the forest, and I followed. A couple of times I looked over my shoulder to see if anyone was watching from the house. But the shutters stayed closed. Rashid didn't even bother looking back.

It took me a minute to figure out where we were headed. Just below the woods, the snow made an odd pattern of small drifts, and it was only when I got closer that I realized it was a graveyard. Some of the markers were stone, some wood, all very simple. There were no monuments or mausoleums, or crosses. A few of the stones had pictures on them of the dead. Rashid started brushing the snow off one, then another. I did the same, reading the names, sometimes studying the faces. Pictures of farmers in their best clothes; old pictures of young brides on the graves of old women; pictures of schoolchildren who never grew up. There were generations here. But none of the stones we found said "Kurtovic" on them.

"Look at this," said Rashid. In one corner of the graveyard the snow was thinner and clumps of dirt still showed beneath it. There were half a dozen wooden slabs with painted names. The most recent was two days old. Most were from a week before.

"Muslim graves," said Rashid. "All Muslim graves."

"What is happening here?"

"I told you, Kurt. There is going to be a war soon. People are getting ready. They are cleaning out their enemies."

"Who's doing this?"

"Serbs. Maybe Croats. They are getting these people out of the way."

"But what have these people done to them?"

"They are not Serbs. They are not Croats. And they are Muslims." He stooped down and delicately brushed the last snowflakes off one of the markers. "Do you remember what I said, Kurt? About justice? You have to fight for justice."

I didn't say anything. But what I thought right then was: Fuck yourself, Rashid. Fuck your "justice." I traveled halfway around the world to find this place that had nothing for me at all. My whole dream of what I was, where I came from, was in this place—and it was empty. And Rashid was talking about his war again—which wasn't even his war—and telling me "I told you so." Fuck your war. Fuck your justice. Fuck you, I thought. But all I did was walk away to the edge of the graveyard and look out over the valley.

"We have company," said Rashid.

Out of the woods a boy and a man were coming toward us. The child was maybe eight years old, but he was leading the way, and the man, his face angular and simple and roughly bearded, his eyes wide open and weirdly innocent, clutched the boy's hand as if he depended on him. There was something wrong here. Like everything here.

Rashid greeted them, and it was the boy who spoke. Soon they were having a regular conversation. "What's happening?" I demanded after a couple of minutes, but Rashid motioned me to be quiet, and kept on talking with the boy.

Finally he turned to me. "The boy doesn't want to say what happened." Rashid started talking to him again. I could hear the name "Kurtovic" in the conversation. The boy shook his head.

"What about the man?" I broke in. "Ask the man if he's ever heard of anyone in my family."

But something was wrong with the man. The boy spoke again. "He's deaf and he can't speak," Rashid translated.

"For God's sake, Rashid, is there any way you can ask him if he ever remembers *anybody* named Kurtovic in this village? Or in any other village?"

The boy listened, then started talking to the man in sign language. It wasn't like the stuff on the TV news. It was slower, and sometimes the kid would touch the man's arm, like that was part of it. The man barely responded. I wondered if his eyes were bad, too. Finally, he shook his head.

"No Kurtovics," said Rashid. "But, Kurt, your father left more than forty years ago. Maybe something happened to his family. You don't know. And these people probably are not the ones to tell us."

I tried to pull my thoughts together, but all kinds of ideas were knocking against each other. Was this the wrong village? No. It must be this one. But I didn't even know who it was I was looking for here. Just people named Kurtovic. It didn't seem like such a big thing to ask. Somebody must know. But there was nobody that I could find.

"What happened here?" I said, pointing at the new graves. "Maybe they can tell us that."

"I don't think the boy wants to say."

"Tell him to ask the man," I said.

As the deaf-mute started to understand the question, he looked back at me with an expression of hope that surprised me. He started to sign quickly to the boy, then stopped, frustrated.

"I think some of these people are his family," said Rashid, listening to the boy talking. "Three cousins . . ." He listened some more. "An uncle. A brother . . . wait. A brother and the brother's daughter and son."

The man looked at the crude slabs of wood and at our faces to see if we had understood. And we had. But what could we do? What did he want? Vengeance for his family? Or sympathy? Or maybe money. What the fuck did he want? I looked at the row of grave markers.

And the man smiled at me. There was that look of hope again. His face was right in mine, trying to look through my eyes like you'd look through the hole in a door. There was something more that he wanted me to understand, and he was really anxious to explain, but signing didn't seem to be enough. Suddenly he leaned down and grabbed the top of one of the grave markers. He started to move it back and forth, loosening it in the frozen ground. I stepped away. He paused a second and looked up at me, to make sure I was watching. I wanted to stop him. But I didn't do anything. He groaned and pulled more violently on the wooden grave marker, frustration twisting his face, his knuckles turning white as he clutched it until, at last, it broke free. I watched, unsure what to think or do. And then suddenly his face relaxed. A look of wonderful tenderness came over it. And he cradled the crudely painted board in his arms like a child.

I don't even remember how it was we left that village. I don't recall how long it was before I spoke to Rashid. But eventually, after dark, I said, "I cannot stand all this pain." And he thought for a long time, and in the silence, in the faint glow of the dashboard lights, I watched his hard features and saw in them something I should have known or remembered long before. Despair and faith can make you strong, I thought. Serenity and anger can work together. And then he spoke. "It is time," said Rashid, "for you to learn about jihad."

XVI

Moving through the trenches at night, you could smell the life in the earth. I broke off a clump of it and crumbled the dirt in my fingers. Tiny roots ran through it like nerves. There were flakes of rotted leaves, and the clay stuck in the creases of my hand. It was a kind of ritual I did every night. I didn't tell anybody about it. Nobody was around to see. But it reminded me where I was, and why. This land was worked by my people. My fathers. It absorbed their sweat in the forests and the fields. It soaked up their blood in their wars. It wrapped itself around them when they died. Sometimes I would taste it. It had that taste of iron. And then I would move out.

There was nothing to guide me through the dark but my senses. Our forces didn't have night-vision equipment. Our guns, our uniforms, everything we had, was thrown together. And part of me liked it that way. I only carried what I wanted. I moved light over the ground, quiet and fast. Rashid had given me a Heckler & Koch MP3, a beautiful little gun for close quarters. He said he took it off a Serb officer whose throat he cut. Maybe he did. Anyway I was glad to have it. I carried six detonators, timers, and at least a couple of blocks of Semtex, which is what we could get instead of C4. On my belt I had my old demolition knife and crimper, and in my pocket, as backup, my old folding SOG Paratool with the wire cutters and the screwdrivers and the blades like a jackknife. Most of the time I carried a combat knife strapped to my leg, but a Libyan muj had borrowed it before he went on a mission, and then he'd been martyred. So this night I didn't have one.

Spring had come, the last of the snow had melted, and the forest smelled of wood and water and flowers. The leaves didn't rustle under your feet and if you could find a hard path, you could move in complete silence. The shadows were deep, but there were no bright lights to disturb my eyes, and by the time I left the trenches I could see my way clearly through the black and gray terrain.

For three nights I'd been probing my way, threading my way, through the mines the Serbs used to defend the eastern approach to their position. The ordnance wasn't very sophisticated. They were just little Yugoslav contact mines, but the Serbs put a lot of faith in them. They felt protected. And that made my work easier. All I wanted was to get across their lines, and if I wasn't blown up they weren't going to notice me. I knew every inch of the clear path I'd finished feeling my way through the night before and, except for a second when I came across a little rock that surprised me, I moved over the minefield without hesitation.

The objective was to reconnoiter a dairy farm about six miles behind the Serb lines. To get there and back the same night, moving fast, I had to track over the movements of cattle or men, taking trails that were well traveled to cut down the risk of mines. I was listening for footsteps or conversation or a cough. The glow of a cigarette, or even the smell, will give the enemy away. And almost everyone smoked. But you can't rely on that. Moving at night like this, you have to have every nerve exposed. And then you settle down.

It was good to be in the night. During the day, when we were awake between prayers, we talked and we thought and we talked some more, Rashid and me, until I figured I knew more about Kuwait, and Palestine and Pakistan, than I ever believed I would. And I guess, looking back, he knew more about Kansas.

There was literally nobody else that I could talk to. The other mujahedin who gathered around Cazin were mostly Arabs and Turks and a couple of Pakistanis and Iranians. They didn't speak much English. They didn't trust me. And I didn't have much time for them. Some were pretty good fighters, I guess, but a lot were not. They were obsessed with death. They tied their green headbands on like they were Rambos for God. Their idea of jihad was not the same as mine. And Rashid understood that. And after a while he understood enough about me to help me find my own way.

Rashid was a kind of buffer between me and the rest of the muj. There was always a lot of potential for blood among us. So many different countries. So many different ways of fighting for God. So many days when we were so close to death, and so ready to kill. If Rashid had not been there, I would have murdered the muj who took my knife. But he held me back, and talked in my ear, and, then, the man just never came back.

In the first days of the war there was no Bosnian army. In some places it was like each village was mobilizing on its own. And there was no company of mujahedin, much less a brigade, like there was later. Our group was about three platoons. But usually we operated as squads or, in my case, alone.

As for the local population around Cazin, we didn't have much contact. They were farmers, mostly, and our house, which had been a Serb house, was away from most of the others. You have to think they were happy to have us. They didn't really have anyone else to defend them. But I think they didn't know what to make of us. Sometimes you'd catch the little kids peering in the windows of our house like they thought they'd find dragons there. I didn't speak the language of the local people, or of the muj. So Rashid and I spent a lot of time in each other's company.

"I have heard of Oklahoma," he said. "And Kansas. They are in the middle of America."

"Yes, they are," I said. "Right in the middle. But what did you hear?"

"There are many Muslims there."

"You could have fooled me."

"It is true. In Oklahoma City."

"How do you know?"

"Faxes. I have seen many faxes from there."

"No kidding."

"They are building the umma there." The community of believers.

"Well, Rashid, don't take this wrong, but they've got a lot of competition. If folks back there are looking for something, it's not Islam. Just say the word, and you know what people think: 'Arab terrorist' or 'Black Muslim.' "

"And justice."

"Nobody makes that connection, Rashid. No white man, anyway."

In Arabic, Rashid cited a verse from the Koran, then translated: " 'They reject the truth when it reaches them, but soon they will learn the reality.' "

"Not soon. Believe me. Right now they've got a new, improved Jesus." I thought of Dave pounding his Bible out at Christ the Redeemer on Route 77.

"How improved?"

"Blonder hair and bluer eyes."

"But you are Muslim," said Rashid, looking into my blue eyes.

"You ought to meet my sister's husband, Rashid. He's a Christian preacher, among other things."

"A preacher?"

"Preaches hate. Blacks, Jews, Muslims. You name 'em, he hates 'em."

Rashid thought for a long time. "Hate is a powerful thing," he said.

I didn't exactly argue. I tried to explain to Rashid what an asshole Dave was, how stupid and how crazy, and how he'd treated Selma. Then our talk drifted off into talk about sisters and brothers and big families and little families, and how Rashid was the only "only child" he knew when he was growing up in Kuwait, and how Selma practically raised me. The question of hate got kind of lost in the talk. But it stayed with me afterwards.

Hate like Dave's was cheap, I kept thinking. If he couldn't hate one thing he'd hate another. There was always going to be someone he'd hate for keeping him down. It didn't matter who, as long as he didn't have to admit he was just a complete fucking loser. What Rashid meant was not hate, but anger, I thought. Righteous anger. And that's not the same thing at all. You've got to separate out the hate before you can really make anger work for you. You've got to make it pure. But if you do that, you can focus anger like a shaped charge so it explodes where you want it to, when you want it to. And you can remain at peace with yourself. And I tried to explain that to Rashid. And I really did think he understood.

One morning when I came in just before dawn, my nerves raw from the race against the light, I washed up and prayed, and found Rashid waiting for me when I finished. He had a present for me. A radio.

"It's brand-new," I said, and really was surprised. It was a National, small enough to carry in your pocket, or hide in your gear, and still in its box with a plastic bag wrapped around it and a little mono earphone.

"Sometimes I forget you are American," said Rashid, meaning it as a compliment. "But because you are, sometimes I think you will not know what is right and wrong. This will help."

"What should I listen to?"

"Your news. The Voice of America. The BBC. These are the best."

"I think I will read the Koran instead," I told him, and was surprised when he shook his head.

"The Koran tells you about hypocrites. But the radio lets them speak for themselves. And when you have seen what you have seen, and then you have heard them talk about these things, you will understand."

And what he said was true. Each morning as I listened, anger rose up in me like the sun. True and horrible stories, what I was living every night, were not even believed by the people who reported them. You could tell by the tone of the announcers. They would talk about massacres, rapes, torture, slaughter, and they would sound—puzzled. Or they would say everybody did that sort of thing in these parts. I thought at first that the people in America did not—could not—know what was going on here. But they did know, in a general sort of way. They just didn't care. They could have done more to learn. They could have done more to help. So much more. But they just didn't. And I started to realize that, in a way, that made them accomplices.

Rashid and I would read the Koran together. We would pray. He would explain the lessons of the Book. And always he talked about justice. And sometimes I thought it was too much. But after a while, he made sense to me.

"Islam and justice are the same thing," he would say. "But real justice? You don't see much in the so-called Muslim world. Did you see it in America?" He shook his head.

"Don't tell me about America, Rashid. America is something I know. It's something else."

"You are right," he would say. "But if we are going to have the justice we want, we have to be ruled by laws and not men. Isn't that something they teach you in America?"

"Where do you get this?"

"It's in the Book," he said. "God's laws. And people who understand them can bring peace here, and everywhere. You and me, Kurt, and people like us, with God's laws we will bring justice."

Long before the world knew about the camps, stories about them came to us like evil rumors, and we knew from the first that they were true. There were already special words for what the Serbs were doing: "ethnic cleansing." But in early 1992, nobody outside knew what that meant. The camps were part of it. A natural part of it. But nobody would believe. The camps were not just meant to hold the men who were there, but to break them, and to infect them with fear like a disease. The burning of the houses, the raping of the women, those were about humiliation you'd feel forever, and feel in your soul: taking away the family's honor, the family's land, the family's existence. What else did you have in these mountains? And all of it was trashed, all of it defiled.

"This is not about enemies," Rashid used to say. "This is about evil."

I don't know why any single Serb did what he did. I used to ask myself. Maybe for blind hate, or greed, or because of old feuds, or for fun, or maybe they were just following orders. But altogether what they did was very systematic. After I found out their leader, Karadzic, was a psychiatrist, I never forgot it. They were fucking with people's heads, and with their souls if they could get at them. They knew just what they were doing, and they didn't give a damn if you knew, too. And after a while there was almost nothing hidden. The Serbs—the Chetniks, we called them —would do what they did and eventually the results that we knew so well would stare the whole world in the face from behind the barbed wire of a concentration camp, in mass graves, in the blown-apart bodies of a marketplace under fire. And the Chetniks would lie, saying it was somebody else's fault. And that happened so many times that the world got bored. Evil became ordinary. Then it hid in plain sight. And every day as I listened to the radio, my anger grew, not just as a Muslim and a son of Bosnia, but as an American.

"You say Americans believe in justice," Rashid was always saying to me. "So why don't the Americans bring some of it here?" And there was nothing I could say to him, because I wondered myself. In Bosnia and Herzegovina, every day of every week, the real suffering just went on and on. And at night, which is the time I was on the move, it got worse.

Before the big camps were created, the ones the television cameras finally discovered months later, there were small ones. Sometimes part of an evacuated JNA barracks would be used, or a school or an old barn. In farming country it's not hard to find a place meant to hold a lot of bodies waiting for slaughter. A dairy farm will do just fine.

It was almost midnight and a wind was moving through the tops of the pines. Here and there, a tree would groan. A dead branch would fall. There was a confusion of sounds, and each one had to be identified. As I neared the edge of the forest, the wind started to hit me in the face, blowing across a small open valley. Once, and then once again, I thought I heard a scream, but the sound swept past me.

There was a small house in the valley, about five hundred yards away. Lights were on. Near it was a bigger building, a cow shed, and beside that an animal pen with a high fence. Through binoculars I could make out a couple of men in uniform talking near the door of the house, and it was a good guess there were a few more inside. Another was posted near the entrance to the shed. A fire had been burning in the pen, and I could just barely see a couple of people on the edge of the light near the fence, but it was too faint to make out any details. If there were many soldiers or prisoners here, they were inside the shed. I settled into my position at the edge of the forest and watched.

The Chetniks were just amazingly, stupidly confident

at that point in the war. They were used to having over-whelming force, and we had next to none. A lot of the Muslims in Bosnia, including a lot of the government, were waiting for the world to help them. And while they waited, the Chetniks got used to doing whatever they liked. It was rare anyone really fought back. People were slaughtered in their homes, in their fields, in the mosques as they went to pray, and mostly they just ran away. In those first few weeks of April and May 1992, whole cities were emptied. And the government didn't know what to do. So in places like this, where nobody saw, and nobody challenged them, the Chet-niks got lazy. They had strung some concertina wire around the house and barn, but beyond that, as far as I could tell, there weren't even any sentries posted on the perimeter. That wasn't necessarily good news. It could mean I'd missed them, or the perimeter was mined, or both. But if my esti-mate was right, I could make it to the buildings without detection.

The door of the little house opened. A circle of light from a flashlight made its way to the front of the barn and disappeared inside. A couple of minutes later it came back out, and as it got closer to the light from the door of the house, I could see there were four people. They looked like two guards and two prisoners. They disappeared into the house. I saw the door close, and then a few seconds later heard the sound of it slamming. I waited, looking for other signs of movement. Then, clear on the wind now, the screams began.

I do not know exactly what happened in that house. The screams went on and on, then suddenly stopped. Then the door opened and a pair of Chetniks came out dragging a man. His legs showed naked, white and streaked with blood. He was curled in a fetal position, his hands clutching his groin. They dragged him across the yard just like that, and into the barn. Then the other prisoner came out, his face and chest covered in blood. He was on his feet, but barely. He doubled over in the doorway, vomiting, but nothing was coming up. One of the guards shoved him toward a tractor that had a low trailer, a manure spreader, attached to the back. I thought for a second in the dim light that the guard had some weird sort of gun, but it was like a baseball bat. He swung it hard against the back of the man's head and knocked him staggering into the spreader. He swung a couple of more times, but he was at a bad angle. The bat hit the side of the spreader. Across the valley came the delayed clang of wood against metal. The guard changed his position to get a clearer, downward swing, like he was chopping wood. Again. Again and again. And now the sound that came on the wind was duller, like a slap. And then the Chetnik with the bat went back inside. Another one came over to look at what was left in the spreader. He used a match to help him see, then he lit his cigarette with it and walked away into the dark.

I was moving now, moving fast, working the contours of the land to get closer to the farm. I had meant to get close on this mission. But only to look. But that wasn't enough now. Not nearly enough. Out there alone, there was no backup, no one to lay down covering fire, but there was no officer to pull me back, either, and there were no buddies to protect. And somebody, this night, this minute, had to do something in this place to make these fuckers pay.

On the side of the driveway not far from the tractor and the manure spreader, they'd left a roll of barbed wire they were too lazy to string. It was in plain sight of the barn and the house, its little razor-edged prongs glittering with reflections from the lighted windows. But as far as any of the guards knew, there was nothing alive around that tractor right now. If people aren't looking for you, most likely they won't see you.

I pulled a block of Semtex out of my rucksack, primed a detonator, set the timer, then walked quickly, deliberately toward the roll of wire and shoved it up against the side of the tractor's big muddy wheel. For just a second I glanced at the manure spreader. There was more than one body in it.

That was clear, even in the dark. But there was no time to count them. The Semtex and timer went right in the middle of the roll, primed to go in eight minutes, which was about as long as I figured it would take to get to the back of the barn and plant another charge if the way was clear. I couldn't know who was on the other side of the wall inside the barn. That was a risk. But the blast ought to create enough confusion for some of the people there to get out. The noise would bring some of the Chetniks into the barnyard. Then my little field-expedient Claymore would blow like a shotgun loaded with razor blades. At best it would kill a few of them. At worst it would help cover my retreat.

I slipped back into the dark, skirting my way through the shadows toward the animal pen. The fire I'd noticed there before was out, but as I moved along the fence line the smell of gasoline grew stronger. And with it was the smell of burned flesh. At the back of the pen, I could make out the shadows of two people. They were just where I'd seen them before. My HK covered them, but they weren't moving. That sick, sweet smell like burning garbage filled my nose and caught in my throat. Prisoners. Or the bodies of prisoners. They were tied to the fence and were slumped against it now. But my eyes were having trouble adjusting after being so close to the light of the house. I reached out to touch the one nearest me. Whatever clothes there had been were burned away and the skin crackled and oozed under my fingertips. The body didn't move.

It was only when I got close enough to see the second prisoner's long hair that I realized she was a woman. A small woman. Her clothes had been ripped open from behind, but left hanging from her shoulders while however many of them raped her. There was a smell of sweat and blood and shit. But mainly there was the smell of gasoline. Her hair and what was left of her clothes were soaked in it. They must have made her watch the other person burn to death, then left her like this, knowing her time would come real soon, but not knowing when.

She was dead already, I thought. But when I touched her neck to feel her pulse, she suddenly shook and let out a stifled scream that was half a gasp for breath. I clamped my hand over her mouth and tried to whisper to her. But now she was really struggling. "Easy, now. Easy. Take it easy. We're going to get you out of here." As I held her mouth and pulled her next to me to try to calm her, I felt the chains on her wrists. They were like old-time shackles. They must have been something the farmers used to tie up the cows. They were solid and strong, and they were fastened around a fence post almost as thick as a telephone pole. "Easy. Easy. I'm American, okay? You can't understand. But—American —not hurt you. Okay?" I took my hand away from her mouth and she slumped against the fence, making low groaning noises through clenched teeth. "Shhhh, now. We're gonna get you out of here."

What I needed were bolt cutters, but all I had were the pliers on the folding tool in my pocket. I checked my watch. Three minutes were gone already on the timer. The chain was wrapped around the post and fixed with a kind of massive iron staple, but I couldn't get enough leverage to pry that out, or even make it budge. I wrenched and twisted the pliers on the chain. The muscles of my hand cramped and the hinge of the pliers started to give. But the links were barely scratched. The woman watched, but didn't seem to understand anything going on around her. Her groaning filled my head.

This was all going wrong. I wasn't controlling the situation anymore, it was controlling me. I had to get the charge set on the wall of the barn, or there was no way out for the men inside. Maybe they were going to die anyway. But if that razor wire blew, and that was all that happened, the Chetniks would just start slaughtering them then and there.

The woman ground her teeth and the sound ran through my nerves. "Be quiet, ma'am. Please, ma'am, shhh. Quiet. Quiet. We're not going to let them hurt you," I said, my hand against the side of her face to bring it close to mine. Like someone roused in a nightmare she started to shout. I covered her mouth again, but she wouldn't stop struggling. "Oh, baby, don't do this. Please. Please don't do this." But I couldn't calm her now, and there was no time. No time now for anything. No time for the other prisoners, and only one thing I could do for this one. I dropped the worthless folding tool and reached for the combat knife on my leg, but it wasn't there. I didn't have it anymore. I knew that. What the fuck was wrong with me? I had to bend down, reach down, feel through the mud for the fucking SOG tool. And from the second I took my hand off her mouth the woman started screaming. High, shrill screams from her gut, filling the valley with her pain. Finally my fingers felt the cold steel of the tool lying in the mud and gasoline. My thumbnail found the ridge on the three-inch blade and pushed it up.

The door to the house opened. Two, then three circles of light came out into the barnyard. I crouched with my left hand over the woman's mouth again, her head pulled backwards almost onto my shoulder. She's so small, I thought for just a second. She's so small. A flashlight swiveled in my direction. It was right in my eyes. I expected a shot, but I made no move. My breath stopped. Through the blade pressed against her throat, I could feel the woman's pulse. Then I heard a laugh. A friendly shout. Another laugh from another direction. The Chetniks thought I was one of them. For just a second I closed my eyes against the light, but its red star was burned in my retinas. The woman shivered against me. I pulled the blade across her throat, fast and deep. The dark red blood gushed into the light, gleaming over the fence post, cascading onto the knife, my fingers, my hands, seeming for a second to fill the air around me, and even when I closed my eyes the red wouldn't go away. And there was another shout. And laughter. And I heard men clapping their hands. And then the roll of wire blew.

XVII

"We thought you were dead," said Rashid.

"No," I said, and kept walking.

"Tell me," said Rashid.

"No," I said.

Little boys playing soccer in the street stopped and stared as I went by.

"Report," said Rashid.

"No," I said. "No." Without looking I saw my reflection in the window of our Land Cruiser. I had slept in the forest for a day and a night, buried in leaves, and now they were in my hair and beard. My face was black with grease and dirt. My hands and arms and shoulders were brown with dried blood. My clothes were stiff with it. My one thought, my one need, was to be clean. Rashid walked alongside me, but didn't try to talk anymore, and when we got to the house where our squad was bunking, he ordered the other muj to leave me alone.

I put my rucksack down in the corner of our room. I took off my boots, my layers of clothes, and let them drop to the floor. A cold trickle from a hose was our only shower. The thin, freezing stream ran through my scalp and down my face. I washed my head and washed it again, but it wouldn't feel clean. I washed my hands, scrubbing each finger, each wrinkle of the knuckles, but the black under the nails wouldn't come out.

"Kurt, we need to talk," said Rashid, standing in the door.

"No," I said. It took a lot of effort to say anything more. But finally I did. "I think that camp is finished."

"Some of the men who got out are already here," said Rashid. "They thought a whole company attacked the place. Many Chetniks were killed."

"What did they tell you?"

"That there was fighting, two nights ago, and they escaped."

"Did they tell you about the women?"

"What women?"

I dried myself off with a rag. I breathed deeply, trying to clear my head, and I thought I had my balance, but when I went back to the room the smell of my clothes, the smell of gasoline and death, filled my throat with vomit.

At noon, I prayed. And then I reviewed procedures. I could have done better, I knew. I could have done differently. I was too hot to act when what I should have done was think. And now I was thinking too much. I needed to get back that separation between my work and my life that I learned in the Rangers. You do what you have to do, you do it right, then you put it behind you and go on with your life. But what life did I have that wasn't this work? I tried to slow down my mind. I had to find some peace. In the middle of the afternoon I prayed again. And then at night. And Rashid checked on me, and brought me food. But I didn't eat, and we didn't talk, not until after the next morning prayer.

"What happened at the farm?" he said.

I told him about the tortured men, and the razor wire, and, finally, about the woman I killed.

The second I finished talking he said, "You did what you had to."

"I couldn't save her," I said.

"Nobody could save her," said Rashid. But I didn't believe him.

He was quiet for a long time. "This isn't the only war," he said. "And in the end, none of the wars will be won here."

I didn't speak. I only half listened.

"You think you can't change anything," he said. "But you can."

"There is too much for us, Rashid. Too much. Leave it to God, and leave me in peace."

"You are tired. But you will come back stronger." I was waiting for him to say something that I needed, something I could use.

"You will come back stronger," he said again. "And with God's help, we can end this injustice."

I listened.

"Don't lose your vision, Kurt. We are fighting for light against darkness. It is as simple as that."

"Spare me, Rashid."

"What do you mean?"

"I want to believe, Rashid. I do believe. But sometimes when I hear you talk, I believe less. All this fucking talk. Leave me alone. I want to be alone with my God."

I expected Rashid to be angry. I guess I expected a fight. But he looked at me without expression, either hiding what he felt, or just planning his response.

"Your God is just a judge," I said. "Mine—the one I find in the Book—is more than that."

"So what is it you want now, Kurt? To go home?"

I didn't respond.

"But you don't have a home, Kurt," he said.

"You son of a bitch." I reached out to the place near my right hand where I'd left the HK. But Rashid was too quick. He had the gun already and he aimed it at me. Then, when our breathing slowed, he eased it back down. "Listen, Kurt. Listen. What is a home? It is a place to be in peace. How are you going to have that in a world like this? You have seen too much. You know too much to live in peace when so many people are suffering, and there's so much you can do to change things."

"Shut up, Rashid."

"Listen to me, Kurt. You can spread the word of God,"

said Rashid. "You can take His message to the unbelievers. You can take His lesson to America. Then maybe there can be peace."

"Forget it, Rashid. I'm not a preacher."

"It is not only preaching that spreads the word of God," he said. He let that idea sink in. "What is important is for America to let us be what we have to be. Instead, it interferes where it has no business. It helps the hypocrites who oppress us. It fights against justice, against freedom. Against us. And for what?"

"Don't tell me about America, Rashid. You've never been there."

"Who needs to go to America to understand it? All you need is to feel it breathing down your neck, listen to it chanting sin, taste its filthy ground-up meat."

"What? Rashid, leave me alone. I have seen real evil right here. So have you. And now you're talking about the evils of Madonna and Burger King."

"The evil of ignorance, Kurt. In America you don't feel what you do. You are in the eye of a hurricane that you create. Pain and suffering and injustice all over the world, and all you see is blue skies."

I didn't want to argue. I wanted to wash and to pray, and to wash again. "Enough," I said.

"The peace of God be with you," he said.

"And with you," I said, hardly thinking.

I touched my fingers to my closed eyes and ran them lightly over my beard. All I could think of was the prayer. Over and over in my mind I repeated the Fatiha. *"Bismallah al rahman al rahim.* In the name of Allah, Most Gracious, Most Merciful. Praise be to Allah, the Cherisher and Sustainer of the Worlds; most Gracious, most Merciful; Master of the Day of Judgment. Thee do we worship, and Thine aid we seek. Show us the straight way, the way of those on whom Thou has bestowed Thy Grace, those whose portion is not wrath, and who go not astray."

My lips were moving with the words and I touched them to feel the silent prayer. *Bismallah al rahman al rahim.*

Under my nails, faintly, I could still smell the blood.

I didn't go out that night, or the night after. Through each day, five times a day, I prayed. I read the Koran. And when I could, I slept. The mujahedin came and went from our room, and once one of them threw a rifle into my lap, to show that they wanted me to come with them to the lines. But I put the rifle aside and picked up the Koran, and that kept them at a distance.

I read through the versions of heaven and the visions of hell, the flowing streams and orchards, the raging fires. I read the tortures of the grave that touched on every sense, the sinners burned and skinned, then burned again. On every page there seemed to be a description of flames and burning skin. And I thought, I've seen this hell already. It's just out there, in the dark.

The muj in Cazin were no good at night. Those trained in Afghanistan knew other mountains, not these. Many were fresh from their hot, flat countries on the Gulf or the Nile, and couldn't get accustomed to the cold. So they crowded thick into our room at night, smelling of sweat and farts, tense with each other and looking for a fight. "The dwellers of Hell will bicker among themselves," I read. True enough, I thought.

There was so much in the Koran to learn, to understand. It wasn't just something to think about, like you would a history book or a textbook. It was something to feel. That was what I was trying to explain to Rashid. There were times when a low current of excitement would pass through my body. And that was a kind of understanding, too. Because you can't just think about God, you have to feel the presence. And in those days and nights, not eating, not sleeping, but reading and absorbing, the feeling came to me. And, slowly, the word that Rashid was always repeating did start to work its way into my soul in a way that, even now, is hard for me to explain. "Justice." Justice is not men in black robes, not a jury of blank faces, not cops on the beat. That is what I hadn't understood. Justice is the design that God made for man. It is the ideal that He understands, but that we can only learn to feel in our souls. There is right and there is wrong. And Islam is the way to understanding in your heart, in your being, which is which. "Keep us on the right path." And if we follow that path, it won't only be paradise in the next world that we'll find, it will be justice in this one.

I would read until my eyes blurred, but I was afraid to close them. The night and the fence would come back to me.

I wanted to get back to that point in my mind where I could divide my life, my personality, my actions, the way I was taught as a Ranger. I wanted to put the horror to one side so Kurt Kurtovic could be something and somebody else. But it wouldn't happen for me. There was too much I had to sort out in my head.

Evil is real, I thought. To pretend it is not is stupid and destructive. It is crazy—it is evil in itself—to make excuses for those who serve the cause of evil. And even if there was some good in people, until they saw the evil that was in themselves and what they did there was no way to save them. That was the lesson of Lot and of Moses and of all the prophets. "As for the disbelievers, whether thou warn them or thou warn them not it is all one for them; they believe not. Allah hath sealed their hearts, and on their eyes there is a covering. Theirs will be an awful doom." It was the work of the prophets to teach and convince. For the rest of us, all you could do was fight. Evil had to be fought and defeated. And enormous, ignorant America was part of the evil. Maybe not the center of it, like Rashid said, but a part of it. Truly a part of it. Slowly I understood this, too, and not just in my mind, but in my heart. And a kind of peace did come to me, like when you finally admit your deepest secret.

Toward the end of the third day, Rashid came and sat in front of me for a moment, saying nothing, then held out his hand for the Book. I gave it to him. He took a small, square piece of paper out of his pocket and marked a place, then handed it back to me, closed.

The marker was a photograph of a young girl with a scarf over her hair. I didn't recognize her.

"She was the daughter of an imam," said Rashid. "She was fifteen years old. Her father was one of those you freed from the camp." I looked dumbly at the picture. "She died there," said Rashid.

It took me a second to understand what he was telling me. Was this a face I'd seen before? I closed my eyes and saw a flash of red. It had been so dark. I remembered the pulse on my fingertips. And then the white light of the flashlights. She had been so small. And the blood, deep and red, gushing up from her throat, covering everything.

"Read there what her father read to me," said Rashid.

It was the third surah, called "The Family of Imran," the favorite of the mujahedin. "You must not think that those who were slain in the cause of Allah are dead. They are alive, and well provided for by their Lord; pleased with his gifts and rejoicing that those whom they left behind and who have not yet joined them have nothing to fear or to regret; rejoicing in Allah's grace and bounty. Allah will not deny the faithful their reward."

Rashid put his hand on the book and turned one page. He drew his finger along a single line.

"We will put terror into the hearts of the unbelievers," it said.

"I'm leaving tomorrow," said Rashid. "Come with me."

IV

Master of
the Day of Judgment

So We sent plagues on them:
Wholesale Death,
Locusts, Lice, Frogs,
And Blood: Signs openly
Self-explained: but they
Were steeped in arrogance,
A people given to sin.

—THE HOLY QUR'AN,
   Surah 7:133

XVIII

"Piece of cheesecake, please." Thick and white and creamy behind the glass of the stainless-steel case, it looked delicious. I was taking my time over lunch, moving against the rhythm in the short-order atmosphere of the Gardenia. Slow, slow. Sipping my coffee, looking around, while the men and women on each side of me came and went, moving from their first glass of water through their Slenderella Salad or their soft-shell crabs on a bun to coffee and the check in ten minutes or less.

Off to the left was a group of dark-skinned men behind a shelf bustling with the traffic of plates and soup bowls: a Guatemalan here, maybe, a Bangladeshi there; all of them shades of brown, all working like hell. "Out Going Department" read a little sign. Above the shelf more dishes were stacked and still higher up, stuck in the wood molding near the ceiling tiles, there were postcards. To the owner? To the kitchen staff? To people who had come and gone and got them and forgotten them. The cards were stuck there unread, in greasy obscurity. One or two looked like they were from South America. One came from the Persian Gulf. "United Arab Emirates" read the red letters written above a little collection of tourist pictures showing wood-hulled boats and brass coffee pots.

The Pakistani waiter brought my cake and I enjoyed it slowly, along with the American-ness of everything around me. The Special K and Frosted Flakes up on a shelf. The paper coffee cups with "It's our pleasure to serve you" written on the side. A strawberry shake overflowed in the machine. So many machines. So much polished stainless steel in an American restaurant. The Bunn Omatic with the decaf. The big Cecilware urn pumping coffee and hot water like premium and regular. Paper buckets full of lemon wedges for tea. Little plastic cups of cole slaw. Covered trays of gooey Danish and frosted doughnuts.

The crowd at the tables behind me and the counter beside me was starting to thin out, but one heavyset character with an earring sat down next to me. He'd ordered something I'd missed on the menu: cottage cheese and fruit and a pile of red Jell-O that covered half the plate and looked, in its cold, shimmering way, alive.

At a booth against the wall beneath a mirror etched with gardenias some of the staffers from the Council were gathered for a cup of coffee. I'd watched them here several times before. They only worked a couple of blocks away on Park Avenue. Most were young, probably younger than me. But one looked like she was about forty. "You go ahead. I can't fight with George anymore this afternoon," I heard her say. "I brought a couple of things to work on. I'll pick up the rest of my stuff later."

"Doesn't he take any vacation?" said a freckle-faced young woman with red-rimmed glasses.

"Next week. I can't wait."

"The Council's like a tomb in August anyway," said a young man with a loose tie and the sleeves of his white shirt rolled part of the way up his arm.

"It's when I get my best work done," she said.

I ordered a cup of coffee to go, and the check, but before I got to the cashier by the door I stopped at the table where the woman was alone, now, and working. "Excuse me," I said. She looked at me like she expected to see a waiter. I looked at her eyes. They were dark brown, deep and alive. She focused on me, and you could see her mind working, trying to place me, and when she couldn't she unfocused. If psychological defenses made sounds, you could have heard the steel doors clanging shut.

"That's that book about the Balkans by Rebecca West," I said. She looked surprised. "I've been looking for that."

"It's just been reissued," she said, and took another look at me.

"I wish I'd had a copy. I was just there."

And she took another look. "In Bosnia?" she said.

"No. Just in Zagreb. Anyway, I guess I can find it almost anywhere now."

She looked at the papers in front of her and suddenly, visibly, was bored with them. She pointed with her chewed-up Bic pen at the paper coffee cup in my hand. "Want to drink that here?" she said.

"I don't want to bother you."

"No, no. I'll bet you've got a better take on former Yugoslavia than most of the people I've been talking to. At least you've been out on the streets, you know."

"A little. Mainly I just went there to see family," I said, sitting down and peeling the plastic top off the coffee. It was still too hot to sip.

"When did you get back?"

"A couple of weeks ago."

"It's incredible what's happening there now. Did you see the NBC stuff on the camps in Bosnia?"

"No, I missed that. Really I was just in Zagreb to see a cousin."

"Well, it's just incredible. They look like concentration camps."

"Yeah. Well. It's pretty crazy over there." The coffee was cooling a little. "How come you're so interested?"

"Everybody's interested right now. Bosnia's the flavor of the month. Ohhhh. Does that sound terrible? But, well, anyway, I'm a research fellow at a place around the corner. Mainly the Arab world, but just about anything that touches on Islam. And you?"

"Retired," I said.

She smiled. "Unemployed?" she said.

"A little of both. I'm looking to start back to school, but that's a project for January, maybe. In the meantime I'm just traveling. I was in the Army before. But I figured I wasn't learning enough or earning enough to stay in."

"I can imagine."

From the little file I'd pulled together, I knew her age exactly. She had beautiful skin, I thought, for a woman of forty-one. The photographs of her on two of her books hadn't shown that life and intensity in her eyes. And in her guest appearances on "The McLaughlin Group" she'd looked tired and exasperated. But she was still pretty, really, and in person her years showed more in the way she gestured than in her face. She was a little tentative, unsure of herself. Like something had broken her confidence. The thin wrinkles on her fingers showed a lot of worries. Her nails were bitten down. And I guess I looked at them too long, because she put down her coffee and then didn't know quite what to do with her hands. And then she became very businesslike. "What do you think the Croats are going to do? Are people in Zagreb sympathetic with the Muslims? Are they going to back them up?"

"I don't think anybody backs up anybody out there. Not for long anyway. I think the Croats are just waiting for a chance to start fighting again. Maybe they'll fight the Serbs. Maybe the Muslims. You can't ever be sure. Tudjman and Milosevic would divide Bosnia right down the middle if they could."

"Iran is getting involved."

"I don't know much about that. You hear rumors, but not a lot you can be sure of. Anyway, whatever Iran or anyone else does, it's the Croats who control the traffic. They're not going to let Iran go too far. I think the whole thing is probably blown out of proportion."

"Don't be too sure—" She hesitated for a second. "My name is Chantal Silberman."

"You're kidding."

"Why would I kid about that?" she said, flustered.

"I'm sorry, ma'am. But didn't you write that article in *Foreign Policy Journal* last year about the lessons of the Gulf War?"

"Yes," she said, a little reluctantly. "And please—" She waited for me to fill in my name.

"Kurt. Kurt Kurtovic."

"Please, Kurt, for God's sake, don't call me 'ma'am.' "

"Sorry. I'm just happy to meet you. Maybe 'honored' is the word."

"Oh, God, this is getting worse. *Pull-ease*," she said, drawing out the word.

"I must have read that article five times. It really helped me sort out some of the things I saw." You could see she was pleased.

"So you were in the Gulf War, too?"

"I was in Saudi. I didn't see much action. But I guess I did see enough to wonder sometimes what the point was."

"Sounds like you've had quite a life. Saudi Arabia. Croatia."

"Things moved pretty fast for me these last couple of years. To tell you the truth, I'm trying to make sense of it all."

"Aren't we all. But if you're looking for more books and articles to read I can recommend a few." She started to write down some titles, but got impatient. "I can't remember the publishers on a couple of them, and they're probably out of print anyway, so they won't be that easy to find. Do you have a fax?"

"Right now I don't even have a phone."

"Where are you staying, then?"

"In Jersey City with some friends. They're not real good about taking messages. Could I just call you later?"

"Jersey City? What brings you to the Upper East Side?"

"Museums. Bookstores."

She was gathering up her papers, and you could see her thinking about a proposition that hadn't been made. "Why don't you just come back to the office with me?" she said. "We can get you set up with a whole bibliography, and I might even have a couple of extra copies I can loan you."

"That's really nice of you—"

"Chantal. Call me Chantal." The name, said out loud, sounded so much smoother and softer than when I read it.

"—really nice of you, Chantal."

"Don't mention it. You can't imagine how hard fresh ideas are to come by. I want to get you thinking about what you saw and heard so you can get me thinking about what I'm going to write."

I opened the door for her. Out on Madison Avenue the full heat of August almost took your breath away.

The Council was more like a mansion than an office building, and when we got to the door I half expected a butler to open it. But Chantal had a key and a card for the alarm system, and when we got inside there was nobody. "Even the receptionist is in the Hamptons," she said. "It's like a tomb."

"Yeah, but it's a fantastic place. A library? Coatroom? Dining rooms? Is this a club or what?"

"We're trying to change that image a little."

"Why?"

"We do serious work here. And the club thing is kind of misleading. You must have heard some of those wild conspiracy theories."

"No, not really."

"The cabal of Rockefellers and industrialists, generals, bankers, and politicians that rules the world?"

"Is that what this place is?"

"Maybe in their dreams, a few of them," she said as I followed her down a long narrow corridor toward the back of the building. "But really it's more like a halfway house for out-of-work assistant secretaries. That's at its worst. And at its best, it's a pretty good think tank. And it pays my bills, so it's a very worthy institution. Do you mind walking up the stairs? The elevator's old, and I have this horrible fantasy I'm going to get stuck in it when there's nobody here."

"That would be grim. Looks like nobody will be here until September."

"*Pull-ease.* That's why I walk the five flights."

The whole character of the place changed once you were away from the big rooms in the front. There were little pantries and tiny service rooms, places where a butler really might hang out from time to time. And the light was dim, like somebody up front was saving on low-watt bulbs for the back. The stairs were narrow, and only took us part of the way to where we were going. Then we had to walk down another hall to another set of even narrower steps. Books in slapped-together metal cases lined every wall. There were offices stuck in every bit of space, even landings, some of them hardly bigger than closets. But nobody was in any of them. The young staffers who'd been with Chantal at the Gardenia apparently knocked off after lunch.

Maybe to save her breath during the climb, Chantal wasn't talking.

"We really are all alone here," I said.

"No, no," she said. "There's always somebody around somewhere." Her voice was tense, like she'd just remembered how vulnerable she might be.

"Is your office in the attic?"

"We're almost there." She took a deep breath and forged on up the last flight of stairs. I followed behind, watching the way she moved her narrow hips in her straight skirt, admiring her pretty legs. And I wondered if I could make love to her. The question comes to you like a reflex sometimes, even when it doesn't make any sense. She might be willing. And I wanted to want her. But it had been such a long time, and I was carrying so much baggage now. Too much to think about. Too much I didn't want to have to explain.

She stopped at the closed door of her office and took one more breath, then shook her head and smiled. She put her finger to her lips to make sure I was quiet. I wasn't sure what was going on. Then she flung open the door. "George!" she shouted. "What the hell are you doing in here?"

A short round man in his late sixties or early seventies was leaning against the desk in the middle of the tiny room, browsing through a book and smoking a pipe. The office was filled with its smell. He didn't so much as flinch at her dramatic entrance. He looked up over his reading glasses with a half smile. "Glad there's somebody still working in this place," he said. "I came up to check on the Bosnia piece. I'd like to give it, shall we say, a prominent position in the journal this issue."

"I told you, George, 'Monday.' You'll get it before you head for Nantucket. Don't you worry."

"Good, good." He looked at me and raised his heavy eyebrows a little higher.

"Kurt Kurtovic," I said, extending my hand.

"George Carruthers," he said, taking my hand and holding it while he delved back into his brain for a fragment of information. "Kurtovic. A Muslim name, isn't it?"

I could feel the blood drain from my face and hands to the center of my body. "Not in my case. Family's from Zagreb."

"But you're an American."

"That's right."

"You're working with Chantal?"

"He's a friend of friends," she said quickly. "He was interested in some books about former Yugoslavia. So I invited him up to look at the ones I've got here on my desk."

"And your etchings?"

"Don't be an ass, George."

He raised his pipe as if he were giving a toast with it, then wandered away down the hall.

"The editor of the *FPJ*," she said. "But sometimes he acts like he's still in the Agency." She stopped herself. Considered what she said. "No. Like he's still in the OSS. I don't think these guys ever got over that. Remember Bill Casey?"

I couldn't quite place the name.

"Reagan's CIA director. Iran-Contra. All that. He was a friend of George's. Kindred spirit I'd say."

She was clearing a pile of papers, pamphlets, and unopened mail off a little armchair in the corner of her office. "I can't believe I let this place get so messy," she said. "It happens every time I'm writing a piece like this. Here. Have a seat. Let me see if I can find a couple of those books." But it was awkward, sitting. She was looking through a set of shelves that went almost all the way to the low ceiling. She stretched for one book or another. I couldn't ignore her. But I couldn't think of anything to say to her, either. My script had run out. I tried not to obsess on that question about my name. I settled into watching Chantal's body stretch for the books. Long legs. There was a little bit of softness right around her middle. Not fat. Just—softness. When she reached up toward the top shelf her breasts rose, and got rounder and firmer under her blouse and her white bra. Damn.

"I can't thank you enough for all this," I said, getting up. "But I think two is about all I can handle this weekend. Can I come back for more?"

She looked distracted, like I'd interrupted something. "Sure," she said. And for a couple of seconds there was nothing for either of us to say. "Sure," she said again. There was another silence.

"When?" I said.

"Late Sunday morning?"

"You'll be here?"

"Afraid so. Take this number and call up from the street. I'll come down."

■

I had never lived in a true big city, and I wasn't ready for the emptiness of the Upper East Side the morning that I went back to see Chantal. I was walking up Park, and there were no cars, no taxis, no people on it. You'd see folks here or there crossing over, headed to Central Park. But mostly it was dead quiet, like all the people had been disappeared and left nothing behind but their bricks, their parked cars, and their litter tumbling in the faint currents of air. As I was about to call Chantal from the street, I watched one of those silver Mylar balloons floating down the avenue. The heat was rising off the black asphalt in waves, but the balloon was only half inflated, and only a couple of feet off the ground.

"Are you down there?"

"Just across the street," I said. I was looking up at the little round windows on the top floor of the old mansion, but I couldn't find her face.

"I see you," she said. Then I saw her waving.

"Do you see the balloon?" I asked.

"Ohhh, some little kid must be so upset," she said. We watched it from our different angles. The motion was hypnotic. But then a taxi turned onto the street. As it roared by, it sucked the balloon after it, forcing it up higher, twirling it erratically, and breaking the spell. "I'll be right down," she said.

"I've got your books—and some bagels," I said as she opened the door.

"You find them around here?"

"Over on Lexington."

"Well, I'm famished. Been drinking coffee all morning. Nothing to eat. Ugh. Time to indulge myself before I faint. I'd like to say 'Let's go to the park,' but I'm really out of time. Can I invite you into the library?"

She spread paper napkins over the top of a little antique coffee table and pulled it close in front of a leather-covered sofa. We sat next to each other. We talked about the bagels and the spreads on them. About nothing, really.

"Is Carruthers here?" I asked.

"Nobody is here," she said, as simple as that, and she took my right hand in both of hers. She examined the palm, then put it against the side of her face, with hers over it, moving closer to me like that until she kissed me. Just very quickly and gently. I didn't move. Then she said, "But there's no time. Got to write. Want to hear what I've written?"

We hiked up the stairs, and she read to me in her office. Then we talked. Or, mainly, she talked and I nodded. But sometimes she'd seize on some little thing I said, and think about it, and use it to trigger other ideas, and she seemed satisfied. Then she wrote. But she asked me not to leave, and I was actually happy to stay. The place was like a refuge, high and hidden away from the world outside, insulated by books in an empty mansion in an empty city, and after an hour or so I felt myself settling in. I browsed the shelves. I sat in that little armchair and read. And somewhere in a chapter of the book called *Black Lamb and Grey Falcon* I fell asleep.

XIX

The ice-green light of the Xerox machine burned across my eyes. I stared at it sliding beneath the glass until it branded my retina with the shape of the book and burned away everything else that was there.

"My dear Mr. Kurtovic," said George Carruthers. It took me a second to see him through the blank spaces, but even when he wasn't carrying his pipe, you could smell the smoke. "If you have the time, could I trouble you to make a couple of copies?"

"Sure," I said. "Put them on the table next to the coffee machine."

"Get them done before the Clinton meeting?"

"You bet."

"Thanks much," he said, wandering away down the narrow hall, peering over the tops of his glasses with his head pushed forward like a turtle. The books he'd stacked and marked were all about ex-Yugoslavia and the Balkans.

It takes a long time to Xerox chapters page by page, and I had a pile to work through every afternoon when I came in. Making copies was one of the things I did around the Council to make myself useful. That, and browsing the card catalogues and the shelves and the Internet, which was a new thing back then. I also made coffee.

Everybody knew me first as "Chantal's intern at the Xerox machine," and I guess there was a lot of gossip. Carruthers, I'm sure, spread hints around. But Chantal and I didn't really spend much time with each other at the office. And the head of the Council was glad to have me working there for next to nothing at the busiest time of the year. After a few days, people focused their gossip on other subjects. I became a sort of fixture. Eventually they remembered my first name. Mostly they never bothered with my second one. Except for Carruthers, of course.

He played a lot of games. He didn't ask me to do much for him, and then only as a favor. But whenever he did ask, it seemed to me there was something else behind it. There would be lists of books he wanted me to look up or pages and chapters to copy, "if I had the time." And those lists almost always seemed to touch on some part of my life, even though I'd never told him about most of it. Bosnia. Desert Storm. Even Panama. Maybe it was just coincidence. The *FPJ* would do articles on those subjects anyway. And he knew I was in the Army and he could have guessed where I'd served. I didn't want to be paranoid. But Carruthers's lists spooked me. They felt deliberate. If he was trying to upset me, then the reaction he'd look for was—any direct reaction at all. So I just did the Xeroxes, very politely, and kept my peace, and sometimes I kept a copy.

I had gotten my foot in the door at the Council at a good time. The United Nations General Assembly opened at the end of September and presidents and prime ministers from all over the world made their way up Park Avenue to the room on the second floor where paintings of past Council presidents hung on wood-paneled walls and the bankers and diplomats and academics who were members sat on folding chairs. At first I was excluded from the meetings. There was always a lot of security around the heads of state, and to tell the truth I was surprised I could even stay in the building. Secret Service agents would swarm through the place, wires in their ears and up their sleeves, guns in gym bags, little badges on their lapels. But I came and went without much of a problem. At the entrance downstairs, the receptionist, Hedwige, knew me by sight. I made it a point sometimes when I went out for lunch to bring something back for her. She liked that, and me. At the Council, just like most other places, being a fixture was better than having a pass. Normally, if I was working on the top floor people kind of forgot I was there. On the lower floors if I was wearing my suit and my black cross-trainers strangers thought I was one of the Secret Service guys.

If anybody ever ran a security check on me beyond the little form I filled out for personnel records, it was so discreet I never noticed. And in any case all they would have found was my record as a Ranger, my honorable discharge, and a few months of travel in Europe. That wasn't going to trip any alarms. As I look back, it's obvious the address in Jersey City could have been a problem. It wasn't the right place for a blue-eyed boy from Kansas to be. But it was clean enough, security-wise. And I never heard anything from the super, or from anyone else there, about people asking questions about me. All in all, what they could have found out was not what I was keeping secret.

At a Xerox machine, you learn a lot. Even when I couldn't go to the meetings and the seminars, staffers gave me their notes to copy, and the papers they wrote, and articles people were sending to them. There were men and women there at the Council who had been very powerful, and some who would be again. But whenever they were writing about things that I'd seen and lived—about Islam, about Bosnia—they didn't seem to have any idea, really, what they were talking about. They were always getting lost in their own information. What was simple, they made complicated, and the complicated things were made too simple.

By the beginning of October, usually when the speaker was so boring nobody else wanted to go, I started getting invited to meetings just to fill up the back of the room. I wasn't supposed to ask any questions, but they didn't care if I listened.

I heard some pretty amazing stuff. One afternoon a former Deputy Secretary of State described the pinpoint accuracy of American bombing, and how well it worked in the Gulf War, and how well it could work in Bosnia, even though the terrain was a little different. It was just incredible bullshit. Like America could change the world by pressing buttons—like it could all be a bloodless process—at least where American blood was concerned. But there was nothing worth saying to him. Not there. Not then. That wasn't my place.

Now, on this particular afternoon, Bill Clinton was coming. He was the Democratic candidate for President. He looked like he was gaining ground. Some of the people at the Council figured they'd be back in government—in his government—if he won. So there weren't going to be any folding chairs left for me to fill. But as the time for the 5:00 P.M. meeting approached, I kept an eye on my watch. When it read 16:48 I went down the back stairs.

I wanted to see this guy. One of the things I had learned in my weeks at the Council, and maybe the most important, was that great and powerful people were not so impressive up close. I was just on the fringes, just the man at the Xerox machine on the top floor. I just caught glimpses, of course. But I got enough of a chance to watch enough of these people to lose my sense of awe. And yet they made decisions that changed the course of the world. That combination of ordinariness and power seemed very strange to me. So I wanted to see Clinton, who seemed to me about as ordinary as it was possible to be, and, yet, who had a shot at becoming President of the United States. I wanted to watch him walk by, to look at his eyes.

I went down the stairs to the fourth floor, then down the long corridor to the back. I was on my way down the narrow stairwell to the third floor when a big man came charging up, taking two stairs at a time, and almost crashed into me. There wasn't enough room for us to pass each other. He was black, broad-shouldered, and surprised to find anybody there.

"ID," he said.

"Why?" I said.

"Secret Service," he said.

I reached for my hip pocket. I was trying to make out his features, but in the forty-watt light of the stairwell the shadows were too strong and the square light of the Xerox was still floating in front of my eyes. He was looking at my hand to see what I brought out of my pocket. I was looking at his face. Then I took another look.

"*Salaam aleikum,*" I said.

His head snapped up and he was staring straight into my eyes. He studied them in the shadows.

"Griffin?" I said.

He took my wallet out of my hand and he took a long time studying my driver's license in the dim light. "*Aleikum salaam,*" he said in a voice almost too low to hear.

"Hoo-ah! Secret fucking Service!" I said. Seeing him here like this was such a weird trick of fate that I felt kind of elated. I held up my hand for a high five. But all he did was hand my license back to me.

"What are you doing here?" he said. It was a professional question.

"Working," I said. "Doing research." He waited for me to say more. We stood there in silence for a long minute.

"Griffin. It's me."

"Yeah. What kind of research?" he said.

"Truth? I man the copy machine. Low pay. Long hours. But it gives me something to do. Going back to school next fall."

"Let me see your ID again," he said.

"How about yours?" He just held out his hand for me to give my wallet again, but I wasn't going to play this game. "Griffin, brother, I can see you on Farrakhan's detail. But Clinton's? What's going on?"

He wasn't going to talk.

"Let's go downstairs and see the great man," I said.

"I'm going downstairs," he said. "You're not going anywhere." His tone was flat, his features were calm.

"Are you shitting me? What do you think? That *I* am a
security risk? I work here, remember?"

"Just stay up here."

I was getting a little riled. "Tell me something, Griffin.
Do they know about you?"

"What do you think you know, Kurt?"

"You were one righteous son of a bitch. Now you're
doing this. You were faking before. Or you're faking now."

"I'm not faking anything, Kurt. You live in the real
world you learn some kinds of righteous make sense—and
some don't. My faith works for me. I got a wife and a kid. I
got a life. But you, Kurt, I don't get that feeling from you."

"Something about the way I smell?"

"Something about you being in this particular place,"
he said.

"A job's a job," I said. "Let's go on down."

"Not you," he said, and there was a long pause.

"I don't have to see Clinton," I said. "You think I'm
some kind of risk? Shit." I ran my tongue over my teeth,
thinking. I could wait. "You're just jumping to some kind of
wrong conclusions. But I am glad to see you again. I mean,
who would have thought? You in the Secret Service, me
here. A long way from Dugway."

"Long way, long time."

"But, hey, when you know as much about each other as
you and me you ought to be able to talk," I said.

A phone was ringing down the hall. You could hear the
gears working in the old elevator at the back of the building.

"Right," said Griffin. "But not now. You call me if you
get down to Washington."

"What's your number?"

"Just call the White House, they'll patch you through."

By the time I left the Council in the late afternoon it was almost dark and it was raining. Steam rose up from the manhole covers on the surface of the street. Down in the subway the water came in, dripping unpredictably the way it does from leaves in a north Georgia forest or the pine woods of Bosnia, but filthy and gray when it hits you here in New York.

It was a long ride downtown to get the PATH train at the World Trade Center, then under the river to Jersey City. There was time to look at the faces of strangers, yellowed and shadowed by the overhead lights, reflected in the windows of the other underground cars.

When I got on at Sixty-eighth Street I would watch the women in running shoes on their way home from work, clutching their bags and briefcases and umbrellas like they were ready to sprint at the first sign of a threat—but where? Here was a girl with hair that looked like it was shaped with glue, her hand in her backpack holding on to something. Mace? Probably Mace. Here was a man in a wrinkled gray suit. Here was a couple: he was thin as the blade of a knife, she was round in every place. I saw these two a lot and every time I wondered if he smothered in her breasts. After a while they'd nod and smile when they saw me. They thought they knew me.

The mix of the crowd got darker as we got nearer the river. Deep downtown the sounds, the languages, the attitude changed, and so did the smells. If I thought about it I could pick out the scent of each individual near me: the cheap musk sold by street vendors, incense and dope smoke that clung to sweatshirts, the earthy stink of unwashed women, beer on the breath, whiskey coming out of the pores, all dense and, always, closing in around me. And this afternoon was worse, because I felt people around who were hidden. This meeting with Griffin didn't compute and I couldn't make it fit into what I was doing or going to do. A wider circle was drawing closed. There would be people blocking me, keeping me away from my mission, and I couldn't control them, couldn't avoid them, because they were part of unknowable fate. All I could do was control myself and watch, and try to keep my bearings. "Thou art not, by the grace of thy Lord, mad or possessed," says the Koran. "Soon wilt thou see, and they will see, which is afflicted with madness."

And then the PATH train stopped and I rode the escalator up into Jersey City, that other world where I lived, and where I knew that my course was the right one. This was a place of real fears and real, desperate desires. Nothing was given to you here, and everything, at any minute, could be taken away. Indians and Paks and Palestinians and Puerto Ricans, a few old Jews—and the high-rise projects full of blacks where none of the others would go if they wanted to stay alive. This was the world of America's longtime losers and raw beginners, rough and violent and looking for something this country wasn't ever going to give them. Everywhere I went on this side of the river, it seemed to me people were lost, and the worst off were the ones who came with the most hope. They lost it with a gun barrel in their eye, a blade across their jugular, or maybe just an immigration raid and the long ride back home to nowhere.

It took me more than thirty minutes to get back to the apartment, ducking under awnings when I could, but mostly soaking in the cold rain. The coat I bought at Marshall's was wet through, and I could smell the damp wool of my suit. There were places where I could see, across the river, rising like massive tablets above the rest of the city, the twin towers of the World Trade Center. I stopped and looked at them for a long time, letting my mind clear. Carruthers floated through it. And Griffin. And Rashid. And the face of a young girl on an old picture. But slowly they drifted away. I had found a line in the sixty-eighth surah. It was helping me. "And the Unbelievers would almost trip thee up with their eyes when they hear the Message; and they say: 'Surely he is possessed!' But it is nothing less than a Message to all the worlds."

There were times when I walked these streets at night and felt like a moving target. But I would remind myself what I'd lived through, and I knew no one was going to take my life from me here and now for nothing. And in the dark shadows of the streets, jogging slow and steady past vacant lots where firelight danced out of oil drums and frozen faces watched the stranger passing, I believed, too, something I wouldn't say to anyone in Jersey City. There were secret saviors here, right here, among them.

XX A couple of weeks before Thanksgiving, I got a call from Joan, my sister in St. Louis, to say she was coming to New York and would like to see me. Maybe we could have tea, she said.

"Tea?"

"Well, yes, Kurt. Don't you drink tea?"

"Joan, it's been—what?—a year? How'd you find me here?"

"Selma told me—"

"Yeah."

"And I was thinking it has been really too long since we talked, you know. And since I was going to be passing through New York with my husband—"

"Joan, I'm very busy."

"Oh, I'm sure you are. But even so, I thought you might make time for your sister."

"When did you think I might make this time?"

"Kurt, I don't know why you are using that tone with me. If this is really too much trouble we can forget it. But—"

"I'm standing in somebody else's office."

"Oh. I see," she said, as if that surprised her. "But I did want to talk to you about Selma."

"Selma."

"I don't know what she's told you about what's going on with Dave."

"We don't talk that much."

"That's why I thought we should talk. You know, you are the man in the family now."

"Un-hunh," was all I said, because I couldn't believe she was saying that. "All right," I said. And we made our appointment. I didn't expect much news of Selma or anyone else. But it was easier to get Joan out of the way by dealing with her. If I ignored her she would see that as a challenge and keep after me. In our family, or what was left of it, she was the only one allowed to do the ignoring.

"Do you know the Mayfair Hotel?" she asked.

It was just down the street. She must have looked at a map. Now that I was working on Park Avenue she thought I was worthy of a visit.

I put the phone back down on Chantal's desk.

"I'm sorry," I said. "Family stuff."

"Want to tell me about it?"

"My family? I don't think so. And we've got too much to do right now, right?"

"Right," said Chantal, looking at half a dozen thick file folders she had spread on her desk like she was laying down a hand of cards. "Right," she said again, like she was convincing herself. She looked at the files in front of her for a good long time. Then she shook her head. "No," she said. "If you don't really mind I'd like to talk about your family."

"I don't think so."

Why was I surprised that she looked so hurt? I don't know for sure. But whenever I saw that pain in her eyes, it shocked me a little. I sort of thought, without really thinking about it, that she didn't feel things the same way I did. Like when you're in school, no matter what you say to a teacher, you don't think her feelings are going to get hurt. You expect her to get angry, maybe. But not hurt. It's an age thing. And there was some of that with Chantal. And there was the control thing, too. What I was thinking about all the time was how to keep Chantal interested in keeping me around, but when I'd say or do something that brought on that look of hurt, I felt like I'd got it wrong. And that could be fatal.

"You want to hear about Croatia?"

"I want to hear about Kansas," she said.

"Chantal, my parents are dead. My father died when I was fourteen. My mother got married again, then she died, too. What else is there? My sisters. Selma is sweet, but she's married to an asshole. And Joan *is* an asshole. Okay?"

She just looked at me and it made me very uneasy.

"There are times when I feel like I don't know anything about you at all," said Chantal. "You've got this shell I can't get through. And I don't like it, Kurt. I really don't like it." She was shaking her head and she turned away from me.

"Whoa," I said. "What's going on here?"

Her eyes were turning red. "That's part of the problem, Kurt. You don't listen."

"That's not fair."

She just shook her head, and in that second I could see everything I'd put together starting to come apart, and I didn't know what I could do about it.

"Am I interrupting something?" said Carruthers, leaning in the open door of Chantal's office. She looked up at him. She focused. And she wiped the tears away from under her eyes. "Dust from the files," she said, but she'd missed a beat. "Got under my contacts."

"Ah," he said. "Shall I come back?"

"I'll be okay. What is it, George?"

"I wanted your input on a Somalia piece."

"I was going to concentrate this week on the Saddam project."

"Hmmm," said George. "Don't you think that could hold? This Somalia business seems to be taking on a life of its own. Bush may do a big humanitarian extravaganza before he takes his leave. It could be a headache for Clinton."

"And Iraq is not?"

"Still, I wish you'd take a look at it." He turned to me. "I'm sure you can help her with it," he said, and smiled, and turned and walked out.

"Stay here, Kurt," Chantal said quickly, firmly. "Don't let him get to you. Stay here."

"He's making me crazy," I said.

"Everything's making you crazy, Kurt."

"I'm okay," I said, but I could feel my defenses failing me. The lines of demarcation between my lives were getting fragile, cracking, breaching. The call from Joan. These tears from Chantal. This bullshit from Carruthers, always probing and testing and smirking.

"Sit down, Kurt."

"I'm tired," I said, and I did sit down in that little chair across from her desk and closed my eyes.

"What's going on with you?" I heard her say.

"Too much and nothing," I heard myself say.

"It's family. Something about your family."

I almost laughed. What I had on my mind was so much bigger than that, I thought. So very much bigger. The sheer scale of the thing dwarfed the concerns of any one man about any one family. And yet here I was with some synapse making a loose contact inside my head because of a call from Joan. And I couldn't say anything, really. And certainly not to Chantal. So I seized on what she was saying to me.

"Yeah, family, I guess." But I didn't want to go into that. I really didn't want to go into any of that. "Or maybe just lack of sleep."

"Why?"

"Dreams."

"Tell me about them," she said, and I breathed a quiet sigh of relief. I thought I could talk about dreams without giving anything away.

"It's like real life most of the time. If there's a problem in the day, I dream about it at night. But I don't fix it at night. I just wake up."

"And you wake up a lot."

"A lot."

"Like what problems?"

"Like—like the Xerox machine breaks. Like—anything."

"But don't you go back to sleep?"

"Yeah. If it's the Xerox I do."

"Do you dream about the war?"

"Which—yes. Yes, about the Gulf War. And sometimes Panama. But, no, I don't think that's it. I wake up. I'm in my bed. I go back to sleep."

"So, excuse me, Kurt. But what are these dreams that keep you awake?"

"Drowning." How had we got to this point so fast? I was telling the truth, which is always the best way to lie. But this was more truth than I meant to let on. And now I had to explain, and be careful about it. "I used to dream, you know, that I was on a boat, a landing craft, and that I fell over the side. And that, just at the moment when I was about to die, or felt like I was, my feet touched the bottom. And I walked. And I breathed. And I walked out of the water. But, now, the dream is different. I am standing, and then the water is underneath me, on top of me, smothering me, and I am trapped in a net, or a car, or, I mean, you know how it is with dreams, the thing that's trapping you is less important than the trap itself. And it's dark. And my throat closes. And no air comes, just the choking. And then I do wake up. And then I don't get back to sleep."

"Terrible."

"I had that dream last night," I said, which was a lie, in fact. But the dream, God knows, was real. I'd had it many times. Too many times. And as I talked about it the idea clutched at my throat and heart, and it seemed so damned unfair to me. I had come to terms with so much in my life. There were so many horrible things that I could see in the eye of my mind, still, and so many little sensations that might bring back too much to think about. But I got them under control. I put them in their place and I closed the door. And when I smelled asphalt burning, or the ripe stink of garbage, or heard a car backfire, or a child scream, I let the sensation pass as quickly as a telephone pole passes the window of a car. So why, God, must there be these new tortures in my dreams? And I wanted at this second to say all this out loud. To say it to Chantal. But I had enough control not to do that. I did have that much control. "Anyway," was all I said, and left the word hanging. "Anyway."

Chantal looked at the file folders fanned out in front of her, then glanced at the window. It was already dark. "Hunan," she said, sweeping the files together in a pile and cradling them in her arm like a schoolgirl going from one class to another. "I'm up for a little Hunan cooking. Let's order some at my place and go over this Saddam shit. Now these files here, they're real nightmares."

Chantal's apartment was tiny, just one L-shaped room in a building that was about as run-down as you could find on upper Park Avenue. Big places had been divided into smaller ones, then those divided again. But with the door closed and the blinds open to the sky, it was Chantal's special world and, after a while, even though I resisted at first, its atmosphere became special to me. One wall was a closet. One wall was books. The bed was hidden in the ell behind a heavy drapery—a tapestry, she said, that she had rescued from a place her grandparents used to have in France. And then there were the windows. And the view. Since there was a low public school building behind hers, she looked out over Madison Avenue, the Metropolitan Museum, and beyond that a wide stretch of Central Park. It was, whatever else I was thinking when I walked into that apartment, day or night, a beautiful thing to see. The buildings made a kind of canyon that drew me in. But this wasn't a canyon made of rock, it was made of windows, and scenes of life, and I would

stand there looking out on the city and be kind of hypno-
tized by it all, the way you are when you look at a television
or a fireplace. I didn't know any of those people behind those
windows. I didn't want to. But a light would go on here, and
there, and there, as people came home from work, and each
time there was a little discovery, a fraction of a secret that
was exposed. All those people. All those lives.

"Don't turn on the lights," I said. "I just want to look
at all this for a minute."

"What are you thinking?" said Chantal.

The cold air on the walk up Park Avenue had cleared
my head. The dreams were behind me. "Just watching the
people," I said. The scene, I thought, was a little like an
Advent calendar.

"What do you see from your place?"

"An alley," I said. "Just an alley." In Jersey City I never
opened the curtain. If I had, all I would have seen were the
windows of a building full of old cardboard boxes. My room
was bare, with a bed on a rolling frame and a card table I
bought to put my stuff on. It was like a cell. And all I did
there was sleep and pray.

"I'm trying to think what this reminds me of," I said.

"Let's just call it Manhattan."

"Sometimes . . ." I took a deep breath and I could smell
the old, old dust in the tapestry behind me and the dried
flower petals in the silver bowl on the little coffee table.
"Saddam," I said. "Let's work on Saddam."

Chantal weighed the files in her arms. "I know what I
want to say," she said. "We know it's there—or almost."

"Almost."

"And nobody pays attention. And Kurt, that scares the
shit out of me. Saddam's nuts, and he's got the stuff to kill
millions of people."

"He doesn't have the bomb."

"He's got chemicals. Have you ever seen the pictures
from the towns he gassed during the war with Iran?"

"Those Iranians—"

"Kurt, he was gassing Iraqis. His own people. Men. Women. Children. Little children."

I didn't say anything.

"Little children. Can you imagine, Kurt? A plane flies over, or a helicopter. It could look like nothing. Like a— what do they call those things?—a crop duster. Probably it wouldn't even be shooting guns. And then down in the street the children would start to cough, and choke, but they couldn't even cry, because their lungs were filling up, and burning. And their parents would start to choke. But the children would be the first, and they'd lie there, all of them would lie there wherever they were, trying to suck in air and getting nothing, and dying. You can see their faces in the pictures."

"War is hell," I said. "I do know that."

"Yes. You do. I'm sorry. But I really am frightened. I've spent so many years watching Saddam, and I know how he thinks, and what he's got to work with."

"But he's got nothing left," I said.

"You sound like Carruthers. But don't you believe it, Kurt. Not for a second. He's got all that he needs."

"No missiles. No air force."

She looked through the shadows for a sign of betrayal on my face. "Are you playing the devil's advocate? No." She shook her head. "Forget it," she said. "Maybe I can feed you something."

"Weren't we going to order Chinese?"

"Yeah. Let me do that."

"You're mad at me."

"No. There's a menu there in the last drawer on the left. Order what you want."

She had the files on the little counter in the tiny kitchen at the back of the apartment. She clicked on the light.

"Terrorism," she said.

"What?"

"That's his revenge," she said. "For sure. Look at this."

It was a news report about a meeting in Baghdad in January 1992. Just a couple of paragraphs. It was called an Islamic Congress. There were supposed to be delegations from as far away as Morocco and the Philippines. "He'd use anybody," she said.

"You're losing me," I said. I walked over to the window again.

"Remember how it was in the Gulf War? He was supposed to unleash all kinds of terrorist attacks around the world. And what did we get? *Pfffft.*"

"So no need to worry," I said. More lights had come on in the skyscraper canyon.

"Wrong."

"If you say so," I said. A couple of hundred yards away, a large kitchen lit up. A young woman—maybe a girl, by the way she moved—opened the refrigerator.

"I do. Listen. He had a very big intelligence operation before the war, but it was conventional, and it was penetrated. Israel, the Syrians, even, God bless, the Americans, had it pretty well wired. The Palestinians were a disaster for Iraq. Supposed to be working with Saddam, but the head of PLO intelligence was singing to the allies. But—never mind all that. The point is—"

I clicked off the light. In the distance I saw the girl sit down at the counter in the kitchen to eat. And now a little boy toddled in. She picked him up and sat him next to her, and started to feed him off her plate. There was something in the scene. A memory.

"—are you following this?" Chantal asked.

"Yeah. Sure."

"Yeah. The point is the old Iraqi operations and networks were all blown. Abu Nidal, Abul Abbas, all of them."

"Okay." The memory was Selma. And me. A long, long time ago. The memory didn't mean anything, really. It was just there in front of me. But it started me wondering again what news there might be from Selma.

"And then what does Saddam put on his flag—his Arab nationalist flag? *'Allah akbar.'* God is great."

"Allah akbar." I turned back to Chantal.

"God is great."

"I get it."

She turned the light back on. "Look at this stuff. Ever since the war, Saddam's speeches have sounded like the Ayatollah's. And now he's holding Islamic Congresses, pulling Koran thumpers together from all over the world. Why do you suppose that is?"

"I don't know."

"Networks. He had to replace his old, blown intelligence and terrorist networks. Sooooo, out go the Palestinians, in come the Holy Warriors."

I put my arm around her shoulders but she shrugged it off like I was hurting her.

"Sorry," I said. "I'm sorry." I picked up the takeout menu and looked at it, but I couldn't focus. "I'm sorry," I said again. "I—I guess—Chantal, I mean, it really is complicated."

"No, damn it, it is not!" she said. "It is not too complicated. Not if people are willing to open their eyes. Saddam lost his old spies and terrorists, and he went out and got himself a bunch of new ones. Some of them were even trained by the CIA in Afghanistan. And he's still got weapons—chemical and biological weapons—that could make any vengeance they deliver more terrible than anything we've ever seen."

I just nodded. I didn't want this to go on. But she waited for me to say something. Finally I just said, "You're right."

"I know. I know," she said. "So why—why—doesn't anybody else know?" She wrapped her arms around her like she had a chill.

It was true that nobody paid any attention to her. The more that people ignored her, the more she obsessed, and the more passionate she got, the more she was ignored. The alarm that she was trying to sound was on a frequency nobody in Washington was trained to hear. "Our Western desire for predictable morality and an essentially Christian logic based on that morality blinds us to Saddam's logic of vengeance," she wrote in one memo. It came back with circles and question marks all over it. So did all the others. Around the Council people were starting to make fun of her. They didn't want to know about this stuff. I heard it in Carruthers's voice: "Don't you think that could hold?" That's what he would say any time she brought up Saddam.

Once I was walking by her door at the Council and Carruthers had just walked out. Chantal was red in the face and so angry she was shaking. "If you had the chance to stop a holocaust—" She was shouting down the hall, but Carruthers was just walking away. "If you had the slightest chance to stop that from happening, wouldn't you? Wouldn't you write what you had to write so maybe, just maybe somebody would do something about it?"

It was all so personal for her. I tried to remember whatever it was she'd told me about her family. She was born in America and her parents had grown up here. But she had lost two uncles and an aunt in France during World War II. Even her cousin had been taken away from his school and no one had ever seen him again. You wouldn't have known any of this about her if you didn't know her pretty well. But she heard those stories all her life and the dangers of the wide, cruel world were real for her in a way they were not for most Americans. She wanted to do something to stop the suffering. "If you had the slightest chance to stop a holocaust . . ." I understood that. I respected it.

She turned out the lights in the apartment and stood beside me now at the window, looking out on the canyon of concrete and glass.

"You think you can stop something like the holocaust?" I said.

She looked up at me suddenly. "I don't know," she said.

"I don't know. I'm probably not the one." She shook her head. "And maybe—don't tell anybody else I ever said this —you know—maybe I'm wrong about Saddam. Maybe it's just some overblown, paranoid delusion." She reached out behind her without looking until the tips of her fingers touched the tapestry hanging in front of the ell. "But you gotta try," she said. "You just got to try."

"And what if you could stop one holocaust by doing something that was, well, almost like another holocaust?"

She leaned back against the wall and wrapped her arms around herself again. "Oh, God, Kurt. Let's talk about something else."

I didn't love Chantal. And at first that made it easier to fake. I could lie to her anytime, under any circumstances, and not care. But over time, it got hard to separate the role I was playing from the person I was. And then I didn't know how to act at all around her. Sometimes the time with Chantal was so comfortable. And sometimes so troubling. I could have seen her as the enemy, but sometimes I felt so sorry for her. After a long time not talking she came back over to the window.

"It's starting to scare me," she said as we looked out on the night and New York. "I feel like Cassandra sometimes."

"Like?"

"Cassandra. Always predicting doom."

I'd heard the name but I couldn't think exactly where. "Cassandra in the Bible?"

"No. Not really. Trojan War. Greek tragedies, like that." I was embarrassed and she was embarrassed for me. "I was about to say something," she said, "about needing to teach the classics in Kansas but, you know what? I can't even remember where she appears. The *Iliad* or one of the plays. But the point is that I'm always predicting doom, and, you know, damn it, probably I am right."

"Probably," I said, "you are."

XXI

The insults were piling up like coals under a grate. In December 1992, at every turn, in every corner of the world, Muslims were reviled, humiliated, murdered, tortured, killed. Whenever I saw the television news or listened to the radio or read the headlines, the message was the same. A mosque was destroyed in India and the police just stood by and watched while it crumbled under the picks and shovels of defiling Hindus. Hundreds of Palestinians were rounded up by the Israelis and sent up to a frozen mountain in Lebanon. In Egypt, to protect a bunch of half-stoned, sunburned tourists, thousands of believers were arrested and beaten, and if they couldn't be found, it was their wives and their children who paid. Algeria was at war. Afghanistan was at war. American fighter planes swarmed the skies over Iraq. In Somalia, 300,000 Muslims died of starvation before, slowly, slowly, slowly the United States started to send aid, then troops, and then pity was played out for all it was worth, and all it was not, right in the middle of the Christmas season. And it all made me sick. God knows how Americans enjoyed feeling sorry for everyone else that December, before knocking back their drinks and sitting down to their turkeys. And in Bosnia? In Bosnia, at last, word started getting out about the slaughter and the systematic, the methodical, the unbelievable industrial-scale rapes going on every day and every night. But many Americans still would not believe, and those who believed still would not act. It would have spoiled the holiday spirit.

The wind was coming down Fifth Avenue like a tidal wave, hard and cold and wet and full of grit. Just as I passed Rockefeller Center, the streetlights went on. The big Christmas tree was erupting with Christmas colors. Angels with wings that looked like spider webs raised their horns to heaven. The avenue was packed with people, denser than the subway. I had to shoulder past mothers and children and office workers and Santa Clauses that looked like bums and bums who looked like Santa Claus, and the blind and the helpless parading their cups and the party girls out of work early in long coats and short skirts, with red lips and hair piled high on their heads that was blown undone by the wind. Umbrellas were sucked inside out. Your eyes teared from the gales of dirt. I'd been through a lot worse, God knows, than December drizzle on Fifth Avenue. But the chill depressed me. The people upset me. The lights disturbed me. I just kept walking.

Every headline I'd seen for weeks worked its way under my skin like a parasite. Every impersonal statistic about Muslims killed just for being Muslims injected me with anger. And there were times, yes indeed there were times, when every ignorant, thoughtless face on the street filled me with rage. It was only natural, really, that I wanted to share the anger and my faith. But I should never have gone to the mosque.

That morning—it was Friday, a week before the holiday—the Council was still open. But I hadn't gone in to work. Instead I'd walked through the half-frozen sleet to Kennedy Boulevard in the middle of downtown Jersey City and to the Masjid al-Salaam there on the second floor above a toy store. The Koran did not require me to pray like this, not when unbelievers might attack. And this mosque, I knew, might be watched. Already a blind sheikh from Egypt who sometimes led the prayers was in trouble with the FBI. I wanted nothing to do with him, or them. But I thought I would trust in God to protect me this day, and to let me pray, and to bring me peace, and, yes, to show me the right way.

I was there a few minutes before the call, but there were already a dozen other men standing around near the door of the room where prayers were held. Out on the street, the gutters were full of trash, the walls covered with tags. Here the carpet was clean, a pretty color of green. The walls were spotless and white. It was not a bad place. There was peace here. Inside. But the men around the door of the room didn't look at my white face with peace. And so I waited. When the call came, all would enter. We would pray. I would leave. And in the meantime I looked at the bulletin board at the top of the stairs. There were notices about big meetings to be held with Muslim stars like Hakeem Olajuwon. There were apartments for rent with little fringes of phone numbers to tear off. There were ads for long-distance services, and halal meats. And somebody had put up an old flier like they handed out in the streets sometimes. There was a picture on it of downtown Manhattan. "If York can cool the World Trade Center, think what we could do for your home," it read.

"Wrong time of year for that," I said to a stocky, bearded Arab who stood near me, watching.

"What do you mean?" he said. It was a simple question, but you could hear something dangerous behind the words.

"For cooling."

He didn't say anything. But he squared his shoulders and moved into my space. I shrugged and turned away toward the entrance to the big room, but some of the others there were looking at this big Arab, and at me, and positioning themselves on purpose to block my way. They didn't know what I knew and they didn't know me, and unless I did a lot of talking, they weren't going to let me pray. Dumb fool that I was, I'd done too much talking already. And now I could feel the heat rising inside me. I couldn't believe they were going to try to keep me from praying. It was all wrong.

It was against the word and the law of God. Did they think I was from the government? Probably. I understood what they must think. But this was wrong.

But this was not the moment to fight. Or to convince. Not today.

I hit the street. "Assholes," I said out loud to nobody. "Assholes." And I set out walking to chill out. I expected to have my head together by the time I got back to my place. I could pray there, the way I always did. Then I could read the Koran. Maybe I could close my eyes and, for a few minutes anyway, maybe I could sleep. But as I walked I couldn't shake the feeling I was being shadowed. I waited in doorways. I watched. I couldn't pick anyone out. But as I walked, and as I looked around, things didn't look the same. Posters, tags, signs, whole buildings were there that I hadn't seen before. Even though I was walking the route I usually walked, I'd look up and suddenly feel lost on unfamiliar ground. Here was the old movie theater that said "Asamblea de Jesus" out front. There was the Temple Beth-El. There were houses of God all over the place, as common as Laundromats and taverns. But they weren't my houses. I didn't have my house of God here. I only had a room. And when I reached it finally and closed the door behind me, and closed my eyes, and tried to clear my head for prayer, it wouldn't clear. There was no one thought in it, there were hundreds. Pieces of dreams and memories bounced around in my skull fast and crazy as pinballs, and they wouldn't stop, and I didn't know what to do. "Bismallah al rahman al rahim." I kept saying the words out loud, trying to begin the Fatihah, but I couldn't hear the meaning. The words were coming out of my mouth, but they were coming from somebody else's head. My muscles started to tie up. My teeth clamped tight together and my shoulders, my forearms, all the flesh beneath my skin, began to contract and quiver. The muscles in my hands were like a tangle of wires, the veins stood out like rubber tubes. I backed up against the wall of the room to steady myself.

"It's not working," I said. "It's not working. It's not working." Over and over and over again. Someone shouted through the door. "What the fuck you doing, man?" And it wasn't until then that I realized I was banging the back of my skull against the wall. I let it rest there for a minute and tried to breathe evenly so my muscles would quit seizing up on me. There was no reason I could think of for my brain to be doing this. Every day, all the time, I could deal with assholes. White, black, yellow, brown. All kinds of assholes. At the Council, at a mosque. Wherever. I stayed on course.

A chill shot through me again and I knew what I needed was a hot shower. A good hot shower. But the one in my room was not very hot, and not very good. The head was lime green with corrosion. The water trickled out of the middle and shot at wild angles out the sides. It would have to do. And as I peeled off my damp clothes, thinking about the shower brought me a little bit of calm. But when I turned it on and the lukewarm water trickled and sprayed, I decided I had to do something to fix it. I felt around in the bottom of my little bag for the SOG Paratool and unfolded the big screwdriver. But the screw in the middle of the showerhead was so corroded it wouldn't budge. The whole thing was wet. It was hard to hold it still with my left hand. I pressed and twisted harder. The blade of the screwdriver slipped and cut across the heel of my hand. Along a thin line the skin was white for a second, then the blood appeared. It began to spill in front of my eyes, and I just watched it. I threw the Paratool into the sink. When I turned on the shower and held my hand under the trickle, the water splattered pink drops of thinned blood all over the mildewed shower curtain, and all over me. But I just let it run. I rubbed the sliver of soap over me with my right hand, blood over me with the left, until slowly the red flow stopped, and slowly I became as clean as I could make myself.

And finally I was calm. And so tired. And I felt like I was half asleep, but no dreams or memories were coming now. There was just the shower, and the little slice across my hand. And then the towel, and then my clothes—my suit. My tie. And then it was time to go into Manhattan. Today was the day I was meeting Joan for tea.

It was interesting to see how uncomfortable my oldest sister was when we sat down. She was the one who wanted to come to this place where the waiters wore tuxedos, and men in gray suits with slicked-back hair drank soda water with lemon, and women with big diamonds on their fingers and heavy gold on their wrists raised cups of tea to twisted smiles. Joan wanted to be here. But she didn't fit. You could tell by the way she sat, near the edge of her chair, and by the way her eyes moved all the time. She didn't feel good about this place.

"Why, Kurt, you look so pale," she said when I got to her little table.

"Working hard," I said.

"No time off for Christmas?"

"Not me."

Her eyes settled on the handbag of the woman at the table next to us and for a second it was like she was in another world. Then she brought herself back.

"I am so glad we could get together this afternoon. Charles and I are only going to be here for a day, you know, before we go down to Florida."

"Yeah."

"Have you tried these little cookies?"

"Not hungry."

"I see," she said.

"Joan, I know we should have a long talk—"

"Yes, we should."

"But I haven't got any time. Really, like, none."

"And you want to hear about Selma."

"Yeah."

"Yes . . ."

"Yes, please," I said automatically, but with a bad taste in my mouth. This was a game of hers that was so old I'd forgotten it. I really did not have time to say "please" to her. I didn't like the reminder or the memories of times when she pretended to be my mother. "You said there's something you want to tell me about."

"You always liked her best, Kurt."

I put my hand down on the table and gripped the edge. "Joan, don't." The table was shaking a little, making rings on the surface of the tea in her cup.

"If that's the way you want to be."

"I'm out of here, Joan."

"No. Stay." She suddenly put her hand on mine to keep me from leaving and I saw, just as suddenly, looking at the back of her hand, how old she had become. If I hadn't been so mad at her for all this bullshit, I might have felt sorry for her.

"I really am worried about Selma," she said.

"Okay," I said, and let go of the table. "Something with Dave?"

"Dave, and Duke Bolide and that whole crowd."

"They're still preaching about niggers, Jews, and wet-backs?"

"It's not the preaching, it's the 'training' that Selma's worried about."

"She ought to be happy if it gets him out of the house."

"He doesn't tell her anything. Nothing. Just disappears for days and doesn't let her know where he's going or when he's coming back."

"Yeah. I bet. She should be hoping he never does come back."

"Even when he's there, half the time he's doing things real secretly. Like he was some kind of spy or something."

"Dave? That piece of shit couldn't spy on a squirrel in his backyard."

Joan stiffened when she heard the word "shit." "I don't

know, Kurt." She folded her hands in her lap. "The things he does. Like the mailbox. He got a new one with a real lock on it."

"What's the problem?"

"He won't give a key to Selma. When he's away, she can't even get in the box to get the bills and things. Can't even look at her catalogues until he sees them first. I don't know how Selma can put up with it."

It sounded like the usual.

"Selma is scared," said Joan. "Real scared. And I'm not sure what it is. She talks about the mailbox and the training and things but to tell you the truth I'm not sure what it is. All I know is that she looks like there's something eating her up from inside. And—and I think it's fear."

"Is he beating her?"

"I don't know," she said in a voice I could hardly hear. "I don't think that's it."

"Well, damn it, what is wrong then?"

Joan looked up at me and past me and in every other direction to see who else was looking at us.

"I don't know, Kurt. I mean, I think she's afraid some-thing's going to happen to him. Like big trouble. With the law. I don't know. I just don't know. I mean, Kurt, why don't you call her yourself?"

"I can't get involved in all that, Joan." I wanted to stay away from those people, as far away as I could. "I've been building a new life for myself here in New York," I said. "You ought to understand that. Especially you."

I wanted to stay away, but in my head, I couldn't. The truth was, almost every day I thought about calling Selma, because almost every day I wondered how she was doing, and if she was okay. But I never picked up the phone. The time never seemed right and there wasn't anything I could do anymore to change things for her. How many times had I told her to leave Dave? And she just wouldn't. And if she wouldn't, then what could I do? She didn't listen to me. She didn't listen to basic common sense. And so, even if I loved her, I couldn't find the time to talk to her.

And looking at Joan as she looked at her hands in her lap, her shoulders hunched a little like she wanted to disappear from this place and this time, I wished that I could tell her what I was thinking. What I was doing. Yes, even Joan. But how would I begin to explain any of it to my sisters? To Joan, sitting here in front of me? Or to Selma? Poor, sad Selma, who didn't even have her catalogues to herself anymore.

The noise of the lounge floated around us, and we added nothing to it, not even the clicking of a cup and saucer. But something went off inside me like a circuit breaker, and for a second it was like my overloaded brain finally cut off and all the buzzers and sirens went silent, and the tension just drained out of me, and I laughed.

"Kurt?"

"I'm sorry," I said, trying to stop myself from laughing any more. "Selma can't do without those catalogues."

Joan smiled, and you know, for a second I was glad. Then I thought about how I would explain to my sisters what I was really doing. I could see how they would react. Joan wouldn't believe me. She'd be confused. She'd tune me out. Selma wouldn't believe me either, but she'd try to convince herself, somehow, I was doing the right thing. Or would she be horrified? What would her face look like if I told her? As we sat there in the Mayfair, I shook my head, trying to shake the idea.

"Kurt?"

"Never mind, Joan. I'll call Selma tonight. Don't you worry."

XXII
The Council's old mansion on Park Avenue was dead empty. I let myself in with Chantal's security card and a key. Nobody was expecting me to be there. I didn't turn on any lights. I felt my way to the corridor that led to the back, and toward the glowing red button on the service elevator. It took a long time to arrive, clanking and shuddering, and then I had to throw a lever to open the heavy door. It made me smile, this elevator. It had that old mechanical reliability of things made in America before silicon chips, even before transistors, like my father used to say, "Back when 'Made in the U.S.A.' and 'quality' and 'dependable' all meant the same thing." My father used to try to make sure everything he bought was made in the U.S.A. He thought, for a long time, anyway, that doing that would make him a better American somehow. More dependable. He drove a Buick. We had a Zenith television. I thought that was really strange when I was little. Nobody else had a Zenith television. But now I understood better. The elevator had that same old solid feel. It reassured me. And we had worked together a lot in off-hours like this, this old elevator and me.

At first when you came out into the basement of the Council, things looked orderly. There was a Xerox machine, which was the one I used any time the one on the fifth floor broke down. And there were metal bookcases with neatly arranged books on them that had numbers hand-lettered on

260

the spines in white ink, which always made me think of the little library at Westfield High School. There was an old furnace over to the right, and the whole place smelled a little like fuel oil.

As you wandered back and to the left of the Xerox machine the junk started to pile up and the order broke down. People had shoved boxes back there full of magazines and pamphlets, then forgotten them. There were a few broken pieces of office furniture that should have been thrown out, but that somebody had decided to keep, then forgotten. There were a lot of old boxes of *Foreign Policy Journal.*

Far in the back of the basement there was a padlocked door to another storeroom. I opened it with a copied key I made the second week I was working for Chantal. An old bare-filament bulb threw spidery shadows inside. Cardboard boxes from moving companies and supermarkets were piled almost up to the low ceiling. Several were open, and you could see they were full of old files and papers, all of them yellowed and dusty, spilling out of boxes that read "Tide" and "Lucky Stars."

The Secret Service had been down here three or four times at least in the last four months, but nothing was disturbed. They would have had to look a lot more closely than they usually did, pulling out all the first and second layers of boxes and getting to the ones right in the middle of the pile, if they were going to find the boxes that counted. But I had bet they wouldn't. And I was right.

There was enough ammonium nitrate in this storeroom to set off an explosion about as big as a five-hundred-pound bomb. The mix was as stable as I could make it. It was wrapped up in plastic so dogs wouldn't pick up the smell, and anyway the stink of the furnace would confuse them. So nobody was going to find it. And all that was required was a detonator, and then this room and the reception room above it and the ones above that, and anybody in them—would be gone.

If things had happened according to the first plan Rashid and I worked out, we would have brought the jihad home to the United States, to midtown Manhattan, right to this cozy little town house full of people who ran the world, sometime in the third or fourth week of November. A few very important people would have been killed, people who knew, and were known to, everybody. The whole government, the whole vast power of America, would have felt it. The jihad would have touched them where they lived.

But the mission was not executed. It had changed a lot, in fact. And that had thrown me off balance.

For quite a while after we arrived separately in the United States, Rashid and I didn't have any direct communication. Basic security precautions dictated that. We sent messages through a cutout who worked near the Council, and I had the impression there might be one or two other people involved who were acquiring and mixing some of the components. But they didn't know me. I didn't know them. The operation was safely compartmentalized, I thought. The mission analysis was holding up just like you want it to. And by mid-October, as far as I was concerned, the operation was a go.

Then at the end of the month Rashid sent word that we were holding off. But there was no explanation. It sounded like an order. And I was not going to accept that. We were going to have to talk.

I had a coded version of Rashid's phone number in my wallet, but I didn't call him to tell him I was coming, and it was after dark when I showed up at the little house where he lived on Ramapo Avenue, a couple of miles from me, on the other side of Jersey City.

He opened the door himself, relaxed as could be. And I didn't like that, either. He was always ready for me, Rashid. I just looked at him. And waited. And studied him. There in the door, standing by himself. Maybe it was his haircut, or his clothes, but he looked different, again. For a second I could have thought he was somebody I never met, just another brown guy on the street. Not even an Arab. A Dominican, maybe.

"Kurt! Come in."

"What's happening, Rashid?"

"Come in," he said. "The plan has changed." He was talking like this was some sort of briefing we were always going to have. Most normal thing in the world.

"I don't get it. What the fuck is going on?"

"One bomb is not enough," said Rashid.

"What do you mean? The bomb we have will do it. And we've got to do it soon."

"We needed something bigger," said Rashid. "And now we have this thing." He was excited. "Ah, Kurt, man, I tell you we are going to change the face of America."

"What thing?"

"We have the Sword, Kurt."

"The sword?"

"Like the Angel of the Lord, we will strike at America," he said.

"We? Is this still our plan? Yours and mine?"

"This is Allah's Plan."

And it was then, and not until then, weeks after we came to the United States, that Rashid told me anything about how the plan—which was not just his and mine anymore—had grown.

"It won't last long. But long enough. It won't kill everybody," he said. "But many."

" 'It' what?" I was tired of this fucking game.

" 'Wholesale death,' like in the Koran—like in the Bible, Kurt. Thousands—maybe hundreds of thousands—will die. 'The sword of the Lord, even the pestilence, in the land, and the angel of the Lord destroying throughout.' "

"What the fuck have you got? What the fuck are you talking about? Hundreds of thousands?"

"But no more than in Bosnia, no more than in Palestine. It will be a great disaster, but then the Americans will know," he said. "Then they will know the kind of pain that you and I have touched."

I looked around the bare room, like that would help bring things in focus. There was a mattress up against the wall with a pile of dirty clothes at one end. A wooden chair in a corner had a fax machine on it. And that was all there was. There was nothing to tell you about Rashid, nothing to tell you what he was doing or planning. I sat down on the mattress against the wall and put my head up against my knees. "Is this some kind of chemical-biological shit?"

Rashid grinned. "This is God's shit," he said.

I was shaking my head. "We aren't aiming at the people who are in control anymore. We are just aiming at the people. A whole lot of innocent people."

Rashid was reaching for something under the pile of dirty clothes.

I watched his hands.

He pulled out—papers. A legal pad. A pencil. "Do you think God does not kill innocent people?" he said, and settled down on the mattress with his own back against the wall, beside me, starting to sketch.

"We have a mission here, Kurt. God's mission, and it is the same like always. Change America. Change the world. Give the real 'innocent people' a chance to live," he said. "Read the Book! This is God's way—and it must be our way." His face was right in mine, close enough to see the veins in his eyes. "Not every man is chosen to deliver God's message," he said. "But I have seen it in you, Kurt. You are chosen."

Like there was nothing else to say, he kept on sketching. And then he stopped. "You are with me," he said. And it wasn't a question.

I thought to myself, No. I felt out of control. And that was the moment to say something—anything—to stop this happening. But I couldn't say the one word. And he accepted that, and went back to his paper. "You are one of God's own," he said, and he was so into what he was doing, and so at ease with it, that he started to pull me along.

Rashid didn't tell me every detail that night, but enough. He wouldn't say where he got this thing that he called the Sword of the Angel. But he gave me an idea of what we would have to build if we were going to use it. And as I thought about it, I thought, technically at least, I could. I asked a few questions. But mainly I just listened, and he went on. It could be done, I thought. But after a while, I was only concentrating in flashes.

The sheer power of the thing was almost irresistible. What we had planned before was just another mission: a quarter ton of well-placed explosives. But this business Rashid told me about now, if we could bring it off, really was like an act of God. And if we succeeded, I thought, that's really what it would be. Because He wouldn't let this happen if He didn't want it.

". . . like in Cazin." The name of the place brought me back to Rashid. "We will make them feel the horror in their guts," he said. "They will feel what they have done."

He was focused on his sketch again. Sometimes he glanced up at me, thinking, filling in details, making notes where I would have to learn more or improvise. He outlined a canister, a cooling agent, an aerosol nozzle. Neither of us had actually said anything for a while when he said, "Everybody has to die sometime."

Every soul shall have a taste of death, I thought. The sin would be if somehow this was all a trick, if somehow God was cut out of the picture. The crime would be if all those people died and somehow nothing changed. But I told myself, again, and over and over, He wouldn't let that happen. I told myself this plan was righteous, and it would work.

And there was something else I told myself: To try this at all, Rashid needs my brain. He needs my skills. If I want to stop this thing I can. I remembered something he had said when we were getting ready to split up in Zagreb and make our separate ways to America. After all those months in the Bosnian war, I was afraid I wouldn't fit into the United States anymore. And he'd just laughed. "You are a dream American," he said. "If you make your anger invisible, then you will be invisible, too." Rashid could not do this thing without me. He needed his invisible man.

Later when doubts did come, like they always do late at night, I would get up and concentrate on building the thing that would make it all possible, knowing that at the end, with God's will behind me, I would make the right and final decision. And in the daytime I worked on being the person I had to be at the Council. And I tried to be patient. But the strain mounted with time.

Now it was almost Christmas. The thing would be finished in a few more weeks. Then all we would have to do was find the right place, and the right time to use it.

I closed the door to the Council storeroom. Nothing had been touched. There was nothing more for me to do down here.

I went upstairs to Chantal's office. Even though I knew she'd gone to Washington for the weekend I half expected her to be there when I opened the door, and when she wasn't I had that feeling you get, that feeling that I always hated, when you come home to a deserted house. I was upset with her for being away. I would be glad when she got back.

Chantal's direct line worked even when the switchboard was shut down. I punched in Selma's number in Kansas, which hadn't changed for as long as I could remember. It rang three times, four, five. I hoped there wasn't going to be an answering machine. It kept ringing. There was no answer at all. I made myself put the phone back onto its cradle slowly and gently. I would have to wait.

If Rashid and I had stuck to the original plan, Chantal might be dead now. She wasn't the target, but if the time had come and she'd been in the reception room there wouldn't have been any way to warn her. Maybe she would be lucky, maybe not. God's will would determine that, and for a long time I thought I wouldn't really care. But after Rashid put the idea in my head of a bigger attack—so much bigger—I saw that the bomb here wouldn't really have much effect. Rashid had convinced me the Council was the secret center of American power, the epicenter of the evil. But he was wrong about that. The Council didn't count for so much in the great scheme of things. I knew that now. I guessed he did, too. Which was why the mission changed. But if he was wrong like that once, he could be again. Chantal might have died for nothing. Just—nothing. I didn't like that idea.

"Rashid, you son of a bitch," I said to the empty room, "don't hold off too long." Sometimes I could feel the rage dying, and that scared me. The longer a mission is, the more it changes in mid-course, the more you get numb, the more you get confused. I had to be sure I was listening to God, not just Rashid—and not to these people here, either. I never should have stayed at the Council so long, I thought. I shouldn't have gotten to know these people the way I did, shouldn't have gotten confused by them.

I tried Selma again. Then again and again. And I never did get her that night.

XXIII

There were a lot of cancellations for the seminar on Technology and Terrorism. Chantal thought it was an important subject, but in New York City and Washington it didn't seem like a big issue. People at the Council were taking a look at all the little wars going on all over the world, but they couldn't make any connections. It's easy to forget, now, that the word, the issue, the idea of "terrorism" sounded, in January of 1993, like an eighties thing. America felt so safe, so smug. The people who did show up for the seminar were spinning out ideas about patterns in the past and the future that seemed, even to them, theoretical.

As she looked over her notes and the papers submitted, Chantal was disappointed. "They're blind," she said. "It will all come back," she said. "But then it will be too late."

"Are those ready to copy?"

"Yeah, for whatever they're worth."

As I read them I felt a little bit the way I used to in night combat when we were wearing night-vision devices. You saw people groping, sensing, feeling what was around them, but they couldn't be sure. They knew the threat was out there. They knew that *I* was out there, but they didn't know where.

And yet there were things to be learned from these experts. Things to remember. One analyst named Carlton Eames, who had been at the Rand Corporation and now worked for a private security company, made an interesting connection between individual fighters—he called them terrorists, of course—and weapons of mass destruction. Chemical and biological agents were already within the reach of some terrorist organizations, he said, especially those hooked up with "state sponsors" like Iran and Libya and Iraq. "But there are constraints on state sponsors and on 'traditional' terrorist groups that have kept them from employing such devices," he wrote. They were trying to build political movements. They had "constituencies," or thought they did. And that made them, basically, very conservative. "They use tried and true methods," said Eames, by which he meant assault rifles and Semtex. "State-sponsored terrorism is more cautious still," he wrote, "because to be caught means to risk retaliation against the state itself."

Chantal had scrawled something in the margin here: "What if the state's got nothing to lose?"

Eames thought the big threat would come from "individual extremists" who didn't have to worry about holding a group together. "These are the ones who threaten water supplies, carry out product extortion, and who have tried to use biological and chemical weapons," he said. "In 1972 two men tried to poison the entire water supply of Chicago using a strain of typhus. Their idea was to start a new master race, with themselves as the primogenitors."

"Founding fathers!" Chantal had written. She hadn't lost her sense of humor completely.

A former head of Lebanese intelligence named George Samiyya, who now had an office in Virginia called Risk Assessment Limited Inc., submitted a paper with the theme "Knowledge kills action." Governments were sucking up electronic information like a vacuum cleaner, he said. But they never quite knew what they had. "Governments increasingly rely on high-technology means for intelligence, security, maintaining law and order. But most of these means work in simplex mode: I can hear you, but I can't talk to you. So communication becomes weaker and the human factor plays a diminished role. In the age of electronic intelligence, intentions have become harder to fathom."

Chantal had scribbled in the margin of this paper, too: "You can tell what Saddam *can* do, but you can't tell what he *wants* to do." I used some Wite-Out to erase her comments before I made the copies.

When I went back to Chantal's office she was out, but she'd stuck a Post-it message for me on her door: "Selma called."

There was hardly half a ring before the phone was picked up in Kansas. A man's voice. "Hello."

"Hello, Dave," I said. "How's it going?"

"Can't complain. Can't complain at all. Doing the Lord's work. Guess you know about that."

"Glad to hear it," I answered, not paying very much attention to what he said.

"How's the weather in Jew York City?"

There was nothing that Dave said or did that didn't make my flesh crawl. "Oh, bad. Rain, sleet, snow, slush."

"Thought so. I hear big storms are on the way."

"Yeah? I guess."

"Yeah."

"Selma there?"

"Yeah. I'll put her on." His voice got fainter as he turned away from the phone. "Selma, your baby brother is on the phone."

"Kurt?" Her voice now. "Kurt, honey, how you doing?"

"I just wanted to know how *you* were doing."

"We are doing just fine, Kurt. Just fine."

For three weeks, ever since Christmas, we'd been having the same basic conversation. And it didn't matter whether Dave was there, she always had the same line. Everything was going fine, just fine. Dave was working hard. She wasn't sure exactly what he was doing with this new job, but he was making money. The church was giving him a regular income now, too. And he was treating her real good.

"Why did you call, Selma?"

"Just getting used to hearing your voice, I guess."

If Selma wouldn't tell me what was going on, there was nothing I could do for her. Just nothing. "Well, I guess I better do some work," I said.

Selma lowered her voice. "Dave wanted me to call you."

"I don't get it."

"Well, everything's fine here," she said, a little bit louder. I heard the sound of Dave's voice in the background, but not the words. "Got to go," she said, and hung up.

Chantal opened the door to her office as I put down the phone. "Was that Selma?" she said.

"Yeah."

"Um, Kurt, I know it's important for you to talk to her. But I got a note from Stella Perkins in Accounting asking why I was calling Kansas all the time."

"Look, I won't call from here anymore. Okay? I thought it was all right, but if it's not, okay. I got to go get some lunch."

She was pissing me off, which is probably why I didn't think more, right then, about that phone call. It just seemed like more Westfield weirdness I couldn't do anything about.

"Kurt?"

"Yeah?"

"Are you coming over for dinner?"

Couldn't let the tension take control. "Yes," I said, and made myself smile, and pushed the door closed for just a second so people in the hall wouldn't see or hear. "Dinner and breakfast," I said.

The winter sun was already fading. The air was so cold it burned your lungs, and each step I took, my pace picked up. By the time I got to Better Bagels over on Third Avenue, I felt alive again, and hungry.

It was late for lunch, and there was only a short line. But there was only one man working behind the counter, and just before he got to me, he disappeared into the back. "Can you believe this guy?" said a fat woman standing behind me. She stamped her foot and her whole body shook a little. But he reappeared after just a few seconds. "I wonder if he washed his hands," the woman said under her breath.

"The usual," I told the man behind the counter, "plus two plain and two raisin cinnamon for breakfast tomorrow." He sliced a bagel in half and dropped it in the toaster. I tried not to look at the woman behind me while I waited. "Coffee," she said, "and a chocolate chip cookie." He seemed to ignore her. "Did you hear me?" she demanded. He looked at her with a perfectly blank expression, then held up a cookie so she could see it. "I'd like it now," she said. "Don't you speak?"

"*Sharmuta*," he said with a wide smile. It was the Arabic word for whore.

"No one in this town speaks English anymore," she said, and took her cookie and coffee and left.

My bagel popped out of the toaster. He spread cream cheese on it, dropped it and the others in a white paper sack, and handed it to me. I ate slowly as I walked back to the Council, and it wasn't until I was finished that I looked for the note lying at the bottom of the bag. It read "Shawwal 12–18. Madison Square Garden. 'We send not angels down except for just cause; if they came to the ungodly, Behold! No respite would they have!' Surah 15:8."

"Yes!" I shouted out loud, then looked around to see if anyone noticed. One old man was looking at me, but he probably thought I won a free Coke with a scratch card. The mission was on.

Then I calculated the conversion from the Islamic dates to American ones. There was still a wait of almost three months. I tried to think why, but couldn't come up with an answer. A terrible feeling of disappointment closed in on me as I walked past the entrance to Lewis College, then over to Park.

I remember the wind was coming really hard down the avenue. The cold was inside my coat, inside my skin and my guts. And I think it was probably then, fighting the cold and the wind, trying to think of nothing, trying to just focus again on what I needed to do to get the job done, trying to make everything fit in my mind—the timing, the place, the wait, the weapon—that I first began to think Rashid might betray me. I tried to push the idea down, but it wouldn't go away. Why did I suspect him? Because he had taken our plan, the one that brought me back to this place and these people, and he had done away with it. Because he had brought in other people. I was sure there were more— maybe many more—than I knew. He had made everything so complicated when it needed to be so simple. When it *was* so simple. Was he working for somebody else? Was I working for him? That was never the way it was supposed to be. With the messages, and the cutouts, and the changes in plan, he had made me, his friend, just another soldier in his organization. And I did not want to be just another soldier, not anymore. Not in this man's army. Not in any man's army.

"You are not God, Rashid," I whispered.

XXIV

The Sword of the Angel was sitting in a freezer in the Biology Department over at Lewis College, just a couple of blocks from the Council, between Lexington and Third. It was stored in a tightly sealed vial with a grease-pencil scrawl across the top that read "No Touch—Aziz Helmy." I guess you would never have noticed it one way or another among the other test tubes, bottles, and vials. You would never imagine, if you opened it by accident, what kind of catastrophe you'd just released.

That would come a couple of weeks later. A blinding fever would burn through your body. Your skin would be covered with craters and pus. And panic would be spreading through America. Thousands of others, eventually hundreds of thousands, would be suffering the same hell. They would fill the wards of hospitals and horrified doctors would see—and not believe what they were seeing—for the first time in their lives: an epidemic of smallpox.

The disease wasn't supposed to exist anymore. At least not here. Not like this. If you looked it up in the encyclopedia, or on the Net the way I did, you'd find the World Health Organization declared it was officially eliminated as of 1980. The last known case "in the wild" was in Somalia in 1977. The last case anywhere was a woman photographer in Birmingham, England, in 1978, who was working near a secure lab that just wasn't as secure as people thought. After that, there was a big effort to round up all known quantities of the virus.

Smallpox was supposed to exist now in exactly two and only two places: at the Russian State Research Center for Virology and Biotechnology in Koltsovo, Novosibirsk— and in Atlanta, Georgia, in a silver-and-blue refrigerator wrapped with a chain, padlocked, and sealed with duct tape inside Room 318B of the Centers for Disease Control. Someday the Russians and Americans would get together and destroy the six hundred beakers of the virus that they had. Then they would declare mankind's triumph over a terrible disease, a victory of science over nature for the betterment of all. They would have played God, and won.

At least, that was the official story. But nobody in the military, American or Russian, really believed it. On the list of viruses tested as biological agents, smallpox was always near the top. And if somebody kept a few test tubes hidden away in his freezer, how would you know? The Americans didn't trust the Russians. The Russians didn't trust the Americans. And nobody could really be sure there wasn't some other country—China, maybe, or Iran or Iraq, or Libya—or just some researcher, that kept a few bottles of the stuff around. Sure, they had all told the United Nations they had no supplies. But who told the truth to the United Nations? So American soldiers were still vaccinated against smallpox more than ten years after it "ceased to exist in the wild" on the chance it still existed in weapons. And even though biological warfare supposedly was banned, and even though the experts at Fort Detrick, Maryland, insisted smallpox wasn't very good for battlefield use—too slow, too easily stopped with vaccine—the scientists were still finding ways to refine it and to improve its killing potential. They were fooling around with its DNA, rearranging the genetic codes. In fact, one reason the American and Russian governments said they were keeping the stocks they had was to find out more about its molecular structure—like that was all just an academic thing.

But if you believed the news stories, even the most

basic form of smallpox scared the hell out of epidemic specialists. Before the first vaccine was discovered in 1790, the disease used to kill as many as 600,000 people a year in Europe. In America, smallpox did a hell of a lot more than soldiers did to conquer the natives. They had no immunity at all, and it just about wiped them out. Even as late as the 1970s, if you weren't vaccinated, you were history. In 1974, an outbreak of smallpox in India killed more than 10,000 people in a single month. Without vaccination, no one is spared, not "from Pharaoh to the maidservant that is behind the mill," as the Bible said. And the world is getting more vulnerable all the time. The virus is living history, just waiting to take its revenge, and you never know where it will be found. In 1985 there was a panic in London when archaeologists digging under an old church found bodies of smallpox victims from a century ago. If there was even the slightest trace of the virus, the whole horror could have started again.

Personally, because I was a soldier and had years of shots and booster shots, I'm probably immune. But civilians today aren't so lucky. Their vaccinations stopped in the 1970s. Their natural resistance is going down, too, especially in cities where they never come in contact with milder animal versions of the virus, like cowpox, that could give them some immunity. And the biggest risk is for the children. Chances are anyone under twenty has never been vaccinated at all.

Smallpox spreads through the air and through simple contact. A handshake, a kiss, a breath, can be enough. If you release droplets containing the virus in a closed space, like a movie theater or a sports stadium, the effects will be huge, and the fact that the effects are delayed makes them worse. You don't know anything has happened. No one will know what has gone on until after the first outbreak occurs twelve to sixteen days later and by then the disease will be all over the map. Inoculation programs could begin again fairly quickly. There are still some reserves of vaccine. But no specific treatment was ever developed for those who actually get the disease. About thirty percent of the people hit by the first wave of the epidemic will die. Many, many others will be left blind or scarred for life. The effects will stare the world in the face for a generation. And to make all that happen, all you have to do is take the virus in a liquid—the same twenty-percent glycerol solution in which it's normally kept—and spray it in the air.

Aziz, who worked behind the counter at Better Bagels to help pay his way through graduate school, did the actual handling of the virus at the Lewis College biology lab. Except for the days when we traded messages, Aziz and I didn't have any contact. But at the chosen time, I was supposed to take him the device. He would load it at some point when he could work in the lab alone, then give it back to me. I would arm it and place it.

When I first started work on the device, I thought there would be a lot of technical problems. But one of the great advantages of smallpox, I discovered, is that it is really easy to store. It's not like herpes or AIDS, which have to be kept super-cooled. Smallpox can be kept at household freezer temperature. When it thaws, it's active. Then all you have to do is spray it.

In December I made up a list of potential targets, not all of them in New York, and passed it on to Rashid. If I was going to be part of this thing, I wanted to be part of the planning, not just the execution. And the way I figured it we wanted the epidemic to be traced back to a place and a time that was important, that would send a clear message about American greed and blindness. But we wanted to create some confusion, too. It would be good if the American government could be blamed for the disaster, at least at first.

One place on my list was the World Trade Center. It was close and it was full of weird government offices, including the Secret Service, and we could release the virus through the ventilation system. But there were some technical problems with that. I was afraid we would lose too much in the ducting. Another possibility was the United Nations. So was the Capitol in Washington. But those were targets where security was fairly heavy already, and the chance of discovery that much higher. Las Vegas and Atlantic City were also on the list. Any one of the casinos with a big show could work, and the message of the plague would be about sin as much as about suffering. I thought Rashid would like that, and Atlantic City was convenient. But the two top sites on my list were farther south.

The U.S. Army Bio-Medical Research Center and the Armed Forces Medical Intelligence Center are at Fort Detrick in Frederick, Maryland, about forty-five miles outside Washington, D.C. Frederick is a small, quiet city with movie theaters and sports facilities and lots of malls, and you wouldn't need to get inside the fort to do the job. Any site in the vicinity would be effective, and once the plague was traced to the area, there would be hell to pay.

The other site that interested me was the Centers for Disease Control in Atlanta. If we released the virus anywhere nearby, then when the outbreak came and was traced in that direction, the whole CDC operation would come under suspicion. "How'd they let that virus leak?" people would wonder. There would be a lot of suspicions. And that would make it harder to take countermeasures. Better still for targeting purposes, Atlanta was a hub, with people flying in and out from all over the world.

But Rashid had picked the Garden, inside Penn Station. It was easy to get to. A closed space with big crowds that would fan out in a thousand different directions and travel all over the country. It was practical. But it didn't really seem like the right choice. At least not to me.

The dates Rashid gave covered the week from Monday, April 5, to Sunday, April 11. When I looked at a calendar I saw why. The Old Testament and the Koran told all about it. It was the time when the Lord brought wholesale death to Pharaoh and his people. The Jews called it Passover.

By early February I figured the device itself was about as good as I could make it. It had to be simple. What I wanted was something that could be hidden in plain sight. After a fair amount of experimenting with different parts and pieces, from Windex bottles to fuel injectors from junked cars, I managed to find the right nozzle. The container had to be able to hold a full liter of liquid, and keep it insulated for several hours. The tubing from the bottle to the nozzle had to seal perfectly, so no virus would escape until the precise moment when we wanted it to. There was a lot going on inside it. But the device, when it was finished, could not have looked more ordinary. In fact, it looked just like what it was: a fire extinguisher. Nobody would pay attention to it when they saw it. Nobody, looking right at it, would suspect what it hid. If it was a little out of the way, nobody would notice when it did its thing. And nobody would notice when it was removed again.

I notified Rashid on February 7 that Judgment Day would be inside the parameters he gave me, on April 10. And on February 8 I moved out of my Jersey City apartment. The room would be cleaned up and I would be forgotten there long before anything happened. I took the extinguisher itself to the Council, and left it in the storeroom in the basement. And I moved in with Chantal.

I had spent nights at her apartment before. I even knew the super, a Pole named Kantrowicz who winked at me every time I saw him. I didn't think of the place as home, of course. But I might have. Chantal wanted me to. And there were times early in the morning waking up next to her when the whole feel of her and her place would get to me with its comfort, and it would take me awhile to remember just why I was there, and what I was about.

Those were real moments of weakness, and they scared me. I would get up, no matter how early it was, long before the first light of the New York dawn, and go down to the park and run around the Reservoir, and then north toward Harlem, looking for a place in the park, looking for a place in myself, where I could pray. Sometimes I carried my father's Koran with me. It was my book of faith and now, too, my book of memories. I had his U.S. Army ID in there, and mine. There was a picture of my mother when she was a little girl in Zagreb. There was a label from a Panama beer bottle, which seemed like a strange thing to put in a Koran, but which reminded me of Jenkins. There was a thin blade of grass, which was green when I first put it there. It came from Josie's place and I thought about throwing it away, but I used it so much as a marker that it seemed like it was almost part of the book, and I just kept it. The grains of sand that worked their way in between the pages and the binding during my time in the Gulf were accidental, of course. But I was glad they were there. They made me think of Rashid walking down that gruesome highway through the dunes when the war was over in Kuwait. The picture of the imam's little daughter that Rashid gave me still marked the beginning of the third surah. I didn't look at it that much. I couldn't. But for a long time, just knowing it was there was all it took to make the anger in me burn a little hotter.

When I first started thinking hard about the scale of death we were about to cause, all this helped. What had brought me here to do this thing? God had willed it. That was why I had these skills, this intelligence, this spirit inside me. It was a design written in the book—in this book that my father had.

I need to see the thing itself.

Aziz Helmy read the note I handed him inside a five-dollar bill, then crumpled it up as he went over to the cash register. He shook his head.

"Today," I said out loud.

He shook his head again and I walked out, but only as far as a diner down the street. I bought a cup of coffee to ward off the February chill, and waited. Aziz got off the morning shift and headed back toward Lewis College. I followed him. He was thinking hard about something, paying no attention to who was around him. A bicycle messenger almost creamed him when he stepped out on Third Avenue. He didn't know I was there until he was walking toward the security guard at the entrance to the biology building.

"Stay cool," I said.

"No!"

"Stay cool," I said, and before he knew it I passed him and I was talking to the guard, an old man with tired blue eyes who looked like he'd been living in his uniform and at that desk for about a century. "Excuse me, sir. I've just got to pick up something from my friend's office," I said, pointing over my shoulder at Aziz. "I'll be back down in two minutes. You want me to sign in?" The guard looked at me. He didn't say anything. He just sort of waved his hand, like I figured he would. I got in the elevator.

The door closed and Aziz turned on me. "You are crazy?" he said, shoving me with both hands. I didn't move. He backed off.

"Chill out," I said. "All I want is to see whatever you keep the stuff in."

"I gave you measurements."

"Yeah, sort of. But I want a picture of the thing in my head. It's got to fit just right."

I could tell he thought I was lying. In fact I wanted to make sure this whole operation was real. I couldn't see the virus, of course. But at least I wanted to see the thing that held it.

It was February 19. We were Judgment Day minus fifty. As long as I was working on the device and the plan, I was able to keep my focus. But now that I was left waiting again —just holding on for that chosen moment—questions started coming up at me like shadows from the deep. And I couldn't respond to them, and couldn't drive them away.

Where did the virus come from? Rashid did not and

would not say. I was hoping Aziz would have the answer. I had a notion he was not only the keeper, but also the source.

"Let's not make this take too long," I told him as the elevator opened.

"Okay, okay," he said, finally, and led me down a hall with dirty green walls and blue-white fluorescent lights. There was trash and graffiti, almost like on the streets outside. A lot of the bulbs were dead, so there were shadows, too. We stopped at a door with a red-and-white warning sign on it. "If there's anybody around, you have to leave," said Aziz, but there was nobody. We walked down another short hallway. The labs didn't look like much. They could have been for a high school chemistry class. I figured I'd pop the question about where the virus came from when we were looking right at the bottle.

Aziz unlocked another door with a red-and-white warning sign on it and a red lightbulb above it. We went inside a small changing room. There were doctors' smocks and a stack of paper masks and paper hats, but he ignored them and opened the second door. "We're just going to look at it, not handle it," he said. "Don't worry about scrubbing." We passed through and turned into a cramped little room. "I keep it in this freezer over here."

There were shelves on each side of us with bottles and beakers. I got a little edgy just looking at them. I tried to look over Aziz's shoulder, but couldn't see exactly what he was doing as he twisted the combination locks and swung up the heavy door. "There," he said, stepping to one side so I could see the simple vial with a grease-pencil label.

"That's it?"

"It is enough," said Aziz. "It is more than enough."

"But where did it come from?"

"Ask Rashid. He brought it."

"You don't know where he got it?"

"I do not, and I don't ask," he said, making a point with his tone. "Have you seen enough?"

"How do you know it is what it's supposed to be?"

"It's my job," he said. "I know."

I studied the bottle for a few more seconds. It looked like it would fit in the extinguisher just fine. Aziz closed the door of the freezer, twisted past me, and started to lead the way back out. I turned for a last look, and for just a second I couldn't think where I had seen a door like that before, with the locks and the heavy insulation. And the label that read "Revco." Then that memory came back to me, and I didn't need to ask, any longer, where the virus was from.

XXV

"Ahhhhhh, shit," she said.

The dream, whatever it was, evaporated and I opened my eyes one at a time. The white walls of the little apartment were gray with the dim light leaking through the blinds. I buried my face in the warmth of her neck and her shoulder. "Ah shit what?" I put my arm around her waist and pulled her closer to me until I could feel the smoothness of her back against my chest, and then I pulled her even closer and could feel her with all of me.

"It's raining," she said.

I had overslept. Now still half asleep, with my eyes still closed, I remembered her with my fingers, running them along her breasts and the delicate roughness of her nipples, the flesh over her ribs, the curve of her waist. I breathed her in. And then I woke up a little more.

"It's raining?" I looked around again at the windows. All the blinds were drawn. I listened for the rattle of raindrops. I didn't hear anything. "How do you know it's raining?"

"Maybe snowing," she said.

"But how do you know?"

She rolled over, wrestling a little with the sheets and with me, until she was facing me, so close my vision was lost in the shadows of her eyes. "I can hear the whistles of the doormen calling taxis on Park Avenue," she said.

284

I listened again. And the whistles reached me, and once I'd heard them, they were loud and clear.

With full consciousness came a chill. "It's going to be a long day," I said, climbing quickly out of bed. "I wonder what time George is going to get into the office."

"He'll be there by the time we get there. Why?"

"Can't hear you," I said from the bathroom as I brushed my teeth. I looked at my face in the mirror. My eyes were tired and bloodshot and the blue in them stood out like the lens of a searchlight. I couldn't see into them, so I just closed them again.

George was only one of my worries today. The other was Rashid. He had sent word that he wanted to see me. It was still almost six weeks until we were supposed to act. Was he going to move up the schedule? Or was there something else? We had been months with no direct contact, and now this. Aziz must have told him about my visit. Maybe Rashid just wanted me to reaffirm my commitment. Or to check on details of the plan. I'd have to wait and see.

Truth to tell, I didn't know what I was going to say to him. When I saw the door of that freezer at Lewis College, pieces of information and memory had started to fall into place as precisely as the tumblers in its locks. The door on that freezer was almost exactly like the one in the beach cottage near Kuwait City I saw that first night that I met Rashid. The little fat man who was with him tried to open it and Rashid blew him away. He said he'd killed the man for risking all our lives to get his own personal fortune out of there. But we didn't know that. We didn't know what was in that safe. All we knew was what Rashid told us. Shit. Then I was supposed to blast it open. If the virus was inside, the blast might have destroyed the virus. *Might.* But I was good at my job. If my charges were right—just right—they wouldn't have cracked an egg inside that thing. And if they were a little wrong, they wouldn't have cooked the virus. They would have released it. As it was, we never found out what the hell was in there. We had to fall back before we could get it open. And then we'd spent that night on the highway of death, and Jenkins was killed, and I hadn't thought about that safe again until this week.

What did it mean if that was where Rashid got our terrible sword? I wasn't sure. Why would he have taken us there, then? Who was he working for? Not the Kuwaitis. Not the Americans.

Chantal was right. I didn't want her to be. But it all fell into place if you knew what she knew, and what I knew, now, about Saddam. He had chemical and biological weapons. And he'd had a program going to develop them since the early 1970s. Like his secret nukes, these weapons were real important to him. Would he have let his scientists destroy the smallpox virus in their arsenal? Would he have turned it over to the World Health Organization? There was no way. He'd have kept it. And in the Gulf War he'd have used it if he could have found a way that wouldn't give him away. Smallpox would be perfect. It might not hurt a lot of the soldiers, but it would devastate the Kuwaitis coming back. He had burned their oil wells, covered their land with fire and smoke, and now he would slaughter and scar their children. And in the chaos of the war, who could say how the plague had started?

But that hadn't happened. Something had gone wrong. Maybe Saddam's governor had left too quickly to carry out the plan. Maybe it all fell apart because of some technical fuckup. The combination locks on the freezer were almost impossible to turn because of the corrosion. Maybe they couldn't get the freezer open, and maybe they were afraid to blast it. I would have been, if I'd known what was inside. Maybe they were scared away by the SEALS who tried to hit the place a few nights before us. Who knew? I didn't. But Rashid and the fat man had known something. That was for sure. And the fat man was dead, and Rashid—

Who was Rashid? He was my friend, I thought. He had protected me. We had traveled together and talked together and shared our secrets. Or at least I'd shared mine. He had listened for hours in late Bosnian dawns about my family, and even my fears. He had risked his life, and he had saved my life. He was my teacher. When I was desperate and lost, he had helped me learn to have faith. He brought me closer to God than I ever imagined I could be. He had shown me the path. And we walked down it together. And now I was doubting him. And doubting him bad.

I thought about all of Chantal's conspiracy theories about Saddam and vengeance and terrorism; about him trading Palestinian terrorists for what she called "Islamist" terrorists. And I knew Rashid fit the profile. He was half Palestinian *and* he was working with the mujahedin. When I met him he could easily have been working for Saddam in Kuwait as a double agent, then helping build new networks in Afghanistan and Bosnia—

No. It was too much. There were no facts here. Just suspicions. This plan of ours was as much mine as his, at least at the beginning.

"Shaving with your eyes closed?" said Chantal, standing just behind me. I stiffened at the feel of her hand on my shoulder, and nicked my lip with the razor. Suddenly I hated her for that, and for all her ideas and theories, and because I couldn't tell her I hated her. I couldn't tell her anything about what had happened. I couldn't tell anyone at all.

"I got to get out of here," I said, rinsing my face.

"See you at the office."

"Yeah."

"Let me know how it goes."

The day before, George Carruthers had taken me to his club for lunch. It was late and we were the last ones served after waiting and drinking—he drank martinis, I had iced tea—for more than an hour. His talk was sometimes slow, sometimes intense, many times interesting, but mainly it was steady. He wouldn't let me say a word. By the time we sat down to lunch, my bladder was full. But he talked, we ordered, he talked, we ate, and he kept on telling me about the politics of Europe and the Middle East and the friends he'd had and the people who betrayed him in the Agency, and the people who were loyal, with little stories and sidelights along the way about kinky German princes and drunken Saudi kings and twisted Croatian Nazis.

One of his few real regrets, he said, was about something that happened almost fifty years ago when he was on the Balkan desk of the OSS. The United States at the end of World War II was desperate for agents to help it fight Communism. And in those days, before Tito and Stalin parted ways, Tito was as good a target as any. So the Americans tried to co-opt fascist officers into their anti-Communist networks, and in the process there were terrible criminals who not only went free, but came to live in America. They were given homes, and new identities, sort of like witness protection for war criminals. And, partly as a result, there were Croatian terrorists murdering people in America as late as the 1970s. But no one remembered that. "Lucky thing." It was all kept quiet—and when bits and pieces of the story leaked it seemed too incredible, too complicated to explore. Who knew who Croatians were in 1948? Or in 1978?

He didn't let me answer. He didn't even pause. "It's not that we didn't interrogate them or that we didn't know who they were. It was just a bad evaluation of what they'd be worth. And, well, you make mistakes." He sipped his drink, but still didn't give me any time to reply. "You make mistakes. But I'll tell you one sure way to judge a man. The Hohenstaufens used to swear by it." He was looking at the way I was holding myself. "And Assad still uses it in Syria. 'You can judge a man's mettle,' so the truism goes, 'by how long he can hold his water.'"

I excused myself on that cue. And when I came back I saw what I had not noticed before, that the whole dining room was empty. The tables had all been cleared but the white cloths were still on them. And George sat there alone at our table, with his back to the room, smoking his pipe, isolated, unlike other men, I thought.

"We were talking about the Croats in America," I said.

"Were we? Oh, yes. Well, more on that some other time. I must be getting back to the office. I've already taken care of the check."

It wasn't just that Carruthers had planted a terrible idea in my head. I had to wonder if he meant to. You could never be sure with him. The games he used to play in the Agency for his work, he played with his acquaintances now for his amusement. What did he think? That my father was some Croatian war criminal relocated to America by the U.S. Army? I told him my folks were from Zagreb, so maybe that was what he thought. He was probing, that was all, trying to get under my skin. But my father was a Muslim, so that wasn't very likely. If my father was a Muslim.

The closer I got to sleep that night, the bigger the questions grew in my head. What had I learned about my father, or my family, in Drvar and Ljeska Župica? Nothing. Nobody ever heard of them. But if he wasn't a Muslim, why the Koran? I couldn't know—and there was nobody to ask, really. And probably George couldn't tell me. But I couldn't just let the matter drop. I had to know more.

I found him this morning in his office, surrounded by books stacked in high, unsteady piles on each side of his easy chair. We talked about different things. I can't even remember the subjects now. And finally I got around to what I had on my mind. "Were there any Muslims given asylum in the United States?"

"Oh, yes, I'm afraid there were. I suppose all of them are dead now, or as good as. Just as well. They were some of the worst of the lot."

"What do you mean?"

"What do I mean, Kurt? The SS Handjar Division. It is famous, really. Or should I say infamous? You should have read your history. It was made up entirely of Muslim troops."

"Muslim Nazis?"

"Why not? But, you know, I think they had doubts themselves. So to prove their loyalty, they were more brutal than anyone. And that, my man, is saying something. Their behavior was so ghastly they embarrassed even the Germans and Italians. Hundreds of thousands of people, mainly Serbs, but also Jews and Gypsies, slaughtered, and the Handjar were right at the head of the pack, swinging the bats, shoving the children off cliffs. What a blood-soaked mess that country was, and is. Anyway, after the war I think we got a few of them, too."

"Do you remember any names?"

"Not yours, if that's what you mean."

"No, no. I'm not worried about that. I mean—" I couldn't think what to say. There was a lot of traffic on the avenue. An awful lot. Horns blaring. People shouting. The noise was really getting to me. "—I mean, they couldn't have been religious Muslims."

"Why not? Some connections with the Mufti in Jerusalem, as I recall. But possibly that was more politics than God. I think the only time most of them looked at the Koran was to use it as a code book."

The sound of sirens in the streets was going crazy, rushing through the closed windows and stacks of books in George's office, invading it with panic. George stood up and looked out.

"Gridlocks as far as you can see," he said. And it was just then that a secretary stuck her head in the office door.

"Someone just blew up the World Trade Center," she said.

I could barely move. Shock filled my gut with blood and my face and hands tingled for lack of it.

"How many people hurt?" said George.

"A lot. But nobody knows yet. It's terrible. Just terrible."

George was paying no attention to me, now, as he turned on his little radio, tuning in his favorite news station.

"Excuse me," I said. "I've got to go make some calls, check on some friends who work down there."

I walked straight down the stairs and out onto Park Avenue, then around the corner. A radio limousine with tinted windows was waiting there. I got in the front seat. Rashid was at the wheel. "We have brought the fire," he said, and he looked more excited, more happy, than I'd ever seen him. "Now the flood," he said, "and the plague."

No words formed in my throat, and if they did, I was afraid somehow they'd betray me. Everywhere I turned I was betrayed. I wanted to think. I needed to think. But my mind was flat-lining. Rashid was sitting right in front of me. There was so much I needed him to tell me.

"I'm leaving tonight," he said.

"Leaving? The country?"

"Leaving."

"I—you never told me—the Trade Center."

"I was protecting that operation, and ours," he said.

"*Ours,*" I repeated.

"Ours." He smiled.

"What now?"

"The same as before. Aziz says everything is ready. So wait. Then move when the time comes. Nothing can stand against Allah's plan." He reached over and shook my hand, and held it. He must have felt how cold it was. "*Maasalama,*" he said. I got out of the car and almost tripped on the curb. I had enough sense not to stand and stare as he inched into the gridlock. I went back into the Council.

"My God, Kurt. Oh, my God," said Chantal the second she saw me upstairs. "Do you know what today is?"

"What?"

"Two years ago today, Saddam Hussein's army was defeated in Kuwait. Two years ago today. Don't you think that means something?"

V

Sustainer
of the Worlds

*Let me fall now into the hand of
the Lord; for very great are his
mercies: but let me not fall into
the hand of man.*

—*I Chronicles* 21:13

*When I get to hell, Satan's gonna
   say,
"How'd you earn your living?
   How'd you earn your pay?"
I will reply with a fist to his face,
"Made my living laying souls to
   waste."*

—*Running cadence for
   U.S. Army Airborne Rangers*

XXVI

We were Judgment Day minus one.

In the middle of the park, in the minutes right before dawn, I faced to the south and east and cleared my mind for prayer. My face and scalp were wet from my ablutions, and the air was chilly and fresh. The branches of the trees, bare as skeletons a week before, were just beginning to blur with life, and the wood around me smelled green. The silhouettes of skyscrapers loomed like palisades beyond the treetops. Ah, God, I thought, it is good to be alive. "Praise be to Allah," I thought. "Cherisher and Sustainer of the Worlds." The words filled me with the spirit and brought a smile to my face. "Most Gracious, Most Merciful, Master of the Day of Judgment." I said the line again and let my mind go still, and then I said my prayers the way I always should have.

That day, in that early, early morning mist as I ran the circuit around the Reservoir after my prayers, I felt like a man who's been in a dungeon and steps into the light. It was the feeling I'd been looking for all my life. And it was crazy that it would happen this way. But it had. In a single February afternoon everything that I believed was *me* was dismantled, betrayed, destroyed. It was like my father and my mother died all over again, and I did, too, and I mourned like I never mourned before. There were a couple of days after that when I was so rattled, so depressed, I look back and wonder why Chantal didn't have me carted away. But she didn't. She listened. And when I could think at all, I was

295

just amazed. She didn't give me any advice. She didn't make any judgment. She just heard me. And it was like being on the bottom of the ocean and seeing, way up there, the thin sheet of silver where the air meets the water. And knowing you're never going to get there. And then one day you do. You break through to the sun and the air. And I had.

But even when I was mourning there were things I did not say. I told Chantal a lot about my father and my mother, about my spirit and my experience with Islam. I thought she'd be horrified, but she wasn't. And I told her about my mother's cousin the nun and my father's empty village in Bosnia—if that was his village. And Chantal might have asked a lot of questions about why I didn't tell her any of this before, but she didn't. It was like she knew it or guessed it, although she said she hadn't. And finally I told her what George had told me about the Handjar. And then there was a minute when she did look almost disgusted, and I pulled away from her. I could see her fighting to control herself. "You don't know that any of that is true," she said. "And even if it is, what your father was is not what you are." I'm not sure she believed what she was saying, or that I did. It was what I wanted and needed to hear, though, and I trusted Chantal even more for saying it. But I did not tell her anything about Rashid. Nothing about any of that.

My business with Rashid, who fooled me and used me, and fucked me up like I was never fucked up before—my business with Rashid was something I was going to settle on my own time. I'd find him someplace. And however I did it, I figured it would be better if Chantal didn't know.

I would have liked to tell her what I'd figured out about Iraq and Saddam. About how right she was. There was no doubt in my mind that Rashid was working for Saddam and, what I hadn't known before, I was, too. I even felt a little guilty about keeping that from her. But anyway, I did. I said nothing about the Sword of the Angel. And nothing about Judgment Day. I was going to take care of that myself.

I ran south from the Reservoir now, down East Drive behind the Metropolitan Museum. There were a couple of places along that run, I knew, where I could catch a glimpse of Chantal's window in the distance. It was not quite six-fifteen in the morning, but the lights were on. It was really early for her to be up. I guessed I wasn't as quiet as I thought when I went out the door. At Seventy-second Street I cut out of the park and headed toward Third Avenue. By precisely six-fifteen I was on the corner near the bagel shop, hanging back a little.

Aziz had had the extinguisher for three days. He'd had plenty of time to load the virus. The actual operation shouldn't have taken more than a few minutes. According to plan he was supposed to show up with it right about now, carrying it in a JanSport backpack I'd given him. He would open up the shop and go in. I'd be his first customer and walk out with the bag and some bagels. I hadn't told Aziz much about how I planned to get the extinguisher into the Garden, or any other operational details. I didn't figure he needed to know. And in fact I had no plan for the Garden anymore. All I wanted was to get ahold of the virus. Then Aziz would have to die.

Usually he was at the shop at six-twenty exactly. But today, no. And every minute that passed left me feeling like a cop in a crack house. Unless you're sleeping under cardboard, five minutes is a long time to do nothing on a Manhattan street corner; ten minutes and your hair starts to turn gray. I looked up and down the street. The newsstands were open. So were the little groceries. Pakistanis and Koreans got up early, or stayed up all night. But I didn't want them or their surveillance cameras to remember me, so I steered clear. A tall jogger passed by, dressed head to foot in black Lycra that showed off a body where every little muscle was hardened and sharpened to an edge. He was wearing a ski cap and dark glasses. He wanted you to look at his muscles, I figured, not his face. For a while, he ran right up the middle of Third Avenue, then turned on Seventy-second and disappeared. And still Aziz hadn't showed.

I started running, too. I couldn't just stand there anymore. Maybe there was a missed connection. At a time like this you can think you have every detail down pat and then you blow the address. A reflex tells you to go one place when your brain should have told you to go to the other. Maybe he was waiting for me at Lewis College.

The street was still in shadow as I turned the corner, and even from a distance the reflected red and blue lights of the police cars filled it with emergency colors. I kept on jogging toward the scene. The cops, and an ambulance, were right in front of the biology building. There was a rumble behind me as more cars rushed down the street. But these weren't the familiar blue-and-whites. They were Army-green Suburban vans. Even at this hour, a small crowd was gathering, and a couple of cops started ordering it back, pushing out the perimeter with yellow tape and sawhorse barriers. But you could still see that the soldiers getting out of the vans weren't in regular BDUs. They didn't have their masks on yet, but they were ready for MOPP-4.

"What's going on?" I asked a woman cop who was ordering us back. She just shook her head.

It's started, I thought. There's been an accident. They know. It probably would have made sense to leave. To get out of there. To get out of New York. But I had to find out what was going on.

Television crews were arriving, their white spotlights bearing down on the front door of the biology building and the police around it as the soldiers went in. There was nothing to do but wait and see what happened. The people around me were starting to stir with rumors. "Poison gas," some of them were saying. They didn't like seeing troops in their neighborhood, and they didn't like the masks the squad was wearing.

"That's the biology building," said a young woman standing near me with a bag full of books over her shoulder.

"So?" said a guy standing next to her.

"So, they do, like, genetic research in there."

You could feel a kind of tremor run through the people who heard that.

"What's going on?" somebody shouted at the cops.

"Everything's under control," said the woman officer right in front of us.

"Hell it is!" shouted a little man in a sharp suit who would have fit in at the Mayfair tea room. His face was red and twisted. "Hell it is! Tell us the truth!"

The crowd was growing fast, and people were telling each other about the soldiers in gas masks, and the mood was getting fearful, ugly, frightening, just on speculation about what might have gone on in there. A middle-aged mother with her baby in a Snugli looked like she couldn't decide whether to stay or go. She covered the child's head with her hand as if somehow that would protect it from whatever unknown threat was lurking in that faceless building.

"Listen up!" shouted a police captain with blow-dried hair and a carefully trimmed mustache. He was talking to the press in front of us. "Some of you have seen the National Guard unit that went into the building and you may be drawing the wrong conclusions. So I want to clear this up quickly. Okay?" The cameras and microphones closed in around him like a football huddle with a hot white bubble of light in the middle. We couldn't see his face anymore, but you could still hear him clear enough. "A man has been killed in the biology laboratory."

"How?" shouted one of the reporters.

"Let me finish. A man has been killed in the biology laboratory, and some of the equipment there has been broken."

"Was it gas? Was he infected? How the hell did he die, Carl?"

"The coroner will determine that. But I can tell you that his throat was cut."

"Multiple lacerations?"

"Just the throat."

"So, Carl, why the National Guard guys?"

"Just to check and make sure there are no potentially hazardous substances. This is perfectly routine in a case like this."

Carl, I thought, you've never had a case like this.

The doors to the building opened and a gurney came out with the body on it, strapped down and wrapped in a plastic sheet. Suddenly the huddle broke and the cameras and lights rushed toward the corpse and the ambulance doors, pressing up against another barrier. A few of the reporters without cameras stayed behind, talking to the public affairs officer. Then when the ambulance doors closed, the cameras came back and the TV correspondents started doing their live appearances for the local news. I stood as close as I could, listening, but trying to stay out of anyone's lens.

"Yes, Jonathan," said one of the TV reporters, a pretty Oriental woman who was adjusting something in her ear. "We're here at Lewis College where a body was found this morning in the science building. According to police sources, this does appear to be a homicide, maybe a robbery." She listened to a voice none of us could hear. "Yes, that's right, there is a group of National Guard soldiers here who entered the building wearing gas masks, but police sources say that's a normal precaution. Apparently there are small quantities —they emphasize small quantities—of hazardous substances in the laboratory." She listened again, and looked at her notebook. "No, we don't have that information. But one source has identified the victim as a Helmy Aziz, twenty-nine, a graduate student here at Lewis College." She listened again. "Thank you, Jonathan," she said.

The virus could be loose by now. Or somebody, not knowing what it was, might be just about to release it. Did whoever killed Aziz have the virus with him? There was no way to get in the building. No way to check it out. Nowhere to start, that I could think of. Aziz was my only contact, and he was dead. The only one who knew about this was Rashid, and I had no idea at all where he was. Bosnia again? Afghanistan? Iraq? Damn him, I thought. Damn him for bringing so many people into this secret, and keeping so much of it secret from me.

The street circus of lights and cameras, cops, reporters, and the crowd showed no sign of letting up, but I wasn't getting anything done. There was nothing to do, in fact, but go back to the apartment.

I jogged up the stairwell, anxious to get to the television. I knocked on the door of the apartment. There was no answer. I opened it. Chantal wasn't there.

There was a note, thank God. "Couldn't sleep. Gone to office to get early start on late projects. XXXOOOO, C."

The news was on all the morning programs, but none of them were telling me what I needed to know. The reporters, the police, the National Guard—none of them had any idea what they should be looking for. Would they notice a bottle that read "No Touch"? What would they make of a fire extinguisher in a book bag? A couple of times I picked up the phone, thinking I would call the police and try to give them a basic idea what was going on. But each time when I heard the duty officer's voice I just hung up.

I was going to have to go back out, but I didn't let myself rush. I showered. I shaved. I put on a white shirt and my suit and the black cross-trainers I used as dress shoes. I figured it might be useful, today, to look like a Fed. And it was always good to be able to run.

I headed down the stairs, as usual. Then something hard smashed against the back of my head. My knees gave way under me. I sprawled down the steps. For a second, in the spinning blur of concrete, I thought I saw someone dressed all in black. Then I lost consciousness.

The next thing I heard was a voice saying, "God almighty." It was Kantrowicz, the building super. "Look at this. You take the elevator next time."

"What happened?"

"You fall, I guess."

"Did you see who it was?"

"Nobody take these stairs but you," he said.

"I got to go," I said, but when I started to stand up, I was shaky.

"You make a big mess here," he said. There was blood on the floor and on my shirt. I felt the back of my head. It didn't hurt as badly as it might have, but my hand came away all red.

The super wanted to call an ambulance, but I just went back up to the apartment. I was being hunted now. And the hunter had given himself away. But he was going to be out there somewhere, circling back, waiting for me. I thought I knew who he was. That runner in the Lycra. But that was just a guess. Whoever, wherever, I had to find a way to find him first.

I ran my head under the faucet to rinse off the blood. It took half a roll of paper towels before the bleeding stopped. My shirt was a mess. The little kitchen and bathroom looked like an emergency ward. Chantal wouldn't be pleased. I was just about to head out again in fresh clothes when the phone rang. I thought it might be her.

But it was Selma, and her voice was desperate. Dave was involved in something terrible, she said, but she didn't know what it was. Only that he and Duke Bolide were on their way to Atlanta to see the big game between the Hawks and Chicago Bulls. I had a little trouble figuring out what one thing had to do with another. Her voice was slurred. She confessed she was calling from the hospital. He'd beaten her really badly this time.

"But what's dangerous about going to a basketball game in Atlanta?" I asked.

Selma said she just knew there was something. She just

knew. She thought they were lying about the game. It was something else. A word here, a laugh there. And all these phone calls that Dave was making to someone in New Jersey. And calls to him. From a man with a foreign accent. Maybe a Mexican.

"Selma, I am sorry, but I don't have time for this."

"Oh, Kurt, you got to help."

"I don't know what I can do, Selma. I got to—"

"You're all I got, Kurt. All I got. Don't let me be alone now. I don't want to die alone."

"Hush, Selma. Nothing's going to happen to you. Maybe I can call this guy who's been calling Dave. How about that? Do you think you can find a number for him?"

"Oh, Kurt, I don't know. I—"

"How about let's talk tonight. Okay?"

"No. Wait," she said, and hung up.

I tried to call back, but it took me a couple of minutes to get the number of Westfield Hospital, and then her line was busy. And then she called me. She'd kept one of her old phone bills with her. She had the number in New Jersey from a few months ago: 329–3868. I called it. It was disconnected. That was that. I rang Selma again.

"Kurt, I'm so scared," she said.

"Don't be. It's okay. I'll talk to you tonight. I promise," I said, and headed back onto the street.

Crowds of pedestrians filled Park and Lexington, folks thinking about those sales reports they had due or that raise they were going to ask for, or that son of a bitch their boss. They were going to work now. But I was going to war. They were the forest I couldn't see through, these people. They were the fog where my enemy hid.

I tried to stay loose as I walked back down toward Lewis College. If he didn't come at me on the way there, that would be where I'd wait up for him. I was letting my mind empty so my senses would open up, readying myself to react at any surprise. But the rhythm of the phone number had gotten into my head and started repeating itself. Three-two-nine, thirty-eight, sixty-eight. Three-two-nine, thirty-eight, sixty-eight. It sounded familiar, but I couldn't place it.

"Three-two-nine, thirty-eight, sixty-eight," I said out loud. "God have mercy." I pulled my wallet out of my pocket and fished a little shred of paper out of one of the folds. There were Arabic letters on it. "Alif Lam Mim. Sad. Nun."

I changed my course toward Madison, toward a bookstore. "Do you have a copy of the Koran?" I asked, and the man pointed toward the back. This couldn't be true, I thought. This couldn't have happened. My memory was playing all kinds of tricks on me and I wanted to be sure I was wrong. I started flipping as fast as I could through the surahs, checking the beginning of each one. The letters "Alif Lam Mim" started the third and the twenty-ninth. Shit. It was a little code I'd made for myself before I knew the Koran really was somebody's code book. It was to remember a number I didn't call very often, and didn't want other people to find. I flipped to Surah 38. The mysterious letter that began it was "Sad." Then Surah 68. "Nun." Dave had been calling Rashid.

This could not be. But it was. And in grim little flashes as disconnected as nightmares the sense of it came to me. All those questions Rashid had asked about my family when we were together in Bosnia, and all that I'd told him. He knew about Dave's ideas. Racial purity. Christian Identity. The Zionist Occupation Government. Rashid had fixed on that, I remembered. "ZOG." He'd said the word over and over, and even laughed. "There is truth in that," he'd said. "Not if Dave believes it," I told him.

Rashid knew about Selma's letters, all the clippings about pipe bombs. "Do you think she thinks he is the one sending these things?" Rashid asked me. "Dave couldn't light the fuse on an M80," I said. Rashid could have known just what he needed to know about Dave, including his address. And maybe he knew more, a lot more, than I did.

"How are things in Jew York City?" The last time I talked to Dave, he'd had this weird tone, like we were sharing a joke. Shit! The idea hit me like a stench in the air. He thought we were doing the same thing, like we were all in on the same plot. But he wasn't sure. Damn right, he wasn't sure. I was supposed to be out of the picture by now.

But Dave, that racist son of a bitch, how could he work with Rashid, who looked like every dark-skinned spic-gook-raghead-nigger he ever hated. "Jew York City." Ah, God. I could hear Rashid's voice now, telling Dave about the Jews, telling Dave about the injustice, telling Dave about the evil plots and the secret protocols—playing with him and playing to him. Rashid didn't use that stuff on me because—he used other things on me. Yes, indeed. But Dave was such a simple, stupid son of a bitch. Rashid could have hit every chord the first time. The Zionist Occupation Government. The Great Satan. All the same thing. "What a perfect fucking match," I said out loud to nobody. "And I brought you together." And this great plan that Rashid and I had, now that it was touched by Dave, seemed even more horrible because it seemed so fucking cheap.

"Are you going to buy that?" said the man at the cash register. I was walking out with the Koran in my hand.

"Sorry," I said, putting it down.

I still didn't know who was out there looking for me, or where. But an empty cab was coming up Madison. I got in. The driver was wearing a turban. *"Salaam aleikum,"* he said.

"La Guardia," I said.

XXVII
The Omni-CNN Center in Atlanta is a huge building that looks in on itself. At one end is the Omni Hotel, all weird pinks and purples and smiling staff. At the other are the offices of the Cable News Network. But in between, the heart and soul of the place is a food court like you'd find in any mall in America. The CNN Center has Taco Bell and a place called Jocks and Jills. I don't think I ever saw one of those before. But the rattle of ice in Cokes, and the sizzle and smell of grease are all pretty much the same. The only difference here was the ceiling, fifteen stories above your head.

The whole feel of the place made me uneasy. There was too much going on. The mezzanine balconies were flying more flags than the United Nations. The walls were decked out with posters for old movies. Offices and shops were all in the same kinds of plate-glass storefronts. There ought to have been people all over. But there weren't that many. The post office was just machines. And the Precinct Five police station was, as far as I could see, empty. A few security guards wandered around the floor, sure. But they were mainly talking to each other, waiting for somebody to call them and tell them what to do. These were not guys you could talk to. I had to get through to somebody who could give orders.

At the bottom of the escalators that ran from the mezzanine to the main floor, just in front of the post office and police station, there was a little bank of pay phones. If I could get through to Griffin, maybe he could pull some strings. But nothing seemed to be working for me. It took four calls and a lot of quarters just to get Information for Washington, D.C., and the number of the White House. Then the operator there said I had to call another number for the Secret Service, at the Treasury Department. I held. I waited. I tried to keep my voice measured and calm, but every click on the line, every second on hold, left me feeling more desperate. I couldn't tell why it was taking so long to find him. I couldn't see if he was there, anywhere near the phone. How many times had I been left on hold in my life? It's not something you think about usually. But now I felt like I was lost in a cave of silence.

"Griffin," came his voice.

And now he had his turn listening to the silence, because—there was just nothing I could say to him. Right before I spoke I realized I couldn't trust him. He was hiding too much himself. I couldn't tell him everything and expect him to keep me out of it. And if I didn't tell him everything, or just about, then there was no way to convince him this was a real plot, a real threat, a real ticket to hell for hundreds of thousands of people. Of children.

"Griffin here. Who's this?"

It was the simplicity of the plot that made it so hard to explain. It was so basic, so easy, so huge that there was a kind of automatic refusal to believe. I was searching for words, for a way just to begin with Griffin, but still I couldn't speak. The horror of what we were trying to do— or of what we'd done—was coming to me like it never had before. Maybe I had been refusing to believe. Or just believing the wrong damn things. But this thing was happening. And it was happening right now.

"If you can hear me, call back," he said. The line clicked off.

I could start to feel the killing. I could start to smell the death around me. Nobody else could see it or sense it, but I knew what was happening, and they didn't, and I could start to feel the weight of the dead on me, burying me, suffocating me with their scarred bodies, drowning me in their thick, cold blood.

There was no time to convince anyone of anything. No time. And I didn't even know, now, where to start the search to try to stop this thing. I looked at all the red and blue and green neon, the spotlights, the sunlight, the atmosphere lights, the reflections off the polished floors of mezzanines and escalators and atriums, and glass elevators moving up and down with bands of light around them. In here you couldn't rely on light or shadow to tell you what was happening. You didn't know, in a lot of corners, if it was day or night. You lost your sense of time. Your eyes played tricks on you. And the noises. I heard all the music that you don't hear, but that works its way into your head. And behind that the hum of big engines—air conditioners—the clatter of dishes; the low, steady motors of the escalators; noises of machines and space; and snatches of conversation; business talk and sports talk and, sometimes, above it all, the hoarse shout of a guide giving the tour of the CNN studios, starting with a metal detector. "Oh, security's tight." I heard a woman's nasal voice. "Just like Fort Knox." The tourists took a long escalator that ended halfway up the side of the building beneath three dummy astronauts dangling in space like something out of *2001*. Behind them, big as a tennis court against an enormous window, was an American flag. The sun outside was setting behind Old Glory. The white stripes glowed a fiery orange.

"And to save energy there are motion sensors that turn the lights on and off automatically," I heard one of the guides explain. When people walked out of their offices, the lights would go out. But as long as they were working inside, they stayed on. I looked over the dozens of glass windows, a little like the cages in the snake house at the zoo.

You could sit in the food court and know just who was working and who wasn't by whether their lights were on. Mostly there were men inside the glass cubes: white shirts and striped ties, rummaging through piles of paper, or surfing the channels on their televisions. In one office on the third floor, the lights were off, but you could see there was still a man sitting on the sofa, his head slumped on his chest. He didn't budge. The lights stayed out. I wondered if he was snoring.

I wanted to talk to Chantal. Maybe she could mobilize some support. It made me crazy that I hadn't been able to get in touch with her. I had to tell her something of what was going on. And I was worried about her. I went back to the phone bank near the escalator. I called the Council. "Ms. Silberman hasn't been in all day," said the receptionist. That was information that didn't fit. There was no reason that I knew for Chantal not to come in. I called her apartment. Her phone rang three, four times. The machine was just about to come on.

Then right in front of me, a hundred yards away, I watched Rashid swing open the door of the CNN Center. I didn't move. On the phone at my ear I heard Chantal's recorded voice. "I don't seem to be here right now, but if you leave your name and number . . ." Her machine beeped. I didn't say anything. Rashid was coming in from the street. I couldn't see his face clearly, but I knew his moves, tight and quick and economical. His hands were in the pockets of his windbreaker but he was walking erect as a soldier. He didn't look around. Didn't seem to care what was going on. Didn't notice me in the shadow of the escalator. He turned quickly to his right toward the steps that led up toward the Omni Hotel lobby in a big spiral. I saw him top the first flight and then the second, and I was after him.

I took the stairs two at a time and halfway up I caught him on the turn. He heard my feet behind him and spun around, reaching behind his back in the same motion. I slammed my shoulder into his chest and flattened him against the wall. I was a good four inches and thirty pounds bigger than Rashid. Bare-handed, there was no match. Before he could catch his breath I spun him, caught his right hand, and brought it up behind him so fast that he loosened his grip. The pistol fell and I reached for it. Stupid move. He twisted away and sprinted. I picked up the gun and slipped it into my belt, scrambling after him, but the seconds I lost let him duck out of sight.

"Shit."

The carpeted stairway ended in an indoor courtyard in front of a restaurant called the American Café. A few yards away, a tall bald man in a suit stood waiting with menus. He was looking off to my right.

"Security," I said firmly, pointing toward the elevators to ask if that was the direction the man had gone. The host in the suit shook his head, then nodded farther to the right in the direction of a short hallway. I waved thanks. "Have a good one," said the man with the menus.

There was a door beneath a red exit sign that read "No Access. Authorized Personnel Only." I stepped through, and heard it lock behind me. Concrete stairs led up and down. But there was no sound. If Rashid was in this stairwell, he wasn't running. Quietly as I could, I went down. There was only one flight. The door at the bottom was locked. He wasn't there. There was no way out but up.

One flight. A second. A third. Every door back into the hallways of the hotel was locked. If he wasn't in here I'd lost him, and lost him bad. I stopped. Listened. But the low roar and hum of the building blocked whatever sound there was above me. At each turn of the stairs I expected Rashid to explode on top of me. Floor by floor, locked door after locked door, I made my way toward the top of the building. Still there was no sound I could pick out as Rashid.

The stairs ended above the fourteenth floor. And the door there was locked as tight as all the rest. Cigarette butts littered the top steps. People had carved things in the concrete. "Bo + Missy," said one. "Anthrax rules," read another.

A thin grate barred the way into the heating ducts of the building. But a couple of feet above my head there was another opening to the air inside the top of the CNN Center. I could see the darkening sky through the glass skylights and steel girders a few feet higher up. It was the only way out. It was small. But the wire mesh was bent back.

All I could do was move fast and hope Rashid wasn't right there waiting. I pulled myself up into the opening, but I couldn't get through clean. I had to put my right arm through first, then my head. My legs were dangling above the stairs.

There was Rashid. He was about twenty feet away on a thin ledge right beneath the skylights. They slanted inward along steel beams above the empty atrium. Fourteen floors below was the American Café. In between: air. Rashid had to lean backward off balance above the abyss holding on to the beams with his fingers. But he was moving easily, cleanly, quickly, like he'd practiced this before. A few more feet and he'd reach the catwalk that the window washers used along the upper edge of the center. Then he could really travel. But when he saw me, he stopped. I was only about a third of the way through the hole. My shoulders were clear. I pushed up on my right arm and elbow. But I was wedged in place, wriggling and twisting, my left arm pinned to my body.

Rashid, leaning out there above the nothingness, turned his body toward me and let go with one hand, waving, relaxed, laughing. "Too late" was all he said.

My left elbow was through the opening now, but as I started to pull myself up and out, the gun in my belt caught and slipped, clattering down onto the stairs below, dropping away, clanging on concrete risers and steel banisters. Lost.

Rashid was on the move again, reaching from one beam to another like a rock climber, the toes of his running shoes

holding on to the concrete shelf more for balance than support. As I got to the ledge, he was already jumping onto the
catwalk. My big hands got an easy grip on the beams. But
in the glass in front of my face I could see the reflection of
the drop behind me. My legs started to stiffen. I couldn't
think about the height. Couldn't look at it. There were five
more beams in front of me, spaced less than the span of
my arms. My eyes closed, I groped for each beam, gripped,
sidestepped, moving easier by touch than I could by eye. But
there was a second when I was right at the end of the ledge,
when I had to jump a couple of feet down to the catwalk,
when I had to open my eyes. My whole body froze, and in
the jump I almost fell.

Rashid was looking for a place to jump or climb off the
catwalk. But there was nothing at this corner. The distances
were too great. He was losing time. He turned away from
the hotel, heading toward the upper part of the main CNN
Center, picking up speed as he heard me closing behind him.
He made a feint toward a balcony just below us to the right,
but he hesitated, and I was almost on him now. He sprinted
for the end of the catwalk.

The giant window loomed in front of us, draped with
the enormous Old Glory and the three dummy astronauts
suspended on their wires. There was a rope piled there at
the end. Maybe a window washer had left it. Maybe they
were going to swing another fake spaceman out there. I
don't know. But Rashid and I saw the rope just about the
same time. He sprawled along the catwalk, grabbing for the
tangled cords. I was on top of him now. Twice, hard as I
could, I rammed my fist into his kidney. He groaned and
twisted with the pain.

"Where's the virus?"

His face was smashed so hard against the metal of the
catwalk and the tangle of rope beneath him he could hardly
talk. "There is no—thing you can do," he said, working hard
just to breathe as I bore down on him.

"I can spread your brains on the floor down there."

His teeth grated on the metal of the catwalk. "The Angel of the Lord is coming," he said. "Nothing you can do."

"You're working for fucking Saddam," I said.

"What?" For a second he almost went limp. "Saddam —shit—he would never guess this stuff."

"Where's the virus?"

"Take a deep breath, my friend." He half smiled. "Let me look at you, Kurt."

Holding him down like a rodeo steer, I twisted a loop of the long, tangled rope tightly around his wrists behind his back and slowly let him turn. Just enough. He looked at me, searching. "You want the secret of the pyramid?" he said.

"I want the virus," I said.

"You, Kurt—and me," he whispered. "We are family."

"The fucking virus," I said.

"More. What I start, you finish," he said, closing his eyes for a second, then opening them right into mine. "You and me, Kurt." He smiled. "We are the Angel."

In that second he turned on me. He must have felt my hesitation and faster than a snake he spun out of my grip, scrambling forward toward the end of the catwalk, working his wrists to loosen the rope. I lunged. I missed. I grabbed a handful of the rope and pulled. He tripped. With his hands still tied behind him he didn't have his balance, didn't have any way to catch himself. His scramble became a stumble, then a dive, trying to catch the far edge of the catwalk with his shoulder to stop the fall. But he had too much momentum. Like a gymnast who's lost control of his moves, he tumbled off the catwalk. The rope payed out, then went taut. I heard a cracking sound, and a choked gasp.

Rashid was hanging about twenty feet below and in front of me, the rope still fastened to his wrists. His arms were wrenched back and up out of the shoulder sockets. His feet, caught in another loop, were suspended a little above him. He looked like he was in free-fall, picking up speed. But he wasn't moving at all.

I lay still on the catwalk, staring through the grillwork at the scene below. At CNN the men and women still working went about their business pulling together news from all over the world without ever looking out their own windows. Straight below me people were moving like herds through the food court on the bottom floor, filing onto the escalators at the end of the building, headed outside. Nobody noticed Rashid was there at all, except for one little girl. Even from fourteen floors up, I could see her blond hair and pink backpack, and her hand pointing straight at him. She pulled on her father's sleeve, trying to make him stop. The father had a bright red jacket with the word "Hawks" written across the back, and a cap with the same logo. He put the hat on his daughter's curls, then put her up on his shoulders, and hardly broke his stride. When he glanced up all he saw was a fourth spaceman floating in front of that huge American flag.

Outside, behind the flag, the lights of an electric billboard flashed bright and relentless. "Hawks vs. Bulls." The game was about to start. And above the billboard I could see the roof of the arena. It was all pyramids.

There was just enough rope left on the catwalk to get me to the top of the big CNN escalator. There were no tourists riding on it now. The north side of the building where I was had grown dark as the office workers left for the day. I started to descend in shadow, trying not to look at Rashid. I wasn't sure what I would do if he was still alive.

As I passed the first plate-glass window, the light went on. I almost lost my grip. I froze. But no one came into the room. As I passed the second window the same thing happened. Motion sensors. I hung as still as I could, waiting to hear shouts from below. But there was nothing. One floor after another, I tried to keep myself to one side of the windows, hoping to dodge the sensors. Sometimes it worked. Sometimes it didn't. But still, no one shouted. No one shot.

At the third floor, the light went on. I froze again. This time there was someone inside. It was the same man I saw before when I looked up from the lobby. But I could see now, up close and in the light, he wasn't sleeping. The skin on his neck above his workshirt was rubbed raw. His face was rigid. His blue eyes were open, but they didn't move. The way death changes you, it's not always easy to recognize a corpse. It took me a few seconds before I realized it was Dave there on the other side of the glass.

XXVIII

"Man, you are lucky," said the scalper in the parking lot. "You got the best seat in the Omni." It cost me a hundred dollars, and as far as I knew it was a ticket to hell. At the entrance the crowd was jamming through the glass door, pressing in all around me. I was exhausted, and I hurt. And I could feel real fear creeping up on me. For almost fourteen hours I'd been trying to beat a clock without knowing what time was set on it, or even where it was. Fear was running through my veins, crawling under my skin. If I let up on myself for a second, I was afraid I'd lose all control. Finally I was inside the door, and I went straight for the first entrance to the stands. Another crowd was there. Children. Everywhere I looked there seemed to be kids, teenagers, little boys and girls. Clueless, all of them. The noise in the entrance, the flashing lights, the smell of people and popcorn and beer, the cheerleading over the loudspeakers rattled my head. I was sweating. I stank of fear. People crammed around me in the little passageway that led to the stands. I couldn't move my arms. I wanted to swing out, to elbow, to clear space. "Easy, buddy," someone said. "Easy. We'll all get in." But there wasn't time now. You're all gonna fucking die, I thought. Every breath you take is gonna kill you, and you people have no fucking idea.

316

I pushed through into the huge hall. An enormous face suddenly flew at me like the horror I felt inside. A cartoon face. Bright colors. Shiny plastic. A yellow beak and angry eyes. It was some sort of Hawk mascot balloon that floated, and turned, and swooped away over the crowd, radio-controlled, driven by tiny propellers. My body went stiff with fear as I realized what it was, then what it could do. If there was a tank or nozzle on it, if there was anything that could pump out the viral mist, then I was too late. Much too late. I was petrified, watching it float away.

Panic destroys judgment. That's the definition of it. And I couldn't afford to waste time on bad judgment. Had to focus. To think. Sort out the facts in front of me. There might still be time to stop the plague. Think. The Hawk balloon would be too complicated for Rashid or anyone with him to rig on short notice. I couldn't spot anything on it. The thermos bottle with the virus in it would be too big. They wouldn't have access to the balloon itself. The device would have to be like the one I built. Or, precisely, it would have to be the one I built. I had to find the fire extinguisher and hope I was in time. But where?

"Can I help you?" said a young woman's voice. She held out her hand for the ticket I still had clutched in mine. She looked at it. "That's on the other side. Go back out here and make a right."

"I'm looking for a friend here," I said. She moved off to help someone else, and I tried to sort out the scene in front of me. The players had come onto the court and started warming up. It wouldn't make sense to put the canister down there. Too many people, including security. And the solution that carried the virus wouldn't be spread wide enough. You wanted to put it higher. At the top of the stands. I scanned the boxes. Press. Officials. Corporate boxes for Delta and Marlboro. And Rankin Mills. I had forgotten completely about this. The company was a big promoter of sports in Georgia. It made sense it would have a box. My stomach churned. The box was all the way on the other side of the stadium and I couldn't see exactly who was in it, but it was full. Somewhere in there would be Tyler, for sure. And maybe Josie.

I backed up against the concrete wall for support.

"Please, sir, go to your seat." The voice of the usher again. "I don't want to have to call security."

"I'm going," I said. I stared up at the ceiling. But I didn't move. I was looking inside one of the pyramids that rose from the top of the arena. When I'd seen them from outside, I thought the pyramids were just an architect's idea of decoration. But they were the key to the Omni's structure. The whole ceiling alternated pyramids and flat surfaces, a little like a checkerboard. Each pyramid was hollow and there must have been more than twenty. From where I stood a hundred feet below I could see a door that opened onto a catwalk at the base of each one to service the lights that ringed the bottom edges. And at the top, inside the pinnacle of each pyramid, there was a square platform suspended like a basket hung from a balloon. You could see where banners were dangling from some of those little platforms, loudspeakers from others. A few had nothing hanging from them. And suspended from the one in the very middle of the arena was the scoreboard. Any of those little platforms would be the perfect site to put the aerosol bottle. The virus would spread over the whole stadium. Nobody would hear anything, or see it or feel it. Maybe it was already happening. Or maybe—this is what I had to hope—the timer was set to start when the stadium was full and the game had begun.

"The secret of the pyramid," I said out loud.

"I'm calling security," said the usher.

"No," I said, and worked up as good a smile as I could for her. "No, don't. I'm sorry. I think I've got the flu or something—and I've never been in here before. It's really impressive." I coughed, then pointed up to the pyramid above us. "Don't suppose I could get a seat up there, could I?"

You could tell from her face I wasn't convincing her I was sane. But at least she wasn't calling security.

"Not unless you plan to go through the roof," she said. "Now please go find your seat."

I coughed again. "Yes, ma'am," I said. I looked up a last time. In at least one of the pyramids I could see there was a ladder from the suspended platform to a trap door at the peak.

There had to be stairs and doors to the roof of the Omni Arena. But I didn't know where to find them or how I'd get through them if I did. I couldn't exactly ask for help. Too many explanations. Too little time. Maybe I could find Tyler? No. No way. Not even here and now. Not to save him. Not to save his family. My God almighty, what could I say to them about what was happening here? There was no more time to call Chantal. Where the hell was she?

Focus, I thought, focus—as I squeezed through the crowd and back out to the main door.

"I left something in my car," I told the ticket-taker as I held up the stub. "Can I get back in with this?"

"You be long?"

"Right back."

"Maybe get an umbrella, too."

"I wish," I said. A chill drizzle was starting to fall.

I wanted to see the outside of the building. Maybe there was a fire escape, a ladder, something to take me to the roof. But there was nothing like that.

Calm, Kurt. Calm. Take the frantic out of your movements. The objective is clear. The means to achieve it are not. What are the options?

The area around the doors of the Omni is all glass, but the solid, structural sides of the Omni are covered with some kind of iron siding, rusted by design, corrugated with deep patterns, crisscrossed by iron braces. It looks a little like a packing crate, and at night, in the shadows, it reminded me of a space hulk in an *Alien* film. The side near the CNN

Center was lit up. But the other side, toward the parking lot, was mostly in the shadows. With the drizzle, no one was standing around to watch. I studied it for a couple of minutes, clearing my head, then outlining the path in my brain. Once I moved, I couldn't stop, couldn't draw attention, couldn't even think about where I was going. The climb had to be quick and clean, grabbing the first iron crosspiece, boosting up on that, and traversing the iron grid to the next. Then the next. It was, at most, a hundred-foot climb. I'd done the same in training on rock faces that crumbled under my hands and toes. That wouldn't happen here. The ascent ought to be over in a couple of minutes.

Shouting. Behind me. Latecomers who just parked their car were rushing to get in before the game began. Shouting at—each other. Not at me. I walked toward the parking lot as if to get whatever it was I'd left there. The four of them disappeared around the corner of the building.

I turned back and jogged toward the wall of the arena. My feet felt heavy at the ends of my legs, but I jumped up with all the spring I could find and tried to seize the iron corrugations. My hands slipped on wet, slick surfaces. I gripped with the points of my fingers, bearing down until the nails were scraping in the surface of the metal. I held. My toes were planted in the ridges of metal below me. I pressed my weight against the wall until I was balanced. And now I started to make my moves. Across. Up. Across. The tendons in my arm quivered from the strain. In my heart I wanted to stop. To get down. To walk away. But I kept going. Up. The face of the wall was in my mind and I moved across it in pain, not thinking, my own face against it, breathing water and rust, gripping with fingers starting to spasm until the edge of the roof was under my hand, and the edge was under my arm, and under my side, straining like a weak child pulling himself out of a swimming pool, and I rolled into a flat puddle, breathing in long, rough gasps, but breathing, and being where I meant to be.

Ah, God, I was weak. What had I done with my life
that I was so weak? Why had I trained all those years? Ah,
God, I'm where I need to be but I can't act. Must act. Now!
I rolled over on my elbow and saw the pyramids all around
me. So many of them. Too goddamned many of them. And
the game begun somewhere beneath them. The crowd below
this roof so big. Why would Rashid wait this long? No one
would wait. It's too late. The thing is done. And I am so
tired. So fucking tired. Just stay here. Survive. Forget. Surrender is not a Ranger word, I thought. Though I be the
lone survivor, I thought. But those words didn't do it for me.
I tried to focus on the faces of the children I had seen below,
but they meant, now, nothing to me. I thought of Josie.
Josie. And couldn't quite see, in my mind, her face. Ah,
God. Our Father, who art in heaven. Master of the Day of
Judgment. Move me. Come on, Kurt. Move. It can't last
much longer.

And some spirit, and what was left of my own spirit,
brought me to my knees, to my feet.

From what I could see, every one of the pyramids had
a heavy door at its top. And any one of the pyramids could
have hidden the extinguisher. Slipping and crawling, I struggled to the top of the nearest one and pressed up on the edge
of the door. It was almost as heavy as the bulkhead in a ship,
and as I lay on the steep angle of the pyramid the hatch was
terribly awkward to lift, fighting me for every inch. Slowly
it cracked. Slowly. And then the light and heat and noise
from below rushed up at me. I had time to look at the
platform and see there was nothing there. But already I was
sliding backward. I let go completely, half rolling to the
bottom.

Think. There is no time to open every door until you
find the prize. Think. You wouldn't put the extinguisher at
one edge of the arena. You'd put it right in the middle. Yes.

But which one of the pyramids was in the middle?
Looking around in the dark and the drizzle at the shapes

towering over me, I was lost in a geometrical mountain range. I counted five diagonally. Or were there seven? The pattern shifted in my head like one of those optical tricks in a child's magazine. Was the design going in—or going out? I shook my head so violently the raindrops spun off my face. I staggered toward what I guessed, as best I could, was the center of the roof, hopeless, half falling. And there, lying against the side of one of the pyramids, was a ladder.

"Thank you, God," I said out loud to any God that was listening.

I hoped, but tried not to let myself hope, that the ladder had been left there by Rashid or Dave or whoever had put the canister in place. God, that would be a blessing. That would make the difference.

I tested it for steadiness. It wasn't anchored on the forty-five-degree slope. It just lay against the surface. There was nothing for it to brace against and it wasn't tall enough to reach the top, but the rubber treads at the foot of it stuck a little bit, and the rungs gave me somewhere to put my feet, however shaky. I got to the top in seconds and pushed the door up, then put my head and shoulder under it to look while I held myself up on the lip of the opening with both hands. The platform was right beneath me. There were wires and cables and ropes strung across it holding the scoreboard and banners suspended beneath. There were hot lights, shining out on the inside of the pyramid, half blinding me. But in one corner of the platform I could just see, looking like it belonged there, right down to the inspection tag, the extinguisher.

I pushed up on my toes, bearing down on the top of the ladder. And suddenly the ladder slipped away. My feet slid. My body went flat and fell—down—back—out of the opening. I hung on. The door slammed down. On my hands. Pain, bright and hot, flashed through my body and for a second I couldn't breathe. The muscles, the bones, the veins of my fingers surged with heat intense as phosphorus.

I had to get my body up again, digging with my toes on that surface that wouldn't give, pulling up against elbows braced against the wet metal, fighting the instinct to pull back, driving forward, using my head, my chin, my face, the back of my skull to lift the door by fractions of an inch, then by a few more inches, pushing my hands and forearms forward, ah, Lord almighty, my elbows were inside now and my head, my shoulders, and I braced myself and held on.

Noise thundered from below, from the crowd, from the loudspeakers. There were no words to hear. Just pure, deafening volume. Far beneath me were thousands of people, and right in front of me, no more than fifteen feet away, the thing that would kill them. But all I could see were my hands. They were white, twisted, starting to swell. Freed from the vise of the door, they started to shake and the quivering moved uncontrollably along my forearms, my shoulders, my spine. All I could do was try to hold steady where I was. Wait. Breathe. Wait. Breathe. Wait.

The first three fingers of my left hand and the first two of my right were broken. There wasn't much doubt about those. The others, I wasn't sure. The thumbs moved, but in moving pulled on the other tiny tendons and muscles in the hands that screamed with a pain that was growing, now, by the second. Wait. Breathe.

There was a ladder on the inside that led down from the trap door to the platform. It was right beneath my face and through its rungs I could see the crowd. Straight down there was the basketball court itself. So far below. I tried to focus on what was closest to me, only what was close, to see only what I needed, to get down, get to the extinguisher. I had to work for every move, every inch. Every fraction of movement called for a lifetime of will, and there was a part of me that said, with more urgency than ever, it wasn't worth it. It was time to give up. To fall away. And down. To float through space. And end wherever, however, I would. It was easy. It was time. It was right to stop.

It's that thing you fight all your life. When it's too hard to work, when it's too hard to live, or to love. It's that second you feel even when you run, and you start on that first hundred yards of the first mile of the first five miles and your body says quit now. Let it go. But instead you go on.

I twisted my body around, bracing on my elbows, holding the door up against my back, and felt with my foot for the first rung of the ladder inside. My neck strained against the weight of the door. The metal of it pressed against my skull. My foot made contact with the first rung. Then the other foot found it. My thumbs felt for the uprights of the ladder and hooked around them, and I stepped down. The door closed above me. My thumbs braced around the uprights. The broken fingers, twisted like broken twigs, stayed open, useless. One rung at a time.

My foot touched the flat surface of the platform. Moving on automatic, barely thinking, I picked my way across the web of wires and ropes toward the extinguisher.

Words blasted from the loudspeakers like thunder. Bells rang and buzzers sounded like sirens. My eyes blurred with sweat and pain. If the extinguisher was hissing, I couldn't hear it. If the mist was spreading, I couldn't see it. The little digital timer and the key wiring that led to the trigger were all covered with black tape so that from a distance they looked like part of the nozzle assembly. I scraped up a corner of tape with my thumbnail and struggled to get a grip on it with the thumb and little finger of my right hand, but the pain was too sharp for me to close them. I used both thumbs, pressing them together. I had to bend my arms from the elbow just to peel back the first strip of tape. The first number on the digital timer read "20." It was set for eight-something at night. The watch on my wrist read 20:14. I gripped the second strip of tape with my thumbs and peeled it back. 20:30. There was time to do what needed doing, even moving as slowly as I was. There was time. If the clock and my watch were in sync.

The third strip of tape covered the red and green leads. I'd tried to keep the device as simple as possible, so Aziz wouldn't fuck it up when he was loading the virus. Simple meant there weren't any real fail-safes, and no traps. The virus was in a thermos under pressure from a CO_2 cartridge. The timer would send a charge to the little cap beneath the lever to the nozzle. It would blow with no more sound than a cork popping out of a bottle. A spring would open the valve, and a cloud much finer than the mist Chantal used on her plants would spread over the people below. It worked, or it didn't. To disarm it, all I had to do was pull the wire off the timer. The red one I'd connected on the left. The green one on the right. It didn't matter which one broke the circuit. I peeled back the tape and squeezed the red wire between my thumbs. The red wire—on the right. I pulled my hands back like I'd gotten a jolt of current.

Ah, shit. I looked again at the leads, closely, really closely. Ah, Rashid, you fucking son of a bitch. This wasn't my wiring. It had to be his. And if he'd wired this trigger, there could be—there probably was—a double circuit. Pull the wrong wire lead, or any lead, and the nozzle blew no matter what the timer said. "You finish what I start," he said. "We are the Angel," he said.

Fuck. I pulled off more tape. The leads disappeared under the hard plastic cover at the base of the extinguisher hose. I pried at it with my thumbs, but it didn't budge, held in place by a ring bolt. I pressed the sides of my thumbs around it and pushed. Nothing. I squeezed harder. The flesh was starting to shred against the burled metal, but it slipped, then turned a fraction more. I twisted with both hands, and it moved, but tightly, not giving anything away. Finally, the bolt was loose enough for me to crack open the top of the extinguisher. Below, the crowd erupted in cheers.

The wires were twisted into a bundle with the red and green going in, and four black ones going out and down into the extinguisher between its wall and the canister on the inside. The surgical tubing was still attached to the canister, running up to the hose of the extinguisher. I hooked the wires with my little fingers and pulled on them one by one. I had to get the leads off the battery itself, just beside the canister's nozzle. My watch said 20:22. And counting. I clamped the hose between my teeth and kept pulling, slowly, on the wire leads. The battery came up in front of my eyes like a treasure from a well. I hooked a thumb over each wire and—pulled. It was 20:23 on my watch.

Through the corner of my eye, I could see the digits flashing on the timer: 20:30, 20:30. Fucking Rashid. Even the time of day was a trick. But nothing would happen now. Without the battery, the device was disarmed.

Gently, gently I slipped the canister out of the extinguisher. The explosive cap and the nozzle were intact. I cradled the bottle in my arms and looked around, aching, exhausted, ecstatic. "Thank you, God!" I shouted as the loudspeaker decibels pounded my eardrums with words too loud to understand.

Below, the players rushed back and forth on the court, looking like toy markers in a toy game. The crowd was on its feet. I could see the Rankin box. In the front row was a woman with sandy brown hair. Lanky. Excited. Clapping her hands and jumping up and down. Was it Josie? I didn't know. And I still don't. I lay back, hugging the canister to my chest. I've got the best seat in the Omni, I thought.

XXIX

"It's me. It's Kurt. Are you in there? I've been really worried."

Chantal wouldn't open the door. "I don't want to see you. I don't want to talk to you," she said.

"Wha—"

"Leave me alone!"

I was too tired to be angry. My hands were bandaged and splinted. My face was scratched, my shoulders bruised. I was wearing a Hawks sweatshirt I picked up at the airport.

"Chantal, I'm a wreck. Open the door. You'll laugh."

"No I won't, Kurt."

"Chantal, what happened? I went out to run and when I got back—"

"When you got back, you bled all over this place and disappeared. I thought you were dead."

"But I tried to call."

"Did you?" She said it like my calling wouldn't have mattered. "Ahhh, Kurt, just get out of here. Just get out of my life, would you?"

"Where were you?"

"Just get out!" she screamed. "Get away from me!" There was hate and hysteria in her voice like I'd never heard, and the door didn't stop the sound. "Get away from here, you son of a bitch!"

I didn't need this. "No! Goddamn it, where were *you* yesterday morning? I came back and you weren't here. I called the fucking office and you weren't there."

"Just leave, Kurt."

"Not until you—"

"Okay," she said, lowering her voice but hardening her tone. "Since you are apparently too fucking young and stupid to figure these things out, I went to the doctor's. Nothing dramatic, just wanted to have something checked."

"Why didn't you tell me?"

"Why? Because I didn't want you to worry. Isn't that just fucking incredible? And then I came back here, and you were gone. And all you left was blood all over the place."

"I fell—"

"Kantrowicz told me. And then I started searching the hospitals. All fucking day, Kurt. Every fucking emergency room in New York."

"I was—"

"I do not want to know where you were. I do not want to know what you were doing. Because—you see—Kurt, what I realized yesterday was that I can't deal with any of this. You are a fucking child. You don't understand me, you don't understand anybody around you, and—hey, it goes without saying—you don't understand anything at all about yourself. And I can't deal with that. I need someone I can be with who will be with me, too. You—even when you're here, you're not."

I'd heard that before. "Chantal."

"I can't have you, and I refuse to need you."

"Chantal."

"That should make sense to you, who never loved anybody in your life."

I butted the door hard, then just let my forehead rest there again against the cool white paint.

"I'm calling the police."

I put my bandaged hands up against the door as if I could feel her through it. But there was no feeling. And I realized all of a sudden that there was no future, either. Not here.

"Chantal?"

"What?"

"My clothes?"

"Kurt, you are such an asshole. I gave them to Kantrowicz. Ask him. And get the fuck away from the door, or I *am* going to call the police."

I didn't want things to end this way with Chantal, but I couldn't tell her the whole truth and I didn't have the energy to lie. I wasn't even sure, now, why I had come back here. I leaned against the door for a few more minutes. She didn't say anything. Neither did I. And then I turned and walked down the stairs. I found Kantrowicz and my clothes and a couple of other things, including my Koran. He was a good man. He let me use his shower, and even made the two of us a pot of coffee. I guess he would have hauled out the vodka if I had given him a chance, but I had to go. I haven't seen him since. I hope he's okay.

As for Chantal, there's a lot I will miss, and that I do miss, about her. But my last memory is always going to be the feel of that cold white door against my forehead.

I got the last flight back down to Atlanta and picked up the Sword of the Angel where I'd left it, in a cold pack in a coin locker at the airport. I didn't want to pass through security with it. I bought myself a Walkman and a bunch of tapes and took a bus for Oklahoma City. Through the small-town Alabama night and the Tennessee dawn I listened over and over again to R.E.M. and to the Allman Brothers' *Decade of Hits*. "Not gonna let them catch the midnight rider." The bus and the music and the mist rising off the fields took me back *into* America. And it seemed like I hadn't been there for an awful long time.

A little after sunup, not too far east of Nashville, we pulled off the interstate on a detour and it looked like the whole little town where we were had turned out for church.

It was really early, and I couldn't figure out why there was such a crowd. I took off my earphones. Sure enough, you could hear the gospel music coming from inside the church, and it made me feel good, truly good. All the little girls were wearing hats and carrying little flower bouquets. It was Easter Sunday. It was just incredible to see.

By the time we got to Memphis it was about ten in the morning, and I felt strong enough to call Selma at the Westfield hospital. Joan answered the phone in Selma's room.

"You've heard," she said when she recognized my voice.

"Heard what? I was supposed to call yesterday but I had a little accident. Let me talk to Selma."

"She's sedated, Kurt. She can't talk."

"What the hell happened?"

"We've been trying to call you, but nobody answers at any of your numbers."

"Joan, get to the point."

"Dave is dead."

"What?"

"Selma was right. He was doing something terrible. Oh, Kurt, this is so awful. The newspapers have all been here and—"

"Just tell me what happened."

"They don't really know what he was doing, but something terrible. They found his body and some foreigner's in Atlanta. The papers are saying it might have been Duke Bolide that did it. He left with Dave and we haven't seen him since. Nobody's seen him."

"I was thinking about coming to visit."

"Oh, Kurt, not now. I mean, for your sake. I even told Charles to stay in St. Louis. You don't want to be part of this."

"Joan, I think I ought to come."

I was lying. The last place I wanted to be was in the middle of the cameras. So I let her persuade me not to come, then I found a cheap motel on the outskirts of Memphis. With the television and the minibar for company, I waited.

Joan was right about the news. There were a lot of reports about the two bodies found in the CNN Center. She even appeared in a couple of them, standing in front of the house near the Wal-Mart and saying she found all this just incredible, Dave was such a good provider, and always a good brother-in-law. I guess she thought she was saving the family's reputation.

From the news that you could watch and the papers that you could buy around Memphis, the Omni Murders looked like a not-very-big story. The first day they were on the front pages, but only the first day. Later in the week, an Atlanta reporter wrote that Duke's fingerprints were tied to some of the mail bombs in Savannah in 1990, and Dave was linked to him. But they didn't know what to make of the body they always described as an "unidentified corpse," with some reports making it of "apparent Middle Eastern" origin, and some "apparent Hispanic origin," depending on whether they were looking for terror connections or drug connections. There actually was some speculation that the body found hanging in the Omni could be linked to the Trade Center bombing. But a lot of arrests were made in that case and apparently the Feds had nothing that tied it to Rashid. At least nothing they talked to the press about.

After a couple of days, interest in the Omni story started to die. The big news was in the Midwest, at Waco, where a little cult nobody ever heard of was holding out against the FBI and the ATF, and it looked like a major showdown was on its way. When it came, the Omni was forgotten completely.

Dave's body, all autopsied and stitched back together, was returned to Kansas about two weeks after he died. Selma was out of the hospital. Joan had gone home. And I came up from Memphis, finally, for the funeral. I didn't want to leave her alone with too many members of Dave's "congregation." But as it turned out, none of them showed up, because they were afraid of police cameras and the press. And, then, the police and the press didn't show up either. So it was just Selma and me and the old minister from Christ the Redeemer, who was probably just as glad that Dave was gone.

Selma leaned on my shoulder and I don't think she heard much of the eulogy. ". . . For many in Westfield, Dave was like family . . ." I put my arm around Selma and squeezed her a little closer to me. We're always "like family" in America, I thought. Because "family" doesn't mean much at all. We've got no families, no history, no ties to the land the way people have them in the rest of the world—that big world we don't know anything about. Selma must have felt me tense a little, because she put her arm around my waist just then. And I guess it was at that precise moment that I thought, Kurt, you've got to come to rest. You want a family, you've got to start somewhere. And this is the only "where" that you really know. I held Selma a little tighter. It was time to stop looking for new histories. Time to stop looking for a new land. Time to come home to my own.

After the handfuls of dirt had been thrown on the coffin and the minister said good-bye, Selma and I stayed behind. "Let's go see Papa," I said.

The grave was by itself. Goodsell and Joan had buried my mother on the other side of the cemetery. There wasn't any choice, they said. The plots next to my father's had been sold. I guess when you've got so many families, or none, it's hard to know where to put people when they die. At least Mama had her stone. Selma had seen to that.

But this corner, where Papa was, nobody came here much. The grass had grown up on the grave, and the taller blades of it blew in the late afternoon wind. "We got to take better care of this place," I said. Selma hugged me real hard, and kissed me on the cheek.

I tried not to think about all there was that I didn't know about my father. I tried just to think about the man I knew when I was six or ten, or in the time just before he died. It wasn't much. Just the feel of that big hand holding mine, or the beat of his heart when I put my head against his chest. It was all hard to remember now. But it was what I had. And I hung on to it, and would.

It's been a while now since real terror came to America. And to the heartland, too. My flat lands have tasted real fear and terror and death, and no place more than down the road in Oklahoma City. And some things have happened that I thought I'd never see, like when Clinton finally bombed the fucking Chetniks and sent troops into Bosnia to enforce a peace. It was too little and 200,000 Muslim deaths too late, but I guess it was something. But all of that, even Oklahoma City, seems a long way away from Westfield now. Maybe even farther away than before.

Rashid was right when he said it would take something more than a single bomb to move America. The boys who took out the Federal Building in Oklahoma City, after all, just gave America another soap opera to watch, like O. J. Simpson or that woman who killed her two little babies in South Carolina. A TV drama, that was all it was. Rashid had wanted something more than that, at least. And so had I.

Of course, his plans didn't work the way they were supposed to. He wanted to kill thousands of people in the Trade Center, not just six. He wanted to flood the Holland Tunnel, as I figured out later. But he hadn't been around to supervise the job, and the idiots he was using wound up bringing in an FBI informer to help them. And I stopped the plague.

There in the tangle of astronauts, in the glow of Old Glory, in the shadow of the pyramids, the whole way it happened was so strange, and so right, that I accept this, now, as God's will. But I can't help asking myself: what if all of those plots, or even two out of three, had worked? I ask myself, would the Plan really have changed anything basic in America?

Maybe. I think the lesson can be taught. But it has to

be clear and it has to be painful and it has to come at just the right time. Rashid's message was too ordinary: revenge for the Gulf War, for Palestine, for whoever was paying him. He had big ideas, but he wasn't really looking to change anything. He was just keeping score. And if the Americans had discovered that, they would never have reacted the way that he—or at least the way that I—hoped. Pity and anger are the only two emotions they ever feel about the rest of the world. They would have felt sorry for themselves. They would have bombed Baghdad, again. Then they would have turned to other business. All those people would have died for nothing.

But I do believe Americans can be made to understand that they live in a universe of suffering, and to do that you can't just tell them about it, they have to suffer themselves. I think about the way they felt when they saw Rangers killed and dragged through the street in Somalia in 1993. Rangers! The best of the best, wiped out by a handful of Muslim warriors. And Americans didn't know what to make of it. They blamed logistics. They blamed the Secretary of Defense and the President. They knew they couldn't blame the Rangers. But it just never occurred to them that *God was on the other side.*

Americans are an arrogant people, steeped in sin, and someday that arrogance is going to be taken from them. They are going to experience a power greater than them-selves—and they will finally *believe* it is a power greater than themselves—and if that happens, I do think they will be closer to God, and the whole world will be a better, safer place. I do believe that still.

But there are other things I'm not so sure about any-more.

How do you find that moment when the wake-up call really will wake them up? It's not that easy. You've got to watch closely. The Internet helps. That's clear. You can take the pulse of the country, even of the world, sitting in your den in Westfield. And I do. I even have a couple of Web sites: "Airborne Daddy," a military affairs service for soldiers trying to keep their home life together, which makes me a little money; and "Cyber Jihad," which helps me stay in touch with the feelings of the umma. I can remain among the believers without raising my profile too high in Westfield. I pray five times a day by myself, now, but on Friday I go to a virtual mosque. I ask for guidance, and I watch for big events. The Olympics was one I thought about. The millennium is another.

And—this is what is hardest to know—could I really be the messenger? If the moment does come, will I know it? Could I truly hear the word? And could I act on it? I keep the Sword in a locked freezer in the garage. There is no way for me to get rid of it. And it is still ready to strike. But I can't tell you when the spirit will move me, or if it ever will. Maybe never.